On the Sickle's Edge

A Novel

Neville D. Frankel

DIÁLOGOS
AN IMPRINT OF LAVENDER INK
DIALOGOSBOOKS.COM

Neville D. Frankel
On the Sickle's Edge
Copyright © 2017 by Neville D. Frankel and Diálogos.
All rights reserved. No part of this work may be reproduced
in any form without the express written permission
of the copyright holders and Diálogos Books.

Printed in the U.S.A.
First Printing
10 9 8 7 6 5 4 3 2 1   16 17 18 19 20 21

Cover Painting:
Alexander Ivanov, *The Appearance of Christ Before the People* (detail)

Back Cover Photo:
Carter Wentworth

Author Photo:
Bryce Vickmark

Library of Congress Control Number: 2016949323
Frankel, Neville D.
On the Sickle's Edge / Neville D. Frankel;
p. cm.

ISBN: 978-1-944884-10-9 (pbk.)
ISBN: 978-1-944884-11-6 (ebook)

DIÁLOGOS
AN IMPRINT OF LAVENDER INK
DIALOGOSBOOKS.COM

Other Books by Neville D. Frankel

The Third Power

Bloodlines

Shtein Family Tree

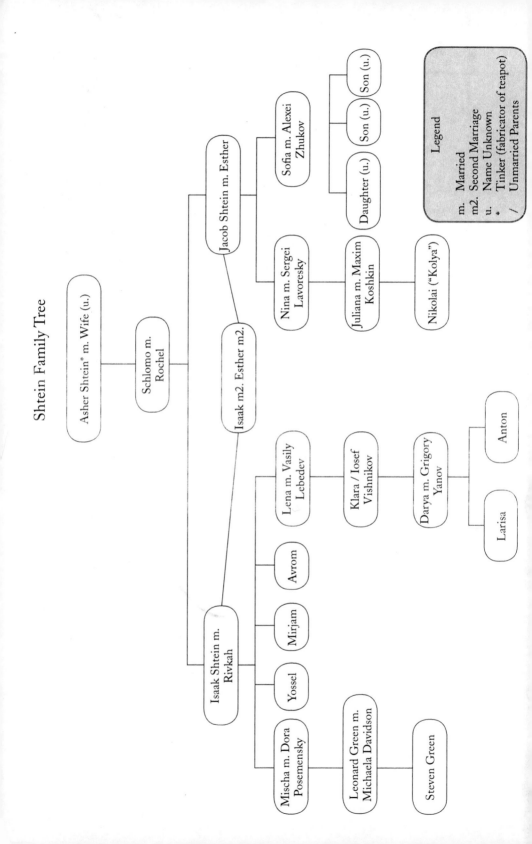

Legend

m.   Married
m2.   Second Marriage
u.   Name Unknown
*   Tinker (fabricator of teapot)
/   Unmarried Parents

Asher Shtein* m. Wife (u.)

Schlomo m. Rochel

Jacob Shtein m. Esther

Isaak m2. Esther m2.

Isaak Shtein m. Rivkah

Sofia m. Alexei Zhukov

Daughter (u.)

Son (u.)

Son (u.)

Son

Nina m. Sergei Lavoresky

Juliana m. Maxim Koshkin

Nikolai ("Kolya")

Lena m. Vasily Lebedev

Klara / Iosef Vishnikov

Darya m. Grigory Yanov

Larisa

Anton

Avrom

Mirjam

Yossel

Mischa m. Dora Posemensky

Leonard Green m. Michaela Davidson

Steven Green

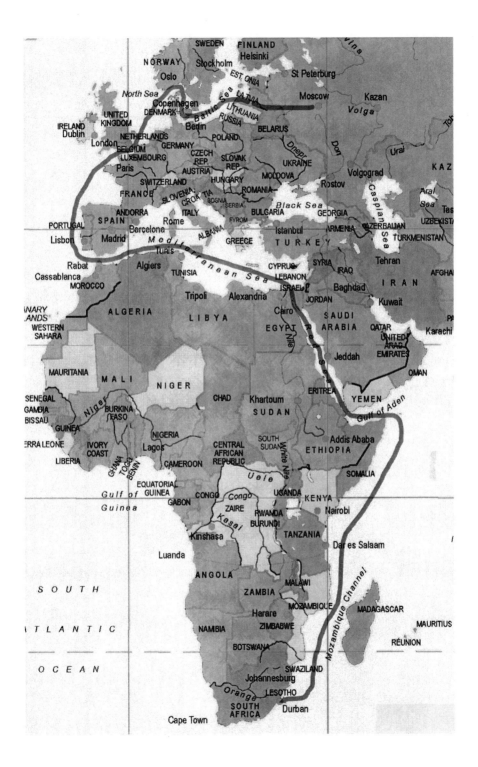

On the Sickle's Edge

Neville D. Frankel

For Charlie and Joe
The boys who were left behind

PROLOGUE

Steven

Moscow, June 1990

Reflections of light from the curtained *dacha* windows billowed out onto the grass, a carelessly thrown satin sheet. Luminous, they draped softly over the bushes. A black Zil limo, recently washed and shined, pulled silently into view, drove past the guardhouse, and stopped outside the entrance. The driver's door flew open and the driver jumped out, took a second to gather himself, and with a flourish, opened the rear door.

Grigory Ivanovich Yanov stepped out of the back seat. I had met him only once, a slender man of medium height, but he moved like a large cat, languid and sleek, almost lazy. Even from a distance, I sensed about him a reckless, compressed muscularity. He had thick, startling blond hair cut short on top, long over the ears and at the neck, and he wore a dark tailored suit. Raising his arms, he stretched skyward, hooked his thumbs and bent to the sides, showing unusual flexibility for a grown man. He looked around casually—although I had the feeling that even his most spontaneous gesture was calculated—brushed the sleeves of his jacket, and walked up the path to the front door. It opened as he approached, and he disappeared within as the door closed silently behind him. The driver got back in the car and drove off.

❦

I thought the loaded pistol in my pocket would make me feel more secure, but all it did was pull down my pants. It was Kolya who, after a hurried tutorial, had given me the weapon.

"Just in case," he said.

Until then, my first and only experience with a pistol had been as a teenager at a shooting range in Arizona. Back then it was never holstered, but this time the weapon felt like an anvil attached to my hip. Ironically, the longer I waited, the more comfortable I became with the weight at my side. I moved with my hands at my waist, trying to hold it all together like an awkward, overgrown urban teenager. The back of my pants hung down below my hips, an advertisement for Fruit of the Loom.

It was early summer, about an hour from Moscow. Kolya and I were secluded behind an overhang of birch leaves and pine branches heavy with needles. We were ten kilometers from the village of Usovo on the banks of the Moscow River, where Russian leaders have built their summer homes since the time of the tsars. Nicholas II had his *dacha* here, as did Lenin, and Boris Yeltsin. The massive gulf between ordinary Russians and their leaders has always been glaringly obvious. At that moment, watching who came and went from one relatively modest *dacha*, I was no more than a hundred yards from the homes of some of Russia's most powerful men.

The residents did not own their *dachas*—use of the properties came with rank and status in the Communist Party and the Committee for State Security, the KGB. The road was unmarked, and the guards in the brick guardhouse at the entrance made sure that the average comrade never found out how well the residents, Party members all, were living. Had I been foolish enough to try snaking my way through the cordon of heavily armed guards and trip wires that surrounded the top-level politicians of the Russian state, I would most certainly have been apprehended, dispatched and probably disappeared.

As I settled in to watch, I wondered what the chances were of an artist, born in Johannesburg, South Africa, and raised in Boston, ending up in the woods outside Moscow, contemplating the murder of a man he barely knew.

❦

My name is Steven Green. At the time of these events I was in my early thirties. I had no military knowledge or expertise with weapons, and had never been with the CIA or the State Department or any other branch of the US or any other government. My intentions were pure, my motivations romantic, and my actions courageous—but my decision-making was careless, foolhardy, and without a doubt irrational.

My presence in the Soviet Union was purely a matter of the heart. I had come to Moscow to rescue the woman I thought I loved. From her husband, no less. And it was becoming increasingly unlikely that this day— or those that followed—would be high points in my life.

I started out as a painter of pictures, but seem to have ended up a teller of tales. Until this point I had done very little worth sharing with others. But my life, it turns out, has been abundantly altered and enriched by the stories of those who came before me and into whose path life has propelled me.

Very little of the story is mine. I'm merely the latest scribe of this particular sequence of events, carefully ordered and strung together. In combination, they are like an ancient heirloom too weighty for wear, laden with opalescent pearls, blood-red rubies and sea-green emeralds bound on an old cord stained by salt and tears, twisted by knots in memory of our forebears, what they lived through, and how they died. That the story is being told at all is to the credit and curiosity of our children, who were as yet unborn when these events took place.

Once our children were old enough to be interested in their own history, they began to ask questions, and it was only a matter of time before they latched on to the fact that their mother and I were distant cousins. It was a toss-up as to whether they were more intrigued or grossed out by this discovery. The fact that we didn't know of each other's existence until we reached adulthood only increased their interest in the details.

In addressing our children's curiosity about their origins, we had to find a way to tell a tale that went back before either of us was born, encompassing five generations of family history. It included appalling life decisions made under duress more than a century ago, decisions that destroyed childhoods and condemned generations to live under terrible conditions in a repressive state; family lost and rediscovered; desertion, isolation and grief; murder and abuse. It was not a story they would be able to absorb in one sitting, and it required going back to the childhood of their great-grandmother, who was born Yelena Shtein. She was already an ancient, gnarled old woman by the time we met, but her story was proof that she had not always been so.

The question, when they framed it, seemed a simple one.

"Mommy and Daddy," they asked, "how did you meet?"

PART ONE

Lena's Story

If you travel to Latvia and drive 160 kilometers inland from Riga, on the Baltic coast, you will find no trace of Illuxt. After the Jewish expulsion in 1915, the deserted shell of our village was razed, the remains buried, rotted away, grown over by forest that flourished on the charred remains of our homes. Stepping quietly among the aspen and pine, some say they hear the faded echoes of laughter from our dead. These thick forests are now the only witness to the disappeared and displaced who once made that benighted place their home.

Our village, in the province of Courland, was once a part of the Russian Empire. Following World War I, Courland became part of Latvia, and was then swallowed by the ravening monster that called itself the Union of Soviet Socialist Republics. Now that monster is gone, replaced by another, and Courland is again a part of independent Latvia. The name Illuxt exists still, a few kilometers distant from where the old village was. It has a slightly altered spelling, *Ilukste*, and with its original name it has jettisoned the heavy weight of its past. Our story, what happened to us, is buried with the wood frames of the shacks we lived in, the ramshackle barns in which we housed the precious cow, the goat, the few laying hens, perhaps the donkey. One day perhaps a historian will foray into the mud of the old place, trying to reconstruct something of how we lived. But Courland will have become part of whatever cancerous empire then sucks the people's flesh from their bones. We will all be gone, our memories of less substance than windblown vapor.

Even so, at every turn, history makes itself felt. Past and present twine about each other, parallel ribbons, always related, always equidistant.

I was only a child when we lived in Illuxt, and it was only for a brief

period. None of us had much of anything, but that didn't make for any less
envy or greed from other inhabitants. The Jews of Illuxt lived mostly in the
center of the village around a dirt square. My ancestors came from Germany
in the mid-1700s. We still spoke German at home, as well as Yiddish. As a
result, the Christians, who lived on their landholdings further out, thought
of us still as interlopers. Foreigners. Like the other Jews in the province of
Courland, we were forbidden to own land, and made a living as tradesmen,
tinkers, and peddlers, selling whatever we could to make ends meet.

In 1898, when my family's story begins, the Shtein brothers—my father,
Isaak, and my uncle Jacob—in their early twenties, lived beside each other
in the center of Illuxt. Both were young men beginning their adult lives.
Both were married, with young children, and their wives had been friends
since childhood. Uncle Jacob left Illuxt to find a better life, intending to
send for Aunt Esther and their children once he had established himself.
His trip did not end well, and he is unimportant in this tale but for one
small detail—his decision to find a better life took him to the goldfields
of South Africa. As a consequence when his brother Isaak—my father—
became a fugitive from the Tsar's army, it was natural that he follow his
older sibling's footsteps.

Before dawn one winter morning, the Tsar's conscription officers
galloped into Illuxt's village square. They cantered around with drawn
swords waving in the air, clattered and shouted and panicked the donkeys
and chickens, whose terrified braying and clucking only added to the chaos.
In the embellished stories that followed, chickens devoured their own eggs,
milk curdled in the cows' udders, mongrels and donkeys took comfort from
one another and curled up together in the warmth of the barn. Children
screamed with fear and clung to their mothers, who were terrified that their
young husbands would be taken for soldiers. The older women cursed their
own husbands, whose softness had prevented them from taking an ax to
their sons' toes—an act that would have crippled them and made them
ineligible for the Tsar's army.

Older men, petrified for their sons, exchanged guilty glances, aware of
the relief they felt at having reached the age when they were beyond the

reach of the Tsar's call. Young men pissed themselves and stood around in their own little puddles, terrified and ashamed. The head conscription officer was a shabby recruiter in an old uniform, but I imagine he appeared to them as a powerful representative of the Tsar, in a gleaming military getup. Those few young men who kept their wits about them might have recognized how absurd it was that the military might of the Tsar depended upon their lean and sallow bodies, malnourished and unpracticed in war. The conscription officer asked laughingly whether any families wanted to buy their way out of service to the Russian Empire—Jews willing to pay five hundred rubles were exempt from serving in the army—but, as my father later told me, the whole village together could not come up with that much money.

All able-bodied men were ordered to line up in the little square beside the synagogue, dressed in their warmest clothing. Three young men were selected at random, to serve in the Tsar's army. The term of conscription was twenty-five years, for all intents and purposes a life sentence. As they were marched out of Illuxt into the countryside, none of those left behind ever thought to see them again. Two of the men were put on a train with other conscripts and sent to serve on the disputed western border of the Russian Empire. Like hundreds of thousands of others before and after them, they were given no real military training, and they died of cold, loneliness, malnutrition, and bad leadership.

The third young man was my father, Isaak Shtein, who was fated not to accompany his two friends on the train. Instead, he was assigned to a troop of rag-tag conscripts making their way to the Lithuanian border. Years later, in a letter to his two oldest sons, my brothers, this is how he described it.

———————◆———————

They gave us badly made boots that we stuffed with cloth to keep our feet warm, and a rough brownish-grey coat to wear over our clothes. We received no training, but were given each a short sword. They took us five days through the snow, walking all the while, carrying provisions in our knapsacks and a rolled blanket wrapped around our shoulders. We stopped at night to sleep around a small fire.

On the fifth day, I was assigned to a group of four men with an officer, and we were separated from the main body. The officer, on an old horse, led the way through an ancient, silent forest of birch and pine trees, and the gorse bushes were so dense in places that when the thorns snagged our clothes, they tore, and we bled. We walked several days until at dusk we reached our destination, a hut at a border outpost.

We had little food, and nothing to do other than look across the hillsides for some unnamed enemy, so we spent most afternoons hunting for something to eat. Anything – edible plants, fruits from a tree, small animals. None of us knew how to use our short sword as a weapon. It was useless for anything other than cutting meat, and I became adept at skinning and eating animals that back in Illuxt I would never have touched, they not being kosher. We had little success—an occasional deer, wild goats and rabbits, and several times a small bird that looked like a chicken but had a foul taste.

Of the four of us, two were Jews and two Christians. We started off wary of each other and not wanting much contact, but we were their only companions and they ours, and we all came to see after several days and nights together that we were none of us as bad as our superior officer. Within days he taught us how to hate him. He was uniformly cruel, and particularly nasty to the two Jews in his little company. He gave us short rations. He assigned us the worst duties and the longest watches. Worst was his contempt for our religious beliefs.

But the Christians, too, were subject to his abuse. One day at the end of winter, one of them accidentally knocked over a pot of soup—water with a few old potatoes and celery root—into the fire, spilling all the liquid and dousing the flame. He burned his hands trying to retrieve the potatoes from the ash, and for his trouble our officer beat him about the floor of the hut with the butt end of a rifle.

We were at the end of the world. We had seen no one else for weeks. For each of us this was the first time away from our families, and we were bereft, lonely and frightened. The idea that we would spend years in this condition was unbearable, and with squinted eyes and hidden looks and not a single word exchanged among us, we knew that at least in the deed we were about to commit, we were brothers.

That night when the officer left the hut and went outside to relieve himself in the hole we had dug in the frozen ground, all four of us rose up and followed him outside. There was a sliver of moon shining on the hills that extended to the horizon, and although it was still cold, there was the feeling of spring in the air. When he saw us coming at him, he tried to rise from a squatting position but his trousers were at his ankles and he fell backward. The first of us hit his head with the stock of the rifle until he was still, and then the other three held him down. I was the fourth, and for all the days of my life I have lived within these events as if in a nightmare that begins and ends and then starts anew.

As I looked down at the terror in the eyes of my officer, I thought of the goat I had killed a week earlier, and there was little to distinguish between them. I drew the short sword from my waistband, ran its blunt edge along the officer's throat, sawing away until the flesh gave and the sinew, and I will recall until my dying day the sound of air leaking from his lungs as blood pooled around his head and he died. I know now that in goat as in man, the tendon resists the knife with the same attachment to life.

Laboring together in the frigid air we widened and deepened the trench, digging through the icy ground until we reached a depth where it was unfrozen. Together we rolled his body into the hole and covered it and we stamped on the soil until it was hard, and then we pulled grasses and rocks and twigs over it so that our work was invisible. We took what little we needed from the hut and left, traveling together in darkness and hiding during the light of day. For six days we retraced our journey. When we recognized our surroundings we separated, each going his own way. I returned home knowing that I could not stay but wanting once again to see my beloved wife Rivkah and my two sons before leaving.

It was early winter when I was conscripted. Now the flowers were budding. Rivkah assumed me long dead. I arrived back in Illuxt in the dead of night filthy, frozen, and starving, haunted by the image of the man I had killed. His eyes were wide open as he lay in the frozen hole, looking up at me as the air bubbled from his throat, his heart no more than a lethal tool whose purpose was to drain the blood from his body in great pumping gouts and mix it with human waste.

I came into the house and in the moonlight I saw my Rivkah sleeping in our bed, dark hair across one cheek and her hand outstretched to where I should have been. Separating our sleeping area from the children was a cloth curtain made of flour sacks cut open and sewn together, and hung on a piece of rope. Crossing the room in two steps I carefully pulled aside this curtain to see my sons, bigger than I remembered them but still my children in sleep, long eyelashes and dark curly hair over their foreheads, even in sleep expressing both their love for each other and the need for independence, each one with an arm thrown over the other as if to embrace and another arm pushing his brother from him.

I thought to let Rivkah sleep while I took the chill off a pail of water on the fire, and tried to wash the filth and the smell of death from my body, standing naked and shivering in the icy room, with the wind blowing through the cracks in the walls. Woken by the sounds of my shivering teeth, Rivkah rose silently from our bed, and when I turned to soap myself I saw her standing behind me, a blanket about her shoulders, her beautiful mouth open in delight and then despair as she saw how thin I had become and how ragged, and recognized, she said, the lost wildness in my eyes. She came to me as I stood there freezing and in silence, both of us shaking with cold and with relief; she washed me and dried me and without a word led me into our bed. And even before she had curled her body around my shivering bones to warm me, I was holding onto her and weeping like a child, she the only force in my life pure enough to erase for a moment the experience of where I had been and what I had done. We woke before dawn, and holding onto each other, I whispered to her what had taken place.

"You have to go, Isaak," she said. "When they find you missing from the outpost, the first place they will look for you is here."

"I know," I said.

"And when they find you, they'll execute you for desertion even if they don't find the body of the man you killed."

"They won't find the body," I said. "We buried it deep, pounded down the soil on top of it and covered it with small stones and undergrowth. They'll never guess what happened. Maybe they'll think we were all captured or murdered by the enemy," I said, hoping, and I realized for the first time at that moment I had no idea who the enemy was. "I don't even know if they kept a record of where I come from. Perhaps they will never think to look for me."

"We can't take that chance, Isaak. What if they force one of the other three men to tell them what happened? They'll find you here and shoot you on the spot. I'd rather have you far away and safe. And if they do find you here, what will they do to the boys? No, you have to go."

"I know," I said, stroking her hair. "You're right. I was dreaming."

"You'll join your brother in South Africa. When Jacob sends money for Esther and the children, you send money for us. We can come to you together. But where will you get the money to buy passage? You'll have to go to my uncle in Riga."

"Perhaps he can get me a job at the port," I said. "I can save money, find out when ships are leaving for South Africa. Maybe get a job on board."

I promised Rivkah I would find Jacob and together we would work hard and save our wages and send for the two families – Jacob's wife Esther and her daughters, and Rivkah and our two boys, Mischa and Yossel. Then we snuggled back down into the warmth of our bed for one last embrace, which turned quickly into something more. Rivkah told me later that she knew by morning she had conceived another child. I left Illuxt before daylight and nine months later Mirjam was born. She was two years old before I had saved enough money to send for the family.

There are no records, no manifests, and no proof of what happened to my father when he went to my mother's uncle in the port of Riga. He refused to discuss this period of his life. I would like to think my mother's uncle helped him; that he worked at the shipyards, saved and scrimped, and bought a ticket in steerage. It's unlikely, knowing the kind of man he was, but perhaps the only way he could collect enough money was to steal it. We will never know. But somehow, he made his way to South Africa.

When he landed at the port in Durban, he traced his brother Jacob's whereabouts north to Johannesburg, six hundred and fifty kilometers inland. From there, he learned of Jacob's route over the newly laid railway to the Witwatersrand Reef—the White Waters Ridge, site of the grandest vein of gold ever discovered. It was wild country, the opportunity for wealth unlimited, and miners flocked there from across the world. He found out that Jacob had opened a general store selling basic supplies to the miners— beer and whisky and reading glasses and boots, as well as food staples like flour and sugar. But when my father arrived on the Reef, except for stray dogs, the gold mining claims around his brother's store were deserted. The store was nothing but an empty shack with an open door swinging in the wind. Jacob was nowhere to be found. With little English and no Afrikaans, it took my father several days to discover someone from the old country who could translate and help him understand what had happened.

The rock in the area was less rich than expected—only traces of gold, and in the hysteria of the time, only the richest veins seemed worth working. So the miners left for greener pastures. Jacob didn't follow them— he was already ill. He might have suffered from tuberculosis, or influenza, or dysentery, or malaria—they didn't yet have quinine, and there was no medical care. He died a few weeks before my father arrived. The people Jacob boarded with had given away what few possessions he had, but they showed my father the makeshift graveyard where he was buried. A year later, as is our tradition, he put up a tombstone. For the rest of his life, even after he left South Africa, he kept a record of where his brother's body had been laid to rest.

Now my father had to make his way alone. He returned to Johannesburg, where there was a growing community of Latvian Jews from the province of Courland, where Illuxt was located. He rented a room to sleep in, found a job in a bakery, and began to save what little he could. It took two years before he had enough to buy passage for my mother and the three children. He felt a deep responsibility for his brother's family, and wanted desperately to keep Jacob's promise to bring Esther and the girls to South Africa. But he knew that once my mother and the children arrived, there was little chance of his being able to continue saving at the same rate.

My mother took the same route that Jacob and my father had, traveling steerage through the Baltic to England, across the Mediterranean, through the Suez Canal, and down the east coast of Africa, to arrive at the port of Durban. Before my mother left Illuxt, her mother-in-law—my grandmother—implored her to take with her a family heirloom—the most precious thing they owned—to this strange and foreign land that had already claimed one of her sons. Although it was bulky, my mother didn't have the heart to refuse. The gift was not only an heirloom, but it had been made by Jacob and Isaak's grandfather, a tinker and metalworker whose talent and craftsmanship had earned him a reputation throughout Courland.

It was a tall elongated teapot made of brass with a rounded belly and a narrow spout that rose straight up from the base. The whole intricate device, which could be cradled easily within the joined hands of a mid-sized man, was covered in delicately wrought silver leaves attached to stems of blue stone and carefully held together with minute, red-tinted metal rivets. It was unusual, and beautifully made. Although not an educated man, the tinker had received a deep understanding of Jewish ceremony and ritual from his father, who had been the synagogue *shames*—the man who took care of the building and was responsible for rituals and for keeping track of holy days. What he had constructed was actually a monument to the memory of his father, a puzzle containing in one place all the symbols and ritual tools necessary to practice the traditions of Judaism. My grandmother wanted to make sure that her son's family, although far from their home and their traditions, did not forget that they were Jews. My mother didn't fully understand what all the parts of the teapot were for, but she knew that the top was a goblet for drinking wine, and that somewhere beneath the body were a pair of candlesticks for the Sabbath candles, and that within the body of the teapot was enfolded a platter that opened out as a Seder plate for use on Passover.

There was much more to it, but she had only seen the teapot at a distance, and on the eve of her departure there was no time for a detailed explanation. She promised her mother-in-law that they would use the wine goblet every Friday night to welcome the Sabbath.

My father met them at the dock. I can only imagine the joy of my parents' reunion after almost three years, and my father's first embrace of my brothers Mischa and Yossel, who were by then eight and ten. My mother would have gently introduced him to his daughter, two-year-old Mirjam, a lovely child with her dark coloring, big eyes, and a shy, winsome smile. They found a house—that is to say, my mother found a house—and quickly settled the family into a routine, taking charge of their lives, as she had back in Illuxt.

In the second year of their arrival, my father was able to open his own bakery. He was forever giving bread away at less than his cost to those who needed it. Mother tried at first to change him but she claimed to love him as he was, and so they were always short of money. She was a big woman, robust and healthy, and she was lively and filled with happiness. She would put her hands on her hips and laugh, and say that money didn't matter, because their lives had been blessed. She loved South Africa—the heat, the landscape, and the richness and variety of the foliage, all new to her, and she didn't feel afraid. Best of all, the children grew and thrived in the warm climate. True to her word, every Friday night she unscrewed the wine goblet from the top of the teapot and the family welcomed the Sabbath with a sip of wine, thanking God for so blessing their lives.

Then she fell pregnant again, her fourth. This one was different from the others. She suffered through her term with spasms and nausea. She was ill and out of sorts, and towards the end of the pregnancy she was so big and uncomfortable that she took to her bed. When she began to bleed, my father closed the bakery, put water on to boil, and sent Mischa to summon the midwife. It was a lengthy labor, more bloody than usual, and by the time my brother Avrom and I were delivered, the midwife knew that this would not be one of her successful deliveries. She had been unable to stop my mother's bleeding, and while she knew from experience that women in childbirth could deal with even intolerable pain, no woman could survive the loss of so much blood.

My twin brother Avrom came into the world a few minutes before I did. He was reluctant to leave the womb, and when he was finally pulled out, he struggled for breath like a fingerling flapping its tail as it landed, wave-tossed, on the sand. As he turned blue and the midwife frantically plumbed his mouth with her little finger, I shot out from between our mother's thighs, a yowling tadpole, enraged, it seemed, that my brother had plugged my exit with his body. It was perhaps the first and only time that I found myself at the center of my world. As I emerged, perhaps ejected by the river of blood that followed, our mother died.

So, life preceded me into the world, and death followed. Like a rabid mutt, Death has nipped all these years at my heels, and even now I am only two steps ahead of that rancid, snarling, thing with foul, matted fur and yellowed fangs. Truth is that as his gains and my losses mounted, he has taken a toll on my spirits. Not that I would ever let it show.

When I was a little girl, an old man took my hand in a silent forest clearing, and looked into my terrified eyes.

"It takes courage, Lena," he whispered, "to laugh in the face of death. If you are going to survive, you need to find that courage."

Even today I hear his rasping voice in my ear, and his advice has served me well.

✿

My father claimed to have looked diligently for a wife—but whether he was capable of such a search is questionable. Besides, what woman would want a depressed, grieving man saddled with a failing business and five children, two of them newborn? Such a woman would have had to love him desperately—and after my mother's death, there was nothing left of him to love.

He fell apart. In the midst of his grief he was unable to manage the bakery. His customers didn't know from day to day whether there would be bread on the shelves. They tried to be loyal to him, knowing his loss, but slowly they drifted away to more reliable vendors. The guilt he must have felt at his failure to provide for us, or to give us any sense of emotional stability, must have been insupportable.

My earliest memories, and some of my happiest, were being carried around on my brothers' backs. I remember standing between them, one of my hands in Mischa's and the other in Yossel's, the three of us running together through a field of long grass. We were laughing, there were dogs running beside us and barking, and the warmth of the sun was on my face. It was an oasis of pleasure in my life, and even this—my single memory of untrammeled joy—is an illusion which I cannot claim as my own. When we left South Africa, Avrom and I were three or four years old. We were too young to recall much of anything, and we could scarcely have run through the tall, rough grasses that reached the height of a man's thigh. Perhaps, trapped in a joyless childhood where my only experience of love was the love I had already lost, I saw another child laughing and running through the grass holding onto someone's hand, and I embraced the vision as my own.

✿

Back in Illuxt, my father's mother and his sister, missing him, took advantage of the desperation in his letters. They tossed him a lifeline, encouraged him to come home for a short visit. He could relax a little; they would take care of the children. There he would still be considered an eligible man, they said. He had his own business, and there were plenty of girls who would jump at the chance to marry him and accompany him back to South Africa.

Whether he believed them is hard to know, but he was a man drowning, and he jumped at the opportunity to escape the wreckage that was his life. While he lived I lacked the courage—or the cruelty—to say to him what I felt. But as an old woman I have learned that there is no alternative to the truth, and I speak to my father often. Too late to make a difference, perhaps, but it makes me feel better. Walking through the snows of Moscow, I tell him what he did was terrible. Beyond measure, beyond forgiveness.

"Your mother snared you with hope," I tell him. "I understand. She meant well. She threw you a line, and you grabbed it to save yourself. But we were all tethered to you, Papa. How could you not see that the anchor at the other end of that line was shackled to the bottom of the sea?"

Where he found the money to buy passage back we never discovered. Perhaps he sold the equipment in the bakery. Perhaps he borrowed. Thank God he didn't have enough money to buy passage for all the children. Mischa and Yossel, at least, were spared the journey back and the pain of the life that followed. But they, of course, had their own story and their own pain—they had lost a mother, and now a father and siblings besides, and their lives were spent waiting for their father to return.

Today we know better, but back then, teenage boys were considered men, able to go out and support themselves. Yossel and Mischa were thirteen and almost fifteen when father was ready to leave. He arranged lodging for them in the rooming house he had stayed in when he first arrived. There was no question of their going to school. They had to earn a living and pay their own way. He found work for them in a coal yard, bagging and delivering coal.

Mischa and Yossel accompanied us—my father, Mirjam, Avrom and me—to the train station in Johannesburg to make the journey to Durban, where we planned to board ship. As we waited for the train, thirteen-year-old Yossel wept openly. He had been a brave boy through our mother's death, and he had done more than could be expected in the face of his father's emotional collapse. Perhaps taking care of us, his infant siblings, saved him from his own grief. But now he was faced with losing both his father, and those of us who had given him his reason for being.

"I'll be back before you know it," my father said, acting bravely.

He rummaged in the bag carried on his back and withdrew the teapot made by his grandfather. He took the teapot in his big hands and unscrewed the wine goblet, the *Kiddush* cup that the boys knew from welcoming the Sabbath, and he handed it to Yossel. Then, as Avrom and I ran about the floor of the station watched by our older sister Mirjam, our father placed an arm about each of his older sons, hugged them to his chest, felt their hearts beating against his.

"My sons," he said, "I go now to find a mother for your brother and sisters. We have among us only one heart. Like my grandfather's teapot, I leave one part here with you; the other I take with me. In this way, although at opposite ends of the earth, we will drink wine from the same vessel. As we say the Sabbath blessings, my heart will beat in unison with yours until we are reunited."

My father was in many ways a foolish man, but he knew as well as Anton Chekhov how to a weave a story that would pull at your heartstrings.

And so my father took us back to Latvia and to the Russian Empire. It would become so corrupt in coming decades that garbage sweepers on darkened streets at midnight and the mightiest officials in the dimly lit offices high above would think the same venal thoughts. In the nostrils of all was the smell of a rotting State, but inured to the stench, they found nothing amiss. For most of my life, we spent our days no better off than the landowners' serfs, knee-deep in the foulest slime, ready to defend the proposition that the muck around us was as pure as spring water.

I remember nothing of the journey back to Latvia, but it took on a mythic quality as I grew up. The journey was long and uncomfortable, boring and dangerous. Most likely, we were housed in airless compartments with steel bunks three-tiers high along the sides, divided into dormitories for families, and separate spaces for single men and women. We suffered from a lack of fresh air, privacy, and toilet facilities. Perhaps there was a sink with cold running water, but there was no hot water, and it was difficult to keep clean. The stench of unwashed bodies, unsanitary bathrooms, sea sickness, smoke and spoiled food would have been overwhelming.

The story was retold in innumerable versions, at first as a tale of homecoming. Then was added the joy of finding a new mother and becoming a family again. As darkness descended, it turned into a sinister fairytale of loss and deprivation, of dying heroes and savaged dreams. Aside from these tales, all I know about those early years is what I have learned as an old woman, from the letters my father wrote to my brothers Mischa and Yossel in South Africa. Like a host of faded shooting stars, as they fell into my possession, each one lit up the past with a momentary trail of light.

They came to me wrapped in yellowing tissue paper and tied loosely with a faded green ribbon, all tucked safely in an ancient, battered ledger box. Carefully I lifted out a three-inch stack of hand-written pages, clipped or tied together into several smaller bundles. Some contained only three pages, others were much thicker. Some piles were held together with a rusted paper clip, others tied loosely with string or ribbon. All had been creased and folded; many were stained. My brothers had read them over and over again.

There were old portrait photographs on card stock, the sepia coloring washed out to light brown, with the backs covered in script. Some were written on small rectangular pieces of paper with edges roughened, as if they had been torn or cut with a blade from a larger whole. There were pages torn from books, with colored swirls on the unwritten sides, and oddly shaped pieces of blank newsprint. Old stationery of different colors, now all faded to faint shades of yellow, on which the sender's address had been scratched out. Used wrapping paper that had been cut into manuscript-sized pieces and covered with writing.

In my first real memory of him, my father was still a big man, already bent of shoulder, the wrinkled lines on his face crisscrossed by broken blood vessels, age spots on hands whose fingers were twisted with arthritis. He was only in his late twenties when Avrom and I were born, so what I perceived in him as age must have been the effect of grief and loss. And his letters tell of his journey and what followed far better than I can.

———————◆———————

My Beloved Sons:

With great sadness I must share with you the news that your sister Mirjam became very ill on the ship out of England. We nursed her as best we could on the ocean voyage through the Baltic Sea, but there were storms, and the sea was rough, and by the time we docked at Riga she was very ill. She survived the journey inland to Illuxt, but she died a few days after we arrived. We buried her with your great-grandparents, here in the Jewish cemetery, and we said the Kaddish for her with love and grief in our hearts. May the Lord who took her from us keep her safe from harm. We take comfort in knowing that she is at peace, and that her spirit has become one with your mother's. Blessed be the name of G-d.

It was a blessing to be among family when this happened. All have been wonderful to us, and your sister Lena and brother Avrom are happy and well cared for. It has been a great relief to see your Aunt Esther and the children, who remained in Illuxt when my brother, your uncle Jacob, went to South Africa. She is in good health despite her widowhood, which has been most difficult for her. I have told her where Jacob's grave is—you will remember that we went several times to visit his burial site—and described for her the place where he lived, and this has given her some comfort.

How strange and wonderful, and how terrible, to arrive back at this place—this place your mother, of beloved memory, and I called home—where we lived with you when you were little boys. Every corner of Illuxt is filled with memories of my own childhood, and with faces as familiar to me as my own, but I also see things now that were invisible to me before.

I think of the hard life you are living alone in Mrs. Wingard's boarding house, and I know that although it is difficult and lonely, your lives are infinitely richer than the lives of your family here. Although Aunt Esther and her children's days are filled with love and with each other, they are very poor, and there is not the feeling, as you have, that life is protected and safe.

The authorities here are unpredictable—sometimes a source of protection, sometimes a cause of great injustice. We Jews in particular are not welcome—they would be happy to see us all gone. The family lives each day with uncertainty, although they seem unaware of it, knowing no other way to be. But I have seen differently, and I feel none of the safety that I felt in South Africa. Our village and all that surrounds it fill me with dread. I will not breathe freely until I embrace you again. The day cannot come soon enough.

Your Loving Father

By the time my father decided to marry his widowed sister-in-law, Esther, Avrom and I were five years old. By then I had already come to love Aunt Esther as my own mother. Of course, growing up, I knew who she was and where she came from. I sensed that there was some deep connection among us all, she and her children and my father and his. But not until I read this letter did I truly grasp how natural their union was, and how in many ways it rescued them both from what would otherwise have been an even more dismal life.

———————◆———————

My Beloved Sons:

I write to tell you the joyous news that your Aunt Esther and I have agreed to marry, so that our children will have the blessings of both a father and a mother. You are already almost men, and so for you it will not be so important, but now the younger children will have both parents, and will be not only cousins, but brothers and sisters. When we return I will be bringing you not only a wonderful new mother, but also two new sisters.

Two long years have come and gone since we arrived here, much longer than I would have thought possible. During that time, your Aunt Esther and I have come to know one another. Together we have wept for all our losses—my child, your sister Mirjam; my brother, Jacob, her husband; and your mother, who was not only my wife, but was also her friend from childhood. As we embraced in grief, I found myself relieved that she feels no anger towards me, that I live while her Jacob is dead; that she bears me no hard feelings because I was unable to send her the money necessary to bring her and the children to be with us in South Africa.

We found ourselves drawn to each other in our mourning, and as the months passed we have discovered, she in her loneliness over the years, and I in my more recent bereavement, that we give each other solace and comfort. I have known your Aunt Esther since I was a small boy. She is a fine woman with a loving heart, she loves your brother Avrom and your sister Lena, and they have become devoted to her, and very close to your cousins.

We will marry next week here in the small synagogue where your mother and I were joined, and although you will not be here with us, you are in our hearts and by my side. I am happy for the first time since

your mother was taken from us, and perhaps, if it p
be the beginning of a happier time for us all. Follo
we plan to leave within the month, and to take shi

Your Beloved Father

Bound tightly to this letter and in the same bundle was a second letter
from my Aunt Esther who was now also my new stepmother.

To Mischa and Yossel, nephews and now sons, I send my greetings
and my love. I hope you will wish for your father and for me, happiness
and health, as I wish it for you. I remember you only as young boys,
and I look forward to meeting the young men you have become. Soon
we will be together as one family, and I will rejoice in making a home
for us all.

With love from your aunt and soon mother, Esther

<hr />

The wedding was a sedate affair between two people who were then
considered middle-aged—she was thirty-five; he, thirty-three. After
the wedding, we moved into her house. None of his letters refers to the
strangeness of moving into his deceased brother's home, or sleeping with
the woman who had been his sister-in-law and was now his wife, or the fact
that his brother's children were now to call him father.

My father and Esther began planning for the return trip to South
Africa, but like a manic spinning top, World War I torpedoed their plans.
Shipping lanes were patrolled by the German Baltic Fleet, and vessels
were already being requisitioned as hospital or troop carriers. The few
ships still carrying passengers were forced to travel in convoy, accompanied
by a military escort. As a result, the cost of passage back to South Africa
skyrocketed, and our trip was postponed until my father could save more

o Esther, South Africa began to feel—yet again—like a lost dream. As the year moved from winter to spring, the German army invaded Lithuania. Immediately they began gathering on the western border in anticipation of a massive advance into Latvia. The Tsar's uncle, Grand Duke Nikolay Nikolayevich, Commander-in-Chief of the Russian Army, attributed the successful German invasion of Lithuania to Jewish espionage. And it was true that many of us still felt more German than Latvian.

Rumors were spread that the Jews of Lithuania had hidden a German unit at the Russian rear, and used it to undermine the Russian effort. The Grand Duke was determined to prevent the Jews of Courland and Riga from doing the same kind of damage, and he ordered that as many Jews as possible be resettled inland, divided among eight cities in Russia. Once it was over, the number of Jews in Latvia had dropped from 190,000 to 80,000. Those who didn't die during transportation in closed railroad cattle cars, and who weren't murdered, may have eventually found their way to the West. Following the end of the war, small numbers repatriated to their homes. Most, like us, were permanently and forcibly resettled elsewhere.

It is difficult for us today, with our watches and clocks and calendars, to comprehend that my father didn't know the date, but in Illuxt, as in much of the rest of Latvia, Jews kept no secular calendar. We lived according to the Jewish calendar, which provided the cycles of the moon and therefore the time of dusk so that we would know when the Sabbath began and what time to light the candles. It told us when the festival days occurred, and what portion of the Torah was to be read each Sabbath. According to differing reports from elsewhere in Latvia, the expulsion occurred either on the second day of Shavuot, the Jewish festival that also commemorates the giving of the Torah, or on the Sabbath. Historians place the date of the expulsion between the last weeks of April and the first weeks of May, 1915. All my father recalled was that the order for expulsion came on a day when the entire community was in the synagogue.

About mid-morning, there was a commotion outside, shouting and stamping so loud that they stopped the service and one of the elders went out to investigate. He returned shortly with the local policeman, followed by one of the Tsar's soldiers, bearded and booted and carrying a drawn sword. The policeman strode through the synagogue, climbed the three steps to the Holy Ark containing the Torah, and as he stood beside the Rabbi, unfolded the proclamation of the Russian High Command, which he read in a booming voice. It ordered that within twenty-four hours all Jews were to proceed to the nearest railway station with only what they could carry, to be transported to the interior of Russia.

By then my father knew there was no passage to be had on a ship leaving Riga. He had to find another way back to South Africa. When they left the synagogue in a panic and discovered where they were to be resettled, he was elated. The community was to be divided among several Russian provinces. He thought that if he could somehow arrange to be sent to Yekaterinoslav, about a thousand kilometers distant, he would have managed to travel almost all the way overland at no expense, and it would be a simple matter to find a means of transportation for the remaining distance to the port of Odessa, on the Black Sea.

They hurried home like the rest of the community, and Isaak explained to Esther what his plan was. He had a valise, but few others did. They wrapped what they could in blankets or bedding, took the few valuables they had. Photographs. A prayer book. Whatever food was in the house for the journey. Esther made sure to take the teapot Isaak had brought back from South Africa, tied in a shawl and carried over her shoulder. Some families buried the valuables they couldn't carry, hoping that when it was all over they would be able to return to their homes. A few, who had cordial relationships with neighbors, gave their possessions into the care of those they trusted.

The train station was several kilometers away. We walked on the side of the road, through the spring mud. Those who could afford it hired local farmers with wagons. They passed us by, hoping vainly that they would not be separated from their belongings once we boarded the trains to wherever we were going.

The entire community spent the night at the railway station, outdoors, surrounded by soldiers, with only the blankets they carried for warmth. The soldiers lit fires and provided them with hot water for tea, but they were otherwise ignored. Some of the local inhabitants came to see the Jews who were being expelled, and through the firelight shouted taunts that Jewish homes and property were already being ransacked.

My own recollection of our journey is unclear, except that in my earliest memories I am never alone. Always Avrom and I are together, and no matter what events are taking place around us, we are able to find comfort in each other.

Until I read the letter my father wrote my brothers, I didn't understand what happened, or how. The act of reading it threw me back in time to the moment in my seventh year when the light in my eyes went out like a dying sun. Since then, I have lived as if by candlelight.

The next day about midday came the trains, with the kind of carriages meant for transporting cattle. Some carried on the sides in white paint the Russian word "spies." The soldiers hurried us into the empty cars, and we tried to remain together, all the family, but Esther's mother, her sister and her husband and their children were pushed into another car and we were separated. It was crowded and stuffy, and with only one small window, very dark. But after being outside all night, it was at least warm inside, and most of us slept once the train began its journey.

We had no idea where we were headed, but any destination inland put us closer to Odessa, where we might find a ship to take us to South Africa. Along the way the train stopped once and we were allowed to go outside, one car at a time, to relieve ourselves. First the women, and then the men. Some of the younger women came back after a long time, some silent, some sobbing, and would not speak of what had overtaken them. Out of respect, we did not press them for information. What would we have done had they told us? There was nothing.

The train started again, and when it stopped hours later, someone climbed up and looked through the little window. We were at a railway siding, the cars being separated. The cars behind us were uncoupled from ours and shunted aside. Among them were the cars into which Esther's sister's family and her mother had been forced when we were separated. Our car remained attached to the steam engine and continued along the track. We have learned, my sons, that one need not be separated from those one loves by continents or oceans in order to have a broken heart. All that is needed is a government of tyrants, and the excuse to issue a heartless edict. In all the years since, despite our efforts, we have found no trace of Esther's family.

We woke after the second night on the train to find ourselves alone. Outside was absolute silence. Through a knothole at the end of the car, we could see that we had been uncoupled, shunted to the end of a deserted line, and the remainder of the train had continued on. For several hours we waited, but no one came to open the freight doors. We tried the door from the inside, to discover that it was indeed latched from without. One of the men in the car was Samuel, a cobbler. We had grown up living in adjoining homes, and had played together in the woods as boys. Samuel had with him his leatherworking tools, and together with a tinsmith who had also brought his tools, and a number of the other sturdier men, they were able to break through the door beside the latch. The hole they made was large enough for an arm, and when it was done Samuel reached out and unlatched the door. Cautiously, silently, one by one, we helped each other down from the car. There were about sixty of us, men, women and children, and we were alone in the forest. It was a warm, spring day, and in the silence, the birds were our only companions. We had just been thrust from our homes with little more than the clothing on our backs. We had no place to go and no idea where we were, but we all felt, at first, as if we were on a summer holiday in the country after a long winter.

Someone found a spring nearby, and we washed ourselves. We built a fire. Among us we had enough tea and sugar for all. We prayed with the Rabbi, who thanked G-d for our deliverance, but there were those among us, myself included, who were doubtful that the unknown we had been delivered into was any better than the fate we had been delivered from.

We left the train and walked along a narrow road several hours until we came to the outskirts of a small village. It was late afternoon, and we stayed quiet in the woods while two of our party went into the village to see where we were, and to determine whether the villagers were inclined to be helpful. They came back smiling. The villagers would give us food and lodge us in a barn overnight if we could pay. We were close to Smolensk, about 400 kilometers from Moscow. I was disappointed because we were further east than I wanted to be, and I was determined that wherever the rest of the group wanted to go, the next morning we would head in a southerly direction toward Odessa, about 800 kilometers distant. We ate bread and cheese, and there were radishes and onions, and some potatoes, and then we slept in a barn, on the hay, lying one beside the other like cattle. In the morning we awoke, drank water, and went on our way with three other families who also had relatives in South Africa, and who had decided to accompany us to Odessa.

When one has no place to call home, any destination is as good as any other. The remainder of the community wanted to return to Orsha, closer to Illuxt, so that they could more easily return to their homes when it was allowed. I thought it folly to return again to such a place, having already returned once and lost a daughter to illness. And so, my sons, it comes time for me to tell you what befell us next. I have carried it with me since—another part of my body severed from me that yet burdens me every moment of my life as if it were bound tightly with thick rope to my back.

Along the road came a farmer pulling a long, empty hay wagon, and offered for a price to take us as far as he was going on his journey.

We accepted, and traveled in silence together for several hours until he dropped us off at a turning in the road and pointed us on to the next village. We continued on foot, staying off the road as much as possible, not knowing whom we might meet. In the middle of the afternoon Samuel stopped us and brought us together in a group.

"Gather around me," he said quietly. "Pretend that we are praying together."

We did, and he knelt on the ground in the center of the circle and unwrapped the roll of smooth leather he carried under his arm. He was a big man, burly and broad, with a soft voice and a dark beard.

"We are not traveling alone," he said. "Several young men from the village last night are hiding in the shadows. They move along parallel to us, waiting. We cannot know what they want, but men who intend peace do not skulk in the darkness. If their goal is to make mischief with us we must be ready to defend ourselves." He looked down at the unrolled piece of leather on the ground, where lay his livelihood, all the tools of his trade. "These are no good to me if I'm dead. But if I live," he said, looking up at us with a smile, "I want them back."

He handed a tool to each of the men amongst us. To me he gave a hammer with a flat face on one side and a chisel-like tool on the other. There were still some tools left, which he handed out to the women and the older boys. Your stepmother Esther picked out an awl, a tool for making holes in leather—a wooden handle attached to a needle-sharp piece of steel. Your brother Avrom was six, and he knelt down beside Samuel, wanting also to be included, to be a man. Samuel roughed his hair and smiled at him, and took from his pocket a little folding knife, which he opened, and cradled the handle in Avrom's small fist.

"Keep this hidden, Avrom," he said. "Let it be a surprise to them if they come upon us."

Then he rose from the ground. We continued on our way, walking closer together than before, and more quietly. I had Esther's girls on either side of me, holding their hands. Avrom walked on one side of Esther, and Lena on the other.

They came out of the forest swift and startling, and they were suddenly around us, no longer silent or hidden. How many there were I do not know. I have tried in the years since to count them, and sometimes there are eight; at others, as many as twelve. Strong young men, and in their eyes there was drink, and greed, and when they looked at the girls, other dark things. But we were no longer helpless as we had been with the soldiers and their rifles, and we were prepared to defend ourselves. They came at us, shouting and pushing, prepared to take what they wanted and expecting no resistance. We were after all harmless Jews, and we were unlikely to have weapons.

The first to strike a blow was Samuel's wife, when one of the louts put an arm about her daughter's waist and attempted to pull the girl away with him into the trees. The girl was fifteen or sixteen, and when she resisted, crying out in fear, he grabbed at her hair and hit her across the face. Her mother shrieked and dove at the boy, and she had a chisel in her hand which she drove into his neck with all the fury of a mother defending her child. He cried out and released the girl, holding on to his neck as the blood pumped out between his fingers.

Everything froze, and we all watched the boy weaving a slow dance to the ground, his wail weakening until it was a gurgle clotting in his throat. Then there was movement again, and the blood seemed to light a fury in our attackers. But Samuel had in his hand a curved blade that he used for cutting leather, and he laid about him with such careless might that he seemed to me a Sampson, and we followed his lead. Our attackers were carrying rocks, which they began to throw, and one struck me in the head, knocking me down. Before I could rise, two of them were upon me, and I used the weighted weapon in my hand to claw at their faces. Other than the rocks they had no weapons, and they ran from me, or fell away, I don't remember which. As they did I saw that another of them had his hands on Esther, who was struggling to free her arm so that she could use the awl to defend herself. But by now her attacker was wary, and he held her arm pinned close to her body as he tried to drag her away with him.

As I watched, my little Lena appeared from nowhere, unarmed and silent, her mouth set. Somehow she had picked up a rock and, seeing Esther in trouble, she smashed the rock against the attacker's knee. He kicked at her and she flew several meters, landing on her back. She remained lying still, struggling to catch her breath, and she watched with wide eyes as her attacker returned to his business with Esther. But my Avrom, seeing both his sister on the ground and his stepmother in trouble, flew across the clearing, a little warrior with the narrow blade in his hand. He reached up and drove its point deep into the back of the man's thigh and pulled down with all his might, and he opened up a bloody gash down to the back of the knee. With a mighty shout Esther's attacker released her and grabbed at the back of his thigh, pulling the little knife from his flesh. He turned on Avrom with such surprise and rage in his face that I was up in an instant. I was halfway across the distance between us before I realized what I was doing, and I flew at him with the hammer held high, ready to cleave his head.

I was clawing through the air, moving as fast as I knew how, and Esther was on the other side of me also moving toward the attacker. Before I reached him the man had my brave boy by the throat, and I saw the little knife thrust into him several times, like the tongue of a snake. Then the man saw that I was almost upon him. He threw my boy aside and turned to me. I flung myself at him, and his raised arms were too late to prevent my hammer from driving down mightily into his forehead. I will remember forever the satisfaction—and the horror—of watching his face split in two. But even as he fell to the ground I was pulling the weapon from where it had wedged in his skull, and I turned quickly back to Avrom. Esther was already bent over him where he lay at the foot of a tree, his little neck bent backwards from where he had been thrust against the trunk, blood seeping from his chest.

I remember nothing of what followed, other than that I was consumed by grief, and fury. Samuel told me I became a man possessed, raging about me with a strength far beyond my own. Of the men *who attacked us, few escaped, every one of them bleeding from wounds I inflicted. Seven remained lying still on the earth, all dead. Great damage we inflicted that day, all without either pride or glory. Our losses were far in excess of the revenge we exacted.*

We hid their bodies with leaves and branches, and we ran, bleeding tears and weeping blood. I carried Avrom in my arms until we were deep into the forest and exhaustion overtook us. And there, leaving the others alone, I took my boy with me and found a stream. I took off my clothes to bathe. As I removed the torn shirt from my back I discovered another loss—the pouch in which I carried my money—my passage back to you—was gone, ripped from my neck, and I cried out for the loss of you, too, my distant sons. After I washed myself I took the clothes off from Avrom and like a naked savage I carried his torn flesh into a stream. When I had washed the blood from his body I lay him down beside a huge oak tree, and I wept. With my hands I hollowed out a grave and I buried your brother, and as I said Kaddish over him, I cursed G-d for bringing us into life. This is the wound I have carried with me since, a wound that will not cease from bleeding—that the G-d I was born to worship has inflicted upon me such grief in my life that I find it within myself to curse his creation.

———◆———

With Avrom's death, and no money for the passage home, my father began the slow decline that lasted for the rest of his life. He lost the ability to make decisions. Since they had no way of knowing where the rest of the family was, Esther decided that we should travel towards Moscow. We avoided roads and villages, traveled by night, hid in the forest during the day. We ate mushrooms, and when we were lucky, caught squirrels and the occasional grouse. We stole a chicken when we could, or a few potatoes, but we were sure to take only what would not be missed, and only when it could be done safely.

One night in a small barn beside a darkened farmhouse, we found a cow with a full udder, and in the darkness Esther took its thick teats in her unpracticed hands. Years later she told me that as she put her hands on its warm and swollen udder, she felt the animal's benevolence, a willingness to be of service to us without any recompense. It was something so lacking in our lives that she wept with gratitude as she knelt on the ground between the cow's hooves, struggling with exhausted fingers to eject milk into a pail. Finally, standing outside the barn in the moonlight, we smaller children greedily drank the warm milk.

When we were done, Esther returned the pail to the barn, and when she came out she found the farmer roused and investigating the noise with a cudgel in his hand. No words passed between them, and although Esther was prepared to drive the awl into his heart, it was clear that he intended no harm. He was an old man, gaunt and unshaven, and he stood staring at us until, from the barn, the cow lowed quietly. He motioned for us to wait, and he went off into the barn, returning a moment later with a few potatoes and some shriveled apples from his root cellar, after which he waved us off, and returned quietly to his farmhouse.

It took until mid-summer before we reached the outskirts of Moscow, still reeling from the loss of all we held dear. We arrived half-starved and in a state of exhaustion, but there was no time to mourn. My father and Esther still had me, and Esther's two children, my cousins and now my sisters, to feed and house.

My father thought this would be a temporary station on the way back to South Africa. Esther was wiser. She knew these Russians, peasants all, and she felt with absolute certainty—as she had when her first husband left on the ship for South Africa—that she would never, ever be able to leave. She was right on both counts, and she was shrewder than he. And she had come to a terrible truth. Being a Jew, at least in the Russian Empire, carried an enormous price, and it gave her no satisfaction that, no matter how hard she searched, she could find no benefit that made the price worthwhile.

All the restrictions we lived with—where we were permitted to live and work, and what work was allowed us; which schools were open to us and which ones closed; the extra taxes we paid for the privilege of what little access we were granted; the constant fear we lived with, of pogroms and violence and deportation and capricious authority—were all a result of being Jewish. And, she thought, enough is enough. Her parents and family were gone, the wise but ineffectual Rabbi she had been taught to revere was no longer there to shake his finger at her. If God is really watching, she thought, what more punishment could he inflict on us? As we lay in the woods outside Moscow, about to enter the city as refugees without identification or status and with only the clothes on our backs, she told my father of her decision.

"Being Jews has brought us nothing but trouble," she whispered, "and in Moscow it will be even worse. Even the lowest peasant will treat us like the mud he scrapes from the bottom of his shoes."

"Moscow," he said to her, "is temporary."

It was a statement made with his finger pointed at the heavens, and in its absolute lack of verifiability, it brought to Esther's mind the Rabbi of Illuxt, who might have eased their passage into the next world, but who had never said or done anything to make life easier in this one. But she had learned diplomacy from him.

"You may be right," she said, "and I hope you are. But for as long as we're here, I'd prefer that no one should know we're Jewish."

"Prefer?" he asked, shrugging his shoulders and raising his arms from the rough bed of leaves and moss they slept on. "You prefer? You think your Jewishness is like the socks you wear, or your hat?"

"What nonsense are you talking?"

"You talk as if being a Jew were something you can put on or take off when the mood suits you. You think we can change our skins so easily?"

"When we walk into Moscow," she said, "we will be no different from thousands of others coming to find food and work and a place to live. We're refugees displaced from our homes in Latvia by the Germans. We have no papers, and nothing that identifies us as Jews."

"We look like Jews," he said, explaining carefully, as if to a child. "We speak like Jews. Our clothing marks us as foreigners. We eat only Jewish food, we have Jewish mannerisms, and no identification. You think they won't know in the blink of a Cossack eye that we're Jews, just as they knew in Illuxt? And besides," he said, speaking with finality, as if convinced that this would end the discussion, "we pray to a different God."

"You pray to whatever God you choose," she said fiercely. "If I pray, it will be to the God who gives us an easier life. We will never have a better chance to take on a new identity—and the children will have better lives."

"Better?" he asks. "How better? How is it better to be a Cossack who rapes and beats Jews than it is to be a Jew?"

Esther sighed and turned away from him.

"Go talk philosophy with the rabbis," she said. "Maybe when we're dead it will be better to be Jews. But while we're alive, it will be much easier to be something else. Anything," she said, "except a gypsy. And if you think your God will be angry," she whispered, "you can pray to him at night in our bed where no one can hear you. Perhaps the Cossacks will come and protect you from Him. Because it's a certainty that He won't protect you from the Cossacks."

When my father first heard Esther speak like this, he was shocked to his core. But the losses she had seen him suffer, and the losses they had suffered together, were sufficient to convince her that there must be a better way. She was determined to hide from outsiders the identity that fate had slung around our necks like a millstone. She had been watching the peasants of Courland all her life—but now she watched with different eyes. Now she was not watching in fear, to see what they would next do to her—she was watching to see how she could become one of them. And she was a rapid learner.

❁

During and after World War I, immigration officials in Russia were given one primary directive: admit no Jews. Applicants were not only asked to state their identity—they were asked to prove that they were not Jews. Their second directive was to keep unwanted foreigners out, and that included Germans. Our last name, Shtein, was too easily identifiable as

German, and there was no way to prove beyond a reasonable doubt that someone named Shtein was not a Jew. Esther was determined that we would shuck off this thing that defined us—our name and our history—like a pair of worn and broken shoes no longer up to the job of protecting us from the road, and toss them into the darkest ravine where they could never be found or linked back to us.

But we could not walk unshod into Moscow—she needed to find something comfortable and secure that would cover our naked identities and allow us to disappear into the crowd. We needed more than a name— we needed a new history, a place we came from, knowledge of what it was like there, and a reason for having left.

Esther knew that the only way to obtain the residency permits necessary to live in Moscow was to buy them on the black market. Thankfully, before my father's pouch was ripped from his neck, he and Esther had divided the money between them. Esther secreted hers somewhere in her clothing, and she still had it. But it represented my father's only chance of ever seeing his sons again. She knew it would not be an easy conversation, and when she first broached the subject, my father flew into as much of a rage as he was capable of at that point in his life.

"No," he said. "Never. I forbid it."

They were in the forest two days from Moscow. It was night, and they spoke in whispers. As she continued talking to him, he covered his ears, rose from his place beside her, and walked off into the darkness. But she was not to be denied. She followed after him. When she told me the story years later, as an old woman, she remembered that it had been summer, that the moon was full, and that they walked together in the darkness, arguing about which children should be the beneficiaries of the money they still had.

"We do not forbid each other, Isaak," she said quietly, sliding her arm through his. "That is not how this marriage works. We talk and we make decisions together—that's what we agreed when we married. Am I right?"

"Of course you're right," he said. "But, Esther, if we use this money, we give up our dream of a better life, and we give up any chance of ever seeing my sons again."

"Why?" she asked. "You made money once—why are you so sure that you'll never make it again?"

"How?" he asked. "Here we are nothing but peasants, without opportunity. Do I have to tell you again that more is possible in South Africa than will ever be possible for us here in Russia?"

"Isaak, my husband," she said, "listen to me. These are not easy words, but I speak them for the sake of the children—all the children. You left Mischa and Yossel in a place where they can make their own way. You gave them the most precious gifts you could have—freedom, and opportunity. We have not enough money to buy passage back, and no papers, and no way to get to a ship. Of the three children you brought with you, only Lena is still alive. The other two are gone, carried off by illness and violence. Yes, you should have left them all in South Africa and come here alone. Perhaps you should not have come at all. But how could you have known? You made the best decision you could; now we have to do the same thing. With Lena and my two girls, we have three children to take care of. Without residence permits they'll throw us into prison or ship us somewhere else, or we'll become beggars because we can't work. What will happen to our children then?"

They walked in silence, and he made no answer.

"Isaak?" she whispered. "Answer me. What will happen to our children then?"

"Esther, you put me in a terrible place. How do I choose among our children?"

"I put you in a terrible place?" she said hoarsely, raging at him but unable to do what she wanted, which was to shout and shake him by his collar. "I? We are all of us in a terrible place, Isaak. The only ones not in a terrible place are Mischa and Yossel. They're free. They have work. They have food to eat. They don't have their father—but if we don't use this money to buy permits our children may not have their father, or their mother, either. I'm not making you choose among your children—you've already done that."

She left him alone and went back through the moonlight to the children sleeping beneath the trees. What she had said was unforgivable, but she knew it was necessary. My father walked in large circles around them for hours, thinking about the awful decision he had to make. Esther heard him moaning, an aimless wounded animal announcing his presence with each footstep as he cracked twigs and shuffled dead leaves underfoot. By the time he came to lie down beside her just before dawn, he knew she was right. It was time to give up the dream of returning, at least for the present, and to ensure that whatever time they were forced to spend in Moscow was made as easy as possible.

❦

It would have been difficult for them to manufacture a believable history. Esther knew only Illuxt; my father was the only one of us who had been anywhere, or who knew anything other than village life. The first friend my father made in South Africa—perhaps the only friend— was a gentile, Genadi Ozolins, who also came from Latvia, where he and his family worked the land on an estate outside Riga. He and my father became friends because although they came from different worlds, they had a common geography, and they could communicate more easily with each other than with the English and Afrikaans speakers they came across. Genadi made a little money in the goldfields and his genius was perhaps that he knew when to quit. He returned to Johannesburg with his earnings, and he started a small coal delivery business. Initially he lived in a boarding house, which is where he and my father met, but shortly after my father arrived, Genadi married and moved to a fine house of his own. In the two years before my mother arrived, he and my father drank beer together every evening, talking about their lives.

Genadi Ozolins was the second of three sons. He would rather have died than become his father, a servile man who bowed and scraped outside the house, but who bullied his sons, beat his wife, and when he was drunk, became a monster. At the age of eighteen, as his mother cowered on the floor with blood in her eyes, and her husband towered over her with bloody fists, Genadi smashed his father's face into the doorpost and broke his cheekbone. He was in the vanguard of those who had the courage to object to the privilege of the landed gentry, and who recognized that there was another—perhaps a better—way, and he refused to serve in the Tsar's army. Instead, with flattery and his handsome, boyish face, he seduced the middle-aged spinster sister of the landowner, and she gave him enough silver to buy himself a way out of the country. She hid him in the wine cellar and fed him stewed chicken and carrots while the Tsar's soldiers combed the countryside for him. After a week, when they had stopped looking, he waited until nightfall and casually walked down the wide tree-lined drive, and out of his own history. He was not sure where he would go—America, Mexico, Africa—until he reached the port and took passage on the first ship he could get. During the voyage, he learned from his fellow passengers about the goldfields in the Transvaal, and when the ship docked in Durban, that's where he went. His timing was perfect.

When he and my father met, Genadi was already well-established in the coal business. What these two men from such different backgrounds had in common, other than the love of their new country, was unclear, but they became fast friends whose influence on each other would last a lifetime. Little did they know that Isaak and his family would soon be leaving and that their friendship would be cut short. They couldn't have anticipated that once we left, my brothers would find employment and family in Genadi's house. Nor could they imagine that years later, being childless, Genadi would leave his coal business to Mischa and Yossel, who had become like sons to him. And what my father learned from Genadi about the Ozolins family became the background for our manufactured history.

We became the family Ozolins, peasants who had toiled for generations on the land of a titled aristocrat. Our story was that at the start of the war, the landowner took his family and whatever wealth they could carry, and went to Europe, leaving the estate to run itself. Of course, it couldn't, and after two years the fields went to ruin. We had no alternative but to leave. And so we joined the stream of peasant families who left the land and traveled until we reached Moscow, the center of the world, where we hoped to find a better life.

Once the decision was made, my father began teaching us what little Russian he knew. As a boy he had some schooling in the language, and he learned more during his brief but disastrous stint in the army. Without knowing how valuable it would be, he and Genadi Ozolins spoke Russian to each other in South Africa. Esther, a girl growing up in a small village, was taught nothing. But she was smart, and she understood much better than my father did how essential it was to blend in. Within weeks she was practicing her Russian on the people we found ourselves traveling with. Once settled in Moscow, it didn't take her long to learn how to read and write. When I think today about how quickly and with what determination she reinvented herself, I am filled with awe and admiration.

Newcomers to Moscow were obliged to visit a police station. Those who were approved to live and work in the city received a stamp in their internal passport, a document issued to every citizen of Imperial Russia. If there were any Jewish refugees from Latvia who arrived legitimately, perhaps they were granted residency permits, or else farmed out to the surrounding villages. I never met any—perhaps they had all been left at deserted sidings to die in locked cattle cars, as we had. We had escaped that fate—but reinventing ourselves was not a simple matter. Until I became an adult, I had no idea what my father and Esther went through to create these new identities. Esther was fond of saying that hardship for some creates opportunity for others, and the influx of refugees into Moscow created a huge opportunity for badly paid bureaucrats who had access to the Department of Passports and Permitting and were willing to risk their lives to make extra money.

I don't know whether, as Jews from Courland, so far from the center, my father and Esther were ever issued internal passports. Esther would have made sure to destroy whatever documents they had; she wanted nothing that could connect them to the Jewish identities they were about to discard. Unfamiliar with Moscow and ignorant of big city bureaucracy, my father and Esther had no idea how to proceed. They knew only that they needed the required documents.

It was not easy to find a corrupt bureaucrat selling forged official documents—such a one was unlikely to put up a sign announcing his business. And it was especially difficult if you didn't even know what you were looking for. Esther had no idea how to go about it—but that never stopped her. It is from her, my stepmother, that I learned all I know about determination and survival—and she taught me two things that have saved my life more times than I can count.

She taught me that there is always a way—and that if there appears not to be, then I could always invent one. And she taught me that in order to discover my way, I had to watch the people around me. The ones to search for were not those wearing the richest clothes or carrying themselves with the greatest authority. No, I was to watch for those with shifty eyes, who seemed to move at greater speed than the people around them, and who seemed to slip among and between the crowds as if they had greater urgency, purpose, and knowledge of where they were going. The people I learned to look for were the ones who seemed to thread themselves through the crowd as if it were frozen in space, as if they were the only ones moving. These were the ones who had knowledge they wanted to keep to themselves— important knowledge, like which vendor had the least rotten vegetables, or where shoes were being sold, or where there was work. And the faster they moved, the closer they were to the sickle's edge, to the line between what was permitted and what was forbidden.

Esther told me how we trudged along the road leading to Moscow, stepping aside for mounted soldiers and horse-drawn carts. She described how she watched the people along the way, all of them in a condition similar to our impoverishment, convinced that she would finally see something of importance. And eventually she did. It was a youngish man in a long, shabby jacket, his hat pulled over his eyes. He wandered along the side of the road, taking big steps, jacket flapping at his thighs, walking towards us, away from Moscow. He looked carefully at those he passed. Just like Esther, he was searching. When he found a likely customer for whatever he was selling, he would stop and reverse direction, enter the roadway beside his target, and talk briefly and urgently before reversing again, moving to the side of the road and continuing his search. When we came across soldiers, he somehow managed to dissolve into the crowd, and Esther watched him as he changed direction, slipped off into the undergrowth, disappeared and reappeared.

"See that one?" she said. "He may not have what we want, but we need to talk to him. He has something to sell. I know it. Watch him—he approaches only men—see if you can catch his eye." She pulled urgently at my father's sleeve. "Remember, Isaak, we speak only Russian."

My father hesitated. He knew that if this was the right man, it would mean the loss of their remaining money, and all it implied. But Esther insisted. Finally the man noticed my father's beckoning head from across the road and made his way over. He walked beside them, looking at my father.

"What are you seeking, friend?" he asked, first in German, and then in Yiddish.

They ignored him, and he repeated his question in Russian.

"That depends," answered Esther. "What do you have to offer?"

"Closed tight as a walnut, aren't you, sister?" He grinned. "I can get you potatoes. Carrots. Onions. Fresh slaughtered chickens."

"Not interested in your food," she said, still walking.

"What then are you interested in? Work?"

"Yes," said my father, "of course. Isn't every man interested in work that will provide bread for his family? But you cannot sell me work, can you?"

"Work is hard to come by," he said. "But in Moscow today everything is hard to come by. And everything costs."

In answer Esther smiled at him, but said nothing. It was enough to inform him that she had the means to pay, at least something, if he could guess what they needed. Which wasn't difficult. If they needed work, they also needed what was required to get work. Papers.

"You are from what part of Mother Russia?" he asked.

"Latvia," Esther said. "Outside Riga."

He laughed.

"With the way you speak Russian?" he said. "Perhaps you want to be from Riga, instead of the other place you come from, wherever that is. I could guess, but that's not my business." He pulled closer to my father. "My business is helping people like us—like you and me—to find the means to get work and to live freely in Moscow. When you can pay for what you need, come to the Jewish soup kitchen."

"Why would we come to the Jewish soup kitchen?" asked Esther.

"Suit yourself," he said. "The Jewish community in Moscow has kitchens to feed Jewish refugees, and they won't turn you away." Again, he grinned, not unkindly. "No matter how much you want to distance yourself from them. Come every day at the evening meal. Don't look for me—we never met, I don't know you. But if you are there, I will find you."

❧

In 1915, 400,000 refugees straggled into Moscow. Although most were displaced peasants, some were Jews who arrived as a result of the massive forced resettlement, and they were assisted by Moscow's Jewish community. But we were no longer Jews, and Esther wanted nothing to do with the food and shelter offered by the Jewish community that we would otherwise have been entitled to and grateful to receive. Despite their determination to be identified as anything other than Jews from the Courland region of Latvia, Esther and my father felt that fate was doing its level best to thrust obstacles in their way.

"No matter how hard we tried," Esther told me, "it was as if the devil himself wanted to goad us back into that godforsaken tent."

Eventually they found the Jewish soup kitchen in the basement of a drab community hall, and when they walked in, they recognized that the task they had set themselves would be like tearing their own flesh. They had little in common with the sophisticated members of Moscow's Jewish community, but the food being served, and the mother tongue spoken, and the warmth of a familiar culture, seemed to wrap them in a robe of welcome. Esther took bowls of soup for herself and for us children with tears in her eyes.

Thankfully, Moscow was in chaos. Some of the city police and security services had been conscripted into the military, and of those who remained, many had been diverted closer to the front, where German forces continued to break through the Russian line. The city was overwhelmed with refugees, and my family was able to lose themselves among the throngs of hungry and dispossessed. Day after day, as the afternoon waned, we made our way back to the soup kitchen, hoping that the young man would keep his promise and find us. On the third day as we sat at a long table eating a thick potato soup with boiled onions and greens, my father saw him briefly at the entrance to the hall. He may have seen us, but he made no acknowledgement. After a while my father decided to disobey instructions and initiate contact, but by then the young man himself had disappeared. My father was disappointed, but Esther took heart.

"At least we know that he appears at this soup kitchen," she said, "just as he said he would. We need to be patient. He'll come to us, as he promised."

She was right. On the fifth day as we ate our soup, the young man appeared at her elbow, as if he were helping to serve food.

"You forgot your bread," he said, loudly enough for those eating beside us to hear, but not loud enough to be too obvious. He placed a bread roll at Esther's place.

She thanked him and he walked off, past us children as we sat between Esther and my father. Almost as an afterthought, he stopped and leaned over my father, smiling, as if he were about to share a confidence, perhaps about his forgetful wife.

"Inside the bread there is a piece of paper with an address," he said in a low voice. "Tomorrow is the Sabbath—one of the families here has invited you for the evening meal. Come at dusk. If you think you're being followed, don't come. And don't come without your money. Half before and half when the papers are ready."

He stood up and slapped my father's shoulder, laughing as he walked away. My father smiled at his back and then turned to Esther.

"Let me have the bread, Esther," he said softly, reaching an open hand towards her, "The children will want it later."

At the appointed time we appeared at the address on the moist paper retrieved from the bread roll. It was a two-bedroom apartment on the ground floor, in a building that seemed to Esther and my father like a palace. But this was before the Revolution—before collectivization, crowding, shoddy construction and shortage became the norm. This was just before the end of Empire, and artisans, shopkeepers and small businessmen managed to live comfortable lives.

It was into one such comfortable life that we were introduced that evening, to a middle-aged couple. The husband was a goldsmith working for one of the elite jewelers who served Moscow's high society. Our hosts apparently knew nothing of our appointment with the young man, who met us in the vestibule as we arrived. Before we went to dinner, he escorted us up three flights to a small attic apartment. It was empty save for a thin, nervous man sitting at a desk, his wrists sticking out of his sleeves like winter branches, and with the longest, finest fingers Esther had ever seen. There was a brief conversation about the names to be placed on the internal passports for Esther and my father. Half of Esther's money exchanged hands but it was not enough, and there was a heated conversation between the young man and the forger. Esther assumed that the forger blamed the young man for not being clear with us about how much was required. But it was clearly all that Esther had, the transaction had already commenced, and so they eventually agreed to go ahead. Perhaps our young man took a smaller cut as a result.

We were taken back downstairs for dinner, and all anyone remembered was the dish we had for dinner, which Esther tried to reproduce whenever she could get the correct ingredients. The dish required a whole fish, from which the skin had been carefully peeled off whole, like a sack, the fish mashed and mixed with cream, spices, potato and vegetables and placed back in its skin to bake. As I was growing up, Esther's description of how that fish tasted became a staple of conversation in our family.

Following dinner we were again escorted up to the attic, where the remainder of the money changed hands, and the thin nervous man presented Esther and my father with two internal passports stating that they were Peter and Inga Ozolins, from the Riga area of Latvia, and that we were approved to live and work in Moscow. Outside the family, we were very careful what names we used. I became Yelena Petrovna Ozolins. When I was old enough to earn money, my co-workers referred to me as Comrade Lena, but the old form of address using the feminine patronymic persisted even after communism, and I responded quickly to the name Yelena Petrovna. But the names Peter and Inga were strangers to me, and I never thought of my father and his wife as anything other than Isaak and Esther.

We found a place to live—one room for sleeping, one for living, and a kitchen. It wasn't much, but at least back then we didn't have to share the kitchen with eight other families. My father found work—first delivering bread, and then, once he was confident in his new identity, he revealed that he had been a baker and was promoted to the kitchen. Eventually he moved to the government bakery that provided bread to the railway.

From then on, we were Russians proper, and what happened to the Jews in Moscow or anywhere else was irrelevant to us. At first Esther and my father lived in fear of being discovered, but they gradually abandoned every mannerism and expression that might identify them as Jews. They listened to speech patterns and accents, and it became a game to guess where people were from. They had to work at speaking Russian with a Latvian accent, because although they had a lifetime of watching Latvian peasants, and although they spoke some Latvian, their original accents would have betrayed them as Jews. They practiced their Latvian accented Russian until it became second nature.

To me, their speech never sounded genuine, and as an adult I would laugh when I compared their speech to Latvians I met who really did come from the area around Riga where we had supposedly lived. But it gave them confidence; no one in authority ever questioned their identity or their speech, and so I said nothing. The subterfuge worked, but our secret burned its way into my soul. I hate the idea that I have been forced to live a lie, and the result is that in my life I have often chosen silence over deception.

Esther was determined to improve herself, and that meant taking advantage of what the city offered. She went to the Imperial Moscow and Rumyantsev Museum, and she discovered that the museum had a library open to the public. It was a place where she could pore over Russian writing without interference or question, and puzzle out what the letters were and how words were formed. And because it was important for us to know the facts about where we came from, she wanted to be able to read books of history and geography. Eventually she learned more about the history of Latvia than any peasant would ever have known, and she discovered in the process where the estate was and what rivers fed the fields, and what crops the estate grew. She learned the names of the nearest villages, and brought home to us the information she had collected. Around the table we discussed our fabricated history, and embellished upon it until they themselves believed it to be true. They shared with us children where we came from and the name of the Duke who owned the estate, quizzed us about our cobbled past until they were satisfied that if we were ever asked, we would reveal only what was safe.

Esther's trips to the library paid dividends beyond the knowledge she gained. As she wandered through the magnificent architecture, awestruck by the world of books at her fingertips, she discovered how easy it was to expand the boundaries of her knowledge. Beyond the geography and agriculture of Latvia, and further even than the vastness of the Russian Empire, she pored over books on South Africa and learned about the gold mines where her first husband, my Uncle Jacob, died. She read newspapers about the war and knew details of the rout Russia was suffering, and she searched for mention of Latvia. And always, she read what she could find about Jews, and their history, and what current insults they were suffering both within Russia and without. She seemed to take a strange and perverse pleasure from what she found.

One day she rushed home from the library, white-faced, to tell us what she had read in the newspaper. There had been a crackdown on the thriving trade in forged internal passports, and a ring of criminals had been arrested. The grainy photograph of the forgers included both the young man who had found us, and the thin, rounded man with long fingers who forged our documents. We waited in fear of being discovered, but within a few days there was a further announcement in the paper that the criminals, privileged government employees who had betrayed the country's trust in them, had been tried, found guilty of forgery and treason, and exiled to an unspecified village in Siberia. The finality of the sentence gave my father and Esther a sense of safety. At least we were in no danger of being identified.

Later in 1915, enraged by the unsustainable demands on Moscow's infrastructure and the increasing cost of food, fuel and housing, there were anti-Jewish and anti-foreign riots in Moscow. Esther and my father watched from a distance, horrified, as the people who had provided them soup in the community hall were hauled from their homes, their businesses destroyed, their families traumatized. I don't know whether Esther ever said anything to my father—perhaps she didn't need to. Perhaps the irony of our situation was so obvious that no words were necessary. We were safe, finally, from the ills we might have experienced as Jews. But the cost was that we had given up one history and adopted another. And I can tell you, having lived under the Soviet system, that although we may have fared a little better than the Jews we once were, there was not much advantage in being a daughter of the soil.

From where I now stand, I imagine that Esther must have lived her life like a woman cooking at a stove on which there are two pots of food, one Russian and one Jewish. The Russian pot bubbles and steams, and she tends it diligently, adding herbs and flavoring, but her eye rests longingly on the Jewish pot from which emerges the rich smells of her mother's cooking, despite the fact that it sits on a cold grate. As she lived in the Russian world, she looked longingly at what she learned of our people, and at the same time the ongoing insults they suffered—the expulsions and the injustice and the pogroms—gave her a sense of satisfaction. They vindicated her decision to abandon the destiny she had been born into.

She must have longed for her mother and her sister. I know this because even though she never spoke of them, she sometimes sat straight up in the early hours of the morning crying out their names, woken by nightmares in which she struggled unsuccessfully to find them. Although her life in Moscow was fraught with hardship and loneliness, she seldom complained. But she was impatient with my father, whose grief, tethered to his face, hung suspended above us like a moist grey cloud. As long as he remained at the emotional center of our lives, the only joy that came into our home was weak and filtered. Esther did her best to lighten the depression around him, and the way she kept herself afloat was to immerse herself in the larger world.

Esther's two daughters, who were older than I, had decided to drop their Jewish-sounding names when we arrived in Moscow, and they became Nina and Sofia. They both flourished in our new home, but Esther saw that I was sinking. After searching for work, scouring the markets and fighting crowds for food that became more and more scarce, ration cards in hand, she would come home exhausted. Nina and Sofia would be out playing in the streets, but I sat alone in our cold, darkened rooms, apparently content to do nothing. I was a silent, unhappy child who wouldn't—or couldn't—grow, had few friends and no interests, who did what was expected of her but seemed to have no inner life. Until the day Esther saved me.

She started taking me to the library with her. At that time you had to walk through the museum in order to get to the library, and when she first took me with her through the entrance and into the granite atrium, I pulled her to a stop before a massive painting. It was of a crowd of bearded men, looking together at something in the distance. Some of the men wore colorful robes, others were emerging or had emerged from a river, and were nude. I had never seen or imagined that such a scene might exist, or that someone might be allowed to paint it. Their bodies were so beautiful, slender and muscular and unblemished, that even today I experience the heat at the core of me that I felt on that day, and I remember the blush that spread from my tiny breasts up into my face. We stood looking at the painting, Esther not quite as taken by it as I was, but watching me curiously.

"What is it, Lena?" she asked quietly.

I couldn't say to her what I felt; I had not yet the words. But as I looked at the painting my eye was drawn to the center, where I saw what the crowd was watching. It was a slight figure in a blue robe, imbued with such peace and serenity that it was easy to understand why he was the source of so much attention.

"Esther," I asked, "who is the man in the blue coat?"

She didn't know, but on subsequent visits to the library museum, I learned that the massive painting was Alexander Ivanov's *The Appearance of Christ Before the People.* It was a very appropriate introduction to art—and to Christianity—for a girl who had lost her mother, her brothers, her sister and her home; who had been told in no uncertain terms that worshipping the God she had grown up with, and reciting the prayers she had once memorized, might bring death and destruction to her and her family.

I was fourteen or fifteen when Esther first took me to the museum. It was only a few years after the Revolution, and already they were beginning to dismantle the Russian Orthodox Church. In the eyes of the Bolsheviks, church and autocracy shared the same bed. Now the nobility was gone, it was time to reduce the church's power and wealth, and to break religion's hold on the people. When I first saw Ivanov's painting, we were already being told that religion needed to be abolished before we could be free and happy. It was to be banned, replaced with something called state atheism, based on scientific principles. It was all the same to me. I've never much believed in religion, and I don't believe in atheism, either.

When I first saw the painting, had I known and understood that the figure in blue was Jesus Christ, I would have been happy to worship him. But by then, it was officially not an option. I suppose, in my own way, I have spent my life adoring the painting. Standing before it became a ritual for me, and I made up stories about many of the figures in the foreground. Not Jesus—I never presumed to imagine what his life had been like, even after I discovered his identity. But by then, I had already come to terms with who I was. It would have taken an act of God to convince me that there was one, and I was certain that my conviction was in no danger of being challenged.

After that first visit, we went to the library together, Esther and I, and while she read the paper, I sat in front of an open book of poems or an illustrated book on geography. She opened the world to me and woke up my sleeping soul. I discovered that not all needed to be sadness, and realized that I would always be able to talk to my brother Avrom, since I carried his memory within me. And not long after, I realized that if I didn't cut the emotional ties to my father, my pity for him would drown me. And not just my pity—my anger, too. For while I was at his side taking care of his needs, he ignored me, preferring instead to mourn Yossel and Mischa, my brothers whom we had left behind.

We lived our lives as if the times were normal. For us, I suppose they were. We felt safer than we ever had in Illuxt, and if we were in danger, everyone else was, too. There was a new comfort in not being singled out for misfortune. But there was nothing normal about those years. In many ways, the twenties were a decade of optimism. The tsars were gone, and all the aristocrats with their pretensions, and it ushered in a new era of hopefulness. For a brief moment in Russian history, there was a great sense of possibility, and it was shared equally by the people and their leaders.

This was wonderful for my father, who managed somehow to raise enough money to open a bakery. It was, he said, a chance to start again, and during that period I remember him as happier, more affectionate, and present. Esther worked in the bakery beside him. They were making a success of it, and they felt, for the first time, that being in Moscow with new identities might just be the way to become independent. If the bakery were successful enough, if they could manage to save just enough money, perhaps there was still a chance of finding their way back to South Africa.

By the early 1930s, it had become clear to our leaders that in order to bring about the communist revolution, the State needed an industrialized base. The only way to build industry was to utilize the wealth of the country—the labor of the peasants, and what they produced. They established the collective. Again, my father lost his bakery, but this time, it was not his doing. It was the State, taking back private ownership of industry.

I don't much care that the nobility was massacred, or that the remnants of their world collapsed, and they were forced to live like the rest of us. But the middle class, too, was hounded into oblivion, and when they were gone, everything went to hell. Life became impossible for the shopkeeper, the artisan, the skilled worker who operated on his own, fixing, repairing, mending, making, designing. They were all taxed out of existence—and those who managed to survive were pulled before a committee of their peers and branded as profiteers. The fortunate ones were allowed to clean toilets or abattoirs. The others found themselves shipped off to Siberia.

Before the war there had been eight hundred shoe stores in Moscow. After collectivization took hold, there were only eight. And as it was with shoe stores, so it was for every kind of enterprise. The communists got rid of everyone with a skill—cooks and butchers and farmers who understood the seasons and the harvest, plumbers and engineers, tailors and boilermakers. They were all members of the middle class. The only really important class of people were the unskilled masses who knew nothing but scratching a living from the soil. I am old enough to know from my own experience that even during the terrible years of The Great War, there was food to be had. But once all commerce and production was left in the hands of the gigantic and incompetent State, the economy collapsed. The Russian Empire, before the war an exporter of wheat, could not feed its own population. And so the black market became the primary market in the Soviet Union, and over the years it gave birth to corruption and graft that blanketed the country.

In politics and industry, the Soviet system favored the most venal and corrupt. They rose to the top like scum in a cesspool. At the end it was so top-heavy that it collapsed under its own weight and brought the magnificent people's paradise to its knees. Six decades it took to prove itself unworkable—a period that coincided with the years of my life.

❀

When I left school as a teenager, I was already as tall as I would ever be. I was the shortest person I knew, lean and slight of body. I worked in the bakery for a few years, but when it collapsed, we all had to find other work. My father found a position at the state bakery. Because he had been one of the suppliers of bread to the trains, he knew people at the railway and was able to get me an introduction. I managed to convince the official transport comrades that I could handle the job of carrier and hauler. They gave me a job wheeling luggage for passengers, and I learned to maneuver the unwieldy carts carrying provisions and cargo to fill the cavernous, near-empty baggage cars for transportation across the country. I also got to unload the locked cars packed with fresh produce that came from outside Moscow. While we stood in line, using our ration cards to get flour laced with straw and mouse droppings, at work I saw fresh vegetables destined for government departments to which only Communist Party leaders had access. During the winter I was occasionally able to steal a few carrots or a squash and hide it under my coat, but that could only happen when there was no chance of being seen, because to be caught was, one way or the other, to disappear. There was no time for lengthy trials or executions—justice consisted of a quick hearing, and then exile.

It soon became clear that if every person in the chain stole a couple of carrots to add to the soup, our poor leaders would starve to death. Besides, the level of discontent among those aware of what the transports contained was not good for morale. Our leaders were fearful —always—of revolution. Instead of coming to the central station, loaded transports were shunted off to isolated railway lines and abandoned stations and off-loaded under cover of dark. The lifestyles of our new Russian gentry, the Communist royalty, had to be protected. And there were plenty of people willing to keep silent in exchange for a few fresh cabbage leaves, a pail of milk for the children, a small basket of beans. A jar of strawberry preserves. Tea. An orange.

Whatever I got, I took home to Esther, whose magic hands turned it into a tasty delicacy, despite what it looked like when it came in the door. One thing there was no shortage of was bread, which my father brought home from the bakery. I quickly made black market friends at work, and I learned to barter. A loaf of good bread was worth a dozen beets, a jar of honey, a half dozen apples. I found that meat cutters—one could hardly call them butchers, since they knew nothing about how to butcher a cow or a goat, in fact few of them had ever seen a whole carcass—frequently had extra meat to trade, and they always wanted bread. It was said that they added my father's bread to the fermenting potato they used to make vodka, but I could never get them to admit it.

My stepsisters Nina and Sofia and I became close during those years. We all left school and found what work we could, but at the end of the day we came home to Esther and my father. We three girls slept in one room, on one straw-filled mattress laid sideways, and extended with sacking, so that we slept side by side beneath two blankets, happy on winter nights to share our warmth with one another. First Nina and then Sofia found boyfriends and were gone.

I was the last one home, and at the age of nineteen I felt that I would never find a husband. When I went to visit my sisters and their partners in their new quarters—a bedroom in an apartment, in which there were five or six couples sharing a bathroom and a kitchen—I envied their intimacy and their privacy, and the fact that they could now make their own way. I'm not sure what that meant to me at the time, but it must have meant something. Perhaps I was jealous that they no longer had to live with my morose father, or that once they were no longer present to dilute his impact, his darkness became insufferable.

"Of course you'll meet someone, Lena," Sofia said one day, sitting on her boyfriend's knee. "You're so conscious of being small—but you don't see how the men look at your bosom, or those jutting hips. And you have such a sweet face." She turned to him. "Doesn't she, Alyosha? Tell her."

Alexei Zhukov was a shy man in his twenties, with straw-colored hair. He would have been handsome, but he already looked worn—he was a worker at a cloth factory, and his eyes and face were reddened from chemicals, his hands raw from handling rolls of rough fabric. He stroked Sofia's thigh, which looked slender beneath his hand. It surprised me, since I always thought of her as a big, healthy girl. She was dark, and her hair fell in black curls about her face. I envied her easy, open laughter and her wide mouth, which carried the promise of sex. There were boys always around her, looking hungrily at that mouth, and I knew they wanted her kisses.

In contrast, I laughed infrequently and with restraint. I knew from the mirror in the library that my mouth was adequate—in fact, I found it strange that my lips were shaped like those on the statues of beautiful women in the museum. But my lips were thinner than Sofia's, and I saw nothing sensual about them. Sofia was all woman, her warm flesh responsive, her roundness inviting. In contrast I was all straight lines, and I might have been marble or stone, like the mythological statues I read about, waiting for the right mortal man to notice me and awaken my flesh.

"You do have a sweet face, Lena," he said, "and a lovely shape." He blushed. "I'm sure you will find someone to love. What about the library? Do you talk to people there?"

Until Alexei spoke, it never struck me that there might be people like me at the library, where I continued to spend what little free time I had. When I finished work I would go straight there, to pass an hour in silence with my books, walking as always through the grand entryway, past Ivanov's magical picture of Christ and of the Jews watching him. Always as I walked by, I felt myself blushing as I looked at the flesh of my brother Jews, men like those I imagined I might have married had we remained in Illuxt. And as my eye was directed to Christ, I felt a confused kinship with him, with his suffering, and his attempts to bring what he thought was the way of God to our kinsmen. It was a strange relationship I established with this painting, spiritual yet deeply visceral; religious yet somehow as secular as the Communist Manifesto; Christian, yet very Jewish. I didn't know what to do with what it made me feel—all I knew was that as I stood before it and gazed into the world it offered, I felt consumed by it, made whole. And the questions it asked and answered were ones I could have spent my whole life thinking about. Best of all, it took me away from the real world, which I knew even then was a diseased place ruled by evil men who had been poisoned by greed.

I had never looked at the people around me in the library, but now I was curious. Could it be, as I sat at my cold reading table, that I was oblivious of young men in the library who thought as I did, for whom the written word was a refuge, who wanted to learn about the world? Men who, like me, were interested in reading between the lines in the newspaper, sifting through what was being said in order to discover what words were omitted, what ideas stifled? And if so, did they notice me?

Slowly, carefully, I began to look up from my books at the faces around me. I began to recognize the ones that reappeared, and although we didn't speak, they became old friends, like the books I had read and later came across on the shelves. There were the old people with sad, patrician faces, who might once have been gentry with their own estates and a staff of servants. I imagined that they came to the library to get out of the one icy room they now lived in, away from the ten families with whom they shared a bathroom and kitchen. The library was not warm, but it at least had some light and the illusory heat of other bodies. There were middle-aged men, ascetic looking, bearded, shabby, but somehow comfortable in their shabbiness. These I thought were the teachers and academics, now relegated to manual labor, who came to the library to remind themselves of what they had once been. There were a few men and women, people like Esther, who didn't fit into any category, but who clearly came to immerse themselves in books. I became fascinated by what their stories might be; wondered whether, if they looked at me, they had any idea what brought me to the library. There were a few young women like myself, and I found myself unable to imagine what they were after. Perhaps it was because in my own mind, I wondered why I was there, and feared that merely by asking the question, my right to return would be revoked. It was a terrible fear. The library was my one escape, and I shudder to think what I might have become without it.

But it was the young men I watched most carefully. As I wandered among the reading room tables, I glanced over their shoulders to see what they were reading. My guesses were often correct. The rangy, disheveled young man with an untrimmed beard was reading the politics of the proletariat, doing his research for the local party meetings he attended. He wanted to fuel his rise with facts. The compact fellow with hair trimmed short and a red wool scarf about his neck was reading Tolstoy. Perhaps he had been studying literature at the university before the war. There were others, plenty of them, but I was far less interested in them as people than I was in imagining their stories. After a few months, I stopped looking for a man who would awaken my womanhood. Instead I wandered the library, content to continue imagining the lives of my anonymous companions.

One evening as I entered the grand entryway and stopped as usual to look at Ivanov's painting, a man stopped beside me. He was closer to me than an unknown man should have been, and I stepped away from him, but he closed the gap I had opened. I glanced briefly at him to see if I had mistakenly stepped away from someone I knew, but he was a stranger, someone I hadn't seen before at the library, and I turned to continue my way into the library.

"Please?" he said. It was a question.

I stopped and turned back to him. He was only a head taller than I was, and I thought I saw green eyes. "Excuse me?" I asked.

"Please," he said again, "don't run off."

"Run off?" I said, letting my irritation show. "What am I, a lapdog? If I choose to leave, I will, but it's not in my nature to run off."

"I intend no offense," he said hurriedly. "I know you are going to the library. I've seen you. Often. Reading and walking around, looking at what others are reading."

"You intend no offense, but you say offensive things," I said heatedly, feeling the embarrassment rise to my face. "I do not watch what others are reading."

"I think it's charming," he said, ignoring my denial. "But you never see me or look at what I read, so I have finally found the courage to speak to you. That's why I ask you, please, don't run off. I may never find the courage to speak to you again."

I looked at him, not sure whether he was teasing me. He smiled. His mouth was the male equivalent of what I wished mine was, and his lips were full, his smile open. His eyes were indeed green, with thick dark brows, and his dark hair curled down over his forehead. He was beardless, and I could see his unblemished cheeks, his smooth chin and the smile lines around his mouth. As I looked at him he removed his gloves and held out his right hand.

"I am forgetting my manners," he said. "I am Vasily Stepanovich Lebedev."

I hesitated before taking his hand. Vasily Stepanovich ignored my hesitation, kept his hand extended, looked into my eyes as I waited. In the past, shaking the hands of men I met, I was often overwhelmed with despair as my hand was enveloped in one so gargantuan by comparison that I felt shrunken, whatever feminine existence I had, negated. Finally I reached out, almost holding my breath, and placed my hand in his.

"Yelena," I said, as I prepared to mumble my father's false patronymic. "Yelena Petrovna Ozolins."

His hand was much larger than mine. But it was not of a magnitude to cause despair. In fact, it was bigger enough than my hand to make me feel protected, but it was warm, and despite myself, I felt something in me begin to soften. Perhaps, I thought, this man might be the one to turn a female form carved in coldest stone to flesh.

"Lena," he said. "What a lovely name." And then, softly, "Lenotchka."

My breath caught in my throat as he took this unspeakable liberty with my name, calling me by the affectionate name my father and Esther called me when they felt particularly tender. It was a familiarity I could not permit, yet I was powerless to say anything. Finally I pulled my hand from him, and he slowly released my fingers.

"I have seen you," he said, "standing often before Ivanov's masterpiece. I would like to paint you as you stand there, studying the canvas. You look quite beautiful, as if you're searching for something." He laughed, something harsh and unexpected in the sound. "Of course, it would be quite impossible. We have no paint. There is no canvas. And no time." He shook his head, and the curls at his forehead followed. "No time. Imagine, Moscow, the center of the world, and we have no time and nothing to paint with."

No man had ever spoken to me like that. He revealed his appreciation
of who I was, his insight into what I was doing, and at the same time he
exposed things about himself that opened him to ridicule. He thought I
was beautiful, and he was a painter. A painter of pictures! Other than the
jewelers who made Fabergé jeweled eggs for the nobility, there was no more
contemptuous bourgeois occupation in communist Russia than one who
painted pretty pictures.

"So," he continued, "tell me, Yelena Petrovna, what do you search for so
intently as you study this painting?"

At that moment I would gladly have opened my soul to this stranger,
with his warm green eyes and his soft voice. But I knew that if I stayed, I
might say much more than was wise. I would have told him of my fear of
being always alone, and of the complex relationship I had with the painting,
and I could have happily spilled my family's secrets, our Jewish origins and
forged papers. It was terrifying to think that anyone could have this kind of
power over me, and all I wanted to do was get away.

"I must leave," I said, turning toward the entrance and buttoning my
coat.

"But you just arrived," he protested, following me. "And we have only
just met."

"I don't want to go," I said, "but I must."

"So you'll be back?" he said hopefully, walking at my side, easily
matching my increasing speed as I tried to outpace him.

"Of course I'll be back."

"And when we meet here again you will talk to me?"

"Yes," I said, "but only if you leave me now."

He stopped short. "In that case," he said to my retreating back, softly
enough that no one else heard, but loud enough to burn my ears, "I will
leave you, Lenotchka, until we meet again."

❦

I shared this encounter with no one, and I angrily avoided the library.

Without asking permission or finding out whether I wanted to know him, this stranger had decided to make himself known to me. Without warning, he simply appeared, took me by surprise, shoved himself into my awareness and so upended my life that I was now deprived of my beloved books. On several occasions when I needed relief from work or home, I found my feet taking me to the library. I knew he would be there, waiting for me, and I dreaded meeting him again. I wanted to see him—I tried out the words—not yet; not at all; very much. They were all true, and I made myself turn around before I arrived.

What I dreaded was how unlike myself I felt in his presence. My way of being in the world—the only way I found that worked for me—was to be controlled and rational. To think and act with deliberation and certainty. As a child I was not so restrained. I remember times of easy laughter with my family, and even, on the rare occasion, joyful horseplay with my father. But what I had experienced in my short life had already washed the playfulness from my soul, and the only way of getting from one day to the next was to get on with the job. I recognized that I was plodding and uninspired, but it was a way to live. Now, thanks to the unwanted attention of this man, it no longer worked. And at night, alone on my cold mattress, missing the warmth of my now grown stepsisters, I tried without success to remember—and then to forget—the way his palm had briefly kissed mine.

When after several weeks I finally ventured back to the library on my day off, there was a warming sun, and the drabness of winter seemed almost about to lift. I felt a lightness as I approached, almost as if I had found in myself a willingness to give over to the process and to let happen whatever might.

But Vasily Stepanovich was nowhere to be seen. I waited before Ivanov's painting in the cavernous entrance, and I scanned the reading room. Most of the collection was not accessible—it required a specific request of the librarians, who would then see whether books on a particular topic were available. But there were a few shelves on which reference books and newspapers were kept, and I wandered among them, my disappointment almost visceral. I kicked at the street furiously as I walked away, careful not to scrape holes in the soles of my cardboard boots, designed with brotherly love by incompetents whose only condition of employment was an unquestioned commitment to Bolshevik principles.

It was myself I was furious with. What right had I to expect that he would be waiting for me? That when I arrived after avoiding the library for weeks he would be there still, and that he would still want to see me? This, I told myself, comes of dreaming, of abandoning what works. I was done now with all of it. He was gone, I was back to normal, and I would resume my plodding life, take pleasure and comfort in predictability.

❦

Several weeks later I stood again before Ivanov's painting, seeing for the first time the two soldiers on horseback at the right side of the painting. Unlike the rest of the crowd, who looked up from the riverbank at the remote figure of Christ in the distance, the two soldiers were on a seemingly raised hillside. While all the others looked up at the godlike figure high above them, the painter had somehow managed to make it appear that the mounted, helmeted soldiers were looking down at Christ from a higher plane. It must be a trick of the eye, I thought, and I walked closer to the painting, hoping to see how Ivanov managed this illusion.

"Comrade, are you Yelena Petrovna?"

I jumped at the harsh sound of the voice at my ear, and the speaker took a quick step back.

"Sorry," he said. "I didn't mean to startle you."

I turned to see one of the guards who patrolled the museum. His face was familiar—grey hair and reddened jowls, puffy cheeks, a kind, tired smile. He wore an old military coat, brown and faded, and a wool scarf around his neck—one of the many old soldiers who were everywhere in Moscow. We had nodded to each other as we passed in the entranceway, but had never spoken before. He knew nothing about me, and I never told him my name. I was naturally cautious, but had learned to camouflage my suspicion with charm. Only once I discovered what people wanted of me was I willing to lower my defenses. I knew that if this was trouble, it would go better if he felt protective of me.

"I am Yelena Petrovna," I said, widening my eyes to show alarm, but allowing a small smile to peek through. "Who is asking?"

"Don't worry," he said, waving his open palm as if to quiet me, "there's not a problem. Your friend asked me to look for you. He waits—up there."

He pointed at the stairs that led to the second floor of the museum, where I had never been. I noticed the old soldier's grimy woolen gloves, whose knitted fingertips had been worn away.

"Does he have a name, this friend of mine?" I asked, realizing that it could only be Vasily. "And why does he wait up there?"

He shrugged his brown serge shoulders up to his ears, gestured at the paintings around us.

"You come here," he said, "because you want to read the stories in these books or imagine what tales the pictures tell. Your friend is no different— like everyone else he earns bread any way he can. He spends his time up there, looking at pictures other people have made. But he dreams of making his own paintings."

"How did you know my name?"

"He told me your name, and what to look for. He said you would stand before that painting, staring, turning your head this way and that. You would be slight, smaller than he, and he swore that in my life I would never have the good fortune to greet a more beautiful little woman." He grinned widely. "And he was right. Since last week I've been on the lookout for you." He leaned in towards me, now my conspirator. "If I know anything," he whispered, "your friend has love in his heart. Go on up. He's waiting for you."

Was Vasily watching me from the upper floor as I talked to the guard? If he was, I would not give him the satisfaction of seeing my eagerness. I forced myself not to look up as I slowly mounted the grand staircase, wondering what I would say to this man who could not possibly be in love with me, not after so brief an interchange as we had. No one had ever been in love with me before. Why should this be different?

At the top of the stairs I glanced around the room at the paintings covering the walls. Heavy landscapes, many of them dark, none as big or as impressive as Ivanov's painting. Vasily was nowhere to be seen. Several wide doors opened on to other smaller galleries, and in the second of these I saw him. He was alone in the room, standing with his back to me, looking intently at a series of small paintings on one wall, his head to one side. I would have been content to stand and watch him, but I knew that if I didn't make my way directly across the room and speak to him, I would turn and scurry down the stairs. When I reached him I stood just to his right and behind him.

"Comrade," I said in my deepest voice, "are you Vasily Stepanovich?"

He started, just as I had, but when he turned his head and saw me, his warm, open smile took form, and his whole face became joyous, even his eyes. "I am," he said in mock seriousness. "Who wants to know?"

"The guard downstairs—the one whose old gloves have no fingertips—wanted me to give you a message," I said.

"I know the guard," he said. "He is an old friend. What message did he give you?"

"He...he said...." I stuttered my way to silence, my cheeks aflame. I had started the game without knowing how to play it.

"What message, Lenotchka?" he asked softly.

I pulled myself together, stood up straight, and took a deep breath.

"He wanted to introduce you to a young woman. He may have said she was a...a short woman." I said, and then I paused, staring at him accusingly.

Now it was his turn to be embarrassed.

"You didn't take offense," he said, "did you? Please, I intended no insult. I think you are perfect. Your height is perfect. What I mean is, you are the perfect height. For me." He groaned, slapped his forehead, buried his head in his hand. When he looked up again he said, "See? In your presence my tongue wants to tie itself into knots."

"The guard was very complimentary," I continued, ignoring his confusion. "He did say she was short. But he also said someone told him that never again in his life would he have the good fortune to greet such a beautiful little woman."

Vasily turned crimson, but he laughed.

"I can't believe he repeated those words to you—they were supposed to be between us. And you," he said, shaking a finger at me, "have you no shame?"

"Why should I have more shame than you do?" I asked. "The guard also told me," I said as I stepped forward and pointed a finger at his mouth, "that when you smile your best smile, you are not quite, but almost, handsome enough for this most lovely woman."

Before I could stop him he leaned toward me and planted his mouth on mine. It was quick, over before it happened, and no one was there to witness it. He looked at me, his eyes soft.

"Do I owe you an apology for that?" he whispered.

In response I could only shake my head.

"I'm glad to hear that," he said. "Now let me show you what I've been looking at."

My heart was racing, but I didn't know until later that his, too, was running at top speed. We did our best to concentrate on anything but each other, and I have always thought that it must have been more difficult for me than for him. That short instant was a momentous one in my life: Vasily was the first man I wanted to kiss, and the first to press his lips to mine.

I followed him back to the wall, where he stood before a series of small oil paintings, portraits of bearded men and a few women. He pointed to them.

"I wanted to show you some of these paintings," he said. "Do you recognize any of these people?"

I peered at them. Some looked familiar, and I moved closer to the wall to look more carefully. They were beautifully detailed portraits of real people, with real expressions on their faces, and life in their eyes. It was amazing to me that anyone could capture the spirit of another person with a paintbrush. Was this, I wondered, some kind of test? Were these important people whose names I should have known, and was I about to be judged or scolded for not knowing them? Vasily placed a hand gently on my arm.

"There is no right or wrong answer," he said. "I know you recognize some of these faces—but do you know from where?"

The answer was there, but I had no words to describe what I recognized. I had never seen a painter at work, never tried to imagine what it was to hold a paintbrush or paint with a wet, richly colored liquid on a blank surface. It never occurred to me that perhaps a painter might first draw an outline on his canvas. I never thought to wonder how long it took to paint a picture, or how long paint took to dry, or whether the artist painted from life or from imagination, and I wouldn't have known how to ask the questions. I had a rich and vivid imagination, but I had little schooling and no exposure to culture other than what Esther had introduced me to at the library. This may not have been a test, but I felt foolish.

"I'll give you a clue," said Vasily. "These are not real people—but you have seen pictures of them before."

In my life I had looked carefully at only one painting. There was only one place I might have seen these faces.

"Yes!" I said. "I have seen them before—in Ivanov's painting downstairs. That's the man in the middle, with the dark, shiny beard, the one that looks like the teacher. And that old man, with the grey beard and the lined face, he's the one in the water, leaning on his stick."

Vasily's hold on my arm tightened, and he smiled. "That's right," he said. "They're for the painting downstairs."

"Who painted them?" I asked. "And why?"

"Ivanov painted them," he explained. "These are the studies he made as he designed the big painting downstairs. You've spent so much time staring at his work, Lena—but do you know anything about that painting, or about him?"

The heat of embarrassment rose to my face, and although I knew he meant no harm, I felt angry with him. I kept my voice down, but I was aware that he would see my anger and hear it in my voice. I have never been able to conceal my feelings, unless I'm haggling with a fishmonger, trying to get a good bargain, or to get a tip from a difficult passenger at the station.

"How would I know about such things?" I said. "I'm a country girl—I know nothing about paintings or painters."

"I'm sorry," he said quickly. "I was just trying to please you. I wanted to share with you what I know about the painting. I thought you would be interested."

"I am interested," I said. "And I'm not displeased—I just don't like it when my ignorance is so obvious."

"All that's obvious about you is your curiosity," he said, standing before me. He took my face gently between his hands, and his fingers were warm on my cheeks. "And your intelligence, and your fresh face, and your spirit, and your beauty." He paused, his green eyes on mine, and a flush in his cheeks. "There," he said, his soft voice hoarse with emotion. "I've said it all. Can I be any clearer in my feelings?"

"I suppose not," I whispered.

I placed my hands over his, and I returned the kiss he had given me. The space between those two brief kisses was only a moment, but it was a moment in which eons passed, and in which certainty was born. Love was only a few steps behind. But the intensity of the moment was too much for me, and as I lowered my hands from my face I took his with me.

"I've been reading about Christ," I said, folding my arms across my chest. I looked up at him, trying to put aside the thoughts that were rushing through my mind. "And his followers, like Saint John the Baptist. And the baptism by water. I know the name of the painting—*The Appearance of Christ Before the People*—but that's all. I would like to know more, if you will show me. Why did Ivanov do all these little paintings first?"

"Will you eat supper with me?" he asked. "Say yes, and I will tell you everything I know about these paintings."

Before I had time to think or object he took my arm in his and we walked together down the elegant staircase, out to the street and into the communal kitchens newly established by our Bolshevik leaders. That's how we ate our first meal together.

This was an essential moment in my life, but much of what followed has eclipsed it. When Vasily and I met, Lenin's 1917 decree expropriating all single family homes had already been in force for a decade, and my family—father, Esther and I—were forced from our small apartment into a "dwelling space." This was the term the Bolsheviks used to describe what all living quarters were divided into.

Our communal space had once been a luxurious apartment. Some of that luxury was still visible in the molding and the woodwork, but now twelve families occupied the apartment. The kitchen was still large, even with each family having its own assigned place for storage, and with so many cooking at the same time. In smaller apartments, families had assigned times for cooking because there simply wasn't enough space to accommodate everyone. In our apartment, some of the rooms were still large, but even a large room soon began to look shabby and worn if it had to contain the life of a whole family.

The standard living space was nine square meters per person. Had I decided to make my own way, as a single woman I would probably have waited years before being assigned to share a room with another single woman. I shuddered at the idea of living with a stranger in whose personal habits and tastes I had no interest, and with whom I had no desire to share my privacy. Was it any wonder I chose instead to stay with Esther and my father? The space allotted to us had once been part of a much larger living room, and someone along the way had managed to get hold of enough pressed board to subdivide it. They must have had material left over, and with it they built a cubicle in one corner, open to the ceiling. It was tiny, with space enough for only a bed and a chair, and it became mine. I was fortunate to have the privacy of my own space, but there was a downside. The board was so thin that when someone in the next room rolled over in bed I could almost feel their cold feet against my back.

Whatever luxury and brightness the original owners had lived with, their doors open, servants running about, Persian carpets on the floors, was long gone. The apartment ran the length of the building, rooms on both sides of a long, dreary hallway. The three dull bulbs hanging from the ceiling wept urine-colored islands of light on the floor. The only natural lighting in the hallway came from the kitchen, which had no door, or from private dwellings when people left their doors open.

In the name of social engineering, the Housing Committee threw together in communal apartments people who might in any other world be at each other's throats. Next to us were two women in their thirties, workers in some government ministry, one of them big-bottomed and sullen, with already grey hair and a harsh face, and the other a tall, fair-haired woman with a sweet smile. If they were more than roommates, no one knew, but they were discreet and quiet, obeyed all the rules for cleaning and the timetables for the washroom, and so no one minded, at least openly.

Beside them was a widowed economist, a bitter man who had nothing but contempt for the communist experiment, and his son, who was studying medicine. Across from them was an inquisitive young couple who always smiled sheepishly when they were discovered pawing through other people's belongings. We all assumed they were informers, but tolerated them because of their little boy, who crawled along the hallway and happily entered all our rooms at will.

At the other end of the hallway was a family of Bolshevik activists, parents and two teenage children. They worked in the Ministry of Transport, and when they cooked together in the kitchen their conversation was always about the revolution and the proletariat and the rights of women. Although it was loud and tiresome—we were subjected to compulsory political lectures on a weekly basis—we were all too frightened of the consequences to tell them to shut up. And beside them, as silent as they were loud, was an elderly couple, remnants of the minor nobility, who had once lived in a gracious home as large as our entire apartment. Their dazed expressions in those years still expressed disbelief at the degree of their misfortune. They made no attempt to live; seemed instead to be waiting for death, and I felt sorrier for them than I did for any of the rest of us.

Living under such conditions was difficult even when we all got along, but that was not the case most of the time. I spent as much of my time away from home as possible. When I was not at the library, I went to the public canteen, where we were all encouraged to eat together.

Communal eating, according to Bolshevik lore, would get rid of the family kitchen, which made women slaves. What it really did was turn the act of eating into an opportunity for political indoctrination, and it put control of the food supply in the hands of the government. No one was fooled. Sheep to the slaughter, we did as we were directed. But they were clever, our leaders. In the 1920s the canteen sometimes had a tablecloth and flowers on the table; there were rooms upstairs for reading and chess, and there were lectures—on personal hygiene, the virtues of thoroughly chewing one's food, and clean teeth. There were even occasionally musicians playing as we ate. This did nothing to improve the quality of the food—watery broth made with half-rotten cabbages or sauerkraut, a stew made of some animal flesh, probably hard-to-find horsemeat, and an occasional morsel of carrot or potato. Sometimes there was a fruit compote, dry and brownish, or a jelly made from fruit puree mixed with potato starch. And then, always, tea.

Although I longed for friendship and warmth, these were gifts I had learned to live without. I didn't know until after I met Vasily that in the grey days before him, my life tasted of ash. That he also brought intimacy, that he desired me, was more than I could at first accept. I wanted to dive into the relationship, but was convinced that he would dissolve into fog and leave me bereft. I remember feeling with dreadful certainty that although I had the spirit of a survivor, my losses were already so deeply layered, any more grief would make my life unlivable. I had no idea that I had a spine of steel—and there was much more I had yet to discover about myself. But I did know enough to be cautious.

Vasily and I sat beside each other at a long table, unaware for the first time of how inedible the food was. On the table there was a blotchy, once-white cloth, many times torn and mended, and a few benches down, drooping poppies in a glass vase. Vasily told me about Alexander Ivanov. It turned out to be less than all he knew, but then, he couldn't possibly have shared with me all he knew about painting at that one meal.

"Ivanov was from Saint Petersburg," Vasily said. "He spent most of his life in Rome. The huge painting you love took him twenty years to paint, and as he designed it he painted hundreds of studies to see what worked—how the landscape should look, and what kind of faces he wanted the people to have. When he brought the painting back and showed it in 1858, people didn't like it. It took a long time before it was recognized as a masterpiece, and many of the studies themselves as great works of art. Sadly, Ivanov didn't live long enough to see that. He died of cholera several months after he came home."

We sat together, my eyes on him as he spoke, and something strange happened—I became less curious about Ivanov, and more and more interested in Vasily, who knew so much about this painter, and spoke about him in a deep voice with such bright eyes and such enthusiasm, and who dipped his black bread in the remains of his soup with delicacy.

"Most great masters like Rembrandt and Titian are known for a portfolio of work —but Ivanov is known as the master of one work—the one you love so much." Vasily smiled at me. "So, even though you may be, as you say, a country girl, you recognize a great painting. In fact, I would say that you have exquisite taste."

"How do you know so much about painting?" I asked.

He thought for a moment, then put his hand over my wrist.

"I'm a painter," he said simply. "I was studying at the Academy in Saint Petersburg, where Ivanov trained. The Academy gave me a scholarship and money to live. I thought I had a little talent, and for a while I felt like the most fortunate man in the world. I studied under Malevich, you know, Kazimir Malevich, the artist?"

I shook my head in embarrassment. "Ivanov's painting is the only one I know. I never heard of this Academy in Saint Petersburg, or of your painter, Malevich." I paused. "And what did it mean, to study under this man? Did he teach you how to paint?"

Vasily looked at me curiously. "You really have no idea how charming you are, do you?" he said.

I wanted to look down, to turn away and hide the heat that flushed my face. But I would not play the guileless country girl to this man. I looked straight back at him, and simply shook my head. "No," I said. "I don't. But you should feel free to educate me on the subject."

"I fully intend to do that," he said, smiling.

"So tell me," I asked, "what did this artist, Malevich, teach you?"

"Malevich," he said, placing a finger softly beneath my chin, "taught me how to see." Slowly he turned my head away from him so that he was looking at my profile. "He taught me how to recognize what's in front of me. When I look at you, I see that the light on your cheekbones reflects up and colors your eyelids. I know that the shadow of your hair at your temples makes your skin appear translucent. That the contours of your ears and the shapes of your lips are as complicated and delicate as the inside of a seashell." He turned my head back towards him, removed his finger from my chin, and smiled. "And I can see how flushed your cheeks become when you are the center of attention."

"I prefer not to be," I said.

"That's part of your charm," Vasily said. "Anyway, I studied with Malevich for several years, starting in 1921. Back then, it felt as if anything was possible. The big industries, steel and oil, were privatized, and people were encouraged to start their own business. You know about that—it's why your father was able to open his bakery. After the tsars were gone, people felt able to express all the creativity in their souls. You've seen it in the new architecture, and it showed itself in art and literature, too. But after a few years, I think it was 1926, the Academy was denounced. The communist press accused us of supporting counter-revolutionary artistic debauchery, whatever that means. The doors were closed. But when it reopens," he said bitterly, "I'm guessing it will be a place where anyone can go to make socialist art, and design posters to forward the revolution."

I looked around to make sure no one was listening. I was shocked by his carelessness. "Such dangerous talk," I whispered, "is foolish. We live in a world where you have to be careful not to wrap your lunch in a piece of newsprint that contains a picture of Stalin. You know that's what one of my co-workers did last week? Someone reported him, and the next day they came to get him at work."

He looked at me, and he smiled. "I'm grateful to see how deeply you care for my safety. I would share any thought with you, Lenotchka, no matter how dangerous. But I'm boring you with my tale of woe. You don't know or care about any of this, do you?"

"It's not that I'm not interested. I'm just—not informed. But," I said quickly, "I would like to know more."

We both looked down at his hand on my wrist, the way his fingers curled all the way around, long enough to touch even his baby finger to his thumb. He looked up and smiled at me again, and he ran his roughened thumb across my knuckles.

"Your hands are beautiful," he said.

I said nothing, watched as he stroked me. It was warm and comforting, my most intimate contact yet with a man—far more than the brief kisses we had exchanged. His touch was a liberty, just like the liberty he took with my name. I wanted them too much to deny him, but it felt as if our talking, and our touching, should have been done in private. I gently pulled my hand away.

"Tell me more," I said, not wanting it—whatever it was—to end. "What did you do when the Academy closed?"

"My world came tumbling down—but I wasn't alone." He shrugged his shoulders. "It happened to everyone who had something to lose. I couldn't help thinking that for the millions of Russians who had nothing, this new world might be a good thing. I wanted to be a part of it. So I came home to Moscow, joined the Communist Party, and became a schoolteacher. That's the short version of my story." He shrugged. "You will find me very pragmatic, Yelena Petrovna. When things get difficult, I become practical and move on. In this new world, where the proletariat is king, part of being practical is making sure no one knows I was ever interested in anything as bourgeois as art. But I feel that I can tell you anything. Besides, I must be willing to reveal myself, because I want to know everything there is to know about you."

He stopped, looked up from our hands on the table, and I felt the heat of his green eyes on my face. "So, my little Lenotchka," he said with a soft smile, "will you tell me who are you?"

Had Vasily invited me in that moment to spend the night sleeping chastely beside him, I would have done so. And had he asked me to go back to his dwelling, wherever it was, so that he could undress me and make love to me on his bed, I would not have refused him that, either. But he didn't offer me his body or ask for the gift of mine —instead he asked me who I was—and there was no truthful answer I could give him. At that moment I was not prepared to lie to him, and I knew that if I stayed, I would betray my family's secret. So I did the only thing I could—I rose from the table. As I rose, he rose with me, shaking his head vehemently, as if he already knew my intention.

"No," he said.

"I'm sorry," I said, "I have to go."

"Not this time," he said. "Somehow I manage to scare you away, without even trying. The last time you left me in a hurry like this you disappeared for a month. I'm not going to let you run away again."

"I'm not running away," I said, hearing the desperation in my voice as I struggled into my coat. "I don't want to go, but I must."

"That's what you said last time," he replied fiercely. "This time I'm not letting you go until I know when I'll see you again. And where. You haven't told me anything about yourself—not where you're from, what you do, nothing."

"You know my name," I said breathlessly. "I work at the main railway. I'll see you tomorrow at the library, after I finish work. In the little room, upstairs with Ivanov's pictures."

Then I ran from the canteen before I could change my mind.

☙

I paced frantically through the frigid Moscow night, my feet like blocks of ice and my face numb. For hours I wandered, several times crossed Red Square, walked in circles through the streets around our apartment building. Most of the time I was hardly aware of where I was. My fingers in the pockets of my coat squirmed of their own volition to avoid freezing. The snow cracked beneath my boots like gunshots, and my breath came from my nostrils like frozen mist that quickly fell away behind me.

What did I run from, that night? From being discovered, yes, but also from the chance to discover who I might become if I allowed Vasily to see who I really was. I had no intimate friends. I was well protected, and my swagger and toughness were defense against being exposed. What I didn't know until that night was how weak and fragile I was without my swagger. Being naked with Vasily, my skin to his, would have been fine—but he was the only person who had ever managed to get under my skin. It was as if he could reach my most hidden thoughts, the private fibers and juices beneath my surface; as if, should he wish, he might coax from my veins the fluids that ran through them. I was terrified, and yet more than I could put words to, I wanted this closeness with him.

I had no doubt that any relationship we might have could not coexist with lies. It would wither and die as surely as a poisoned plant. And until that point in my life, there had never been a living thing I wanted more to nurture and protect. If there was a way to have it all—to have Vasily as lover and friend, and at the same time to protect my family—I would find it.

❦

When I arrived at the library the following evening I stopped downstairs to wash my face and run my fingers through my hair. I was excited, and I looked pretty, not like someone who had been wheeling luggage and provisions all day at the railway station. My friend, the museum guard, smiled at me. I smiled back, and then ran up the stairs to find Vasily already waiting for me. He was alone in the little exhibition room, looking at Ivanov's paintings, and I walked straight up to him, slipped my arm through his, and kissed his cheek. He turned to me with surprise on his face, and I saw the pleasure in his eyes.

"I'm so glad you came," he said, showing his top teeth. They were white and not very straight, but when he smiled, his face took on a glow, and I was sure that what I was doing was right. I laughed at his words.

"I said I would be here, and here I am." I paused. "But I have made some decisions."

"Yes," he said. "Something is different." He searched my face for a clue, and then touched my cheek. His brow was furrowed, and he looked very serious. "Whether or not I like it, I will respect whatever decision you make."

"Thank you," I said. "Last night I had some thinking to do, and I ran away from you. I wanted to apologize, and to promise you that it will never happen again."

"That would be good," he said solemnly. "Now we can have a conversation from beginning to end." He paused. "Is that what you've decided?"

"That's one of the things," I said. "But there are others."

He started to speak but I put my fingers to his lips.

"Let me finish," I said quietly. "This is not the easiest thing I've ever done."

He nodded his head in agreement, and he kissed my fingers as I lowered my hand to my side. Quickly I looked around to be sure we were still alone, and then stepped back and stood tall, with my shoulders straight and my head up, as Esther had taught me.

"I don't want to do anything you don't like—quite the opposite," I said, and discovered with pleasure that when I stood tall, I could look up directly into Vasily's eyes. I spoke slowly, all these words, more words than I could remember ever speaking before to anyone. It was as if I were taking a vow, witnessed by Ivanov's paintings of Jews and Pharisees looking over our shoulders.

"My life has been like a rope," I said, "twisted and tied into knots. Some of those knots belong also to other people, and some are truths I have promised not to reveal. So some things that are not mine alone to share with you. Not now, and perhaps not ever. But I promise never to tell you anything that is not true." I stepped forward and took his hand. "Vasily, I cannot completely give myself away. Not yet. But in this new world we talked about last night, I believe everything is possible. If you can accept what I offer, I will share with you whatever is mine to share."

Without speaking he wrapped his arms about me and hugged me to his chest. I felt the warmth of his neck against my cheek, and beneath it the particular smell of his skin—first tobacco, and then his sweat, which never changed. As long as I live, the bittersweet, musty smell of dry leaves on a summer wind will remind me of Vasily.

"When first I saw you," he said, his voice muffled in my hair, "I knew I would never find a woman more gracious or honest. What you offer is more than I could have hoped. Of course I accept."

"So," I whispered, "what happens now?"

"When we come to a more private place," he said, "I am going to take your lip between my teeth, as you were doing standing before the picture downstairs, on the day I first saw your face and was turned to stone. And then my plan is to kiss you as I have imagined kissing you since that day."

He smiled his gentle smile, a smile that seemed always to start with his eyes opening wide, and the flesh at his temples creased, pulling up at the skin over his cheekbones, which only then lifted the corners of his mouth and opened his lips to show those crooked teeth. I loved watching it happen, and I learned that once his eyes opened, the dawn of his smile was never far behind.

"But before that," he said, "I want to know something about the woman I plan to kiss, because afterwards she is likely to be speechless."

We went back to the canteen where we had eaten the previous night. On the second floor at the far end of the building there was a small reading room. In it there were several people sitting and reading, and an old grandmother at the entrance, knitting socks, watching and keeping order. We sat together in one corner, at a plain wood table with two straight-backed chairs. Vasily selected a book at random from the shelf and opened it on the table before us.

"This is after all a reading room, and we need to be seen to read," he whispered. "So, Lenotchka, again I ask, will you tell me who are you?"

"Yes," I whispered back. "I will tell you whatever is true, even though it might hurt me, so long as it doesn't hurt those I love. Ask me what you want to know."

"I will. But first tell me, why do you think my questions might hurt you?"

"I have never shared the difficult parts of my life with anyone," I said haltingly, not quite knowing where I was going. "It's always been easier to remain silent."

I wanted desperately to be worthy of this man, and although I had promised him the truth, I wasn't so sure that the truth would show me in the best light.

"What is it?" he asked, alarm in his lowered voice. "You are suddenly pale. Are you ill?"

"No," I said, adjusting myself on my chair. I sat up straight, reminded myself that I had reason to be proud. "I'm fine. My life has been what it is. My answers will be what they are." I shrugged. "We will like each other's history, or we won't."

"So," he grinned, "we're both fearful of disappointing each other. At least we start out on the same foot." He bent his head towards mine so that our hair touched and tickled my forehead. "Tell me, how does a country girl come to be in the center of Moscow?"

"When I was a child," I whispered, "my family came to Moscow." I looked at him as I spoke, sure that I would be unable to lie while he stared at my face. "We came from Latvia, my father, stepmother and two stepsisters."

"What happened that you left Latvia?"

"During the war we lost our home, everything. We became refugees."

"From German forces?" He asked. "Or from Russian soldiers?"

"Does it matter?" I asked wearily. "The war came. It didn't care who we were. Everyone was a victim. There was no winner, and the Russian people lost."

He looked around us.

"These days that's a dangerous opinion," he whispered.

"I said I would tell you the truth." I answered defiantly. "That means more than the facts of my life. What I said about the war is based on what I've seen, and it's my truth. Do you not like it?"

"It's not that I don't like it," he said. "I think you're right. But that doesn't make your opinion—or mine—any less dangerous."

"Then it's a good thing we're only telling each other," I said. "What's your next question?"

"It's your turn," he said. "Is there nothing about me you want to know?"

"Everything," I whispered. "Where you grew up, how your childhood tasted, how you feel about your mother and your father, what you teach, what foods you like, who your friends are. What you think, and what you believe, and what you want for your life. But I have time. And I know you'll tell me what you need to, when the time is right."

"You make me ashamed of my desire to know you all at once," he said. "So I'll put my curiosity away, and we can feed it slowly, as we feed yours. Just answer me one more question. How does a country girl come to spend so much time at the library?"

"I knew you would ask me about the library," I said, smiling, "and about Ivanov's painting." I closed the few centimeters between us and kissed his face. "I have never spoken of this because it's the part of my life that hurts most. But I'm glad you asked, because you need to know."

For the first time I told the story of my twin brother Avrom's murder, and how I was never really aware of how close we had been until he was suddenly gone. I described how worried Esther was when she came home to find me curled up against the wall, nursing my bereaved heart; how she took me to the library in the hope that I would find something there to make me want to live again.

"I'm so sorry," he murmured. "How fortunate for you that your stepmother was looking out for you." He paused. "Or do you think of her as your aunt?"

"Much more than a mother," I said, "she has been the saving grace in my life."

He gently stroked my hair. It was cut short, chopped around the ears in the fashion of the time, and at his touch I felt a tingling, as if the skin of his fingers was in direct contact with my scalp.

"If I invited you to come home and share my supper, what would you say?"

"Would I need to say anything?"

He took my hand and we walked through the darkness together, purposeful and silent. His room was ten minutes away. When we arrived, we left our boots and coats inside the front door of the apartment, and he walked me quickly down the dimly lit corridor, ignoring his neighbors' curious glances. He unlocked his room and ushered me in. Then he closed the door behind us and took me in his arms.

"I've wanted to do this since the first moment I saw you," he murmured.

I was twenty, waiting for my chance at love. But I was dry and parched, a dormant plant in the desert of my life. I thought myself hardened, my skin thickened and scarred by incessant battering, and I had a hard time believing that Vasily found me appealing. But he put his lips to mine, and when I felt his tongue I was unsure what was expected of me. He showed me, softly, insistently, and I opened my lips to him. The taste of him, and his gentleness, and the intimacy of what we were doing, were like unaccustomed rain, and I flowered like a desert plant. My arms locked about his neck, and I opened my mouth to him, returned his kisses with a passion I never imagined existed in me. He taught me more than I ever thought possible about how tongues could talk to each other, and about how deep a kiss might be.

That night I remembered I was still a girl, and at the same time I became a woman. I gave myself to him with such joy and openness, and I took from him all the gifts he offered—the sharp musk of his scent as I kissed his underarms and the soft hair on his chest, the pleasure of his warm skin against mine and the long muscles in his legs. When he came into me I felt a brief moment of pain, and then surprise—at his hardness, and at what happened when, very gently, he took my breast into his lips, first very gently and then, sweetly, carefully, with his teeth. The silent cry that came from me lasted until I had slowly emptied all the breath in me and the room began to spin. Had I not made Vasily stop and taken huge gasps of air I would have fainted.

❦

Vasily introduced me to love, and when he came into my life I discovered what it was to have something—someone—worth living for. He became my best friend, and eventually the repository of all my secrets. By the time I shared with him that we were Jewish, it was a non-issue between us. He had already guessed that I was protecting my family and that our identities were forged. We were so in love that no truth I could have revealed about myself would have lessened the intensity of his feelings for me.

It astonished me that he loved me as deeply as he did, but it was constant and all-consuming. He was considerate, always tender, often funny. We laughed our way through the days, thinking of each other, waiting to be together in the evenings, and at night he couldn't get enough of me, nor I of him. We discovered to our surprise that cardboard walls result in heightened passion; that having to make love in silence leads to careful, leisurely movements, soft whispers, holding of breath, and to pleasure stretched out, staggered and prolonged.

But by 1928 the country was in turmoil, confused and barely functioning. We learned to live as if in two worlds, one foot planted in each, never sure when the balance was about to shift from one foot to another. The more I came to love Vasily, the more I dreaded losing him. It didn't take much imagination. There were the epidemics of disease, which gave radio and press an opportunity to trumpet Soviet medicine's advanced treatments for flu and dysentery and cholera, and to extol the skill of our dedicated physicians and nurses. There were revolts, always in distant provinces, by greedy peasants unwilling to sell their produce to the State at mandated prices, and always put down successfully by the proud and brave members of our Soviet military. Closer to hand, there were the regular arrests of minor officials or important Party members, on charges of mismanagement, fraud, or anti-Soviet behavior.

Most frightening were the periodic arrests of our neighbors, often the most unlikely ones. Many never returned, having admitted under interrogation that they had mixed ground glass into bread or diluted wheat with sawdust. They had overcharged at State stores and pocketed the excess, or sold food on the black market at exorbitant, capitalist prices. They were banished. Later, when isolated villages could no longer cope with the number of exiles, punishments became more varied. Some were executed. Siberian exile was institutionalized in the form of the Gulag, about which the world already knows enough from those determined enough to have survived.

The few of our neighbors who did return gave credence to our worst nightmares. After absences of weeks or months they would suddenly reappear, gaunt, limping, nursing broken fingers or infected jaws where teeth had been pulled, minds twisted from enforced wakefulness, bodies wracked by exposure to iced water, wet blankets and unheated cells. But their withered souls, visible through their eyes, were most terrifying. They had been damaged beyond repair, the damage inflicted by their brothers. For them, and for us, there was no retreat from knowing that unspeakable brutality is camouflaged by only the thinnest veneer of civilization. They had been flayed alive, the veneer pulled back, their lives—and by extension, ours—revealed to be hell on earth.

But in this fearsome environment there was still room for hope. Love bloomed, young couples wed and children were born. Small victories took on significance. And we were fed a diet of how wonderful our leaders were, of the radiant future they planned for us.

We were exhorted to love the Motherland, to work for the triumph of the proletariat, and there was a constant stream of celebrations and festivals with balloons and music and food, and massive colorful posters of happy, healthy workers with thick wrists, full heads of hair, and the joy of work blazing in their eyes. We were all caught up in this strange combination of deprivation, delusion and mania. It lasted for a long, long time. In fact, it survived the collapse of the Soviet Union. From what I can see, it remains the frame through which the Russian people still view the world.

✿

I took Vasily first to visit my stepsister Sofia and Alexei. I had not been to visit them since Sofia told me I had a nice bosom and a pretty face. We brought a bottle of vodka, and as we sat on their bed, we toasted one another and ate pickled sardines and bread that Sofia got from my father.

"See, Sofia," said Alexei, looking at her as he raised his glass of vodka to toast us, "I was right—I told Lena to look in the library for someone to love."

"It was the right place," said Vasily, putting his arm about me, "but she didn't do any looking. I had to do all the hard work. Finding her was difficult enough—convincing her that I was good enough was exhausting. But finally she came around." He put his hand under my chin and gently lifted my head until he could see my eyes. "Right, Lenotchka?"

"I always knew you were good enough," I said. "It was me I wondered about."

"Look, Alyosha," laughed Sofia. "Neither of them thinks they're worthy of the other. Don't you think they're a perfect match?"

They sat together on the bed, he leaning against the wall, and she resting her full body against his chest. He put one big, raw hand on her shoulders, slipped the other around her waist, and spoke into her ear.

"Whereas you and I both agree," Alexei said, "that you're way too good for me, right?"

Sofia giggled and turned her face up to be kissed. I remember feeling for the first time as an adult a sense of place, of belonging to a community and of playing an important role in my own life. It was a lovely moment— two young couples in love, comfortable enough with each other that we could be honest and joke about our relationships.

A few weeks later we celebrated their wedding in our kitchen, inviting all our neighbors in the apartment. My father managed to exchange bread from the bakery for eggs and pickled fish, and he brought home a loaf of bread baked with raisins. We drank tea, toasted the couple with vodka, and

I introduced the rest of my family to Vasily. As usual, my father was distant and tearful, but he managed to pull himself together enough to make a toast, and to show some interest. Esther was wonderful, enthusiastic and gracious, and she welcomed him with her big, open heart.

Vasily got along well with Alexei and with my sister Nina's boyfriend Sergei, and after the wedding we spent several evenings together. It felt to me that our lives might just have turned a corner. Perhaps, I thought, there was the possibility of ease and safety for us, that the decisions my father and Esther had made were about to bear fruit.

Then the foreman at Alexei's mill was arrested for not producing his quota of cloth. Sofia came to me in tears, fearful that Alexei would be denounced. He had complained to the foreman about the danger of running the looms too fast, which caused flaws in the fabric. He also pointed out that fabrics were being rushed through the dye, which ensured that the colors would quickly fade. The foreman took no notice, but once arrested, he was pressured to name workers whose lack of cooperation was responsible for unmet quotas. Alexei's name was at the top of the list.

Production quotas were set by the State, and the State was never wrong. When quotas were not met, it was because some poor unfortunate worker lacked the necessary commitment to our "Glorious Future." Someone always had to pay. The foreman disappeared, his wife and children left to fend for themselves. Alexei and Sofia were relocated to a Siberian mining village somewhere in the frozen *taiga* reserved for enemies of the State. It was not a prison sentence with a set term. It was lifetime banishment.

We all wept together, found ways to give them something that would remind them of us and at the same time warm them in the frigid Siberian winters. I gave Sofia the blanket from my bed; Esther and my father gave her the teapot we had brought back from South Africa. Sofia wanted me to have it—it had been made by my great-grandfather.

"No, Sofia," my father said, "you take it. The wine cup we left with Mischa and Yossel in South Africa; the rest of the teapot goes with you. It's the last remnant of our lives in Illuxt. I want you to have it."

Sofia ended up taking it, and as we embraced at the train station, under the watchful eye of the guards, she whispered into my ear.

"The teapot is yours, Lena. The only reason I'm taking it is because it binds us together until we meet again and I can return it to you."

We watched the train pull out of the station, Nina and I holding Esther between us, grieving for the daughter she knew she would never see again.

"Is this," she whispered to no one in particular, as the tears coursed down her face, "why we came so far? Threw away our history and our birthright? So that they could separate us, peel us one from another, and send us to live out our lives in frozen places at the ends of the earth?"

None of us had an answer. We were all thinking the same thing.

Sofia gave birth to three children in a mining village so remote that the *taiga* was visible in all directions as far as the eye could see. Esther ached to see and touch her grandchildren, but all she knew of them was from her daughter's letters, and she died without ever seeing or embracing them.

❦

Vasily Stepanovich Lebedev came from a middle-class family. His father and grandfather before him had been paper fabricators. They manufactured the fashionable papers on which the aristocracy wrote their letters and printed their calling cards. In their small factory outside Moscow, they bound their handmade papers into blank books used by the idle rich to write memoirs, and by their estate managers to keep accounts. The Lebedevs were talented artisans accustomed to bowing and scraping before their entitled clientele, but the quality of their product was such that they had no competition.

With the disappearance of the aristocracy and the decline of the affluent, the market for their product was wiped out. There was no need for expensive handmade papers—our lives were not worth memorializing, and we worked so hard and so long that there was neither time nor energy for writing. We lived cheek by jowl—we needed no calling cards to know when someone came to visit. The whole idea was laughable, something imported from the minor nobility in France or England, to whom the

Russian aristocracy had always looked for example.

The Lebedev paper factory fought to remain in business, producing small boxes and more affordable, utilitarian writing paper. But they were unable to give up their commitment to quality.

"What we produced was too expensive," Vasily told me. "We had to close. If we'd stayed in business a few years longer, we would have been taxed out of existence, and then taken over by the State. At least we failed honestly," he continued wryly. "My parents were able to sell off their equipment."

By then the doors of the academy where Vasily was studying had been shuttered, and he moved back with his parents in Moscow. His brother was living in Paris, where he had been a student since before the Revolution, and somehow he managed to get a letter to his family. He said he had studied the French Revolution, knew what was coming, and advised his family to join him in France. But it was too late. When his letter arrived, his parents had barely enough money to make the journey from Moscow to his mother's village.

They assumed that Vasily would accompany them to the safety and isolation of rural life, but he had no interest in leaving. I was amazed, unable to imagine a life far away from Esther.

"You lost everything," I said, "including your dream of being an artist. Why did you not want to go with your family?"

"I miss my family," he said, "but I thought I could be more useful here. The Revolution was just the beginning. I knew some policies would be too extreme—but there are always extremes in times of great change. I thought that under Socialism, things would have to be better for the average Russian than they were under the tsars. And I wanted to be part of the new Russia."

He remained in Moscow, granted a room in the family home which had been converted to a communal apartment housing eight families. As a member of the Communist Party, he proved himself a tireless worker. Committed to the belief that a socialist Russia would benefit everyone, he quickly became an articulate speaker, able to enthrall his audience. His enthusiasm and energy prompted high-ranking Party members to propose him as a lecturer, traveling from school to school to educate and inspire budding young communists.

One evening I went to listen to him lecture to members of Komsomol, the youth division of the Communist Party. He spoke with such confidence, and his green eyes glowed like embers embedded in the fire of his beard and his dark, curly hair. There were moments when I wanted—almost—to believe in the flawless socialist world he envisioned, peopled by vibrant, healthy, committed workers who loved their lives and their reborn motherland. But I suspected even then that the perfect communist state and the flawless men and women who lived in it, existed only in fairy tales.

If I could not buy into his vision, my love for him would have to suffice. There was a kind of desperation in his oratory, and I found something about his vision frightening. Deep in me a disturbing question was trying to ask itself. How was it possible for a man of Vasily's intelligence and rationality to be so convinced by a dream?

At the same time, it terrified me that he might be struggling to maintain his own waning idealism. In addition to lecturing, he was now also in charge of selecting and training a staff of other lecturers. The accuracy of their message, and their success at motivating their audience, was his responsibility. I knew that he would find it next to impossible to inspire others if he doubted the message.

In the spring after we met, we walked along the banks of the Moscow River one Sunday afternoon, and for the first time, he revealed his misgivings about the Party.

"I've looked into the wheels of this grinding machine for long enough," he said quietly, "to see how the sausage is made. It's not pretty. Much is destroyed in the process, waste as well as what might be put to better use whole. At first I thought it was the price we pay for difficult change. But I've come to believe that Russia will never be a true socialist state until the people are willing to commit their lives to it. And so far, they've been unwilling to make that sacrifice."

"The people?" I said. "You mean those, like us, who spend half our time terrified of being pulled out of bed and disappearing for no good reason?

We're not committed, Vasily, because we don't trust; we've seen what our leaders are willing to do to us, and we watch them living corrupt lives just as we watched the wealthy aristocracy before the revolution. Our Communist Party leaders are just a different species of aristocrat."

"Lena," he said, looking around uneasily, "you mustn't allow yourself to say what comes to the tip of your tongue." He pulled me close to him. "It scares me sometimes, how freely you speak what you think. I chew my words through six times over before I say them, because I'm scared. Of sounding unpatriotic when I lecture, or of having one of my speakers say something terrible and get us all sent into exile. But for you it's all black and white—and that makes everything seem so easy."

"Black and white seems easy to you only because I seem to have fewer questions than you do," I answered. "But having fewer questions doesn't mean I have clearer answers. I have fewer answers than you do because I see just how little is possible."

I came to a stop in the spring sunshine and pulled him off the path so that we were closer to the water, out of hearing of other couples strolling hand in hand along the riverbank.

"What is it, Lena?" he asked.

"I love you," I said, looking up at him, "for your compassion, and your commitment, and your brilliance. But you make me fearful for us."

"Why?" he asked. "I'm good at my job, my supervisors like me, and I am rising in the Party as I had planned. What are you fearful of?"

"You wrap your idealism around you like a protective cloak," I said, "but it can't protect you from your own doubts. You are in danger, and you can't see that you—we—are exposed."

"You're talking in riddles. I promise you, everything will be fine."

He spoke in that dismissive, patronizing tone men use when they're afraid of hearing the truth from a woman. But he forgot for a moment that he loved me because I would not be dismissed, and because being patronized was a guarantee that I would find a way to have my say. Then, perhaps because he looked into my eyes, he remembered.

"Very well." He sighed, and smiled anxiously. "Please. Tell me how I'm exposed."

"You promise everything will be fine. Does that mean none of your patriotic comrades will ever denounce you? That you'll never be sent into exile, or executed? You can't promise me those things, Vasily. None of us is safe, even you, although you don't see it. That's why you have to think everything through six times before you speak."

We huddled together, his arms about my neck and mine about his waist, our bodies pressed together as if we were simply lovers exchanging sweet nothings. Vasily looked at me gravely, his face pale. Perhaps it was only the afternoon sunlight at my back, but even his green eyes looked washed out, as if the light behind them had been extinguished.

"I sometimes question," he said, "but I didn't think my doubts were so obvious, even to you. Perhaps I need to measure my words more carefully."

"You already measure your words. What you need to do is decide what you believe, and whether what you say in your lectures is really true. But," I said, "while you're deciding, I want something from you."

He tightened his arms about me.

"What, Lena?" he said. "What can I give you?"

"Forever," I said, "I want forever, but life tells me there is only now." I kissed his mouth. "I want you for my husband. And I want your child. Now. Before they take you from me."

He clasped me gently to his chest as if I were a treasure. "If you're willing to bring a child into the world, you must feel there's some good in it. You need to have faith," he murmured, "as I do, that no one will take me from you, and that our future will be better than your past."

A few weeks later my father and Esther gave us a small wedding party. Like all our celebrations in those days, it had a manic overtone. Vasily was right—it would have been a relief if I had faith in the future. But I could have faith only in myself and in him, in what I could see and control. Beyond that, there was little to believe in. The best I could do was hope for a better future, but in my mind I was prepared, always prepared, for more of the past. I didn't know how to have faith in something I had never seen.

❦

Vasily and I were married in 1928. For seven years we tried to have a child. They were long years because I spent them waiting—for my body to conceive; for my period to stop; for morning sickness. I waited for the next of our friends to be denounced and disappear, or for Vasily to fall out with his masters. And the more time passed, the more certain I became that when the knock on the door came and Vasily was taken from me, he would leave me childless.

Nina and Sergei were by then married. They worked at whatever jobs they could find, always struggling, and their daughter, Juliana, brought the family closer. I did what I could for them, as we all did, bringing food when there was extra, buying clothes for Juliana whenever children's clothes were available. We seldom spoke now of Sofia and Alexei, except when letters came, or rare photographs of their children, when we pooled our money and bought clothes for them, too. It was almost as if we closed ranks about them protectively, aware of how fragile our connections were.

I loved Juliana, and I imagined taking her to the museum when she was older. But being with Nina and her family heightened my awareness of my own childlessness, and Esther suggested that perhaps I couldn't fall pregnant because my work was too strenuous. I appealed to my supervisors for a change within the railway. After so many years of proving myself, I thought I might be promoted to a supervisory level with less hauling and lifting, but apparently I was thought too rigid—which meant I would not tolerate the graft that went on everywhere. Instead, I was transferred to a different department within the railway, and was made a conductor. They put me on the local trains, so that I came home to Vasily every night. But by then he was traveling, too.

He worked in the Commissariat of Enlightenment, which was the name they gave to the ministry in charge of education. The department he ran was responsible for speakers throughout the province, and after three years he was promoted to manage motivational lecturers in schools throughout the country. It was a huge promotion, and with it came a higher salary—but the salary itself was less important than the other changes in our lives. Suddenly I had access to stores reserved for higher-ranking Party members, and the food I had once lugged from the trains, stealing an occasional fresh carrot, was now displayed before me, accessible and affordable.

I had spent years standing in lines for everything, only to discover once I reached the head of the line that I was waiting for half-black cauliflower or wilted, rotting spinach. Now I had to pinch myself when I showed my card and entered the store. The food didn't all come from the trains anymore—Stalin had finally realized that collectivization had ruined the food supply. Small scale enterprise was encouraged, and much of the food in Moscow now came from small businesses. So we had fresh-laid eggs and onions pulled right from the soil, and crisp cucumbers and cabbage still smelling of garden moisture. I brought home fish that smelled like seawater when I put my nose to its shiny scales, and chicken so fresh that when I opened it up I imagined I could still feel its body heat. It was not always possible, but whenever I could, I bought more than we needed. Esther would not accept the food from us without recompense, but she enjoyed cooking and she was creative in the kitchen. We agreed that she would cook whatever I gave her, and share what she made with us and with Nina and her family.

With Vasily's new position, we qualified for a much nicer dwelling space. Our communal apartment was in a converted mansion with stone walls and an elegant marble spiral staircase. Best of all, we had part of the original kitchen, with the old estate stove, and room in it for a big table. We had two rooms, which had been part of one of the mansion's dining halls, and there was a window in each room. In our bedroom the window was small, but it was one of the few remaining original stained glass windows that had graced the mansion. At sunrise on cloudless days, the sun shone through the yellow, red and gold feathers of our glass peacock, bathing our bedroom in amber and rose-colored light. We mentioned the magic of our stained glass window to no one, fearful that it would be taken from us.

When we first realized how beautiful the sunrise was, Vasily stood me naked before the window, my arms raised, looking up at the window over

my shoulder. On those few days when all the stars were aligned—sun-filled days when we were both home, and we had the time, and the weather was warm enough for me to stand unclothed—he asked me to pose for him. It was the only time I saw him weep. I asked him why, but never truly believed his explanation.

"A goddess come to life," he said softly, looking up at me from his brushwork. "Your beauty is so still, it pushes you into the background even as it makes you shine. And you are so defenseless as you stand there, all revealed. I know how frightened you are of trusting anyone, and of how much strength there is in your small body. That you are mine moves me to tears."

It was the best answer he could come up with, a wonderful explanation, and perhaps it was even partly true. Yes, I was slender and young, and I never doubted that he loved me, but I hardly think my tough, skinny body and small breasts would have brought him to tears. His father sometimes sent him a package of handcrafted drawing paper that he had saved from the factory, and this is what Vasily used when he drew me. I think the act of drawing, on paper his father had made, brought home to him just how much his family had lost, and how deeply sad he was that he had been deprived of his life's work. But whatever the reason, I loved being drawn, looking down at the colored light bathing my legs and belly, and he continued drawing me whenever there was time, and as long as the paper lasted.

Several things about our new situation surprised me. I had always looked at high-ranking Party members with their more expensive clothes, their limos, their access to fresh food and foreign goods, as arrogant, greedy, and entitled. Now I was on the way to becoming one of them, and I found that not all my assumptions were accurate. We may have had more room, but we still lived in close proximity to six families, most of them young couples like us, a few with children. To my relief, most of them welcomed us. It was as if we had qualified for membership in an exclusive club, and having met the requirements, there was no question that we were worthy of admission.

There was an ease among us that was absent in all the communal apartments I had lived in. Perhaps it was because compared to where we all came from, we lived in the midst of plenty. We cooked in the spacious kitchen, often contributing food to a communal meal, and the atmosphere was most often friendly and casual—as long as we all obeyed the rules. There were many, both stated and assumed, and I learned them quickly.

We had our own space for storage in the kitchen, and the first rule was, never touch anyone else's food. In winter, we kept food cold in the narrow space between double layers of window glass. These were real double windows separated by eight or twelve centimeters, plenty of space for a string bag full of food. We never prepared food or washed dishes directly in the sink. It dirtied and stained the sink. Instead, we were expected to have our own basin, which had its place on our shelf, and which we placed in the sink when we cooked or washed. There were many rules for the bathroom, which fifteen of us shared, and a timetable for washing in the morning that was determined by when each of us started work.

In the toilet, aside from cleanliness, the most important requirement had to do with how one sat on the commode. In this new apartment, every family had its own toilet seat. This was new for me. I assumed that everyone either squatted over the toilet or wiped the toilet itself before sitting down. We had never had a toilet seat before—but here every family had their own detachable toilet seats hanging on the wall—red ones, green, blue and yellow. After a while, I became used to our system. It would never have occurred to me to use my neighbor's seat, and the idea that someone else might place his sweaty, hairy cheeks on my seat filled me with revulsion.

I was surprised at how quickly I became comfortable with these new norms, and how little guilt I felt at having so much more than others. My rationale for this preferred treatment fell into place with ease. Vasily worked very hard, and his job often took him away from home; he had huge responsibility for the young minds he was charged to inspire, and most importantly, his visibility made him a target. In exchange for all these inconveniences, we were rewarded with an easier life.

Somehow Vasily managed to avoid mistakes and continued to rise in the Party. His travels took him away often, and he was sometimes gone for weeks at a time. As a result we were together infrequently, and I began to accept the idea that I would live my life without ever having a child.

Then Vasily went on a three-week trip to Ukraine. It was a relaxing interval for me—I was settled in my new job, and for the first time in years, I wasn't worried about him. I stopped worrying about conception, too. It was a given that since we were not sleeping together, I couldn't become pregnant. It was the longest period we had been apart since our marriage, and I even enjoyed missing him, knowing that he would be back soon. Our bodies had a chance to recover from each other, to learn again the longing we felt when we were first together.

When he returned we rediscovered each other as if for the first time. I was so hungry for him that I couldn't tell the difference between my own pleasure and my longing to feel his within me. I remembered again the feel of his body and his scent; knew the vibrations of our intertwined limbs, and the steps in our dance as if they were home. As we lay together afterwards, face to face, exhausted and quivering, I ran my hands over his shoulders and his hips, and he kissed my fingers. I felt that if ever something was going to take seed within me, it was now.

I was twenty-eight when we brought Klara into the world in our new rooms. Thankfully, she was a tiny newborn—birthing a big baby from between my hips would have been like trying to force a ship from the neck of a vodka bottle. As it was, I labored for twenty-seven hours. The midwife told me later that she feared neither of us would survive the birth. But Klara emerged with long dark hair, and at the sound of her full-throated cry my milk came down, dripping from my swollen nipples like melting ice in spring sunshine. It was a good thing, because she stopped crying only long enough to take the breast. When I held her in my arms as she suckled from my body, the love I felt for her was so fierce it took me by surprise and at moments left me breathless. She was so tiny, with her perfect fingernails and rounded elbows, and her little mouth that would purse and root for the nipple at the slightest touch on her cheek.

Vasily was in love with our daughter from the moment she was born. I, too, knew that I would protect her with the final beat of my heart. At that recognition, I joined the sisterhood of mothers, and my eyes were opened. I understood finally what my grandmother felt when my father left for South Africa, imagined what my own mother must have felt at the dawning recognition that she would not live to suckle me and Avrom, the rending of Esther's heart when Sofia went into exile with Alexei. So I discovered that the present moment contains within it all moments past, and that the experience of becoming a new mother holds in its lap all the joy and all the sorrows of motherhood.

❦

Klara was born in 1935, the second year of Stalin's Great Purge. Fear was so thick it oozed from our pores like sweat. In the streets and standing in lines for food, the air was filled with an unpleasant, yellowish odor. Some said the smell came from a huge warehouse of rotten eggs in the city. Others identified the smell as the nauseating fumes from petroleum.

But it was neither. It was instead the stench of our own fear. Even those who didn't notice it or weren't bothered by it were affected. We all became hyper-alert, suspicious of everyone, over-protective of what was ours. Like horses, skittish in the presence of predators they can't see, we all sensed threat everywhere. You could see it in people's eyes—wide open, darting about in search of danger, evaluating every face and glancing around for the men in black coats to come and separate mother from child, and drag them away for committing a crime—undefined and unknown—against the State. And when someone was taken off the street or from an apartment, bystanders and neighbors breathed a sigh of relief that it was not them, and turned away. And we all wondered what the crime had been—although we knew from the evidence, and from the huge numbers being arrested, that in most cases there had been no crime.

Anyone with eyesight could have seen that we were being targeted to meet the quotas established by a wolf pack gone mad. It was either the NKVD or Stalin's ministers, cringing and corrupt. Perhaps we convinced ourselves of the guilt of our fellow citizens. To do otherwise would have made us participants in a continued abomination.

But I was oblivious. For the first and perhaps only time in my life, my guard was down. If I saw evil around me, I discounted it, refused to acknowledge it. I enjoyed my work and couldn't wait to get home at night to collect Klara from Grandma Esther, where she spent the day while I was on the trains. She was a beautiful child, with full cheeks and dark curls, and she was happy and loved and cosseted in a way I had never been. Having a child allowed me the opportunity to spill on her all the love and tenderness I longed for from my own mother—and in giving it to her, to experience it firsthand for myself. In feeding her, I fed myself. But I could not maintain my blindness forever, and eventually I had to look up and see that for the first time, Vasily was openly scared.

How do you describe a million and a half people, many of them loyal members of the Communist Party, being taken out and shot? The fact that Stalin was mad doesn't answer the question—he didn't do the shooting. He just gave the orders, and everyone followed like sheep. Even those in charge of carrying out his orders, who thought they had miraculously become wolves, were themselves identified as traitors and executed. When the purges began, the Chief of the Secret Police was Genrikh Yagoda. The mere mention of his name made the ordinary man shudder. But Stalin tired of his influence and replaced him with another would-be wolf, Nikolai Yezhov, who was himself led to the slaughter and replaced by Lavrentiy Beria, whose feet rest in a fetid pool containing the blood of millions. The purges became so vast that they consumed their own ranks, and when they were over, Stalin was the only original Bolshevik leader left. He tolerated no threat to his authority. Anyone who showed an inclination to independent thought found a place on one of his many lists.

Between 1937 and 1938, over a thousand people a day were executed. At first, the condemned were driven to execution sites outside most big cities to be shot and buried. But there were so many it became impossible to handle them individually. Instead of loading prisoners into vans to be taken out and shot on arrival, they were stripped and muffled. Naked and bound, they were loaded into sealed vans. During the trip to the burial site, carbon monoxide piped into the sealed compartments did its deadly work, and all that remained was to unload the still bodies into mass graves.

The whole country became a charnel house. The Nazis may have developed it into a perfect instrument of mass murder, but the parents of the rolling gas chamber were Mother Russia, and Stalin.

And so we come to Vasily, who tried, again and again, to tell me what he saw. There were three Moscow Trials, and he knew from the first two what was likely to happen to those who were taken.

"If they arrest me," he said as I lay quietly in his arms, with Klara in her crib at the foot of our bed, "you can be sure I'll be tried and convicted. If that happens, Lena," he said, "don't waste your time looking for me. You'll never find me. The men responsible are moving heaven and earth to conceal what they're doing. All of them—including Stalin—will be long dead before it all comes out. It will come out, and they'll rewrite this time in history, but it will take several generations. Your job will be to get on with your life and do the best you can for Klara."

Afterwards, I remembered what he had told me. These things he told me in bits and pieces. They were too difficult for him to say all at once, or for me to take in. A week would pass, and he would try again, whispering in my ear as we lay together. I think he would begin always by saying 'if I'm taken...', and I became accustomed to tuning out his words after that. I didn't want to know, until I had no choice.

"When ten years have gone by and you ask where I am, they'll tell you I died of exposure or dysentery. It will all be lies. I will have been a decade dead. Promise me, Lena, if they take me, you'll carry on with your life. Don't wait for me."

I promised, of course. What else was I to do? Vasily knew I would do everything I could for Klara—his concern was whether I would do anything for myself.

His crime, when they had to find one, was no crime at all. He had the bad judgment to have written an article praising Leon Trotsky, long before Stalin banished him from the Soviet Union. When Stalin got around to naming Trotsky in absentia as an enemy of the people, those who wanted to get rid of Vasily took the opportunity to include him among Trotsky's allies.

Vasily had taken the three-day journey on the Trans-Siberian Railway to visit several major cities, including Novosibirsk and Omsk. He was already in Siberia—perhaps they arrested him there, close to the camp where, as he predicted, they would claim to have sent him. I never found out whether it happened there, or whether they lay in wait and snatched him at the train station when he returned to Moscow. All I know is that one day it was announced in the news that Trotsky's allies had been charged, found guilty, and executed. I had no reason to think that Vasily would be among them, but that night Vasily didn't come home. And then he never came home.

Where he was tried and sentenced, where he was executed and buried, I never found out. But Vasily was wrong in one particular. I didn't have to make a fuss before they told me anything. A week after he went missing, two members of the Secret Police came to the apartment to vomit on me the words that I already knew were in their mouths. My husband Vasily Stepanovich Lebedev had been convicted of anti-communist activity and sentenced to ten years in an unnamed prison far distant, family correspondence forbidden. And by the way, they said, since I no longer had a Communist Party affiliation, I had two weeks to leave our rooms and to apply to the Ministry of Accommodation for dwelling space befitting the family of a man convicted of treason. They left me immobile at the door without saying good-bye, and as they went down the stairs I heard them talking about what they would eat for their midday meal.

❀

I can admit now that after Vasily died, I fell apart. It was not clear to me at the time just how distressed I was—I still went to work, and went through the motions of taking care of myself and my infant daughter. But they took from me the love of my life, and even though his disappearance was not unexpected, something within me died. If I believed we had souls, I would say that my soul gave up the will to live. Only one thing kept me going—something I have revealed to no one until now. Not to my stepmother, Esther, or even to my father, who would have understood, and from whom I took the idea. I watched him all through my childhood writing letters to my brothers, Mischa and Yossel, and I saw his obsession with his inaccessible sons as a rejection of me. But long before the beginning of The Great Patriotic War, the writing of such letters became impossible—there was no way to send or receive mail from the West. And so he stopped sending them letters. But he never stopped writing to them.

All trace of Vasily was gone, wiped away as if he had never lived. I became his only mausoleum, and I had nowhere to put my grief. I began writing letters to my brothers, whose faces I knew only from the ancient photographs beside my father's chair. I wrote to them of my love affair with Vasily and our marriage, and of my fear that they would come for him, and of what happened when he disappeared. The letters, had they been discovered, would have been sufficient evidence of my treasonous thinking to end my life. I had enough sense to destroy the most dangerous of them, but many I kept. There was a vast distance between me and my unknown brothers. I didn't know whether they were dead or alive, but it was a given that they would never read my scribblings. That made it easier to express what I was unable to say to any living person. It was like shouting into the void. And so I unburdened myself to them, spilled all my anguish onto the paper, which I hid in an old biscuit box under my bed.

Klara and I were assigned housing in what became known later as a Soviet slum. Our dwelling space was in an apartment on the fourth floor of a concrete slab building without an elevator. This communal apartment was several steps down from the one we had been forced to leave, and we shared a bathroom and kitchen with twelve family units. However, it turned out to be a good move, because our neighbors treated us like family almost from the beginning. For a year I lived in a fog, unaware of who they were, and when I finally emerged, it was to realize that almost to a person they had been unaccountably kind to this dazed young woman and her little girl. They helped cook, sharing what little food they had when I was physically unable to cope. They were warm and gentle with Klara, who was immediately at home with the other children in the apartment.

Most of our neighbors were workers who made the system function. There were two servers in a communal cafeteria, and several factory workers at plants on the outskirts of Moscow, one of them making wooden furniture, and another involved in manufacturing machine parts. We had a nurse and her husband, a low-level engineer in the water department, two young unmarried teachers who shared rooms, and several young couples. There were also several students in the midst of taking their degrees in physical sciences and engineering, who were given a stipend and accommodation until they graduated. These were all people in whose lives there was little ease, and for whom hardship was a given. Most didn't know any differently— we had all grown up under similar conditions, and so accepted the cramped quarters, bad insulation and insufficient heat in winter, long workdays and unending waiting in lines for food, clothing, kitchen supplies and whatever else was needed. They were good people, and kind to us, and I learned from them much about compassion and community.

We had one room, big enough for a single bed and a small cot. Most nights until Klara was seven or eight, we slept together. We also had room for a chair and a little table, and eventually some shelves on which I placed a glass vase for flowers and some little green plants. I bought a piece of fabric with flowers on a light blue background, and Esther made me curtains for the windows. I did my best to make our room into a home. But I was seldom there.

My job did not go well for me after Vasily disappeared. I was still naïve enough to believe that my performance at work was sufficient to ensure my employment, but there were others after my job, people with connections I no longer had. My circumstances were well known, and by then it was understood that a conviction for treason was an undeclared death sentence.

My supervisors received orders to give preference to Communist Party members, and they had no choice but to comply. They had the decency to be embarrassed as they informed me that I was being reassigned back to being a cargo and baggage handler.

My body had been delivered of a child, and I was no longer a youthful woman. It was exhausting work, far more difficult than I remembered. I left work each evening completely spent—but still had to go shopping for whatever meager supplies were left at the end of the day. And I had to do my shopping in time to pick up Klara from her little school. I was late often enough that I can repeat today the lectures I received from her teachers.

"Competent Socialist mothers set a good example for their children by being always on time. They are considerate of other workers, like teachers, who also have to leave on time because they, too, have families to care for."

I resented those lectures because the teachers held all the cards. They were not interested in my story, and if they were angry with me they might take it out on Klara. As it was, I could not compete with some of the other parents, who gave the most lavish gifts they could afford to the teachers in the hope that their generosity would lead to preferred treatment for their child.

Sometimes I would go to the markets early so that I could at least have food to prepare, and then arrive late to work. I would receive the obligatory lecture there, too, but these were still men and women I had known since I was fifteen, and they often winked and let it pass. The system was broken, but everyone knew it, and many of us did our best for each other.

Each year I worked as a cargo and baggage handler, I made the request to change back to the ticketing system. In the fifth year my request was granted, and I became a conductor on the local trains. But even then, I had to work a full day, and it was still evening when I returned home to Klara.

Vasily had been a warm and loving father, and Klara waited each evening for him to come home. She was three years old when he was taken from us, and she never recovered from losing him. She had nowhere to turn but to me, and I was unable to comfort her. I never understood what she needed—all I knew was that I could not provide it. The one child I gave birth to turned out to be the one I was incapable of raising.

From her first days at school her teachers described her as a troublesome child, and I was frequently called in to talk to teachers who told me I needed to give her more discipline, administered with love. By the time she was thirteen, she had run away several times, stolen money from Grandma Esther, and refused to play with her cousin, Nina's daughter, Juliana, who was two years older than she.

For well-adjusted Soviet children who toed the line, there were plenty of after-school activities to fill a young life with ideas and ambitions. The activities and the lessons were all intended to make children into stalwart Communists. I despised the hero worship of Stalin, and the lies they told about how wonderful our lives were. We lived in a deep hole, in darkness, looking up at glimpses of weak sunshine, and somehow people convinced themselves that we lived on the surface, with sunshine on our faces. There were some fights I knew I could not win, and I encouraged Klara to be involved. But she was one of those who fell between the cracks, and for them, there was no place to go, and no remedial help. She became one of those children who left school in the afternoon, with no place to go and no parent available to make sure she was occupied productively. She could choose to go home and spend the afternoon alone, or she could make other choices—which she did. She made friends with other disaffected children and became one of the young delinquents who frequent the streets of Moscow, stealing where they can, drinking vodka, coming home drunk—or not coming home at all.

At sixteen she left school, despite all my efforts to keep her there, and when she left school, she also left home. For two years she lived somewhere in Moscow, with a boyfriend whom I knew only as Iosif, and she came home only when she needed money or when he became drunk and abusive. But always she went back to him. When she turned eighteen, they both applied for jobs at a new factory town several hours from Moscow. She never told me what kind of job it was or what the factory made. She simply appeared one day and told me she was going.

I wrote to Klara each month. Once or twice a year she sent me a card.

She never came home. I became used to my life as a single woman, and when my bosses asked whether I would like a transfer to the Trans-Siberian route, which would take me away for weeks at a time, but where the pay was much higher, I jumped at the chance. I thought I could design a new life for myself, and dreamed that perhaps there would be a rail line built between Moscow and the factory town where Klara worked.

Then in 1957, when Klara was twenty-two, she gave birth to a daughter. She sent me a letter containing a photo of her newborn baby. On the back were a few scribbled words: 'your granddaughter, Darya, born two weeks ago.' I sent her clothes for the baby, encouraged her to come and visit, asked if I could come spend my vacation days with her. She always found a reason to say no. I told myself she was an adult. She had the right to live her life as she chose. My life would continue on its own path. And it did, until it was stopped dead in its tracks.

One day at the beginning of June, 1959, there was an explosion at a munitions factory several hours from Moscow. In trying to meet his production quotas without sufficient respect for the materials he had to work with, the plant manager ignored safety warnings from his employees, kept the blast doors open when they should have been closed, allowed smoking too close to explosives, and failed to monitor workers for drunkenness. The explosion required only a little negligence, one drunken worker, one spark and an open blast door. It was a three-line item in the daily paper, and several passengers on the train that day clucked their tongues as I punched their tickets, and said what a shame it was that forty workers had lost their lives due to the negligence of a plant manager. One man said it was a shame the manager was killed in the explosion. Had he lived, he would have received the sentence he really deserved.

This was one of the many disasters mentioned briefly in the papers, disasters that were always sandwiched between longer reports of increased productivity, happier peasants, healthier children. I thought nothing of it until I arrived home after seventeen days on the rails. I had four days off before my next trip, and I was out of food. On my way home I went first to see if I could buy some tea and perhaps something for my supper—a piece of chicken, some potatoes, carrots and onions. If not, I would get a *pirozhok*, a meat pie, for my lunch. By then commercial meat pies were available—mostly bread dough with just enough meat sauce in the middle to let you know that the meat was missing.

When I arrived home with my groceries, it was to find that someone from the Youth Ministry had been to visit me several times, and had left behind a note requesting me to come to their office as soon as possible. I was to ask for the Child Affairs officer. I couldn't imagine what this was about—I thought perhaps Klara was in trouble and had asked for my help—but quickly realized that at the age of twenty-four she would have long before aged out of the Youth Ministry. It was a late afternoon in June as I came up from the Metro underground and walked along the street towards the office of the Youth Ministry, and I remember enjoying the feel of the sun on my face.

The Ministry secretary looked at the letter I showed her, and told me to wait while she called the appropriate person. I waited for almost two hours before a woman my own age called for me and led me upstairs. We went through a door on which the words "Office of Abandoned Children" was stenciled, and then to a desk on which the nameplate read M.I. Petrova. She sat down behind the desk.

"We have a lot to talk about," she said. "Would you like some tea?"

This was a big surprise. State offices seldom offered citizens anything at all. In fact, they usually wanted to get rid of you as soon as possible. Suddenly it struck me that being in this particular office might have more to do with my granddaughter than with Klara.

"I don't know what we have to talk about, Comrade Petrova," I said, "but yes, please. Tea would be very nice."

She rose and went into another room, and when she returned she had two cups of tea. She placed one before me and sat down again, a weary looking woman, a little on the round side, so that her face was full and without wrinkles. She had grey hair cut short like mine, and she had a warm smile.

"Please," she said, "call me Maria Ivanovna."

"Thank you," I said. Not just tea, then; also I was being invited to address her informally. This was not a good sign. Suddenly I was worried. "What is all this about, Maria Ivanovna?"

"Your daughter is Klara Vasilyevna Lebedev?"

"Yes."

"When did you last see her?"

"It has been several years," I answered, ashamed. "We had little contact once she left home. Why? Is she in trouble? Is there a problem with my granddaughter?"

"I must give you some difficult news," she said. "A few days ago there was an explosion at the factory she worked in. Forty people were killed—among them your daughter and Iosif Vishnekov, the man she lived with."

I watched myself responding to this news as if I were my own reflection, sitting on the window sill and looking out of my own eyes at the middle-aged woman being told that her daughter was dead. What was she supposed to do? What would she do?

I did nothing, simply sat, staring across the desk at nothing in particular. I stopped breathing—or at least, I was not aware of breathing. Mostly I was thinking—of the little baby Klara had been, of all the promise in her life, and of how it all turned to dust. And I was thinking of what her life must have been, the life she closed to me. Without information, I had to imagine what kind of factory Klara worked in—and I always assumed that it was some kind of furniture or industrial plant. I envisioned her on the assembly line, packaging machine parts or attaching the cheap aluminum table legs to the table tops that were a fixture in every apartment in Moscow. It never entered my mind that her place of work was a munitions plant, or that she might be handling live ammunition.

I dropped my head into my hands.

"Yelena Petrovna?"

"Yes?"

"Can I get you anything?"

"I have no more tears," I said quietly, raising my head and looking at her. "Why am I here? What happened to my granddaughter?"

"Darya was at the child center when the explosion occurred—three kilometers from the blast. She was not harmed. I will not say she is fine— she has lost her parents. But she is being well cared for."

I felt my lungs expand in a gasping, shuddering breath. It was as if my heart had stopped beating, and these words were the electric shock that brought me back to life. I rose from my chair.

"Where is she now? I must go to her."

"There were several children orphaned in the explosion," said Maria Ivanovna. "She went home with the family of one of the other children at the child center. We had to go back to the factory records to find your name and where you lived. It took some work to find you. As you can imagine, it makes our job much more difficult when the deceased is estranged from family," she said, and I imagined a hint of resentment in her voice.

"I thought I did everything possible to love my daughter and keep her safe," I heard myself say, and I tried without success to stop the words before they were out. "If I'd only known our estrangement would make your life more difficult, perhaps I would have tried harder to prevent it."

"I'm sorry," she said, the color rising in her face. "I meant no offense."

I put my hands on her desk and lowered my head. "I'm not myself. Your job must be difficult, dealing with death and abandonment every day. I am sorry I spoke harshly. I can't expect you to know what happened in my family."

She looked at me without speaking, but in her eyes I saw that she did know. And I wondered for a frightening moment whether she knew everything, and whether they would keep me from my granddaughter.

"Of course you know," I said bitterly. "The State knows everything, doesn't it? How easy it must have been for you to pry into the facts of my life, to open up the little box with my name on it."

"You are more than the total of what you have suffered," she said gently, choosing to ignore my anger. "And yes, I do know your story. I've read

Klara's school reports and I know what happened to your husband. Your life has not been easy." She paused. "You know I asked you here because despite your estrangement, Klara did love you. She listed you as her closest relative."

My legs suddenly gave way, and I lowered myself to the chair. She came around the desk and put her arm about my shoulders. As she placed her own handkerchief in my hand, she slowly raised my hand to my face and helped me wipe my cheeks.

"You see?" she said. "Your heart is not closed. You do have tears to shed for your daughter."

She sat with me, this government official, this kind stranger, as I sobbed silently, and she rubbed my shoulder.

"This is not your first time, is it?" I said eventually, after taking a moment to catch my breath.

"No. And it never becomes easier. But I know how much I can do, and I know what is beyond my control. I've learned that a few minutes of kindness cost me nothing." She looked at her watch, rose from beside me and went back to her desk. "But now I have to do my job—making sure that children are cared for. Darya's father was himself an orphan, and he listed only Klara as his next of kin. That makes you Darya's closest relative. But you are not obliged to care for your granddaughter, if it will be a hardship. I have looked into your work, and I know you travel many days in succession. There are State institutions that provide care for orphans if you are...."

"No," I said as I rose again from my chair. Anger lay like bitter sand on my tongue. "Never. My granddaughter will not be raised in an orphanage."

She smiled.

"I'm glad to see that you feel so strongly about this," she said. "I'm on your side, Yelena Petrovna—no one wants her in a State institution. She will do much better in your hands."

We dealt with the necessary papers—always papers—and she gave me a stamped document appointing me Darya's guardian. When I left the office I went straight back to the Metro and rode to Nina's stop so that I could share the news with her. Then I went home to prepare for the introduction into my life of a little girl I didn't know. Whoever she turned out to be, I knew I would protect her with the ferocity of a wounded mother bear.

❧

The following morning I boarded the local train headed to Kalinin, a four-hour ride, with detailed instructions on what to do when I arrived. The area where the explosion took place, a factory outside Kalinin, was now under a military cordon, and no traffic was allowed within several kilometers of the site. It wouldn't have made a difference—even before the explosion, the factory and living quarters for the workers were in a restricted military compound, and no visitors were allowed. It differed from one military installation to another, but in some places visitors were discouraged, and workers had to request permission to leave the compound. At best, it would have been difficult. Had Klara been granted leave, she could have found transportation to Kalinin, but we would have had no place to meet. Maria Ivanovna suggested this might have been the reason why Klara refused to have me visit. And perhaps, she said, if outside visits were frowned upon, Klara didn't want to make waves.

A kind woman, Maria Ivanovna, I thought, staring out of the train window as we left Moscow behind us. She tried so hard to make me believe that my relationship with Klara was not poisonous, that Klara naming me her next of kin was proof of her love. It may have been true—but it didn't make me feel better. If there had indeed been a chance of reconciling with her, I should have been more aggressive. I should have pursued her with more love and less anger in my heart.

And yet here I was, on my way to retrieve her daughter; to undertake yet again the raising of a child. I watched the countryside clatter by, rolling hills and grassland, and small villages up against the rail tracks, ancient wooden houses with peaked roofs, leaning into their little vegetable gardens, and a worn track leading to the outhouse. Their lives were untouched by what happened in Moscow. They lived as they had for a century, the only change being the introduction of electricity a few years earlier. Many homes had no running water, and the fields were still tilled by a man behind an ox-drawn plow.

I wondered whether I was mad to take on this burden, whether I could find in myself the tenderness necessary to raise another child. I was fifty-two, alone, and my adventures were over. I had predictable habits and my life was a known quantity. After Klara left, I made sure that I would not again be hurt, and I had learned to love from a distance. I saw the people dear to me in my life on my own terms. When I began feeling strangled by the emotional pull of my stepsister and her daughter, I quickly found ways to distance myself from them. Work was a good excuse, and my multi-day rail trips made the excuse real. I still went to the library whenever I was home. The library and the museum were now housed in separate buildings, and sometimes I went instead to the museum to see what was on display. And always, I would stand for a moment before Ivanov's masterpiece, from which I drew strength, and which never lost its fascination for me.

As we approached Kalinin, I went through the woven bag I had brought with me, containing a few things for the child, and a worn brown bear that had been Klara's. It was threadbare and soft, and had mismatched eyes— one was a black button, and the other a larger brown button. I remembered sewing them on. As I left my rooms with the bag, I reached under my bed for the biscuit box. There would be at least four hours on the train during which I would be unoccupied. It was an unusual luxury, and something in me wanted to read what I had written in the years since Klara left. I was in a rush, and I grabbed a handful of papers at random.

One of the unsent letters to my brothers was written after our father died in the influenza epidemic of 1953, two years after Klara left home. At his funeral I wept in anger and despair. My brothers, I reasoned, would never know that our father had died, or how, and it was my duty to inform them.

My Beloved Mischa and Yossel:

I write to share with you in great sadness that we are all together orphans. Our father is dead.

As the winter approached, he became ill and took to his bed, where he spent the cold months lying in silence, coughing and drinking only hot water. At the end he drank a sip of hot wine, and in his mouth were prayers for his children, both those taken from us in death, and for you, from whom we are cut off in life, and whom he missed most terribly. In the middle of April he died, at evening, close to the anniversary of the death of our brother Avrom, my twin. His death came as a relief to him—his time on this earth was hard, and in his last years he was not happy. He leaves Esther alone, but it's perhaps something of a relief for her, too.

It's strange to think that you never knew Esther as the woman our father married, intending to bring her back to you in South Africa. She was wonderful to me, the mother I never had, and she was a loving grandmother to Klara. We have our father to thank for her presence in our lives—she carried the burden of his sadness, and tried her best to make up for it.

I share with you my sadness that my daughter, Klara, has left home. Our relationship is not good. I wonder sometimes, thinking about our father, whether I failed her in the same way he failed me. Was I so full of grief at Vasily's death—as full of grief as our father had been—-that I had nothing left for my child, just as he had nothing left for me? What could I have done to her so terrible, that she chose to leave her family, to go and live with a man who beats her, and to work on a factory assembly line hours from Moscow? I hope you have experienced no such failures in your lives. I dream that perhaps, in time, she will come to realize how much I love her and return home to me. The family asks about her, but I have no answers. I watch our sister Nina's daughter, Juliana, as she finishes school and studies to be a doctor. You can imagine how painful it is for me to see the contrast between our two daughters.

In the meantime, I live my life from day to day, carrying my losses in the pockets of my apron, weights banging against my thighs at each step, reminding me that they are there. I could take off the apron—no one forces me to wear it. But it is the closest reminder I have of what I have lost, and I would be desperately lonely without it.

Your sister in grief,

Lena

As I read this letter, a half-dozen years after writing it, I sound like a mad woman crazed with grief, reaching out in her mind to brothers she would never see, about losses with which she refused to part. But was she the mad woman—or was the mad one on the train, the one who had established in her life some peace and predictability, and was about to throw it all away for a child she had never known? I considered getting off at the next station, tearing up the document in my pocket, returning home to resume my life. Let the State take the child. With my history, why did I imagine for a second that I could do a better job?

But getting off the train would have meant never being able to look in the mirror again. It would have meant living in shame for the rest of my days. And when my panic subsided, I reminded myself that of course I could do a better job than the State. My love might not have saved Klara, but a grandmother's love must be better than having to cozy up to the orphan in the next bed.

I closed my eyes for the last leg of the journey, I breathed deeply, and I tried to remember. It had been a long time since I left myself open to whatever might be coming.

✿

As the train pulled into the station and passengers began stepping down, I watched people on the platform staring at me—a very short middle-aged woman with a red and green woven bag, jumping down from the train with the nimble step of a dancer. What they didn't know is that I could have done it in my sleep, that I had spent years jumping down from moving trains all across the Soviet Union. Maria Ivanovna had given me a round-trip voucher which I used when I got on the train. As a result I didn't have to identify myself as a railway employee, and I realized that this was the first time I had traveled anywhere as a passenger.

My instructions were to go to the station entrance, where a military presence had been assigned since the explosion. Four soldiers in camouflage fatigues stood at the main entryway, two on each side, each with a rifle slung over his shoulder. Large, dour boys, boots planted wide, looking around them for menacing civilians. I approached one of them and looked up at him.

"I was told to speak to one of the soldiers about picking up my granddaughter, who was orphaned in the explosion last week. Can you help me?"

While I was speaking, he looked over my head, disdaining to glance at me. But when I was through he lowered his eyes, and his expression softened.

"Speak to that soldier over there," he said, pointing at one of the other uniforms. "He's in communication with the base."

I gave the other man my name, and on his shortwave radio he announced that I had arrived and was waiting at the station for my granddaughter.

"It shouldn't be long," he said. "They will bring her to you."

"They?" I asked. "Who? I thought I would be able to go to my granddaughter."

"I'm sorry, Mother," he said. "No civilians are allowed. One of our off-duty comrades will bring the child to you." He smiled. "There are several little ones waiting for family to come. All the nurses want to take care of them."

"How many?" I asked.

"I'm not sure," he said. "Seven or eight."

Seven or eight children orphaned in the explosion, I thought, and young nurses bringing them one by one to meet whatever family had come for them. If they were lucky enough to have family. Children being handed over from one stranger to another. I had no knowledge of who Darya was, of her likes and dislikes. I would have no chance to see where she and my daughter lived together with the father I had never met, or to collect the clothes and toys Klara had accumulated for her. And no memento of Klara, either.

I supposed Darya was the best memento I could have. But it would be like receiving a newborn baby with no preparation—only this newborn was already two years old, with her opinions, patterns and habits. I steeled myself to take possession of a frightened, screaming child.

I sat on a bench outside the station to wait, watching travelers coming and going, all in a rush to get somewhere fast. Pensioners huddled in groups around me, having emerged like reptiles from the darkness of their caves, to bask in the June sunshine. They smoked, turned their faces to the sun, talking sports scores loudly and everything else in muted voices, mouths hidden behind their hands. It was like this, I imagined, in every city in the Soviet Union, when the sun came out on a June afternoon. But I was not out to enjoy the weather, and I watched the road for a military vehicle to appear, a vehicle from which a uniformed woman would emerge carrying a little girl.

Several camouflaged trucks drove by without stopping, soldiers under the canvas cover in the back. Non-military vans stopped outside the station to drop off boxes, and I saw how hard the porters and baggage carriers worked, scurrying back and forth from the road to the rail track. They pushed carts and two-wheeled carriers loaded with packages and suitcases, followed by well-dressed Communist Party members keeping a close eye on their belongings. It was a grueling job, and I breathed a sigh of relief that I had left it behind me.

A small, two-door van painted military green pulled up in the area marked for police vehicles. The doors opened, a uniformed soldier emerged from each door, and walked over to the soldiers at the main entrance who had been so helpful to me. I didn't hear what they said, but one pointed to me. The two newcomers looked towards me and approached. I met their eyes as I rose to greet them.

"Grandmother?" one of them said. "Are you Yelena Petrovna Lebedev?"

He removed his cap, perhaps out of respect. But I think he was puzzled. He scratched his stubbled scalp. Both young men towered over me, and it was clear that I was not what they expected, a tiny woman in a faded black coat, carrying a bright woven bag.

"I am. You have my granddaughter?" I asked.

"What is your granddaughter's name?"

"Darya," I said. "My daughter—Darya's mother—was Klara Vasilyevna Lebedev. Do you have her?"

"Yes, but before I take you to her, we need to make sure you are approved to receive her."

I pulled the certificate from my pocket and handed it to him.

"Will this do?" I asked.

He unfolded and read it, carefully refolded it and handed it back to me. Then he smiled.

"Come, Grandmother. We have a lovely little girl for you. A delight. If the Ministry had not found you, my comrade or I would have been happy to take her. And you will have to pry her out of the arms of the nurse assigned to care for her."

I picked up my bag and followed him to the back of the truck, and he opened the tailgate and glanced in. Then he turned back to me and put his finger to his lips.

"She's sleeping," he said.

Before I looked into the truck I reached into my bag and pulled out Klara's worn, stuffed bear and held it under my arm. Then I looked into the truck to see a woman in a nurse's uniform sitting sideways on the bench. She looked up at me, smiling, a pretty young woman with blue eyes and straight fair hair.

"Yelena Petrovna?" she whispered. "Darya's grandmother?" she whispered.

I nodded.

She introduced herself as Irina, and looked down at her feet.

"Here is your angel," she said quietly.

I climbed up on the back step so that I could look down into the bottom of the truck. There she was, sleeping in a bed of blankets on the floor. Long eyelashes, round, smooth cheeks, apple-red; she was sucking her lower lip in sleep. Full lips, just as Klara had. Her little fists were clenched. I could see how fine her skin was, and how soft.

"I made sure she had a long nap," said Irina. "I didn't want her to be tired when she met you."

"Thank you," I whispered. "Let her sleep a little —I have so many questions for you before she wakes."

"What questions, Grandmother? I don't know whether I have any useful answers—I don't know much about her."

"How is her eating? What foods does she like?" I asked. "And her sleeping—does she go through the night? She must miss her mother. Are there nightmares? How does she like to be comforted?"

I wanted to communicate to this young woman the importance of the moment, to let her know she was the connection between Darya's past and her future. That once we separated, the connection would be broken. In the few moments before we parted, I wanted all the knowledge she had.

"How is her speech? Does she have many words? Does she like to have her hair brushed? And what about baths? Her mother used to love warm water in the little tub…"

"I've only known her three days," said Irina, taking my hand in hers.

She smiled at me. I remember her pretty, smooth face, unlined and unworried, trying to comfort this anxious old woman.

"She's happy and calm. She loves her food—so far she eats whatever she can get her hands on. She already drinks from a cup. They said she was toilet trained—but she seems to be regressed a little so we put a diaper on her. She's a good sleeper, and when she awakes, a comforting hand and a lullaby puts her right back to sleep. She doesn't have many words, but she knows how to communicate what she wants." She leaned forward and put her other hand around my shoulder. "Maybe she doesn't yet realize what's happened—and even if she could, would she understand that her life has changed? I suppose this changes your life, too," she said. "But how lucky she is to have you!"

She rose to her feet and jumped from the truck, and then reached in and gently pulled the bed of blankets towards the lowered tailgate. As she did so, Darya opened her eyes. They were green, as Vasily's had been, and more than the color, it was as if he looked at me through her eyes. It was shocking, to see the depth and calm of his soul, clear and wise, peering out of her pink, unformed face, still warm and drowsy from sleep. Then she rolled onto one elbow and pulled herself to a sitting position, and opened her mouth to yawn, showing a mouthful of perfect little teeth. Suddenly all my doubts disappeared. She was mine, and at that instant I knew we would be fine. I had promised myself that I would not cry at our first meeting, and I didn't—instead I smiled, showing the love I felt in my heart, but I cannot deny that there was moisture in my eyes, and a lump in my throat as I reached for her, my arms wide.

"Come, Dashinka," I said softly, "come."

She looked for a moment from the young soldier to me and back again, trying to make sense of the situation. And it looked as if she made a decision. She opened her arms towards the young woman.

My heart fell as Irina scooped her up. Of course I understood—she was a pretty young woman, she was familiar, and I was unfamiliar, old and wrinkled.

"Dashinka," she said, turning the child to face me. We were two paces apart. "This is your Babushka. She's come to take you home with her. And look what she has for you."

I reached under my arm, withdrew the stuffed bear, and tickled her nose with it. She smiled uncertainly and looked back at Irina. Then she turned and looked at me. Her glance moved across my face, and something like recognition came over her. She reached for the bear with one hand, and with the other she reached for me.

"Mama," she said.

I heard Irina's surprised intake of breath.

"She recognizes you," Irina said, handing Darya to me. "Did her mother look like you?"

"Yes," I said, kissing her cheek. She smelled of wet diaper, but we would soon change that. In my woven bag I had brought two diapers just in case. But beneath the wet diaper, I smelled the sweet little girl smell I had all but forgotten. "We looked very much alike—we had the same eyes and cheekbones. Didn't we, Dashinka? We looked very much alike, your Mama and I. But I am not her—I am Babushka. Can you say that? Babushka."

She clung to the bear, but she was not uncomfortable in my arms. My heart was full, and I was ready to take her home. Irina walked me back to the track, carrying my bag and a canvas carrier containing Darya's clothes and what toys could fit.

"Good-bye," said Irina, her eyes filling. "You be a good girl, and listen to Babushka."

"Thank you, Irina, for taking care of her," I said. "We're going to be fine together."

She smiled and waved as she turned quickly and walked back to the truck, and we were alone for the first time.

"I'm going to put you down now," I said, "because you're a big girl and you know how to walk, don't you?"

I sat on a bench as we waited for the next train, and she stood beside me and watched with big eyes as I went through all her clothes and repacked both bags so that I could manage them. I was thankful to see that Klara had taken good care of her. Her clothes were bright and clean, pinks and purples and light blue and yellow; she responded to my voice, smiled, was interested in what I had to show her. I changed her diaper, and we had a drink of water and some bread and jam.

When the train finally came and we boarded with the help of a young man who carried my bags, she was tired again, and I pulled out a book to amuse her. She sat on my lap, and it was difficult to know which one of us was more entertained as she pointed with her chubby forefinger at pictures of puppies and kittens, trees and tractors, apples and whales and seagulls. I sounded out the name of the picture, and she looked back at me with a little frown of concentration between her dark emerald eyes, and with a serious expression she repeated the word.

"You don't want to frown, Dashinka," I murmured, smoothing out the lines between her eyes. It was something left over from my own childhood, when Esther would smooth my frowns away. They thought in those days that frowning as a child would result in a permanent early wrinkle. In response she twisted around in my arms and solemnly traced the wrinkles between my eyes.

After a while she yawned, snuggled down on my lap and fell asleep in my arms. As we rolled home towards Moscow, I felt happier and fuller than I could remember. I would bring up this child as Klara would have wanted me to. Without hovering, I would watch her like a hawk; guide her, without being directive; love her, without smothering. I grew up not loving myself, and was unable to give the gift of self-love to Klara. But I was determined that whatever else she became, Darya would grow up loving herself.

There was no force on earth strong enough to make me avert my eyes or my attention from this child, not for an instant. Not Mother Russia, waiting patiently with her ever open, always salivating maw; not even Death snarling at my heels. I made a vow that I would be wholly present at every step of this child's life.

I have done everything in my power to keep that promise. Vasily would be proud.

❀

I was able without much trouble to return to the daily local trains so that I was off work to pick up Darya at the end of the day. The little nursery not far from our rooms was bright with colored paper flowers and images of animals on the walls, and filled with other beautiful, well-loved children, and once she adjusted to the new routine, she couldn't wait to get there. She made friends easily, and everything I worried about fell away as I saw how quick she was to understand, how rapidly she learned and accepted what was expected of her. She was quite the opposite of her mother—malleable, agreeable, easily satisfied. I began to worry that she was perhaps too passive and accepting, but I had nothing to worry about. There was nothing passive about her.

Everyone in the family was delighted with her. Nina and her daughter Juliana, who was not yet married, could not get enough of her. There was no shortage of people to hug and entertain her, first while I readied our rooms, and then when I was out shopping or taking a well-deserved hour at the library. Just as Klara and I had done after Vasily died, Darya and I slept in the same bed.

Esther was eighty-one and in ill health when I brought Darya back to Moscow. Arthritis made it difficult for her to get around, her legs were swollen, and she had trouble catching her breath. Walking up and down stairs had become almost impossible for her. Like many of the elderly in Moscow, who lived on third or fourth floors without an elevator, she was confined to the floor she lived on. She was no longer able to get to the library, and so her world began to shrink. Juliana, by then qualified as a doctor, asked her boyfriend, Maxim Koshkin, to come and examine Esther. He had already been a doctor for ten years, and he agreed with her that Esther had heart trouble for which there was no remedy.

Despite her ill health, Esther was alert, she kept her sense of humor, and she was interested in the world. She couldn't wait to get her hands on Darya, this beautiful child who was her first great-granddaughter. With great joy she watched Darya playing with blocks and dolls, busily toddling around the floor in her own imagined little world. At every opportunity she hugged and kissed her, tickled her and laughed loudly at the peals of joy she elicited. But as I watched all this, I could see that despite her happiness, there was something on Esther's mind.

On one of my days off, while Darya napped, Esther and I drank tea together at her little table, covered with a worn oilcloth on which the yellow lilies were faded to a creamy, eggshell color, and the red background worn to pink. It was quiet, most people were at work, the afternoon sun shone through the little window in her room. We were tranquil and at peace with ourselves, and with each other.

"I need to talk to you, Lena," she said, "about something we've not mentioned since you were a child. But it's been on my mind since your father died—and especially since you brought Darya home."

I looked at her expectantly.

"We've always been able to talk to each other, Esther. What is it?"

"As long as my body will allow, I'll keep on being a nuisance to you and Nina," she said. "But one day soon I'll be gone. To join your father, I suppose." She paused. "Whatever that means. I only hope," she continued with something between a smile and a grimace, "that he'll be complaining less than he was when I last saw him."

"For your sake I hope so, too." I reached across the table to take her hand. Her knuckles were swollen, but her fingers were as thin as matchsticks. "You were the one who carried his sadness for all of us."

"You know your father died with Mischa and Yossel's names on his tongue. We have lived with the absence of those two boys—now middle-aged men older than you are—for almost fifty years. I last saw them when they left Latvia with your mother before you were born—and I am still haunted that we were never able to get back to them." She paused, sighing deeply. "Sometimes, Lenotchka, I feel that it's my fault."

"We were caught in a war—how could you possibly feel responsible?"

"Come sit next to me," she said, putting a finger to her lips.

I went around to the other side of her little table and as I sat beside her, she put her mouth to my ear.

"We never know who might be listening," she whispered, and for the first time she told me the story of our arrival in Moscow. Until then I didn't know that it was her idea to forsake our Jewishness, that my father was reluctant to use the money he had left—the money for passage back to

South Africa—to buy forged papers.

"Perhaps," she continued, "if we had not spent that money, we might have been able to buy our way out of the country."

"You did what you needed to do to keep the family safe," I whispered back. "We all thank you. It has made our lives much easier."

"So," she said, counting on her fingers, "your father is gone, and I will soon join him. Vasily and Klara are gone. Of all the children your mother gave birth to, you are the only one we are sure still lives. Now you have Darya to care for. Don't you wonder sometimes, whether your brothers are still alive?"

"Of course," I said. "I carry them with me always." I decided not to tell her that I had been writing unsent letters to them, just as my father did.

"Once I'm gone, Lena, if something happens to you, the link to South Africa will be completely broken. There will be no one who remembers how to find Mischa and Yossel, and if they ever try to find us, it will be impossible."

"Why?"

"Because we have erased every path that might have led them to us."

"What paths? What are you talking about, Esther?"

"Did you never wonder whether they think of us here? Or whether they ever tried to contact us?"

"Yes, of course."

With crooked fingers digging into my shoulder, she pulled me closer.

"Have you forgotten that when we entered Moscow we changed our name from Shtein to Ozolins?" she whispered. "That when you married Vasily you changed again, from Ozolins to Lebedev? We could never let them know our new names without putting ourselves at risk. Even if they had been able to send us letters, who would they have sent them to?"

I was struck dumb. In all the years since I became Yelena Ozolins at the age of seven, I had never considered that my brothers had no way of knowing where we lived, or what our new names were—or even that we had new names. Even when it became possible to send and receive airmail letters from the West in the early 1950s, we didn't consider it. No one wanted it known that they were in communication with family outside the Soviet Union—it was only asking for trouble from the KGB. Suddenly I understood why my father died with Mischa and Yossel's names on his lips. He was aware all along that we were not just cut off from them, but that without their knowing our names, it was unlikely that they would ever find us.

"For most of the years since then," she continued, "it wasn't an issue— whatever channels of communication might have existed, were closed to us. There was no way for them to contact us," she said, "or for us to try and find them. Now I think we have a way—but only if you agree. If not, I will never talk about this again, because it is not without danger."

"All of a sudden we have a way to find out if they're still alive?" I asked. "What is it? I need to know—how else can I decide what the danger is, and whether I want to expose Darya to it? I'm all she has, Esther—I have to be very careful nothing happens to me."

She beckoned me closer, and I placed my ear next to her mouth.

"The next time you're alone with Juliana and Maxim," she whispered, "ask him about the people he works with at the International Red Cross."

❦

Once Esther mentioned the Red Cross, I began to be aware of rumors. The Red Cross had a presence in Moscow. I heard that they helped someone I worked with connect to her brother in London. Someone else in Mexico. A third person in Argentina. But the risk one took in making such a connection was not insignificant. Would I have to meet with someone from the Red Cross, and if so, how could I be sure the KGB was not listening to my conversation? To have it be discovered after all these years that we were Jews with false papers would be a disaster—and I would have nothing interfere with Darya's safety and with the opportunities available to her. And so for months I did nothing but think about whether to speak to Maxim.

About three months after our conversation, Esther fell and broke her hip. In the hospital she contracted pneumonia, and she died a few weeks later. We buried her beside my father. She was a wonderful mother to me and a great role model, and with her death the last link to Illuxt and our family history was gone. It was a very small ceremony—a few of Esther's friends, my stepsister Nina and her daughter Juliana, and Juliana's now husband, Maxim. As we walked from the gravesite, Juliana and Maxim in front of us, Nina and I embraced each other and wept. I decided that this was a perfect time to act on Esther's suggestion.

"Maxim," I said, pulling them to a stop. "We need to talk."

I wiped my eyes and made sure no one was close enough to overhear our conversation.

"Several months ago Esther told me to ask you about something. Will you tell me about the Red Cross?"

Maxim was in his thirties, built like a bricklayer, with a shock of grey hair and deep blue eyes. He was as solid as they come, reliable, confident, and practical. The first thing he did was smile, and then he casually looked around.

"I would be happy to tell you everything I know about that fine organization," he said. "Why don't we walk together a little. Juliana, would you mind?"

She shook her head and shooed us off, and stayed behind to talk to her mother. It was the end of summer, the leaves, red, yellow and gold, were falling around us, and there was a pleasant breeze, containing within it the seeds of winter. Maxim took my arm as we walked down the path back to the bus.

"What's all this about the Red Cross?" he asked quietly. "Have you decided to try and contact your brothers?"

"You know about my brothers," I said. "What else do you know?"

"I know the whole story," he said. "Just as Vasily did. He died long before I came into the picture, but did he know? Of course he did—you told him. There can be no secrets in a marriage, Lena. How else can we understand and protect each other?"

"We live now in easier times than when Vasily and I met thirty years ago," I said. "But even then he knew everything. You're right—there can be no secrets in a marriage."

"You want to find out if your brothers are still alive?"

"I want to know how it's done and how dangerous it is. This is something my father would have wanted, and Esther, too—but I won't do anything to endanger Darya."

"Neither would I," he said. "All I can tell you is that in the hospital, I work with people from the Red Cross. They have branches all over the world. They don't talk about it publicly, but they will make contact between people here and family in the West. They act as messengers, that's all. We can find a way to get a meeting between you and one of them—that's not a problem. They'll make an inquiry in South Africa. If your brothers are no longer alive and they have no family, that's an end to it. But if it turns out that they are alive and want to communicate with you, are you willing to receive letters from the West?"

"I'm not sure. After the war there was no way to receive such letters—but you tell me that now it's possible? How?"

"The world you grew up in is changed, Lena," he said. "I think there will be more and more contact with other countries. There are now mail agreements between our government and the West, so that letters can be sent almost anywhere. But it's still wisest to assume that the KGB has eyes on everything we send or receive."

"So this is not without danger," I said.

"Not without danger," he agreed, "but much less than before."

"I have to think about this," I said.

"That's fine," he said. "You just let me know if you want to start an inquiry, and I'll arrange a meeting."

We turned to go back to Juliana and Nina, but halfway there he put his hand on my arm and stopped me.

"Lena, I have a suggestion," he said. "Why not take this one step at a time? We could initiate the inquiry and see what happens. It could take a year to get an answer—and who knows what the politics will be by the time the answer comes back? Your brothers may be dead or untraceable. Perhaps they emigrated to another country, and you'll never find them. If that's the case, at least you've tried, and you can move forward knowing that you've honored your father's wishes, and satisfied your own curiosity."

"And what if that's not the case? What if we find them and they want to write to me?"

He shrugged and ran a hand through his thick grey hair.

"You would have found your brothers, Darya would have uncles and perhaps cousins overseas, and think what a gift it would be to your brothers to know that you're still alive." He smiled, and threw his arms wide. "Wouldn't that be a wonderful problem? Why don't we see what happens, Lena? Let the worst thing be that your brothers are well and want to write to you. If that happens, we'll find a way to do it safely."

❀

Maxim made it painless. He was a natural healer, and part of his skill was to make the lives of others easier. His colleague at the hospital was a French doctor, working in the USSR to establish a domestic equivalent of the Red Cross. He was stationed in Moscow through the French embassy, and had the protection afforded diplomats, but in Moscow even diplomats— especially diplomats—were shadowed by the KGB. We had to choose a meeting place that was not out of the ordinary for us, and so we chose the Tretyakov Gallery. It was certainly within my own normal routine, and fortunately, Maxim enjoyed taking foreign doctors to a different museum or historic site whenever he could. There would be nothing strange about Maxim bumping into his aunt in the museum atrium, where she often stood looking at Alexander Ivanov's massive painting.

Maxim reminded me that this was a chance meeting, and that I should dress and behave as if it were any other day. At the appointed time I walked slowly through the atrium, so nervous that I could feel my heart beating, and I was reminded of my first meetings with Vasily as a young woman. The painting was in a different building back then, but the memory of our first kiss in the little exhibition room on the second floor was still vivid, and I recalled it every time I stood before Ivanov's masterpiece.

As I sat down I saw Maxim and his friend enter the building, talking and laughing together. Behind them was a group of university students, and after them came a man in a belted raincoat, his head down, and when Maxim and his friend turned and stopped before the painting, the raincoat man stepped to the side of the room and pretended to be reading the newspaper. Everyone knew that he was KGB, and everyone pretended not to know. My first, fearful impulse was to rise from the bench and walk out of the museum, but my initial reaction to events is always followed by a second, much stronger impulse, motivated usually by anger. This time was no exception. I would not run—but I would act so that he would never know what we were doing. I rose from the bench and walked quickly across the room, clapping my hands.

"Maxim!" I said loudly, throwing my arms about him and kissing his cheeks. "*You're being watched,*" I whispered, and then pulled back and continued in a loud voice. "I've been trying to get you into this museum for years—how lovely to run into you! And here you are, standing right in front of my favorite painting! Who is your friend?"

He was so taken aback by my enthusiasm and lack of secrecy that he appeared genuinely surprised to see me. He kissed me back on both cheeks.

"We know he's there," he muttered. "I didn't realize you were such a wonderful actress."

He introduced his friend as Claude, a French doctor he worked with, and we shook hands. I remember nothing about him—which is strange, since he was the first foreigner I had ever met.

"You like Russian art?" I asked Claude. "Do you know this painting?"

"I know nothing of this artist," he said in Russian so thickly accented that at first I thought he was speaking a different language.

"That makes two of us," said Maxim. "I know nothing of this wonderful painting."

"So shall I tell you what I've learned about Alexander Ivanov?"

"That would be marvelous," said Claude.

I began to talk loudly about Ivanov's history and how the painting was executed in Rome over a period of twenty years, and I mentioned the many small studies he painted in preparation.

"What mastery he had of the human body," said Claude as he pointed at the nude teenage boy emerging from the River Jordan. And then he whispered, "*Where did your family live in South Africa?*"

"*Johannesburg,*" I answered softly, pointing to the mountains in the distance. "He was also a master of landscape, wasn't he?"

"Indeed. *And what were your brothers' names?*"

"*Mischa and Yossel Shtein,*" I said, pointing to the small figure in the distance, standing alone. "And you know who that is, of course?"

"It must be Jesus," he replied. "*What year did you leave, and how old were they at the time?*"

"Yes, that's right. See how the whole canvas directs the eye to where Jesus stands in the distance? *We left around 1912- they were thirteen and fifteen.* And see how all the figures in the foreground have turned to look at him, including John the Baptist?"

There were a few more questions. He asked me our father's name, and how to spell Illuxt. It was over in a matter of minutes. Claude shook my hand and thanked me for the lesson. I kissed Maxim on both cheeks. They walked off to continue their tour of the museum, leaving me standing alone before the painting, so exhausted that I completely forgot about the raincoat man until he tapped my shoulder.

"Comrade," he said, looking down at me from under the rim of his hat. He was much taller than I was, but still he felt the need to speak in that soft, threatening voice they all cultivated. "You know it is unwise to socialize with foreigners. How are you acquainted with those men?"

I laughed loudly, drawing attention to our conversation. "One of them is my nephew—he's as Russian as you or I. I don't know where the other one is from—but both are foreigners to art. How about you? Are you a foreigner to art? Would you like to know about this marvelous painting, painted in Rome by a very talented Russian?"

I took his arm as if to pull him towards the canvas, but he shook me off and turned away. I was just another clueless grandmother, hardly worth intimidating, and he had far more important quarry to track.

In the months that followed, I had little time to think about anything other than what was in front of me. It was how I had lived most of my life. And with Darya to care for, I had no choice but to resume that grueling schedule. She was a handful, with a very determined streak. The idea that I had worried about her passivity became something of a grim joke. She was up at the crack of dawn, snuggling into my arms and pulling at my nightgown.

"Wake up, Babushka. Babushka, I'm hungry. Babushka, I need water. Babushka, I have to pee. Babushka, I want to read a book to you. Babushka, let's play."

I could have eaten her up. I loved her with such deep intensity, but I no longer had the energy of a young woman. I dragged myself out of bed to supervise her dressing and washing—but she insisted on dressing herself. She chose which clothes she would wear, allowed no one to help her brush her teeth, and screamed in frustration if I insisted upon wiping her bottom for her. She wanted to be—and she was—independent from the first day. As a result I was always cleaning up after her, and everything took longer than it needed to. But I vowed to be patient and always present, and I was determined to keep my vow. Nina and I had very different schedules, but she was always willing to help with Darya when she was free. Very soon after their marriage, Juliana and Maxim announced that she was pregnant. And so it became clear even after my father's and Esther's death that life would go on, and that it would drag us all with it as it had always done. The Red Cross and the inquiry we had started fell to the back of my mind, and so did the uncertainty about what I would do with the results. I thought I would be obsessed with the outcome, worried about how I would react if the inquiry came up blank, and equally concerned about how I would respond if my brothers were found alive and well. It was almost as if, having finally found a way to inquire about them, I was able to get on with my life.

And then seven months after my chance meeting at the Tretyakov Gallery, Maxim came to my rooms one evening after work and sat me down at my table.

"We have an answer, Lena," he said, handing me an envelope with my name written on it in Russian.

"Where did you get this?" I asked.

"From Claude, "he said. "The man you met at the museum."

I looked at the envelope in my hand. It was shaking. After so long, I dreaded the idea that I was about to open a form letter containing copies of my brothers' death certificates.

"Open the letter, Lena," urged Maxim quietly. "Let's find out what it says."

There was a tremor in my fingers and a catch in my breath as I carefully slid my thumb under the flap and pulled open the envelope. Inside was a single sheet of paper folded into thirds, and on the outside fold were printed the words, "To my dearest Sister, Lena." As I unfolded the letter, a small photograph fell into my lap. I picked it up and looked into the faces of two balding, middle-aged men wearing business suits and ties. Both had sad eyes and wide, expressive mouths. They stood side by side in the shade of a large willow tree, a flower garden behind them. Both were short, one thin and stooped, the other a little heavier in the face and belly. They had my father's face and his sad, lost expression. I knew immediately which was which—the short, stooped one was Yossel, and the heavier one, with broader face and bigger belly, was Mischa. But to me, both were strangers.

"Oh, my poor father," I heard myself say as I unfolded the letter. It was written in blue ink, in Russian, in a hand I did not know.

"Claude said your brother doesn't speak Russian," explained Maxim. "He wrote it in English, and had a friend translate it so that you would understand. Read it aloud, Lena."

I tried, but my voice broke, and I handed it to him.

"You read it aloud," I said. "I can't do it."

And so I first heard my brother Mischa's words in Maxim's voice. He read it quietly, without speed, so that I could savor each word. I sat with my hands over my mouth, my breath coming in shudders, and as I listened, I stared at the photograph on the table before me. I understood for the first time what it meant to experience something bittersweet—it was to feel through a breaking heart an almost unbearable sense of joy and elation.

——◆——

My Dear Sister:

I thought my life would pass without ever saying those words. At long last we have found each other. Thank God. How we have waited for this moment! Since we were boys in our teens, Yossel and I hungered for word from you.

When father first took you all—you and Mirjam and Avrom—back to Illuxt, we talked late into the night about where you were, what you were doing, and when we would next see you. But as World War I became inevitable, we realized that you were unlikely to return before it was over. The last letter we received from father was the news of his marriage to his late brother's wife, whose name I have forgotten. Esther, I think. She must be long gone by now, but she would have been all these years your stepmother, while we here had to be both father and mother to each other and to ourselves.

And then nothing. No news. No more letters. We knew you must have been caught in Illuxt. After the war we continued writing, but there was no way to get mail to Latvia, and our letters were returned. All our inquiries led to dead ends.

After World War II we hired a Latvian to do research for us. He found our home village, Illuxt, razed to the ground after the first war, and rebuilt a few miles away, its name modernized to Illukst. We felt even more distant from wherever you might be, but we never gave up hope that one day we might be reunited. Now we find you in Moscow. What a story that must be! I long to hear from you how you arrived there.

Sadly, this wonderful news comes too late for Yossel, who never married, and who died from a stroke two years ago. He and I were all our lives more than brothers—we were partners in business, and best friends, and since his death I have been sunk in the most profound grief. He was all I had left from the family of my youth, but now I have my family back, and that knowing lifts my heart and fills me with hope.

As for me, I was happily married for many years, but my beloved wife of forty years, Dora, passed away recently. I have a son, Lenny, and a wonderful grandson, Steven, who is three. Perhaps one day soon we will all meet.

You must know by now that we changed our names, and I want to explain that we did not lightly throw away our birthright. South Africa before World War II had a divided population, a powerful portion of which belonged to the Nationalist Party, was against Britain, and wanted to go into the war on the side of Germany. Anti-Semitism was growing, and there was talk in the 1930s of depriving Jews of their citizenship. That never came about, and today it all seems like an impossibly bad dream. But at the time it was terrifying, and there was no knowing in which direction history would take us. It seemed prudent to change our names to something less obviously Jewish. It was a difficult decision—we knew that it would make the task of finding us far more difficult for you, if any of you still lived. So we kept Shtein as our middle name. We knew wherever records were kept, buried in some government office, there would be a trail leading to our birth names. So Yossel Shtein became Joseph Shtein Green, and I changed my name from Mischa Shtein to Mike Shtein Green.

Our father would be over eighty, if he lives still—but that would be too much to hope for. Still, perhaps it will be given to us to look into each other's eyes once more. What about our stepmother? Are you married? Do you have children? I remember that our sister Mirjam died on the journey over—but what of our brother Avrom?

We know that conditions in the Soviet Union are not easy. I am not a wealthy man but I have been fortunate in my life. Long before Yossel died he and I agreed that if ever we found you, it would be a great joy for us if we could make your lives more comfortable. Let me know, please, please, if there is anything you need.

The man who brought me this wonderful news shares with me that much in your life is not as I might assume, about which I will say no more here. I would do nothing to cause harm or discomfort to you or others in the family, and will follow your wishes in all things regarding contact between us.

From across the wide and distant oceans that have kept us apart for half a century, I send you and our brother and I hope all the nephews and nieces I have never met, fifty years of kisses, and, my deepest, deepest love.

Mischa

<hr/>

The first thing that struck me was that Russia was not the only place in the world where being a Jew was dangerous. They, too, had changed their name in order to be safe. Esther would be smiling at the irony.

What to do with such a letter? It revealed such a vast chasm between our lives that I was thrown into a state of panic and fury. Yossel is dead—how do I mourn for a brother I haven't seen in fifty years? The man who tells me Yossel is dead, and who calls himself by my brother Mischa's name, writes to me, offering to make my life more comfortable. What would he give me? A house? A big car? A thick carpet for my floor? American movies and chewing gum? He wants to know what I need. Why? So he can send them to me? How can he not know that anything he gives me will make me suspect in the eyes of the State?

For fifty years I've lived with Avrom's absence—only to find that Mischa never knew. Never knew! Of our journey to Moscow and of Avrom's death and the pain of my loss. Never knew! What a wonderful mother Esther was. Never knew of our stepsisters Sofia, exiled to Siberia and Nina, my closest friend. Never knew of my beloved Vasily and our dead Klara and her baby Darya. How to tell him how hard our lives have been, how hard I have worked, how desperately our father missed them? And does it matter if he knows? He doesn't know me—can't know me.

But the opposite is equally true. Can I possibly know him? He says he has done well in his life—what does that mean? His wife, like my husband, is dead. Can I ever know who she was? And does it matter?

Perhaps, I tell Maxim, this was all a mistake. Fifty years is so long that we can never really be reunited—we have grown so far apart that we are related only by blood. I was better off not knowing how vast the gulf between us has grown.

"Did you think for a moment that this would be painless, Lena?" he asks in his deep, soothing voice. I think, this must be the voice he uses with his very sick patients. "You searched for your brothers so that you could find them, wherever they are and whatever they've become. Now you realize that whatever else has happened to them in their lives, they didn't remain the young boys you remember. You didn't share their lives—just as they haven't shared yours."

"And so? Now what happens?"

"Now you've heard his voice. Wouldn't you like him to hear yours?"

"If I write him a letter, who will take it to him? Remember, Maxim, I must be safe."

"Claude will be our mailman. He went to South Africa—he was the one who told Mischa you're alive."

"What did Mischa do when he heard?"

"He wept, like a child. They talked for a long time—he told him all about our life here." He paused. "Claude liked him. Your brother is warm and funny, but there is a great sadness about him."

"Why does Claude do this for us?"

"He's my friend, Lena, and he likes to help people. Once the Red Cross found Mischa, he arranged a business trip there. He wanted to meet your brother and to tell him that he had spoken to you at the museum. Claude goes to Paris every two months. He'll take letters out of the country for you whenever he goes. Mischa will send letters to him in Paris, and when he comes back here, he'll bring the letters to me. For the moment, that's all we need."

I suddenly realized how much Maxim was putting himself out for me, in ways that made both him and Juliana vulnerable. I felt ashamed at my caution.

"Maxim, thank you," I said. "I am being so ungrateful. I do appreciate how good you are to me."

"You don't have to thank me. I do it because I love you." He kissed my cheeks and patted my shoulder as he left. "Besides, if I didn't, my wife and her mother would have my head." He smiled. "Just write to Mischa," he whispered, and I watched him walk down the darkened hallway.

❦

I pulled out from the box under my bed the unsent letter I had written to Mischa and Yossel in 1953, when our father died, thinking that now, finally, I had someone to send it to. But I couldn't. It was a letter written to myself, not for anyone else's eyes. I would have to start again, and what I wrote would be very different.

———◆———

My Dear Brother Mischa:

How wonderful to learn that you live, and to discover where you've spent your life! Your letter scratches only the surface of the joy and sadness we've not shared, but from that scratch flows blood and tears. All at the same time I mourn for Yossel. I cry tears of joy at your marriage and the birth of your child and grandson, and I weep for the loss of your wife, whom I will now never know. It is like being forced to imagine and relive in a single moment the fullness of fifty years. Since your letter there have been moments when I felt I could not bear the intensity of the joy and desolation in my heart.

I also have news—some of it by now ancient—much of which will sadden you.

We lost our brother, my twin, Avrom, a lifetime ago, in 1915. It is hard to comprehend that all these years you had no knowledge of this event, which in many ways shaped my life. Father died six years ago, in the 1953 flu epidemic, and Esther last year. Just as you are alone on your side of the ocean, I, too, am the only one of our mother's children left on this shore. I, too, was married, but am now alone—my husband Vasily and our daughter Klara are gone. I am raising my granddaughter, Darya, who is three years old. She has been a sweet gift in my life, and gives me new purpose.

There is much more, my brother, to tell you and to ask you, but this is not the time. Perhaps we will meet again, if not in this life, then in some other. In the meantime, it is gift enough to know that we have found each other, that our long silence is broken, and that, at least for now, we have a way to exchange words.

With all my love,

Lena

PART TWO

Darya's Story

My world starts with Babushka. She and I joked that we belonged together like onions and garlic, borscht and potatoes, skates and ice, hammer and sickle. My first, warmest memory is of waking up next to her in the morning, snuggling and giggling together. She made every morning of my childhood a game, and she quickly became my best and closest friend.

If my first memory is waking up beside Babushka, my second memory is of a doll, a gorgeous soft thing almost as big as I was, and of the man who gave her to me when I was barely four. She was the most beautiful object I had ever seen. The container she came in would have been a gift by itself—a big, pink box almost big enough for me to climb in. It was big enough to hold my toys and books, and until it fell apart, it was home to my most precious possessions.

She was made of flesh-colored plastic with a happy, painted face, pink cheeks, and cherry-red lips. Her brown eyes opened when I picked her up from her nap, and closed when I laid her down to sleep beside me. She had long, dark lashes and thick brown hair that I could fashion and braid, and she came with her own hairbrush. Her head turned left and right so that as she sat beside me on the floor or as I ate at the table, I could turn her head and she could always have me within eyesight. Her body seemed wonderfully real—she had a belly button, and her arms and legs were jointed and rotated just like mine so that I could dress and undress her like a real little girl. Best of all were the two sets of clothes that were tidily folded in one corner of the box—a purple skirt and a pale pink blouse, and a set of pink pajamas with little mice printed on them. And to my absolute delight, the man from a country across the ocean who brought me the doll managed to find a set of pajamas for me to wear that were identical to the pink pajamas the doll wore—pink with little brown mice.

His name was Uncle Mischa, Babushka's brother. He came to visit us from a faraway place, and I remember vaguely an old man with a mostly bald head and a warm smile. His eyes were sad and red, and for much of our time together he carried a white cloth in his hand—it was my first exposure to a handkerchief—with which he constantly dabbed at his eyes, sometimes covering them completely for a few seconds. I thought at first it was a game, but I noticed that whenever he covered his eyes Babushka's face took on an expression of grief so deep that it shook the foundation of my universe. Much later, when I understood the significance of his visit, I realized that much of his time with us he spent with tears in his eyes.

Uncle Mischa wore a dark suit and a red striped tie. On the first day he came to visit us in our room he brought the doll with him. I sat on his lap and he showed me how to dress her, and smiled and talked to me softly in very bad Russian which improved over the few weeks he spent in Moscow. He smelled different from all the people I knew. When he kissed my cheeks I smelled his after shave, wonderfully rich and tart. Babushka sat on the bed and watched us together. When she smiled, I smiled back at her, and when she cried, I jumped off Uncle Mischa's lap to wipe her eyes as we had done for each other since the beginning, but Babushka waved me back.

"No, my angel," she said. "You stay there with Uncle Mischa. I want to watch you together. I'm not crying. These are happy tears that my brother and I have a chance to see each other, and that you and he can know each other. Happy tears."

The doll itself was memorable, and by all accounts Uncle Mischa was a warm and generous man. But the vividness of my memory has to do with the emotional tone of his visit, and the way it touched Babushka. I was at school when they first met—Babushka arranged it that way, not knowing how she would react to Mischa after so many years. I don't know where he stayed. We were not allowed to visit him. Intourist, the official state travel agency, would have assigned him to a hotel where foreign visitors were housed, either The Metropole or The National, which was one block from Red Square. He and Babushka were never seen together in public. He had a driver assigned by Intourist, a man who watched his every step, and took note of where he went and whom he visited. We saw him whenever we could, and then Uncle Mischa was gone, traveling on an airplane back to his city across the ocean, and everything went back to how it had been before.

But not quite as before. Clearly the politics had eased, which made it possible for him to visit in the first place. After he left, the letters Babushka received from him were major events. It was drummed into me early that these were not to be discussed outside our rooms. I learned later—much later—that when Mischa saw our rooms he was so distraught at the conditions we lived in that he went back to his hotel and wept. I was not aware as a child of being deprived or of living in substandard conditions, and I was an adult before I had sufficient exposure to the world—and to how others lived—to comprehend the level of his shock at how his sister lived.

Two events in my life brought an end to my innocence, and they were both stories Babushka told me. They were revelations about our lives and who we were, and in my memory, they came about organically. But there was a fierce intelligence behind the way she told these stories. In retrospect, I am in awe at how well she understood me. To my mind she remains an apolitical woman unschooled in the world, who, until she revealed herself to me, never uttered a word against Stalin or communism. As a mother of teenage children, I now recognize with amazement how politically astute she really was. I marvel at the risks she was willing to take in revealing what she did—not only political risks, but risks to our relationship, which has always been the most important thing in her life. Yet she made the decision to expose herself, and our whole family, to me—an immature teenage girl—whose reactions she could only have guessed at. She was never a religious woman, but she had faith in her intuition. She was determined to do the right thing by me, and let the chips fall where they may. What touches me most deeply is how much faith she had in me, and in my ability to see things as she did.

Most of my friends had already started menstruating when I had my first period at the age of thirteen. My best friend, Manya, had a mother who was practical and educated, and who knew me and Babushka well enough to recognize that I could benefit from the advice of a younger and more educated woman. When she sat Manya down for the traditional mother-daughter conversation about becoming a woman, she made it a point to include me. I also had my older cousin Juliana, to whom I was very close. She made sure I was informed, and that I felt comfortable with my body. In the dangerous innocence of childhood, I thought I knew all there was to know about becoming a woman. But something happened a few weeks after I got my first period, something that, at the time, I was convinced would forever change my relationship with Babushka.

Every week my grandmother and I went to the public baths. Most Muscovites did. It was a change from the apartment, where bathing took the form of a lukewarm sponging while standing in the bathtub. The public baths were clean enough, and there was plenty of hot water. There was even a pool to soak in, redolent of mineral spirits. It was a communal event, and it was a way for the women to relax away from the pressure of work and family.

She was generally firm, but she never, ever did anything harsh to me. She was unfailingly gentle, and in her old world way, as loving as any grandmother could be, given the pressure of working and raising a teenager. But on this occasion, a few weeks after I announced the start of my first period, we were sitting in the communal pool, and she beckoned me to her. Muttering something under her breath, she placed her hand on my head, which she did often. It was a sign of affection. But this time without warning she pushed my head underwater and held me there. It was so sudden and I was so surprised to find myself submerged that I breathed water into my lungs. When she released me I came up choking.

I was furious, and in the midst of my fury, embarrassed as I coughed and gagged and the water ran from my mouth and nose. I glared at her, stormed out of the pool, dressed without drying my hair, and made my way home. All along, she was only a few steps behind, trying to keep up with me, calling my name. I ignored her. It was a frigid January and snow was falling. After a fifteen-minute walk home through the icy streets, my hair was frozen to my scalp and I was shivering. She came into the apartment behind me, joined me in our bedroom, and closed the door behind her. Her hair too was wet and frozen, but she came and stood behind me with a towel, hugging me to her and gently patting my hair. I had dark hair with red highlights, it was thick and long, and had she dried it the way she generally did, it would have snapped off in frozen strands.

"Dasha, my angel," she whispered. It was the only way to have a private conversation in our room. "Don't be angry with me. I was wrong to surprise you, but I didn't want this to pass without some kind of ceremony. I'm sorry I did it so roughly, but I know nothing about what it all means. I don't know how to say the words, may my father and my mother forgive me—but I must tell you the truth."

What she was saying made no sense. I thought she was talking to herself. She continued to pat my head in silence. I was already a head taller than she, and standing behind me as I sat on the bed, her head was level with mine. Eventually she leaned forward, turned my head a little towards her and kissed my forehead.

"Now you are a woman," she whispered. "A Jewish woman. You should be proud—both are honorable. But you need to be careful, Dasha. In our lives, we bleed from both."

I jerked away from her in horror. "What terrible curses are you wishing on me?" I whispered.

I didn't know what anti-Semitism was, but I knew that Jews were reviled. There were a handful of students with Jewish names in my school. It was understood that they were seldom admitted to the most desirable professions, and the best schools were usually closed to them. They were routinely embarrassed by teachers and mocked by students. I don't know if I believed the tales about what Jews had done to deserve the treatment they received, but I knew for a fact that they were greedy and dishonest, and that Israel, where they all wanted to go, was an illicit country stolen from the Arabs and supported by the United States. We were all aware of the Doctors' Plot, an event in 1953 in which the story was spread that Jewish patients of Jewish doctors recovered while their non-Jewish patients died at an alarming rate. Several Jewish doctors were dismissed and arrested. Anti-Jewish publications—and violence against Jews—proliferated.

In later years, when I was better informed and more curious, I researched the Doctors' Plot. At the time, some in the Kremlin believed that Stalin was readying camps for the Jews, ostensibly to protect them from violence, but in reality to attempt his own version of something he was a master at—ethnic cleansing. Stalin died in 1953, and shortly after his death, it was announced that the case had been fabricated. But when we were taught about the Doctors' Plot, there was no mention of fabrication, and the implication was that it had been a Jewish plot to assassinate high-level Soviet leaders.

I was a Russian, a good person. I intended to be a member of the Party, and to make a contribution to the People's State. I was going to be a valuable part of the system, and none of those things would be possible if Babushka spread crazy accusations about my being a Jew. My first thought was that she had lost her mind, but I was savvy enough to recognize that even if what she said had no foundation, it would be enough to taint me and ruin my prospects. I could not report her—that would be a way of spreading this awful lie. I would have to find some way to keep her quiet. It crossed my mind that I might have to kill her—but only for a split second. Then I couldn't decide whether I was more horrified by her words, or by my instinctive response to protect my political prospects by murdering the person I loved more than anyone else in my life. As I sat on the bed, weak with the horror at what I had contemplated, Babushka came and sat beside me. She embraced me, and I threw my arms about her.

"Babushka," I whispered into her ear, "I think you're not well. But don't worry. I'll take care of you."

She released me from her embrace, put her hands on my shoulders, pushed me far away enough so that she could look at me, and stroked my cheek. In her face, the wise, crafty, gentle face I loved, there was something that looked like amusement.

"You think I'm talking nonsense, Dashinka? Losing my mind?"

There were tears in my eyes as I nodded.

"I think maybe you're not well in your head."

To my surprise, she smiled, a deep, sad smile filled with the pain of complex and difficult knowledge. The permanent furrows from the ends of her lips down to her chin deepened, and the web of lines at the corners of her eyes tightened like a purse string.

"There's nothing wrong with my head, child," she whispered. "But it's time for you to learn about your place in the world."

Suddenly I knew she was not crazy, and that there was at least some truth to what she had said. I didn't learn the whole story until much later, but what she told me—and what she showed me—was sufficient to change my life and the way I thought about everything in it.

"I have never told you anything about our family, Dasha," she whispered, "and you have never asked me any questions about it. Have you never wondered, where do we come from?"

"We are Soviet citizens," I answered. "We come from Moscow. What is there to wonder about?"

"Yes, yes," she scoffed, still whispering. "All of us in Moscow are Russians. We have pure Russian blood, we are Russian born, Russian educated; we have Russian temperament, and we are descended from the red earth of Mother Russia, from Russian peasants. We are not related to the landowners or the nobility murdered at the time of the Revolution, and certainly none of us comes from anywhere else. Right?" She shook her head in the negative. "No, my love, not right. The truth is that many of us Russians in Moscow come from other places, some by choice, and some by force. We come from Latvia, and Lithuania, and Belarus. All those countries are now a part of the Soviet Union, but not all the people who live there feel like Russians or want to be a part of the Soviet Union. But they have no choice."

I put a hand up to cover her mouth. "Babushka," I said, pleading softly. "You shouldn't say such things."

She pulled my hand from her face and held it in her lap.

"Don't try and teach this old woman to suck eggs," she said sternly. "This is not a day for you to teach—it is a day for you to learn the truth."

She was quivering, her eyes bright, and in later years I realized that it was with anticipation and excitement. She had held onto what she was about to reveal all her life, until it was safe to pass her knowledge on. This was the day. At the time, I didn't understand. How could I?

"We never talk about family," she said, "because our silence leads us to assume there is nothing to discuss. We go about our lives as if we were as Russian as vodka. It makes life simple."

We sat together on her bed in our little bedroom with the white lace curtains she had made on the window, and she stroked my hand.

"But life is not simple. It is true that we live in Moscow, the best city in the richest country in the world, and we are Russians. But there are other truths. One is that Moscow is not the center of the world, and that far from being rich, our country struggles every day to feed and clothe its people. Another truth is that no matter where in the world you live, it is easier to survive if you are not a Jew."

She paused, looked into my eyes, and continued to stroke my hand. Her hands were work-hardened, her finger joints swollen with arthritis.

"We pretend, like many others in Moscow, to be descended from the serfs who worked the land, and we convince ourselves that we are fortunate to be a part of our great Soviet experiment. But the truth is that we come from a little village in Latvia, and that our blood is Jewish. Your great-grandparents were Jews. This old grandmother is a Jew. Your mother was a Jew. You, too, Dashinka, are Jewish. No one else need know this—but I can't keep it from you any longer. If you continue to work hard, you will be noticed by the right people, and they will invite you to become a member of the Communist Party. You can rise as high as the men in the Kremlin will let a woman go. But after this day, when anyone suffers—when anyone is punished or denied a position or a place in school because she is a Chechen or a Christian or a Jew, you will know that it could just as easily be you. Do you understand this?"

"I understand. But—" I hardly knew how to phrase my question "— how can it be? How do you know? And if it is true, why does it not say so on our identity cards?"

"My father and Esther and all their children were expelled from Latvia in the Great War because we were Jews," she said. "We arrived in Moscow without identity cards and without permits. My stepmother Esther made a decision. She said all the bad things that happened to them in their lives happened because they were Jews. Now they were starting new, without a history. No one knew them. There would never be a more perfect time to stop being Jews."

"How can people just stop being what they are?"

She shrugged.

"That's what my father said. He asked her, 'you think you can take off your Jewishness the way you take off your socks?' And she said, 'I can do anything that will make our children's lives easier.' That's what they did. They got false identity papers. They became Russian. They stopped thinking of themselves as Jews—which is to say, they stopped behaving like people who are different and expected to be treated badly. Instead of watching to see what the people around them were about to do to them, they started watching to see how the average Russian behaved. It was a different way of being, and it worked. They became like every other refugee in Moscow trying to make their way in the world."

I was shocked almost to speechlessness.

"If this is true," I stammered, "then your parents were liars. And you. And now me, too." A thought struck me. "And what about Nina, your sister? And Juliana? Are they Jews, too?"

"Yes, my child, all of us who are children of my parents. This is how the real world works," she said gently. "The people in the Kremlin have access to everything—we have access to nothing. They say Jews stick together, that we care about our own and nobody else. It's true that Jews help each other—how else would we have survived? The Communist Party you think so pure is an illusion to keep us all believing we are the best and the richest in the world. The KGB knows it. Time you did, too. And yes, my parents lied. All my life I've lived this lie. Perhaps there will come a time when you can reveal the truth, but until then, you too, will lie. It is a matter of survival, and it works." She rose from the bed. "I have something to show you."

I sat in silence as she took the wooden chair from my desk, carried it across the room and propped it under the door handle. Then she waved me over and together we lifted the little table at which I did my work and at which we ate when we were alone. We carried it next to the bed and lowered it to the floor, careful not to make a sound that could be heard from the next room. She knelt down beside our single window and, using the little knife she carried in her pocket, pried the floorboard closest to the wall from its place. It came up easily, and she laid it against the bed, reaching down into the space beneath the floor to withdraw a dusty package wrapped in a piece of ancient newsprint. Gently, as silently as possible, she unfolded the crumbling paper, and from within she withdrew a big Russian nesting doll—a Matryoshka. Holding it under one elbow, she put her other arm on the bed, levered herself up from the floor, and set the Matryoshka on the bed.

"It's a Matryoshka," I said, reaching out to touch it. "It's beautiful. But what's so special about a doll?"

"Not yet," she said, firmly moving my hands from the doll. "You know so little—but how can I expect you to know anything if no one tells you? Before I show you this—this doll—I have a story to tell you. Come, sit next to me."

I was thirteen. I prided myself on my drive, my organization, my commitment to The Cause—something much bigger and more stable and more solid than I was. It gave my life purpose, and perhaps it was what I needed, having lost my parents so early. But at that moment, my ordered, ambitious world was being dismantled. Another story seemed more than I could stomach. I leaned in to her and she cradled me as she had when I was a baby, only this time she could barely get her arms around my shoulders. I didn't pull away.

"This is very hard," I said. "I don't think I can do anymore tonight."

She rubbed my shoulders.

"Of course you can," she said, chuckling. "As always, you're much more than you think you are. And besides, this is the good part."

"So there is a good part?" I asked.

"Well, there's always a worse part and a better part," she said. "This is the better part. I've waited a long time to tell you, so don't you dare fall asleep in the middle of my story. Promise to listen?"

"I promise," I said.

The tale she told me was about her stepsister, Sofia, who, in the 1930s, was banished with her husband to live in Siberia. All Babushka knew was that her sister and husband had disobeyed Party doctrine, and for that they lost their right to live in Moscow. In those years, banishment was forever.

For decades these two sisters wrote letters to each other, and each tried to protect the other from the knowledge of how deprived their lives were. Years later Babushka shared with me all the letters she had received from Sofia, and I was deeply touched by the care she took to describe her life in the brightest and most lively language. I don't doubt that reading and writing these letters were some of the sweetest experiences of both women's lives. Neither had any schooling to speak of, yet Sofia's writing, filled with errors of grammar and spelling, was clear and forceful, descriptive, humorous, even flamboyant. It shocked me, and once again I was ashamed at how little I had known who my Babushka was.

Sometime towards the end of The Great Patriotic War, what they call in the West World War II, Babushka and her young daughter—my mother, Klara—were sent away to Lake Baikal for a month, with other women and children. She couldn't remember why, but when I investigated years later, I discovered that it was a way of getting some of the most vulnerable people out of the city in the event that the German army ever reached Moscow. From Moscow to Lake Baikal was a seven-day train ride through Siberia. Somehow, before leaving Lake Baikal, Babushka was able to get word to her stepsister Sofia, letting her know on what train they would be returning to Moscow.

There was only one rail line through Siberia. The train had to pass every stop on the line. It took Sofia and her husband three days traveling by the only method available—a horse cart—to reach the closest station on the rail line. There they waited. Babushka never found out for how long; there was not time to ask. It could have been days. When finally the train pulled in, stopping at what was barely a hut in the middle of a cleared space among the pine trees—Babushka disembarked, my mother in hand, searching anxiously for the sister she hadn't seen in twenty years. A few people boarded the train, some left, to be met by horse-drawn carts, or to begin walking off into the flatness to some unknown village. A handful of peasants waited, sitting on barrels or benches, talking and drinking vodka. And there was a cart on which sat two old people, a man and a woman, vaguely recognizable.

The man lowered himself from the seat, walked around to the other side and helped his wife to the ground. Together they hobbled over to the tracks, waving their arms, calling, "Lena! Lena!"

Babushka said that once she got over her shock at their appearance, she thought, my sister has become the Russian peasant our parents wanted us to pass for. But this was not passing—they had become the real thing. And what a price they had paid.

"Our train stayed at that station only a half-hour," she concluded. Her lips quivered as she cried through her words, and tears ran down her cheeks and followed the wrinkles in her chin to drop like jewels on her sweater. "That's all the time we had to greet each other, kiss cheeks and then say good-bye. We knew we would never meet again. It's in the nature of things that we all suffer many losses. But this separation from my sister was so unnecessary, such a waste. An order given by a crazy man and carried out by cowards."

She stopped, wiped her eyes, breathed a few ragged breaths before continuing.

"As the train whistle announced that it was about to leave, my sister pulled me to the cart and took out a big old box. It was full of biscuits, she said. And I thought, such a big box. Enough biscuits to feed the whole train."

" 'My recipe,' she said, holding tight onto my arm. 'Baked specially for you. Traveled three days on the cart to get to you. Carry them carefully, Lena,' she warned, 'or all you'll have is a box full of crumbs.'

"We kissed each other and she waved us back to the train. By the time we found our seats, the cart and the hut were just a speck in the distance."

I didn't quite know what to say, or how the story had anything to do with being Jewish or with the Matryoshka doll. But I knew Babushka needed to be comforted.

"It was thoughtful of her. Did you and my mother eat them on the train?"

"There were a few biscuits at the top of the box, and yes, we ate them. But there was something else in the box, too."

She leaned across to the Matryoshka doll and carefully pulled apart the two halves. Inside was an ancient shawl, bordered with faded, barely visible designs of red, purple and yellow. It was wrapped around a heavy object, which she set on the bed. The shawl was ripped and shredding, and she was gentler than I would have been as she unbound the old rag from around whatever it protected. Perhaps she sensed my impatience, because she stopped and looked up at me. Her hands rested lovingly on the torn cloth.

"Don't be so quick to judge what you see, Dashinka," she whispered. "This old thing was my stepmother's shawl. It's older than I am, and it kept her warm as she carried us children through the forests, not knowing whether we would live or die, or where we might end up. It is a rag now, but still it has a purpose."

"I'm sorry," I said.

She looked down again and set the shawl aside, revealing an intricate ornamental device that appeared at first to be a teapot. It was made of brass, covered in delicately wrought silver leaves attached to stems of blue stone. It was by far the most intricate, ornate thing I had ever seen, much less touched.

"What is it, Babushka?" I asked breathlessly. "What is it for?"

"It looks like a teapot, but it is something other than that. I don't know—I was never taught these things. When my sister was sent to Siberia, our father gave this to her, the only thing remaining from his past. My sister gave it to me in that box at the train station. It was meant for your mother."

She lifted it from the bed and handed it to me. I took it. It was heavy and solid. In the back of my throat I smelled the metallic odor that was the oxidation of metals. I turned it in my hands, noticed the parts that moved, and the latches that opened to reveal other vessels and containers, and the strange writing on the bottom, with a star in the middle.

"This is the only thing we have left of my father, the only thing that shows we once lived as Jews. My father's grandfather—your great-great-great-grandfather—was a tinker when we lived in that part of Latvia called Courland. He made this, perhaps as early as 1840. Somewhere on the teapot are his initials in this script I can't read—his name was Asher Shtein. I don't know what any of these symbols mean, or what the containers are for, but my father treasured it all his life."

She put her hand on the teapot that now rested in my lap, and she pushed it towards me.

"The teapot is yours, Dasha. A piece of your history. One day when you grow up you will take it from me and become its guardian. Perhaps by then you will be able to show it on a shelf in your home. And maybe you will find out what it all means."

Again, she stroked my hair. Eventually we got ready for bed, and as I lay down to sleep she curled up behind me and put her arms about my shoulders.

"This is all I have to give you, my angel," she whispered into my ear. "This, and my love, and my stories of the past, and the efforts of a stupid old woman to bring you to womanhood with an ancient ritual I don't even understand.

"When I became a woman, my stepmother Esther went with me to the public baths. She prayed in silence to her Jewish God, and she pushed my head under the water, and when I complained to her, she slapped my face. When your mother became a woman I took her to the public baths. I didn't know the words. All I remembered was that I had been pushed under the water, so I pushed her under, too. She refused to speak to me for days, but I never raised a hand to her. I was a young woman then, and not very courageous—and your mother was very different from you. So I never told her the truth, and she died not knowing why I pushed her head under the water. I made myself a promise that I would deal with you differently. And now I have. I've revealed to you what your great-grandparents tried so hard to hide from the world. I only hope I've done the right thing."

Until that night, I was proud of my Russian peasant blood. It may not have been the intent of my teachers, but what I took away from their constant drumbeat is that I had the purest blood in the world. Each day on my way to and from school, I was aware of being thrilled and energized by the knowledge of who I was. I belonged to the people, and because of who I was, my destiny was integrally woven into the fabric of the People's State. It sounds ridiculous today—frightening that such a complete indoctrination could have been achieved in the mind of a thirteen-year-old child. But that provincial view, so in conflict with the populist inclusiveness implied by the People's State, was the message we all took home. How difficult it must have been for those children who, unlike me, knew that their blood was of poorer cast.

For several years, I managed to simultaneously live the two conflicting versions of my history. Outwardly, I remained the steadfast Russian student, passionately involved in celebrating the magnificent achievements of the Union of Soviet Socialist Republics. Inwardly, I was terribly conflicted. I had Jewish blood but there was nothing Jewish about me, and having Jewish blood made me ineligible for the future I had planned—unless I was willing to live a lie. Gradually, as Babushka had hoped, I developed a growing awareness that the State was capable of injustice, and that our leaders were not as uniformly heroic and ethical as we were led to believe.

Even after all her explanations, I still had no idea why she had pushed my head underwater. So I began to read, surreptitiously, books on ancient and discredited religions. I couldn't ask the librarians directly for what I wanted— it would not do to have an interest in religion on my record. But I discovered that there were ways around the system, ways to get what I wanted without setting off political alarm bells. I couldn't be openly interested in religion— but I could certainly be interested in learning how primitive human ritual had been made obsolete by the advent of the modern Communist State. And when I phrased my questions appropriately, monographs and books on the history of religion appeared. What I found was written through the jaded lens of Soviet sociologists and ethnographers whose mandate was to discredit the rituals and the people they were studying. But in the process, they had to describe the rituals, and that was all I needed.

I knew nothing, and what I took from my reading was incomplete and tainted by the contempt of the writer for his subject. But it was the beginning of understanding. At night as we readied for bed, brushing each other's hair, I would whisper what I had learned into Babushka's ear.

"The ancient Jews had a ritual bath called a *Mikvah*, where the women bathed and purified themselves for their day of rest and prayer, their Sabbath. It doesn't seem that girls went into this *Mikvah* before they became women—it was only after their period began. It was a good thing you were trying to do. You were trying to make me pure."

"I had no idea what it meant," she whispered back to me. "How could you be more pure than you are already? And what a primitive thing— the idea! That women need to be purified once they begin their period is nonsense forced on them by male priests."

"The Christians had priests," I said. "The Jews called their priests a different name—Rabbi."

I didn't recognize the irony of my teaching Babushka about Jewish ritual, or explaining to her why she had pushed me under water. But she was aware of it, and it touched her soul. Somehow, she said, although she couldn't understand or agree with what I reported to her, it connected her to her parents. And I was touched, too. She wanted to give me something from our heritage—a benediction of sorts—but her parents had shared with her only snippets and vague memories. For her, it all built into a mystical edifice of superstition, fantasy and falsehood, littered liberally with half-true biblical stories and isolated factoids from Jewish history. Her misguided attempt to purify me in the public baths was the only way she knew to introduce me into the Jewish sorority from which she had been excluded.

Until I was sixteen I lived in conflict with myself, unable to give up the Russian blood that I now knew did not run in my veins, but equally unable to embrace the blood that did. Gradually, however, I was coming to clarity about the true nature of the Communist State. It took another story to bring me around.

❧

There were times in my childhood when we were blessed by material riches that I knew were not possible on a ticket-taker's salary. I assumed all along that my Aunt Juliana and Uncle Maxim, both doctors, had paid for them, and Babushka didn't correct my assumption. But when I turned sixteen, she bought me a pair of boots that I knew we were unable to afford. They were of soft, luxurious, leather, clearly of good quality, warm and comfortable, with fur on the inside. But they were not ostentatious, and no questions would be raised at school. I think they were more expensive than the ostentatious boots worn by the children of high-level Party members— one paid a price for superior workmanship and quality materials so good as to be invisible. When I asked whether I should thank Juliana, Babushka said no. It was time for me to learn the source of the things we couldn't afford.

"You're so full of secrets," I said, smiling at her. Secrets had become something of a joke between us. "You keep secrets so well—until you decide to share them. You love to turn my life upside down."

"Not secrets," she said, "truths. I give you truths when you're ready to hear them. I only hope I'm right about your readiness."

As a physician, Juliana could travel outside the city to visit patients without raising suspicion. At the age of six or seven, I accompanied her several times to see an old couple who lived in a small village sixty kilometers from Moscow. We took the train, which stopped briefly at an almost invisible station, and we walked through the unpaved frozen streets to a small house off the main square. An old woman answered our knocking and bustled us into the living room, which served as a kitchen as well. Sitting at the stove was an old man who wore his overcoat across his shoulders, draped on top of a long-sleeved woolen undershirt. On his feet were a pair of ancient, cracked shoes without laces, the toes curled up and the tongues hanging out over his shins.

At the end of his visit to Moscow, having seen how we lived, Uncle Mischa made it known that he intended to send us a package every month containing goods that the family could sell on the black market. Exactly what the discussion was and how he knew what to send, I never discovered. But letters went back and forth, and perhaps Babushka underlined particular words or wrote items in a particular script that indicated what was needed or what was selling well. Each month, Juliana went to visit this ancient couple. They were old family friends who had agreed to be the recipients of the monthly parcels. In exchange for something from each parcel, they were willing to take the risk. They had no children and little to lose, and because they lived in the country outside Moscow, were less likely to be tainted by contact with the outside world than we who lived in the city. The parcels were always opened and rifled—a sign that the someone in the postal service had taken his or her share—but the excitement of receiving such bounty from the free West was overwhelming.

I remembered how Juliana always carried an expandable net shopping bag in her doctor's case. It was not unusual —most of the people we knew carried a net shopping bag crushed in a briefcase or a pocket, in case they came across a store that actually had something to sell. When I went with her, she brought a net bag for me, too. I watched as Juliana went through the motions of examining the couple—taking their temperatures, their blood pressures, their pulse, looking at their throats and their teeth and their feet.

They would offer us a cup of tea, and then the old couple would bring out the big brown paper package tied in string and taped closed. In silence they would cut the string and pull off the tape, careful not to tear the paper—it could be reused. They would lay out the contents on the floor, while I was stationed at the door to watch and see if anyone approached, glancing backwards occasionally to see what was being unwrapped. Yards of the finest blue wool pinstripe suit cloth rolled inside yards of silk suit lining; a dozen men's belts of fine unmarked leather softer than any average Muscovite would ever see in his lifetime, six brown and six black; a dozen pairs of ladies gloves, the leather so soft and fine-smelling you could put them on and never know they were there. Sometimes there were dozens of pairs of wool socks, and warm silk tights to keep girls' legs warm in winter. Dozens of men's silk ties, the latest fashions from France and Italy, in colors so rich they made your eyes swim; women's designer wool sweaters from Ireland and Switzerland and Italy, fashionably cut, magnificently colored in designs of teal and royal blue and raspberry on ivory backgrounds.

The old couple looked carefully at these riches, glancing at each other, and he shyly selected one item for her—a pair of tan gloves that she could wear in the house, never outside. She went straight for a warm pair of dark navy woolen socks for him, and I watched her kneel on the floor at his side. She helped him off with his shoes, revealing socks stretched and threadbare, darned at toe and heel. These she slid off and carefully unrolled the new socks onto his cracked and gnarled old feet.

Juliana stuffed as much as she could fit into her expandable shopping bag, and put the lighter items into mine. We kissed the old couple good-bye and left, and we caught the next train back to Moscow. I went with her several times, and then, one day, without warning, I was told that there would be no more parcels. Besides, they said, I had school activities, and was busy with my own life. But the parcels didn't stop—they continued for years. The real reason the family decided that I should no longer accompany Juliana is that I was a bright, talkative child who noticed everything, and I was beginning to understand some of the subtle—but lethal—distinctions we lived with. There were periodic stories in the paper or on television of brave, patriotic children who informed on parents or relatives for un-communist activities, and the paranoia generated by these tales infected everyone.

When Babushka reminded me of Uncle Mischa and told me that parcels were still being sent to us from Uncle Mischa's son Lenny, who now lived in Boston, I was aware that most of what we received was sold on the black market. At sixteen I had a much better understanding of what a difference the monthly parcels made to the food, clothing and small luxuries we were able to buy.

If the Soviet Union was the richest country in the world, as we were taught, why was it necessary for our relatives in the capitalist West to send us luxuries to sell? Was this, I wondered, charity? It was deeply ingrained in us at school that because we all had everything we needed, charity was unnecessary in our country. In fact it was forbidden, even to religious organizations. It made no sense to forbid something because it was not necessary—until I realized that if institutions were allowed to dispense charity, they would generate a massive sense of loyalty in those they provided for. The last thing the Kremlin wanted was to encourage loyalty to the church.

My doubt about the Communist catechism was now in full flower, and I was bereft. I had nothing to take its place. Without awareness, I became very much a political animal. I learned to read between the lines in my textbooks and to interpret what the newspapers had been instructed to exclude from their stories. Without being observed, I watched and listened to others, and I began to hear what was not being said.

Even then I was smart enough to keep my thoughts to myself. I confided only in Babushka. I knew nothing about the culture, history or religion of the people I came from. But at least I had a history and past to learn about, one that descended deep into the well of time. By the age of sixteen my doubt about the Soviet State had mushroomed into anger and resentment. The Soviet State had betrayed me. It was only a matter of time before I returned the favor.

✹

I was nineteen when I met Grigory Ivanovich Yanov, and in my first year of journalism school. He was in his late thirties. As an official in Moscow Komsomol, he came to our meeting one afternoon to present leadership awards to the winners in a literary competition I didn't know I had won until the award was given.

The competition—an essay on the subject of patriotism—was run jointly by the Literary Gazette and by Komsomol. Although I had no desire to write an essay on the subject of patriotism, as one of the elected leaders of our unit, I felt obliged to participate in the competition. My essay parroted the accepted opinions of the Communist Party, using language taken directly from textbooks and pamphlets, but changing it enough to make it mine. I made liberal reference to The Great Patriotic War, which was a touchstone for every Russian. The patriotism of our soldiers was held up to all school children as the highest virtue, and adults of all stripes found themselves deeply touched by the sacrifices of our people and our military. It was an easy essay to write—I learned early to litter my essays with the old virtues. Grigory Ivanovich Yanov read the essays. He awarded me the medal, putting it around my neck with a crimson ribbon attached.

"Congratulations, Comrade Darya Iosifovna," he said, shaking my hand. For a moment I thought he looked more deeply into my eyes than was appropriate.

I learned early that men found me physically appealing. But I was disdainful of women who used their looks to gain advancement, and I downplayed my appearance. I hid behind a mask of shyness, avoided eye contact, hid my long, dark, lustrous hair in a bun under my cap, and wherever possible, wore clothes that showed my figure to least advantage.

But this man, I thought, was in a different category. Comrade Yanov was so senior, so much older, so experienced and so attractive, he couldn't possibly be susceptible to my appearance. I let my guard down, smiled at him openly, met his glance. The way his blue eyes widened when he returned my smile let me know he was not immune. Even from his lofty position he could see me, and he didn't hide the fact that he found me desirable.

I was secretly thrilled.

Within the week he sent me a note asking me to come to his office overlooking Red Square to discuss Komsomol. I was ushered past two male secretaries in his anteroom, and into his office. He used a large, handsome straight-legged table as a desk, papers in three neat piles on one side. There were filing cabinets against one wall. The office was spartan and streamlined with the exception of a thick, richly-colored grey and purple carpet, and a handsome German shepherd who rose from the carpet to sniff me, remained aloof even as his tail gave him away, and quickly returned to sit beneath the desk. There was one other item in the room. Hanging on the wall was a single wheel attached to what looked like a bicycle seat. I must have looked at it strangely.

"I see you notice my unicycle," he said with a smile. There was a gleam in his eye.

"I've never seen one before," I answered. "What is it for?"

He shrugged casually.

"Oh, it's for entertainment," he said. "A circus prop. But it does improve the balance. And who would you rather watch, a man on a bicycle or one balancing on a unicycle?"

"I suppose I would be intrigued more by the unicycle. Do you ride it?"

"No," he said. "But I like to think of myself as the man on the unicycle. Intriguing, and with fine balance."

I smiled, not knowing what to say. It was a strange comment, and I didn't understand what it meant until sometime later.

We sat on straight-backed chairs and drank tea. He wanted to know what I thought about Soviet youth, whether their idealism and commitment to the goal of universal communism was sufficient. He peppered me with questions on Komsomol, how it was run, whether I thought it was a strong and useful organization, how it could be improved, whether I wanted to play a role in its future. He was curious about my interest in journalism, and what I saw as the role of the Soviet journalist. He wanted to know about my life—my home, my family, what happened to my parents. And at the end of our very formal and proper interview, he said he would consider it an honor if I would accompany him to dinner the following week. I wouldn't have known how to refuse, and I didn't want to.

He sent his driver to pick me up in his official limo. I assumed that, as a Komsomol official, he would frown on an excess of show, and that my clothes would not be important. This was a very good thing, since I had little to choose from. I wore the only good dress I had. Juliana had copied it from a magazine and showed it to Babushka, who sewed it out of cloth sent in one of the packages from Lenny in Boston. It was made of a soft, burgundy fabric that draped easily. She had given it three-quarter-length sleeves, and it had a cut that Juliana said flattered my figure without giving everything away. I wore my hair up, revealing my neck.

But I was wrong about the importance of dress. The driver took me to a hotel across from the French Embassy—the Hotel Oktyabrskaya, which was known as a symbol of the massive power and wealth of the Communist Party. It was not a hotel I had ever thought of entering, and I was not sure that under ordinary circumstances the average Russian would have been allowed entrance. The vestibule leading into the restaurant was all mirrors and marble, and when the maître d' approached me I said in a barely audible voice that I was here to meet Comrade Yanov. He recognized my nervousness and smiled warmly, trying to put me at ease.

"Comrade Yanov is waiting for you." He put his mouth to my ear. "If the other diners stare, young lady, just imagine they're paying you homage. Walk tall, and follow me."

"Thank you," I whispered, but my feet would not move; they remained rooted to the floor. I think I would have turned and walked out, but the maître d' had other ideas. He stood behind me, blocking my path.

"No need to be nervous, my dear," he said in a low voice as his hand gently steadied my elbow. "Keep in mind that Comrade Yanov is only a man, no matter how much power he wields."

As he walked me to Comrade Yanov's table, I was aware of being perhaps the youngest woman in the room, certainly the least well-dressed.

Unlike the women at the tables I passed, I wore no jewelry. But I walked straight, with my shoulders back. I knew the dress was flattering, and as we approached the table, I watched Comrade Yanov watching both me and the other diners as they marked my progress through the room. He was clearly more than satisfied with what he saw. As I reached him he rose, took my hands in his and kissed me on both cheeks. We sat down without a word.

"You look as if you need a glass of wine," he said, raising his arm to the waiter. "You probably feel a little out of place. It was thoughtless of me—I should have told you where we were dining."

His eyes followed the contours of my face, across my ears, down my neck. I found myself blushing.

"I'm glad I didn't forewarn you," he continued. "Watching you cross the room without any warning of what you would be facing when you walked in was a gift. You were magnificent."

"Thank you, Comrade Yanov," I said. "My grandmother taught me that it's important to show grace under pressure."

"Calling me Comrade Yanov," he said earnestly, "forces me to be my most official self. Please, Darya, I would much prefer you to call me by my first name."

"I would like that, too," I said, bowing my head in a brief nod. "Grigory."

Already we were Darya and Grigory. What comes next? I remember thinking that nothing in my life had prepared me for this, and immediately realized that perhaps this was the moment everything in my life had been readying me for. Either way, this was where I had landed, and there was no way but forward.

We looked at the menu together and he explained what many of the French-sounding dishes were. Then we ordered, and he watched me as I looked around the restaurant.

"Who are all these people?" I asked.

The restaurant was open only to foreign guests with foreign currency, and to high-level officials. I could not have imagined such opulence. There were floor-length velvet curtains on the windows and massive Persian carpets on the floor, shining cut-glass on the table and polished silver cutlery, crystal chandeliers hanging from wood-paneled ceilings, and waiters in spotless uniforms. I'm sure the wine was the finest to be had in all of Russia, rich and full-bodied, and I quickly learned to appreciate it. But the food was beyond the wildest imaginings of my palate, and I had no language to describe it. There were moments when I found myself so overwhelmed by the depth of aromas, the subtlety of the spices and the multilayered tastes that rolled across my tongue that I found myself unable to breathe. He ordered the sirloin and offered me a mouthful, and it was unlike any beef I'd ever tasted. I ordered my first roast duckling, with a delectable fruit sauce, fresh baby carrots and roasted turnips and a crisp salad with walnuts and dried berries and a white cheese I didn't know.

But I was aware that the plates going back to the kitchen contained sufficient food to feed a multitude. I thought of the riots that would take place if the hungry in Moscow had any idea of the waste and excess, and I was sickened by the image of Babushka, standing in line for hours hoping to buy a chicken that wasn't grey and half-rotten. And so I learned the meaning of ambivalence—I loved the experience, and I despised myself for loving it. Learning to live with a lie was easy. What was difficult was learning to live with who I was becoming.

But Grigory took everything into account. Once he had decided that I was what he wanted, and learned how important Babushka was to me, he went out of his way to court her, too. He was careful not to overdo it. When he first came to pick me up himself, he brought her a gift from the special closed store to which we had no access—a basket containing half a dozen fresh mandarin oranges, bananas, and a can of Spanish olives. Whenever we went out together, he presented her—or had his driver deliver—a gift. And once he came to know her better, he offered her the things she really appreciated. A small package containing a cut of fresh meat, beef tongue, or a freshly skinned rabbit. Once he arrived with a whole pineapple, which we had never seen before, and didn't know how to prepare. We were on our way to the theatre, but he took off his jacket and rolled up his sleeves, and put on Babushka's apron. In anticipation, all the others who lived in the apartment gathered around the kitchen table. With a showman's flourish he removed the thorny crown, cut off the thick peel, and sliced it into thin rounds. I don't know where it was flown in from—Cuba, perhaps—but Grigory was no stranger to it. The fruit was ripe and delicious, and as she tasted it, Babushka's eyes wrinkled with pure joy.

The play we went to see that night was Chekhov's *The Cherry Orchard*. We arrived late, but for Grigory, it was a worthwhile effort. He knew that, like every other woman, my heart could be had by any handsome, charming man willing to show kindness to those I loved. And, like every other man, he hoped that my body would go along for the ride.

Where politics and advancement were concerned, I was fully capable of subterfuge and manipulation. I knew how to lie and withhold information, and to smile with delight even when all I felt was repugnance. But where love was concerned I was an open book, writ large, and I assumed that others would have a similar incapacity for false display. He took me back to his apartment afterwards, where we discussed *The Cherry Orchard* over a glass of French Sauvignon Blanc, and then I gave myself to him, eagerly, and with gratitude. Afterwards, basking in the warmth of what I thought was love, I was still impressionable enough to mistake his narcissism for contentment and post-coital bliss.

Then there was the ballet, and the concerts. Opening nights and the best seats were reserved for high-ranking officials and foreign dignitaries, with only a few available for the public. But Grigory had tickets to whatever he wanted. He took me to hear Beethoven and Mozart and Tchaikovsky, and he insisted that Babushka accompany us to see Swan Lake. She came, reluctantly, but filled with anticipation. She was awed by the seats we sat in, and by the magnificent dresses and jewelry of the women around us. But the majesty of the music, and the grace of the ballet, and the tragic magic of the story, overwhelmed her. We both wept during and after the performance. I have wondered since whether she wept because she was so deeply touched by the magnitude of the spectacle, or whether it was something else. Anger, perhaps, and a sense of betrayal, that our leaders lived in such opulence, in a country supposedly belonging to the people. But anyone could get tickets to symphony and opera. All we had to do was buy a set of tickets, some to events we wanted to see, and some to events no one had any interest in. It was only the most desirable seats and the most prized dates that were unavailable. Babushka had not been deprived of exposure to culture and art. I think, for example, of her lifelong love affair with the museum and the library. Of Alexander Ivanov's painting, which became in many ways the centerpiece of her life, and through which she met my grandfather, Vasily.

But music had never been a part of her life, and she never took me to concerts or ballet. As a young woman, she believed, as she was taught, that it was all wasteful bourgeois entertainment. Even when she knew better, she continued to believe the party line. Perhaps she felt bitterness that she was an old woman before discovering that such rapture was possible, and despair that she had lived a lifetime without it.

"There are lies, Dashinka," she whispered to me later that night, "and there are lies. Some we tell other people to make our lives livable, and some we tell ourselves so that we can get through each day. I didn't know until tonight that for getting through each day, we pay a price —and the price can be a life that sometimes feels not worth living."

Grigory and I were already a couple, and I thought myself in love with him, when Juliana and Maxim invited us to supper at their home. Their son Nikolai—Kolya—still lived at home, and was in his last year of high school. We had always been close. We could talk to each other about almost anything, and I felt for him what I imagined I would have felt for a brother. He was a soccer player, muscular and taller than I was. He had his mother's light brown hair and her grey eyes, and the smooth skin on his cheeks gave him a boyish appearance. He came in from studying as we sat down to dinner, hugged me enthusiastically, and I took great pleasure in introducing him to Grigory. Kolya was half a head taller, but Grigory, the more senior, the more powerful, seemed to expand in stature.

"So, this is the young man who wants to make a career in the military," he said.

"Yes, Comrade Yanov," said Kolya. "I hope to qualify for officer training school." He looked at his father, smiling. "I think my parents prefer me to become an engineer, where I seem to have an aptitude, but I have always dreamed of serving my country."

"Good engineers are always in demand," said Grigory, unsmiling, looking at Maxim, whose face had turned ashen. "Of course, as a parent, one prefers to see one's son in a profession that does not put him in harm's way." Now he smiled. "Isn't it a good thing parents don't get to make these decisions? If they did, we would have a weak defense force unable to protect the infirm and the vulnerable." He turned to Kolya. "Perhaps I can be of assistance to you. We should talk before the evening is over."

Maxim rose to pour vodka and filet the salmon, while I helped Juliana put the vegetables and potatoes on the table. Out of the corner of my eye I watched Grigory and Kolya bent over the eating table, deep in conversation. When Maxim looked at me I thought I saw fear in his eyes, but when I met his glance he quickly turned away. I hoped I had done the right thing by introducing his son to a man who could help him achieve his dream.

Grigory never told me what he did—who owed him favors, who he was able to influence or lean on—but in both my own career and in Kolya's it was clear that some force was at work behind the scenes. Admittedly, we were both bright and motivated enough to achieve high marks. But even the star student without connections was denied admittance to the best institutions. Without push from somewhere, the door to honeyed postings and the most prestigious jobs was closed. We had no such problems.

At Grigory's suggestion, Kolya took the exam for admission to Bauman Moscow Higher Technical Institute, one of our finest engineering schools, as his parents wished. Kolya was surprised at how easily the application process and the interview went. When he was admitted, he said it felt as if someone had greased the rails. It was wonderful that Grigory took such an interest in Kolya, whom he clearly liked. I thought he was grooming my cousin for some future role, but we never discussed it.

Kolya worked hard and graduated in three years, which was in itself unusual. Somewhere along the way, Grigory suggested that he make an application to the Moscow High Command Training School, a four-year institute for future military officers, from which graduates emerged with the rank of major, and the possibility of a non-combatant staff position.

The interview went well, despite Kolya's concerns. He had heard from other applicants that they had been asked absurd questions, like having to quote the page numbers in their textbook that dealt with Stalin's military achievements. But the questions were reasonable, and at the end the interviewers wished him good luck. He left feeling disappointed, as if the whole process had been little more than a formality, and was not surprised when he was accepted. His parents were delighted. It was the best of all possible worlds: the stability of a prestigious military career, without the danger of combat. Kolya felt that he was well on his way to achieving his goal, but he admitted to me that he entered this phase of his training with some misgivings. It had all been a little too easy, he said. He could not have achieved it without help, and he wondered whether someone, sometime, would come to collect on the favors. In the back of my mind I wondered vaguely who he thought the "someone" would be.

Grigory's star continued to rise, and I must have known that only one engine had the power to grant him the escalating access he had to goods, services, property, cars and vacations. But questioning him would have been terribly unwise. It would have ripped the scales from my eyes, forced me to turn my back on him and what he represented. Instead I focused on how wonderful it was for Kolya to have Grigory as a mentor, and I was proud to have been a part of making it happen. How bad could it be, I thought, for Kolya to have his continued support?

As for me, I thought I was already wise in the ways of the Communist Party. There was no way to avoid the conclusion that our media's primary goal was the spread of Soviet propaganda. They were forbidden to discuss only the obvious, like military information, but also crime, drugs, low crop production, industrial failures and accidents, and natural disasters. Even the names and sizes of our population centers, and how far they were from each other, were closed subjects. Foreign powers already had other means to access such information, and the only possible conclusion was that it was being kept from the Russian people, for reasons I could not understand.

It soon became clear to me that the prestigious school I had been admitted to was a training ground for high Party positions in charge of the media. Once I realized what journalism really was, I lost all interest in pursuing it, and had no idea what I would do with my degree.

Grigory, however, had many ideas, and he set before me interesting positions that he had the power to make mine. How, I wondered, could he have such influence? Who exactly did he work for? No one who worked for Komsomol had the kind of access he did.

In glowing terms he would describe a position in the Ministry of Agriculture, and he made me believe that I would be able to ensure the food supply for every Soviet citizen. And then, in an instant, he would show me how unrealistic the fantasy was.

"Of course," he would say thoughtfully, "you would be working under Sergei. He's a micro-manager; he'd drive you insane. Not a good idea. Let's see what else we can find."

When all the positions that turned out not to be right for me were eliminated, only a few remained, all in Ministries where he had influence. He never asked my opinion, but he must have suspected that we had major political differences. He kept me where he could watch me, and where he could find a use for me. As I reconstruct events, the logic behind his actions begins to make sense. He was far-sighted, and trust was never part of his plan. From the beginning he followed the old advice to keep your friends close, but your enemies closer.

❦

In 1979, when I was in my early twenties, Grigory invited me to a major event—the first performance of Handel's *Messiah* since the Revolution. There was a mostly silent, lowering crowd outside the theatre, resentful to see the usual bejeweled party officials and foreign diplomats taking all the seats. Somehow, I managed to live a dual life—in my own mind I was the secret rebel, loyal to the people, contemptuous of our leaders' hypocrisy. At the same time I was able, without giving up the role of secret rebel, to exit Grigory's chauffeur-driven car and walk between the crowds on his arm, wearing the expensive perfume he bought me, and, by then, the gold and sapphire necklace and pearl earrings. It made sense to me then—I was there not through any achievement or status of my own, but as his guest, and I could be uninvited at any moment. All I had to do was put one foot down in the wrong place.

Grigory and I had established a routine—his driver picked me up, we went out to dinner or to a show, or to a Party event, and returned to his apartment. He undressed me slowly, instructed me to lie or move or twirl or bend or twist so that he could look closely at my breasts or the spread lips of my vulva. Sometimes we stood before a full-length mirror in his bedroom, he behind me, and he grasped my hair in his fist, turning my head one way or the other as he roughly stroked the curves of my belly and my hips with his free hand. Or he would stand behind me and run his fingertips firmly down my vertebrae, from the top of my head down to where the cheeks of my buttocks separated, and down further, exploring every crevice of my body. I took it as a tribute to my beauty that he was so taken by every part of me. It was acknowledged that what he extracted from me was a performance which he orchestrated and sometimes acted in, and once I had performed to his satisfaction, he lay me down in one position or another, always carefully choreographed, and he had sex with me. There was something furious in the way he thrust himself into me. His orgasms were loud, and he shuddered inside me with such violence that I remember still the sensation of my bones shaking uncontrollably, as if I were in the grip of a rutting animal. Sometimes, when I was excited by something in the performance he commanded, I would be ready for him and prepared for my own orgasm—but regardless of whether or not I was ready, when he was primed he took his own pleasure. Occasionally it was pleasurable for me, too, but my pleasure was never his concern. It was years before I discovered that for most people, the greatest aphrodisiac is experiencing a partner's pleasure. That was seldom true for Grigory. When he was finished, it was over.

I am embarrassed by how anatomical and functional those words are, mortified that as a young woman I was so uninformed and so easily misled. I think back now, and what I remember is the pain. How he wrapped his fist tightly in my hair, pulling at the roots, and used it as a lever to turn my head this way and that. How tightly he gripped my shoulder, or my thigh, twisting and leaving bruises that blackened and remained for days. It was not merely that I confused love with sex, or that I came to see his violence in our coupling as a normal part of love-making. It was also that I was so willing to discount my own satisfaction. There was nothing mutual in our sexual encounters. He didn't even have sex with me—he had sex with parts of my body. He fucked me. In every way possible. All the more astounding that following Handel's *Messiah*, when he asked me to marry him, I accepted.

That's not actually what happened—he didn't technically ask me to marry him. When we returned to his apartment he took my hand and led me straight into his bedroom. There he pulled back the bedcover, and began to remove his clothes.

"Get undressed," he said. "Slowly."

He watched me. When we were both unclothed he put my hands between his legs and I did what he showed me until he was hard. Then he sat me down on the edge of his bed. I remember well his grey satin sheets, the likes of which, not long before, I could never have imagined. Grigory knelt on the floor before me, slipped his hands beneath my thighs, easily lifted me up and slowly lowered me onto his erect penis.

"We're suited to each other, you and I," he said in a soft, throaty voice. "The spring will be a good time for us to marry." He took my wrist and placed the forefinger of my left hand on my clitoris. "Come," he commanded.

I did. Then he did. And in the spring we married.

✲

Babushka did her best to convince me that I was making a gigantic mistake. She had his measure, and she never gave up trying to share with me what she recognized in him from the first moment. I remained impervious to her cautions.

"It's not in your character to play his little mouse," she warned. "Not for long. You'll soon tire of pretending to be what he wants, and what will you do then? Make no mistake, he won't take kindly to being made a fool of. How are you going to live from day to day with a man like this?"

"A man like this?" I scoffed at her. "You make him sound so ominous. He's just a man." I remembered the maître d's words. "No matter how much power he wields."

We sat together at her little table covered with a faded oilcloth, purple and yellow flowers on a white background. She scrubbed it clean after each meal, and we joked that it was sterile enough to rent out to surgeons at the hospital as an operating table. Babushka reached across and took my hand in hers, holding it firmly as she spoke. With her other hand she stroked my forearm. It was an old habit, something she did absently, and even at her fiercest I found it comforting. Perhaps it was a way of showing that her words were motivated by tenderness and concern.

"Long ago I said you would have to keep our history to yourself, just as I have. About your politics I said nothing. At thirteen you had no politics, and neither of us knew then how deeply you would feel, or how much your opinions would differ from accepted views. I helped to shape your thinking," she continued, "so it's no surprise that we share the same politics. I've always kept my opinions to myself—but you're a different animal. A new generation. You have an education. Silence is not easy for you. What you believe is dangerous, Darya, to you and all those you love. Your views are a threat to all those in power, including Grigory. The policies he carries out are against everything you stand for. Eventually your views will conflict, and then what will you do? This is no basis for a marriage. What do you think your life will be, when you live every day a lie?"

"We both live a lie every day," I said, stung by the accusation. "Is there some other lie you're talking about?"

"I'm talking about the lie you tell yourself," she said, exasperated. "You behave like a blind woman, Dasha. Can't you see he's already connected at the hip? He may be marrying you, but his first commitment will always be to the Organs."

The Organs. The Organization. The Security apparatus, the KGB. This was the first time I had been confronted with the truth, and my response should have been indication enough that I had suspected all along. I shrugged it off as if it were unimportant, remembering as I did so Maxim's fearful glance the first time I took Grigory to his home. He had known right away.

"I'm in love with him," I said simply.

"Don't talk shit to me," she whispered, and her words came out as an angry hiss. Her lips were two brittle twigs, a frightening twisted slash on her face, higher on one side than the other, something she had never shown me. Had my mouth not been hanging open in shock, I would have grimaced in pain at the tightness of her hold on my wrist.

"Babushka…"

"Don't interrupt. You've always been able to talk rings around yourself. I've watched you do it since you could put two words together. I'll never stop loving you more than I love my own life, whatever you do with your own. But don't you dare try and talk me into this ugly fantasy. This is not a man for loving. You might use him, just as he uses you. But be careful, Dasha. Between husband and wife there can be no secrets."

"Really?" I said. "When you married my grandfather, did he know? Or did you wait for the right moment to tell him the truth?"

She hesitated, taken aback. I had never challenged her in this way, and I watched myself stepping outside the bounds of our relationship, nervous, exhilarated by the power it gave me, saddened by what I was doing, but powerless to do otherwise.

"This is not the same," she said, heatedly. "Vasily was not in the KGB. Who I was made no difference to his position. And he didn't have the resources to dig into my past. You think you can marry a man high up in the Organs without having your background unearthed like a rotted coffin?"

"It's all ancient history," I said. "You told me yourself your parents bought new identities. If nothing's been revealed until now, what makes you think there's anything in the records, if the records even exist after all this time? How many hundreds of thousands of people came to Moscow as refugees after 1914? How long do we have to live in fear of the past?"

"You talk like a child. I don't know what records there are. If we're lucky the coffin will be empty, the corpse rotted away. Perhaps even the coffin is gone. But nobody marries into the KGB without a deep background search. Perhaps it's not as dangerous now as it once was to be a Jew. By marrying this man you take on your shoulders the risk of exposing us all. If that happens, can you keep us safe? All of us? Juliana and Maxim? And your cousin Kolya, whose future you've already put into Grigory's hands?"

As always, she was right—I was running rings around myself. Grigory was handsome; he had the capacity to make himself charming; he was already in a position of power, and he wanted me. He made me feel that I was beautiful, desirable, and important, and that my opinions counted. In that, he proved himself a far better liar than I could ever have been. I even managed to convince myself that by marrying him I would have access to hidden information, and perhaps be in a position to influence his actions. I was too young to see who he was, to recognize what he really wanted, too young to know that wisdom comes at us in uneven bursts, and in random order.

By the time I realized how much I despised him and all he stood for, it was too late. There were signs, but I didn't know enough to read them. One was the nature of the men he kept closest to him. Damaged, uneducated men, primitive and physically intimidating, with battered, swollen knuckles and scarred faces. They leered at me when he was not looking.

Another was that I was unable to tell him the truth, which should have set off flashing warning lights in my head. I didn't reveal our history to him on the grounds that it would expose the rest of the family—but the real reason was my fear of how he would respond. If he did investigate my past, I hoped it would reveal nothing. So I began our marriage with a lie, which set the ground rules for a union replete with distortion and deceit.

✥

It was not until we had been together several times that Grigory asked me whether I remembered the unicycle in his office. We were lying on his bed, which still seemed gigantic to me, both of us still unclothed, and I was in that warm, satisfied and hazy place that follows sex.

"Of course I remember it," I answered. "You said you thought of yourself as the man on the unicycle—intriguing and finely balanced."

"Yes. And you thought it a very strange thing for me to say, didn't you?"

"Well, I didn't understand what you meant."

He took my hand and placed it between his legs.

"What do you feel?" he asked.

I hesitated, not knowing what he wanted me to say.

"You have my scrotum in your hand," he said impatiently. "Tell me what you feel."

"I feel your balls," I said.

"No," he said, "you don't. Feel again—carefully—and tell me what you feel."

I knew enough anatomy to know that the scrotum was a delicate sac, and I didn't want to feel it too firmly. Despite his encouragement I was not eager to cause him pain—but without a more detailed examination I couldn't feel well enough to answer his question. For the first time in my life I made a clinical examination of a scrotum, feeling first for one testicle and then for the other. It was a cool night, and his sac had contracted tight up against his body, thickening the wall. I had to feel very carefully to identify what I was touching, but it didn't take long.

"So," I said with a dawning smile as I looked up at his face and continued to fondle him. "How intriguing. This is what you mean by being the man on the unicycle."

"Now you know my secret," he said with a grin, "I'll have to find a way to keep you quiet."

I thought he was only joking.

"What happened, Grisha?" I asked. "Were you born with only one?"

He brushed my hand away, rolled quickly off the bed and pulled on his undershorts.

"It's getting late," he said brusquely. "I have an early meeting. Get dressed—Viktor will take you home."

At the start of our relationship we often walked hand in hand, and as lovers do, I would run my hands over his, learning his shape and feel. His fingertips were coarse and roughened—more so than was normal. Usually he pulled away when I began to caress his fingertips, and when I wanted to look more carefully he closed his hands into fists. Eventually, lying in bed as he slept, I cautiously examined his hands, and saw that the coarseness at his fingertips was really a network of minute scars. Even before he proposed, he joked that he would tell me what happened to his hands once our first child was born. I dream today about what I might have done differently in my life had I been able to elicit the truth from him before we married. But I had no choice—I was on his timeline, and I had to wait to discover his story. By the time he told me his truth, Larisa was already born, and I was unwilling to do anything that might endanger her.

❀

Even before I graduated with a degree in journalism, I received an invitation to join the Communist Party. It was not unheard of, but it was unusual to be invited so early in a career. It was Grigory's doing, of course, and I felt unworthy of the honor. I soon realized that this was not the Communist Party I aspired to join as a girl, but then I had an epiphany. The Party had always been less than I thought it was. I was the one who had changed.

Grigory knew it would take time, and he was willing to wait and watch.

As he did so, he planned my ascent to the level where he knew I would be most useful.

It started at the lowest rung in the Ministry of Foreign Affairs, responsible for overseeing our interests abroad. I wanted to improve communications with western governments, but Grigory insisted I would be more valuable working to support foreign communist parties. An impregnable wall existed between these two departments, for obvious reasons. It would have defied credibility to claim that with one hand we were working to improve relations with a democratic, capitalist government, while with the other we gave support to a communist organization in their midst dedicated to undermining their system. The Ministry was responsible for both, but it had a separate department for each. To use the same people for both jobs would have been an invitation to schizophrenia.

Much later I began to understand why Grigory felt so strongly that one option was better than the other. His network of informers and the men who owed him allegiance were all domestic. But he needed international connections to reach the level of power he wanted. He was also innately suspicious, and he sensed even back then, before there were any visible signs, that an underground dissident movement had been born and was gaining momentum. It was a natural conclusion that some dissident support came from outside the country. He wanted to know who, and where, and how. Without being aware of it, I became an essential part of his strategy. I became his eyes and ears.

Grigory knew I would be expert at writing propaganda. My English was good enough, and I had all the necessary people skills. He also saw in me something I was too inexperienced to recognize. I was the naïve believer, someone who still clung to a belief in the best of our utopian dreams—full employment, free education and medical care, a dedicated safety net. These things I would be happy to share with Communist parties in the West.

My first position was on a team that wrote and reviewed articles for western communist party newspapers. *The Daily Worker* in the United States, *Morningstar* in the United Kingdom, *L'Humanitaire* in France. It was eye-opening. Communist party members in the West would have laughed out loud at how little information was available to the average Russian. The propaganda we wrote for an international audience had to be far broader. Very quickly I learned to compartmentalize. What I was permitted—even encouraged—to give our allies outside the country, had to be kept separate from what I was allowed to know as a Soviet citizen.

The irony was that I excelled at writing even about restrictive doctrines that I didn't in the least believe in. My bosses soon considered it safe to have me communicate with the foreign press, and eventually to have me participate in meetings and conferences with foreign representatives. At first Hungary and East Germany, and then Romania, Poland and Cuba. Once I had proven myself with Communist bloc countries, I was allowed to travel more widely, and my education began in earnest.

My first trip to Western Europe was to France, where I had to be careful not to reveal just how happy I was to be out of Moscow. It was spring, and I felt myself blossom as I strolled down the Champs-Elysées beneath vast, shaded horse-chestnut and plane trees. I felt lighter, more at peace. When I sat at a café and sipped my first café-crème, I breathed more easily, as if the air were clean. The elegance of the women everywhere, beautifully made up, with light scarves draped just so around their shoulders, brought a lump of sadness to my throat. I visited Notre Dame Cathedral, and even though we had equally magnificent architecture in Moscow, perhaps for the first time I felt free, aware of not being watched. I soon realized that most Communist Party members we met in European countries were really only Communist-wannabes, political flower children, dreaming about utopia. They were blind to the vast chasm between theory and practice—and it was my job to preserve the illusion.

❧

When I was twenty-seven, I made my second trip to Cuba on behalf of the Foreign Ministry. My task was to address Cuban youth leaders, and to convince them that the lives of young adults in the Soviet Union were indeed as idyllic as they were painted. I was the guest of honor in a drab community hall in Havana, and following my talk to an audience of about fifty young Communist leaders, there was a celebratory meal along with a jazz band proudly playing Cuban music. As we ate chicken and rice, and I had my first fish enchilada, the young Cubans asked me about Moscow. One question in particular I will remember for as long as I live. It was asked by a young man, dark and intense, wearing scholarly tortoise-shell glasses. He was sitting across the table from me, and he leaned forward as he spoke. Those around us listened intently as he phrased his question with quiet confidence, and it was clear that they saw him as a leader.

"We hear about clandestine protest meetings in Moscow," he said quietly. "Rumors that reasonable people—artists and students and scholars—are dissatisfied with current policies. It is said that many such groups meet regularly, camouflaged as literary or musical gatherings."

"It's difficult enough to inspire a cohort of young socialists," interrupted a heavyset girl beside him. She had dark braids and smooth dimpled cheeks, and she was as serious and intense as he was. "But when we hear that in the cradle of communism people are punished for expressing their views, it makes our task even more difficult."

I smiled at these candid questions, posed by idealistic young Cubans. They were only a few years younger than I was, but to me they seemed like children, and sitting among them I felt like an ancient, battle-weary charlatan, so accustomed to enticing young recruits into battle with half-truths and lies that the words came unbidden to my tongue.

"The question has been asked," I said loudly, "whether those who protest against current policies in the Soviet Union are subject to unreasonable punishment." I rose to my feet and waited for silence. "Let me address the question openly, because among us there is no room for dissembling." I looked out at the sea of faces. "Every system has its share of dissatisfied troublemakers, who would destroy what others have built. Sometimes there is reason for anti-government demonstrations, as there was during the anti-war riots in the United States in the 1960s." There were nods of agreement around the hall. "In the Soviet Union there are accepted channels for bringing issues to the leadership. So one has to ask, why would people choose to express their dissent outside accepted channels? The answer is that a few misguided individuals would take great pleasure in showing the world that our magnificent Socialist experiment is a failure. We cannot allow these people to affect the course of history. So, yes, there are destroyers amongst us, and they must be stopped. Social, political and economic revolution is delicate and fragile, and the process needs to be protected so that future generations may benefit from the sacrifice of those who came before them."

The hall rose as one person, and I sat down to thunderous applause. I was shaking, appalled by my own deviousness, and by how eager this group was to embrace the party line.

The question about dissidents blindsided me. Grigory had mentioned dissidents on occasion, with contempt and irritation, but without any detail. I knew they existed, but I would have been hard-pressed to describe what they wanted, who they were, or when and where they met. If rumors about anti-Soviet activities were spreading as far as backwaters like Cuba, I needed to know more than I did. I decided that when I returned to Moscow, I would find a way to attend these gatherings. With the support of my superiors, I could attend meetings without fear of being arrested in a KGB raid. But my bosses were party hacks whose primary objective was not to lose their jobs, and that meant not taking risks.

Immediately upon my return from Cuba, I started the long bureaucratic process of convincing my bosses that we had something to gain from discovering who the dissidents were and what they were about. A month into the process, I discovered that I was pregnant—and I was suddenly much less interested in increasing my visibility to those in power. But by then it was out of my hands. Behind the scenes Grigory was working his own sources.

※

Nothing in my life had even remotely prepared me for the experience of childbirth. Perhaps for the first time, I allowed myself to feel that not having a mother was a disadvantage. Babushka, Juliana and the other women in my life had done their best to give me a childhood filled with love and acceptance, but as the day of my delivery approached, I felt very much alone. I spent the nights tossing and turning, woken repeatedly as the baby kicked. I thought I would be delighted, but I began to resent what the presence within me was doing to my body—and then I was filled with guilt for my lack of motherly feeling. I was so sleep deprived that I became depressed. My feet swelled during the day. The slightest movement exhausted me, and I began to appreciate how slender and graceful I had been before my pregnancy. Babushka was a great comfort but there was little she could say to help me, and Juliana seemed caught up with her work. Grigory was scheduled to be away for several weeks around the time of my delivery. This came as no surprise. He had made his essential contribution, and I already suspected that his interest in babies or small children, even his own, would be negligible. But his position and his status in the Party gained us access to the hospitals for the politically powerful. For that I was grateful, especially later, when exposure to hospitals in other parts of the developed world showed me how substandard our state medical care was.

My labor lasted thirty hours. It was painful, and it felt interminable. The nurses were pleasant enough, and quietly efficient. But they seemed unaware that although the sounds and smells and stages of childbirth were a daily experience for them, I was going through it for the first time. No visitors were allowed, the isolation felt absolute, and I had no idea what was coming next. It was terrifying.

I had imagined that the first contact with my baby would be on my terms, that she would be with me, and that I would be able to gaze into her new face, cuddle her, feed her and kiss her. But the moment Larisa was born they swept her away to clean and wrap her, and I was wheeled into a ward with five other women. We had three days of post-partum hospitalization, and they were intended for us to rest and recover. But rest and recovery included very little interaction with the newborn, which is what I most needed.

When they first put Larisa in my arms she was heavily swaddled. I didn't see her body or her hands until I took her home. They brought her to me to

feed two or three times a day. When she was hungry between feedings, the
nurses fed her water in the nursery. At the time I didn't know any different,
but even then it seemed a cold and impersonal way to introduce a child to
the world. I was discharged from the hospital with no idea how to diaper
or swaddle my baby. One imagines that mothers are born knowing how to
give the nipple, but there was far more to breastfeeding than that. I was
relieved—and delighted—to discover that Larisa herself had the rooting
impulse, and she knew immediately what to do when my nipple touched
her cheek.

Babushka was waiting for us at the apartment, and she welcomed us
with open arms. Together she and I gently unwrapped the swaddling cloth
until my Larisa lay on the changing table in all her pink glory, and for the
first time I was able to run my hands over her smooth shoulders and her
warm little belly. It was the first time I had seen a cut umbilical cord, and it
made real for me the way she had taken oxygen and nourishment from me
even before she was born. I counted her fingers and toes, held her naked
against my skin as she drank from my body. Babushka showed me how to
position her when she was feeding so that she took milk and not air; how to
burp her gently; how to change her without making her cold. Larisa stayed
in the bedroom with me for the first weeks of her life. I watched her as she
slept, talked to her gently when she was awake. She learned the sound of my
voice, and I learned to recognize the many meanings of her cry.

Soon after Larisa was born, Grigory clawed his way to the next rung
on his carefully constructed ladder of privilege. We moved across the city
to a luxurious apartment in the tower of the massive Kotelnicheskaya
Embankment building on the northern bank of the Moscow River. On
either side of the tower were communal apartments, but the tower itself
had been built to house the most elite members of the Kremlin. There
were guards at the gates, a beautiful garden, halls filled with billiard tables,
swimming pools, and a special school within the structure for children of

the residents. Our neighbors included Central Committee members, and men and women in the highest ranks of the military.

One of them was the man Grigory reported to in an unnamed division of the KGB, a big man with massive shoulders and a belly to match, old enough to be my father, with balding grey hair swept back, white eyebrows and puffy cheeks. When he looked at me with undisguised lust in his pouched, reddened eyes, I had to hide my revulsion. The idea of him touching me was like a physical assault. Had he made a move to seduce me, I don't think Grigory would have tried to stop him, and may even have offered signs of encouragement. I avoided being in his presence whenever I could, but I was uncomfortable living in the same building. I felt vulnerable and unsafe—ironic since it was probably the safest dwelling in the city.

I hired a nursemaid for Larisa, a young woman selected by the agency that provided domestics to families like ours. She came from a simple peasant village in Ukraine, and they put her through a security clearance so comprehensive and invasive that she came to us terrified. Her name was Anna, and she lived with us in one of several small bedrooms. I realized only when she arrived that our apartment had been constructed, long after the Revolution, with live-in domestic help in mind. If my eyes had not already been opened to Communist Party hypocrisy, that realization would have done the job.

Grigory wanted me to go back to work a few weeks after Larisa was born, but I insisted upon staying home with her. I asked Babushka to come and live with us, but she was adamant that she wanted to maintain her independence. She didn't need to tell me again that she would never live under the same roof as Grigory, nor did she mention that in her mind, the inhabitants of the building were the same kind of Kremlin men who took and murdered my grandfather, and she wanted nothing to do with them. But she came to see Larisa every day, and she and Anna got along famously. They made our meals together, talked about cooking, exchanged recipes, and laughed in the kitchen as the baby napped during the day. And, following his instructions, they made ice cream for Grigory.

I had known almost from our first meeting that he loved ice cream, but somewhere in his travels he discovered the difference between our commercial product and fresh, hand-churned ice cream made in small batches. One day as he talked about how much he loved ice cream, and how difficult it was to find the good stuff, Babushka began to laugh. That was still in the days when he pretended to treat her with respect.

"I'm glad to see," he said, "that you find humor in my love of ice cream."

"I don't think it humorous at all," she retorted. "I'm laughing because you're not alone. And I can make you the best ice cream you ever tasted. All I need is a churn."

"And how does an old train conductor know how to make ice cream?" he teased. "I suppose you learned it on the trains?"

"That's not far from the truth," she said, gesturing with her chin at me. "Darya knows—she's tasted my ice cream."

"Tell him," I answered, and turned to Grigory. "You guessed right. She learned it on the train."

"When I first started," she said, "they put me with an old conductor who knew everything there was to know about running the rails. On long trips he took with him an ancient ice cream churn. At stops along the route, he introduced me to the peddlers who crowded the stations, and he showed me how to buy farm ingredients from them. Fresh milk, fruit when it was in season. Pears. Peaches. And he showed me how to use the machine. It was hard work, I can tell you. We sold the ice cream to passengers, and it went quickly. When he retired he gave me the churn, and I used it for years. Kept repairing it until the parts fell off, and there was no one around who could fix it."

"I hope you still remember how to do it," he said. "Say yes, and I'll get you the finest ice cream churn in Europe."

"My head remembers," she answered, "but my hands may not be able to turn the handle fast enough. I suppose I can teach someone younger to do it."

"Perhaps we can find a churn with an electric motor," I suggested. "Then you won't have to depend on anyone else."

And so Grigory imported two electric ice cream churns from Italy, one for our apartment in Moscow, and one for the *dacha*. If he could have it fresh in town, why not at our country house? We were not the kind of people, he said, who had only one churn, and needed to carry it back and forth with us, like peasants.

❦

When our daughter Larisa, was born, I reminded Grigory of his promise to tell me what happened to his fingers, and he told me his story. By then he had nothing to lose by confiding in me.

"I grew up in a factory town a few hundred kilometers from Moscow," he said. "A grim place, rows of concrete slab buildings to house factory workers. When I was a baby my father disappeared. One day he just didn't come home from his shift. My mother was convinced he'd been imprisoned for some minor offense, but he could just as easily have deserted us, or been murdered. She never spoke about him, but after a few years she remarried. Gave me a stepfather worse than any father I might have had.

"My mother was a small woman, passive and timid. She was the kind of woman bullies are drawn to, with no ability to speak or stand up for herself. Her new husband was three times her size. He turned out to be violent by nature, and when he was drunk he was vicious as well. She lived in terror for our safety."

When Grigory was eleven he arrived home to find his mother lying on the floor with a bloodied face. His stepfather stood over her, his huge hand around the neck of a half-full vodka bottle. His mother implored Grigory to leave, but he bent down to touch her face, and as he rose he picked up the first thing that came to hand—his stepfather's muddy boot—and threw it with all his might at its owner's face.

"My stepfather forgot he had a bottle in his paw, and he raised his arm to protect himself from the boot. The stupid asshole smashed the bottle into the side of his head. I hoped he would break the bottle and cut his own throat, but we weren't that lucky. It didn't break, but he lost hold and dropped it. I watched as the vodka slopped out onto the floor and mixed with my mother's blood."

For a moment Grigory's stepfather stared at the expanding pool of clear liquid rimmed with pink.

"You spilled my vodka, you little bastard," he growled.

Grigory stood between his mother and his stepfather.

"Go, Grisha," she pleaded. "Please, leave. I'm all right."

"No you're not," he said. "You will never be all right as long as he's around." He pointed to his stepfather. "You will never hit her again," he said quietly.

His stepfather grinned and feinted towards his wife, still supine on the floor, and as Grigory bounded forward to prevent his mother from receiving another blow, his stepfather sidestepped and lunged at him, catching him a fierce blow to the side of his head and knocking him out.

Grigory said that when he came to, his stepfather was kneeling at his side, one hand on his chest, holding him down, and the other at his groin.

"I didn't know what he was doing to me, but it was impossible to breathe. I haven't felt such agony, not before and not since. From that moment, I knew one of us would kill the other."

"You think you're such a ballsy fellow," his stepfather said with a drunken leer. "Let's see how brave you are now. You don't ever threaten me again. You understand?"

Grigory passed out from the pain, and the next day he was barely able to move. He dragged himself out of bed and went to school. When he passed out again, the nurse was called and he was sent to the clinic, where he waited for hours. His scrotum was blue, the size of a grapefruit. When the doctor arrived he took one look and diagnosed a ruptured testicle.

"How did you say you got this?" asked the doctor.

"Soccer," mumbled Grigory.

The doctor looked at him skeptically. "Your testicle is mangled. Crushed like a plum. We'll have to remove it before it turns necrotic and kills you. I've seen more soccer injuries than you can count, my boy, several of them to the groin." He shook his head. "Never seen one that looks like this. You want to change your story? Tell me who did this to you, and we can make sure he doesn't hurt anyone else."

Grigory insisted that he had been playing soccer, and was kicked in the groin.

"Why didn't you tell the truth?" I asked him.

"Don't you know yet that I'm a planner?" he asked quietly. "I plan for every possible outcome." His eyes were focused on me with cold detachment, but I would have sworn he didn't know I was present. "Even if they sent him away for a year or two, I knew he would come back. I had to get rid of him before he had a chance to kill us. I didn't want his dead body traced to me. There could be nothing in the medical record to show I might have reason to want him dead."

Under local anesthetic he was operated on and the ruptured organ removed, leaving him with only one testicle. At home he became quiet and obedient. Like all bullies, having asserted himself, his stepfather thought himself safe.

But Grigory began to plan, and he stayed up night after night imagining how he would take his revenge and protect his helpless mother from the monster who ruled their home. He watched his stepfather carefully—how he moved, where his strengths were, and his weaknesses; how he ate and drank, and where he sat after supper in a vodka-induced stupor before his wife cajoled him into bed. On his days off, when he drank more vodka than on workdays, he often fell asleep at the table as he read the paper, his shins hooked around the chair legs. On such occasions his stupor was deeper, and when he woke his mind was less clear.

"I began to scavenge around the town after school," Grigory told me, "and at night I went out with the metal shears my stepfather had stolen from the storehouse."

He went to the furthest fences he could find around the factory, mostly unguarded, and from them he filched the materials he needed—strong, slender poles and lengths of razor wire—and he started constructing the engine of his revenge and freedom. Using shoelaces stolen from workers' shoes at the factory, he tied the poles together to form a sturdy T. He made a hole at each of the three ends of the T, and using ropes stolen from the factory's supply, he tied loops at each end of the top of the T, practicing for hours until he could rapidly secure the loops with knots that would not come undone.

He spent hours each day honing the razor barbs and the flat wire itself with a sharpening stone. Even though he used a pair of pliers to hold the wire, the tips of his fingers were sliced with crisscrossed cuts so numerous and so deep that they left permanent scars. But even as his fingers bled he took satisfaction in the knowledge that the clean cuts were a sign of how sharp the wire was. When he was satisfied, he looped the razor wire into a coil of three strands, with a tail, and into the tail he securely bound a piece of wood as long as his forearm. Then he waited.

When his stepfather had the day off, he drank in the early afternoon and generally fell asleep. His mother had learned not to be home when he awoke. She went to see what meager provisions the stores might have received, even if she had sufficient food for their evening meal. Grigory waited until his stepfather was sleeping at the table, boots untied, shins as usual twined around the front legs of his chair, head back so that he snored loudly at the ceiling. In absolute silence and without so much as touching his stepfather, Grigory slipped the tail of the T between the front legs of the chair until the top of the T came to rest against the legs. Carefully he wound the rope attached to the left side of the T around his stepfather's left ankle and the left chair leg. He did the same on the right, tying both so that the sleeping man was unaware of the binding—but secured so that struggling against the knots would only make them tighter. The tail of the T now ran back between the rear legs, extending out behind the chair. At the end of the tail there was a hole, through which a rope was threaded and looped at both ends.

Now Grigory brought out the second part of his machine, identical to the first. He tied the top of that T to the rear legs of the chair, just beneath the seat, securing it with shoelaces running through holes he had drilled. The tail of the second T angled down behind the chair, coming to rest at floor level, on top of the tail of the first T that extended from between the front legs and ended behind the chair. Grigory lined up the holes at the

194 Neville D. Frankel

ends of both Ts, inserted the final shoelace through both holes, and secured them together so that each kept the other from rising.

He had cut open lengthwise one of his stepfather's socks, and loosely wrapped the razor wire in it. Very cautiously, he slipped the sock over his stepfather's head and allowed it to come to rest softly on the sleeping man's shoulders like a lethal necklace. At the back of his neck, the rope attached to the razor wire hung down behind him. Grigory carefully threaded the end of the rope through the holes at the ends of the two Ts. Now all he had to do was tighten it.

This was the most dangerous part, and he had only one chance to do it right. Through all this his stepfather snored unaware, occasionally snuffling or scratching his crotch.

"I stood behind him. From where the rope emerged from the holes in the Ts on the floor, I wound it around my hand, and I took a big breath. With every muscle in my body I jerked the rope upward as fast as I could, and when it was as tight as possible, I wound the end of the rope around the short piece of pole I had inserted into the razor wire, and tied it tight."

As the necklace tightened against his Adam's apple, Grigory's stepfather gagged and opened his eyes, but Grigory had already stepped around the chair to the other side of the room, so that he was in front of the chair, facing his stepfather.

He knew the poles would hold and the razor wire would cut, and he had tested the shoelaces. They were strong enough. But he was concerned about the knots. He had practiced tying them, using a book about knots, over and over until his hands were raw. But he knew already that it was dangerous to put complete trust in anything.

"I wanted him to see it was me who did this to him," said Grigory. "I was going to watch him die, but if anything went wrong, I'd only have one chance to get out the door. Just in case, I had a bag hidden downstairs with food and clothes, and whatever money I could get my hands on."

The first thing his stepfather did was to raise his hands to his neck, trying to loosen the pressure around his throat. But all he did was slice his fingers, and as he struggled to get his fingers beneath the razor wire, he rubbed it up and down on his neck, slicing and cutting through the flesh. Grigory watched the blood begin to flow down his stained, long-sleeved undershirt. Now his stepfather was suddenly alert, unable to breathe. He looked around him, saw Grigory, and panicked. He tried to step forward and rise but his feet were secured to the chair. Terrified, with no idea of the nature of the device restraining him, he began thrusting his head forward and back, and at each thrust the razor wire slashed deeper into his throat.

The only thing left to do was also the worst —he tried to get away from the thing throttling him. He rose straight up with explosive force, and as the rope behind him stretched, the razor wire tightened and bit into the bones of his clavicle, piercing the front and sides of his neck. The pressure became so intense that he began to hyperventilate, whipping his head from side to side. The cutting implement was held in place while the substance being cut gave itself to the blades in a submissive frenzy. The razor wire gashed his carotid artery and the blood arced from the side of his neck at each pump of his heart. But he continued to thrash around and finally the razor wire sawed through his windpipe. By the time he fell back in his chair, ragged breath coming from the hole in his neck and his shirt red down to his waist, he had little life or breath left.

"I watched the air spray pink from his throat," continued Grigory calmly, "as his lungs emptied themselves." He looked through me and I knew he was watching the scene play out. I wondered how often he had replayed it in his mind. "I moved forward, right into the center of his darkening focus, so that the last thing he saw before he died was the smiling face of his ballsy stepson."

Grigory removed the bloody necklace, untied and dismantled the wooden structures, and placed the pieces in a bag. He took the bread knife from the kitchen, ran the blade through his stepfather's gaping neck, and clasped the dead man's bloody, lacerated hand around the handle. Then he washed the blood from himself. There was no one else in the apartment as he let himself out. No one saw him leave. He went down to the basement and threw the bag into the building furnace. Before he went to play ball with his friends, he returned his clothes and the food he had taken from the apartment.

The police found it difficult to believe that a man might be capable of ripping such a ragged hole in his own neck with a breadknife, even one with a serrated blade, but there was no other evidence. They questioned his mother, who was seen to be out of the house all afternoon. She may have had reason to murder her husband, but she was clearly incapable of such a violent crime. They questioned the neighbors, all of whom had reasonable alibis, and eventually they questioned Grigory, the eleven-year-old stepson of the victim. He, too, probably had reason to want his stepfather dead, but he was small for his age. The interviewing officers felt sorry for this little boy with an angelic face, who sat through the interview slouched in his chair, hands buried in his pockets. No child would have been capable of planning or executing such a diabolic act. With no further avenues to investigate, they called it suicide and closed the case. The life of factory workers was no picnic. Depression and alcoholism were rampant, and drunken suicide was not uncommon.

I had little insight as a young woman into the kind of trauma that might lead a boy to kill his stepfather with such meticulous butchery. Nor did I understand how the initial trauma, or the success of his planned revenge, might distort a child's mind, or determine the kind of man such a child might become. As Grigory told me his story, our infant daughter Larisa slept in her crib not a hand's reach from where we lay in bed. I felt the hair on the nape of my neck tingle as it stood erect, and my instinctive reaction was to grab Larisa in my arms and carry her as far away as I could.

As rapidly as I had the reaction, I knew to hide it from Grigory. I looked away, not wanting him to see how appalled I was. I couldn't help but be sympathetic to the boy who had been so badly mistreated. I could even have understood if, as his stepfather lay in a drunken stupor with his neck exposed like a ritual sacrifice, Grigory had taken the kitchen knife and in an act of spontaneous rage slit his stepfather's throat. But the satisfaction and the detail with which he related his brutal, choreographed sadism seemed beyond the bounds of sanity. It was evidence of a mind unhinged. All I could think was that he had become the same kind of monster his stepfather was. And I had linked my life to his.

From that moment, little pieces of the puzzle began to fall into place. The secrecy around his work. The feral nature of the men who were drawn to him, and to whom he gravitated. The abject, round-shouldered, fearful way most people approached him—they knew instinctively that he was to be feared. His inability to trust anyone, or to make the distinction between affection and sexual arousal. And, most distressing to me once I recognized it, the absolute absence of tenderness in his relationships, even with Larisa.

My need to find him trustworthy drained away, replaced by a gradual awareness that it would be wise to fear him. Being his intimate was dangerous—it meant being always under observation. Fear would keep me alert, prevent me from reacting in ways that might elicit unimaginable behavior from him. Over the years I worked hard to ensure that the monster within him remained buried, and I intended to give it no excuse to emerge. This was not simply a matter of self-preservation—just as Babushka had been my sole bastion of safety against the world, I became the only safety for Larisa.

I came to think of him as a huge, black spider, ruthless calculation in every move. With an imperceptible adjustment of a hairy, multi-faceted leg, he would cause one strand of his web to vibrate slightly, and without knowing it, his prey would avoid the vibrating strand and so be driven in whatever direction the spider desired.

Grigory made no issue of his preference for perfect young bodies, and he tired of me as soon as I had given birth. But once I began to see him as a spider, all I could think of was his round black abdomen being carried on silent, stilt-like legs about his web, and I was unable to wipe the image from my mind. It was only a short step to revulsion, and I was relieved that he wanted nothing to do with me. But very soon none of it would matter. Shortly after arriving back from Cuba, I was to discover how little I, or anyone else, meant to my husband.

In my free time I began thinking about work, and reading what I could about the dissident movement. There wasn't much useful information in the newspapers, but Grigory started bringing me information to read when he came home late at night.

"What is this?" I asked, the first time he dropped a stack of files on my bedside table.

"Nothing important," he said casually as he took off his Italian silk tie and carefully unbuttoned his shirt. "Reports. I thought you'd like to catch up on what's going on, who's opposing Kremlin policies. I assume," he said dryly, "that one of these days you'll want to go back to work."

The first reports he gave me rehashed what everyone knew—where the major dissidents like Sharansky and Solzhenitsyn were and what they were up to. As the weeks went by the reports he offered became more detailed, containing names of local dissident leaders and what they were talking and writing about. But the reports were vague and there seemed nothing dangerous in what these critics of the regime had to say.

"What do you think?" he asked me one night.

"About what?"

"The reports, Dasha." He sat on his side of the bed and carefully took off his shoes. "The updates I've been giving you to read."

I lay in bed, reading. I had on a light blue silk nightgown, and I felt attractive and sexy. He glanced at me, his gaze resting on my still full breasts, and then our eyes met, briefly, before he turned his head away. One side of his mouth tightened and the corner of his lip turned down sharply into a grimace of distaste. He hadn't touched me since long before Larisa was born, and while I had no particular desire for him, any touch would have been welcome. His silent rejection reminded me how much I disliked and feared him, and I was furious with myself for wanting something I despised. I was filled with embarrassment. If he noticed the flush of anger that rose to my cheeks, he would see it as one more little victory in our domestic war.

At the same time, a part of me wanted him to recognize my self-loathing because I knew it would arouse him and lead to the physical intimacy I craved—and hated myself for needing.

He missed nothing, of course. My flushed cheeks had exactly the effect I expected. He undressed without haste, hung up his suit, and in one careless move grabbed a fistful of bedclothes and ripped them effortlessly from the bed. They billowed across the room and landed in a snowy pile on the thick Afghan carpet. My nightgown had ridden up and was gathered around my waist. I was naked from the hips down, and the suddenness of my revealed flesh and the shock of cold air made me look at myself as if for the first time. I saw a belly still heavy from carrying Larisa, my pubic hair thick and dark, the triangle coming to a point where it thinned below my navel. My thighs were long and smooth, and against the white sheets they seemed muscular and toned, dark and flushed. I was surprised at how much I liked my body, even, I thought, if he didn't.

Grigory knelt on the bed. I watched him as if in a trance. He was lean, his sides taut, the skin rippling and supple over his ribs. The long muscles in his buttocks and thighs were tight and hard, dancing across his bones. At one instant I saw in him the repulsive spider, gliding silent and stiff-legged towards me. Then my eye was drawn to the erect cock standing out from between his legs and suddenly he was a prowling male animal, sleek and predatory. I knew he was my predator because his cock hung off-center, pulled to one side by the botched surgery that had removed his testicle.

I was without volition—my muscles and my will, frozen. As if I were a marionette with locking joints and he the puppeteer, he rolled me over onto my stomach and with powerful, expert hands at my waist he lifted my hips so that I was on my knees, and he knelt behind me. Holding my arms at my sides, he butted his head into my back, forcing my shoulders to the mattress. And then, a rumbling growl emerging from deep in his chest, Grigory opened his mouth and took the back of my neck between his teeth and I was suddenly the female panther, dark and sleek, and he the dominant male, looming over me, subduing me by locking his jaws in the fur at my neck. The sound coming from deep in his throat reverberated down my spine and pulsed up into my skull. The part of me that was panther loved it, but the woman, unprotected by fur at her neck, felt the pain of his locked jaws.

"Grisha," I heard myself say, voice muffled by the mattress, "you're hurting me."

As ever, he was oblivious to other people's pain. He mounted me from behind and pushed into me with such urgency that the pain rose up from my vagina into my throat and blocked my voice. Anger mushroomed in me at the intensity of the pain, and I didn't care whether or not he drew blood at my neck. All I wanted was to get him out of my body and away from me. I tensed all my muscles, trying to throw him off. But the immediate demands of his erection were all he cared about, and I couldn't move him. My own desire, like breath withheld until my lungs were about to burst, came flooding from me in shuddering gasps as if I had been drowning, as if by inserting his penis into me and thrusting violently he gave me access to oxygen and allowed my lungs to fill with air. Even as I gasped with relief, and with pain and pleasure exquisitely combined, I wondered what thoughts passed through his mind, and what he saw from his vantage point behind me.

He took exactly what he wanted—and at least on that occasion I got what I needed. I rose and showered, scrubbing myself beneath the jets of steaming water, trying to remove from my skin the abhorrent parts of what had just happened. I was horrified by Grigory's capacity for violence, and filled yet again with self-loathing at my craving for the physical attentions of a man who clearly felt nothing for me, and whom I despised.

As I dried myself I vowed that he would never violate me again. If I gave him permission to fuck me, it would be because I wanted him to, and it would be in a way I desired. I was done subjugating my desires to his. When I returned to bed he was already there, lying naked on the bottom sheet, waiting for me to remake the bed over him. I put on a fresh, silk nightgown and over it, my robe, picked up the sheet from the carpet and waved it so that it bellied above the bed and came to rest over him. I did the same with the blankets, and then climbed into bed.

"You were whining for it like a bitch in heat," he said without looking up from the file he was reading. "Anna won't be able to look you in the eye tomorrow. Neither will our neighbors. Good thing the old woman doesn't live with us—imagine having to face her after that performance."

He closed the file and set it on the blanket between us. He was gloating, filled with satisfaction.

"Now that I've given you what you wanted," he said, "tell me what you thought of the reports I left for you to read."

I ignored the first part of what he said—there was no possible response that would lead anywhere good.

"The reports are useless," I said. "Your agents find sedition and treason wherever they look. Their accusations make even the most innocent grandmother sound like a danger to the State—and anyone who might be really dangerous gets lost in the crowd. I'd have to listen with my own ears to know if there was really anything treasonous going on."

"So you don't want the little fish," he said with a thin smile. "You want the kingpin, if there is one. Well, I think now you have your chance."

"My chance to do what?"

"You've received official approval to participate in dissident meetings," he said. "Go back to work. Let's see what you find out when you sit in such meetings yourself."

❧

So I went back to work, unsure whether I was going back to the same job I left. I wanted to learn about the dissident movement—not to spy on them. It didn't worry me that my superiors expected intelligence reports from me. I knew how to prepare reports that had value, without revealing information that would bring down the heavy hand of the KGB on people who were simply getting together to share their ideas. But I had been too smart for my own good. Once Grigory became interested in what I was doing, control of the process was wrested from my hands. He would do whatever was necessary to protect his interests—which included knowing whatever I discovered.

Just as I returned to work, Mikhail Gorbachev began to implement his new policy of openness, *glasnost*, to reduce corruption and abuse of power in the Communist Party and in the committees that ran the country. It resulted in less censorship, and soon all the social problems denied by our government were being trumpeted in the press, openly acknowledged and discussed in public. Our perfect Socialist State suffered from rampant alcoholism, domestic abuse, endemic food shortages, substandard housing and building codes, widespread pollution—and the problems mushroomed from there.

The gusts of openness blew the secrecy out of Moscow, and we all breathed the fresh air deeply into our lungs. At first, small groups gathered in each other's homes. Once they realized the authorities didn't really care, they began meeting more openly. By the time I returned to work, several organizations were holding regular sessions. I went to several meetings of The Moscow Tribune, an organization of academics and writers, at the headquarters of the Filmmakers' Union near the Peking Hotel, but learned nothing that was not already public knowledge. Then, in the spring, there was a meeting at the Central House of Writers. It was billed as An Evening of Remembrance.

When I arrived, an audience of about sixty people stood around in small groups or sat on folding chairs, talking quietly as they smoked cigarettes or drank coffee from paper cups. I knew no one personally, but recognized a few men and women who had been exiled but then returned, gaunt, grey and bent. Andrey Nikolayevich Sakharov was there, recently permitted to return from exile in Gorky, a city off limits to foreigners. And there were others who had paid their dues to the dissident movement, some having spent years of their lives in remote camps in Siberia for refusing to be silenced. As I looked around I saw several people sitting alone, as I was, trying to be invisible. There seemed no agenda until an elderly man rose and made his way to the front of the room. He was balding, with long thinning white hair at his sides and down his neck, and he leaned heavily on a cane. His open windbreaker hung down at his sides almost to his knees, and once he reached the podium he waved his arms as he spoke about 'crimes of the past.' These were code words from the language of repression, when it was forbidden to talk openly about the horrors that took place under Stalin. One could hint, telling stories from memory or hearsay—but because there was no real information, the greatest complaint people could voice was that there was no access to the facts. But this was a different time, and while the old-timer was treated with respect, some of the younger people in the audience were impatient with his outdated caution, his circumspect language.

As the speaker drew to a close and took his cane in hand, a young man in his twenties detached himself from the side of the room. He was thin and scholarly, with rounded shoulders as if he spent his life at a desk. Hands twisting nervously before him, he stood at the front of the room and introduced himself as Dmitry Yurgachev. He had dark hair shorn almost to his scalp, and he wore faded jeans and a ripped denim jacket. He was defiant as he stood before us, and exultant, his eyes bright with excitement. He said he had important information to share.

"Few people know," he said, "that since 1929, all anti-Soviet crimes— anything that gave Stalin an excuse to purge the population—were recorded in the archives of the Interior Ministry. We don't know the exact number— but we all have someone who disappeared. When they died, how they died, and where they're buried, is all either hidden or lost. But I have proof that what actually happened is far worse than our government admitted, and far worse than any of us could have imagined."

He wore heavy dark-framed glasses that kept slipping down so that he was peering over them. As he spoke he jabbed periodically at the bridge of his nose with a practiced forefinger, pushing the glasses back as if they would eventually learn to stay put.

"I spent years working in those Archives, and I have recorded names and dates and the descriptions of crimes. Under Stalin there were at least sixteen million citizens arrested or executed. And I have copied a letter—a confidential letter from the Chairman of the Supreme Court to Nikita Khrushchev reporting that in the decade after 1953, at least a million two hundred thousand people were posthumously rehabilitated." He paused.

"Posthumously rehabilitated," he said again, slowly. "What an absurd phrase. Without admitting any wrongdoing, without letting family or country know, the State had admitted that these people were murdered by mistake. How can our country have executed a million people in error?"

Even the pale, craggy, survivors in the audience, walking on sticks, bowed over by arthritis and a diet even worse than that of the average Russian, were impressed by Dmitry's words. They agreed that it was time for his research to be made public. He was flushed with pride by the end of the meeting, surrounded by veterans of the struggle whose interest and praise validated his obsession and his years of secret labor.

Dmitry was an academic researcher working on his own, unlikely to have contacts outside the country, and I had no professional reason to cultivate him. Besides, if I showed any interest in him, Grigory would have quickly found out, and any attention I drew to him could only have caused him harm. But I did have personal reasons for wanting to talk to him.

As I sat listening to Dmitry, I found myself thinking of my grandfather, Vasily. Babushka spoke little about him, but I knew he had been executed under Stalin's rule. I had no idea what his crime was, how and where he was tried, where and when he was executed. We would never discover where he was buried—but perhaps, I thought, Dmitry might be able to find out whether he was important enough to have been posthumously rehabilitated. Babushka would, at the very least, take grim satisfaction in knowing that, at some level deep in its metaphorical subconscious, the State recognized itself as a murderous thug.

I remained in my folding chair pretending to read my magazine. Dmitry's admirers gradually began to trickle in ones and twos towards the exit. He waited until they had all departed, and as he gathered his papers and left, I put on my coat and followed him out onto the street. I intended to shadow him until we were several blocks away, and then to approach him, but he was walking fast, his long loping stride rapidly widening the distance between us. I increased my pace so that he didn't get too far ahead of me—but at the first corner, a figure unfolded from a doorway and I had to abandon my plan.

Dmitry was unsurprised by the newcomer. This was clearly a planned meeting. Without pause they fell into step and continued walking together. The newcomer was tall, with broad shoulders and long arms, and a hip swing as he walked that was particular to men with muscular legs. He and Dmitry glanced at each other as they talked, giving me momentary glimpses of their profiles. Before I knew it at a conscious level, my body recognized the newcomer, something in my chest leaped with excitement and before I could stop myself I found myself shouting his name.

"Kolya! Kolya!"

My cousin turned when he heard his name. At first he registered surprise, and then he recognized me. Even from a distance I could identify his expression as one of terrible alarm. His forehead creased upward, his eyes opened wide and his mouth, which usually wore a gentle smile, turned down at the ends, dragging his lips into an open grimace. I could almost feel his jaws clench. He shook his head at me as if in warning, and he and Dmitry increased their pace. I ran towards them, but they turned at the next street and when I reached the corner, winded, they were nowhere to be seen.

I turned back unsteadily, knees trembling, hands quivering as they held on to my bag. I was aware of being confused, but had no idea why I would be so deeply shaken by the unexpected appearance of my cousin. As always, when unsure, I began to analyze what I knew. I was reacting to something I didn't even recognize at a conscious level. Certainly, I was surprised to see Kolya with Dmitry—it was not the kind of association I expected, and I didn't think the people Kolya reported to—including Grigory—would have approved. Unless Grigory was behind it. Had he given my cousin some clandestine assignment parallel to my own—and then not said a word to me? Nothing would have surprised me. Or so I thought.

I was not pleased with Kolya, nor with his parents. We had all been very close—when I was growing up their apartment was a second home to me. But when I married, everything changed. Our contacts became few and far between, and we had had no contact at all since before Larisa's birth. Even Babushka had commented on how strange it was that Juliana had not even made a new baby call. Kolya I could forgive—he was on active duty, and

I never knew where he was or what he was doing. How long, I wondered, since we saw each other? I calculated that I had been away on several trips, and then my pregnancy, and now Larisa was six months old. With a shock I realized that I had not seen or heard from him in over a year. In that time, I had never asked about him, and as usual, Grigory had said nothing.

Kolya and I played together all our childhood. We knew each other well, and I was sure that his shaking head was a warning to me. A warning not to follow him? Not to be seen with him? And the distress on his face when he recognized me—was I so upset because of his reaction to me, or was it something else?

I tried to replay the moment I saw him. What was it I had responded to so viscerally once I recognized him? The first thing I saw as he stepped out of the doorway was a heavy boot—old military, perhaps—followed by the leg of his pressed military trousers.

No.

That's what I expected, but not what I saw. What I saw was workpants. Dark green workpants, stained and discolored from wear. A plaid quilted work shirt, torn at one elbow. A worker's grey cap, the brim pulled down in front. His hair was shaggy, sticking out over his ears at the sides, and down below the level of his cap in back. Not the Kolya I knew, who prized his appearance and was proud of his military uniform. And then I knew what had so distressed me. It was the brief glances of his profile, and his face.

He had a sculpted profile with a nose a little too broad; high Slavic cheekbones; full lips for a man, but offset by the maleness of his square chin. He had been a gorgeous boy, and he was a most handsome man. But this face was neither. It was worn. His bloodshot eyes submerged in their own bags, cheeks hollowed out as if weight had suddenly dropped from his body, as if he had stopped eating, or been deprived of food. I had never seen him unshaven, but he was grizzled, a week's growth blurring the outlines of his cheeks. It was not just distress I saw on his face—it was fear. And I knew without asking the question that the fear he felt was for both himself and for me.

✿

My first thought was to share my concern with Grigory, but I quickly decided not to. It would be foolish, or worse, harmful—especially if he had anything to do with Kolya's unexpected presence. A much wiser course of action, I thought, was to speak to Juliana. She would know what was going on. But she didn't return my telephone calls, and I finally sent her a note.

My Dear Juliana:

I long to see you and to introduce you to Larisa. We have important things to discuss—worrying things that affect us all. Please let's arrange to meet. I will bring the baby to you, wherever you choose. Will you come to my house, or shall we meet at the coffee shop in the Peking Hotel? Perhaps we could have lunch at the International. Let me know.

With much love,

Darya

Juliana called me the evening she received my note. She was distant and uncommunicative on the phone, but agreed to meet me for tea. She would love to see Larisa—however, not at any of the places I suggested. We arranged that she would call me the following day to let me know the place and time. When she did call early the next morning, it was to announce that she wanted to meet me on the street, near the Kitai Gorod station. It was near the Kremlin, only a few kilometers and two stops from my home. It was within walking distance of several hotels and coffee shops.

She made clear that she would decide which place only once we had greeted each other on the street. This was unusual behavior for Juliana—

she was a strong, straightforward woman—everything she did in her life was above board, and she tackled obstacles head on. But this was the kind of clandestine plan that reflected a fear of being recorded or videotaped, overheard or spied on by men in dark glasses. It began to explain her avoidance of me—and I began to suspect that whatever fear she might have, it was not her own safety she was concerned about, but the safety of someone close to her.

On the morning of our meeting I called into the Ministry and reported to my bosses that I was attending a dissident meeting. Anna and I dressed Larisa in a pretty pastel jumpsuit with white fluffy kittens on the chest—the light color brought out the depth of her eyes, and I wanted her to look beautiful for Juliana. I put her in the stroller and told Anna that I was taking the baby out for a walk. We took the Metro, exited at one side of Red Square, and waited at the corner we had agreed upon. It was an autumn day, the winds were blowing, and a weak Moscow sun was trying to break through the clouds. Juliana emerged from the Metro just after we did, nodded to me without even looking at Larisa, and led the way to a small coffee shop inside one of the older hotels, where few international visitors went. Only when we had sat down together and taken off our coats did she turn her attention to Larisa. Then, for a brief while, it was as if nothing was amiss. She held my daughter in her practiced hands, smiling and cooing, and Larisa responded with her own sunshine smile, looking at Juliana with serious green eyes.

I watched Juliana carefully. She was a full-bodied woman of medium height, with an animated, expressive face. Like most professional women of her generation, she wore no makeup, and her grey hair was cropped about her ears, with a short curl over her forehead. Kolya got his warm, grey eyes from her, and his easy smile. On that day she wore a dark plastic raincoat, and under it a red cardigan. She held Larisa against her cheek, kissed her warmly, and then cuddled her close.

"Lena said she was beautiful," said Juliana. "She was right. It warms my heart that you've been able to give her a great-grandchild."

She looked over Larisa's head at me, and her smile faltered as she pursed her lips. I saw for the first time that her full face was now more angular than round, the warmth in her eyes diminished, almost the way a light bulb loses light and power as it expires.

"You know, Dasha, what I wish for this child," she said, her voice dropping almost to a whisper. "Only the most wonderful, joyful life."

"I know," I said. "Thank you."

"Here," she said. "Take her now."

There were tears in her eyes as she removed Larisa from her bosom and handed her back to me across the table. It was almost as if she didn't want to give up holding my baby, but what had to happen between us could not transpire over her head. We sat in silence as I settled her back in her pram and the waitress took our orders for tea and bread rolls with cheese.

"What do you want with me, Dasha?" she asked.

There was anger in her voice, and beneath it, something that sounded like desperation. It was not what I expected, and I didn't know whether to be offended by her question or to feel sorry for whatever she was going through. The surprise I felt at her response must have registered on my face, because even before I answered, her expression changed to one of relief.

"I want you back in my life, Juliana," I asked, reaching across the table to take her hand. "Why are you so distant with me? What have I done?"

She pulled her hand away and slumped back against the bench, shook her head as if in disbelief, and closed her eyes.

"You know nothing of what's happened to us, do you?" she said.

I stared at her pallid cheeks, the skin pouched at her neck from loss of weight, the weariness. It was cancer, I thought. She was dying. That's why she had been avoiding me.

"What's happened?" I asked. "Are you ill?"

She waved away my concern. "No," she said grimly, sitting straight again. "My health is good. But a piece of me wishes I were dead—and after you hear what I have to say, you'll wish me dead, too."

"How can you say such a thing?" I asked, horrified. This was my beloved Juliana, my much older cousin who had played aunt in my life, who along with Babushka had taken care of me and given me the love and mothering that made me a secure and happy child. "I would die before wishing ill on you. Juliana, what is this about?"

"I should have guessed that you knew nothing," she said, her voice low, almost a whisper. "I didn't want to be the one to tell you. But we have no choice now. I'm going to tell you all of it, from the beginning, even though you will hate me for it."

"Whatever it is, I won't hate you. Maybe I can even help. Tell me, please."

"In your note you wrote that we needed to talk about things. Worrying things. What did you mean?"

I hesitated, but I could tell her what I had seen without disclosing the nature of my own assignment. I explained to her that I had seen Kolya on the street, looking shabby and unwell.

"I shouted to him. When he recognized me he looked frightened, and he ran away. I followed, but I couldn't find him." I opened my hands in bewilderment. "He didn't want me to find him. And he ran from me, Juliana—from me! He's the closest thing I have to a brother. Why would he avoid me? Do you know about any of this?"

"We've had a terrible time." she said. "It continues still. I think it will never end." She took a deep breath, tightened her mouth, exhaled the words. "A year ago Kolya was convicted of a crime. He received a dishonorable discharge and spent six months in jail. He was only released last month."

"Kolya?" I was stunned. "In jail? There must be a mistake. I wish you had come to us. There must be something Grigory can do."

Juliana looked at me, shaking her head.

"No? What are you saying? There's nothing he can do?"

"It will do none of us any good for you to tell him. He already knows. He chooses to do nothing."

"How can you say that with such certainty?"

She hesitated. "You haven't asked me yet what Kolya's crime was," she said grimly.

"Whatever crime he was accused of, there has to be an explanation. Kolya's no criminal."

I tried to feel indignant at the very idea, but what I felt was a weak substitute, a fraud. I knew what my husband was capable of—or thought I did. He made it his business to be aware of every detail of his employees' lives. How could he not have known what was happening to Kolya? It was infuriating and terrifying to think that he might know, and chose to say nothing; that he might have been coming home at night to me, pretending nothing was amiss, caring so little about me that he felt no obligation to share what he knew about someone so close to me, someone he had mentored and helped.

Helplessly, Juliana shrugged her big shoulders. "Grigory knew everything," she said. "I'm sure. And in a minute you will, too. Ask me now, Dasha, what was the crime?"

"Okay, what was it? This crime I don't believe he's guilty of?"

"What he's guilty of shouldn't be illegal," she said, "but it is. Your cousin was caught in a hotel room. With a man. Both of them in the military, which makes it worse, even thought they were off-duty. But that doesn't matter. They were found guilty, dishonorably discharged, and sent to prison like common criminals."

What surprised me most about Juliana's words is that I was not surprised at all. I thought back, and remembered all the signs I had misread. When we were growing up, homosexuality was not discussed. Officially, it didn't exist. Aside from being socially unacceptable, it was a punishable offense, and being openly gay would have been political suicide. As teenagers, we used to go out in groups, and couples would pair off to neck and fondle. Kolya was always with those who were alone—usually because they were themselves not chosen. But he could have had his choice of girls—they were all after him. He seemed disinterested, and in my ignorance I assumed it was because he was too good, too determined to be the perfect Soviet man. I put it in the same category as Kolya's refusal to have more than one drink. We had discussed it, and I admired his determination not to be controlled by his emotions or his sexual needs. Now that I understood, I could see that he was simply an ambitious young man trying to be discreet.

"My Kolya may have seemed perfect, but he wasn't," she continued. "I recognized that he was different, even as a young boy. Maxim and I hoped he would outgrow it, as most boys do. We knew if he didn't get beyond it, it would ruin his chance of success, and make difficulties for all of us. But I could never have imagined this."

"We shared everything," I said. "I thought there was nothing we couldn't discuss, but he never told me this. I had no idea."

"You had no idea—but you're not shocked, are you?" asked Juliana. "No, not shocked. You love him—somewhere inside you, you always knew, and you accepted the truth about him. But how could he reveal this? To you?"

She leaned forward, intense, bitter, and she threw open her arms in mockery. Her red cardigan pulled open, and as she waved her arms I saw that her breasts were unhampered, dancing loosely beneath her faded beige blouse. I turned my eyes from where they had fixed on her jumping nipples, shocked by how much her breasts sagged and how low down on her belly they were. I was embarrassed and saddened for her —for her age, and her grief, and her unkempt appearance. Her mouth turned down in distaste, and she held back nothing as she described my youthful enthusiasm for the Soviet ideal. How cruel and callow I must have seemed to her.

"Darya, the staunch Communist, Komsomol leader, prize-winning essay writer on Soviet history—the Kremlin approved version. There were no cracks in your ideology. Your convictions were absolute. Kolya could never have risked sharing his secret with you. And just when you began to open your eyes and see the flaws in Communist philosophy, along comes Grigory. With his outward charm and his big car, and with his gifts of pineapples and plums and turkeys, and the fashionable dresses that showed your cleavage and the pearls to hang between your tits and before you knew it he charmed your underpants right off and you jumped into his bed. Oh, don't look so shocked. I've been around a long time. I watched the whole parade. Once he set his sights on you, you had no chance." She paused, turned her head away from me, towards the door. "Lena tried to tell you. You couldn't hear. Now look where we are. All of us. You included. What a mess."

All I could think was, what have I done? But I said, "Oh, Juliana," as the tears welled up in my eyes, and I reached across the table again to take her hand. "I'm so sorry."

In answer she looked at me sadly, and her eyes filled with tears that rolled down her cheeks. Again she pulled her hand away. It was almost as if she refused to take comfort from me, something I didn't then understand. From her sleeve she withdrew a crumpled handkerchief and held it to her eyes.

"Help?" she asked. "Who do you want to help, Dashinka? You can't even help yourself."

"What do you mean?" I asked.

"I can't blame you for what's happened—you were a child. You knew nothing. And still," she said, taking a deep sigh, "still, you know nothing. And it's left to me to tell you."

I was about to ask again what she was talking about but she held up a hand to silence me.

"Be patient. You'll know soon enough," she said. She settled herself in her chair, sipped her tea. Her hand was trembling, and her cup rattled in the saucer as she lowered it. "Do you remember the first time you brought your husband to our apartment?"

"Yes," I said. "I wanted to introduce you. You made dinner for us."

"Do you recall that Kolya was there?"

"Of course. He came in from studying—or from sport. I don't remember. He and Grigory talked. Kolya wanted to go to officer training school, and Grigory offered to help guide him in his career."

"And what happened?"

"He did guide him. Made introductions. Paved his way."

"Anything else?" asked Juliana.

"Yes," I said. "He took Kolya to events where he might meet influential people."

"Correct. Did you ever wonder why he did all this for Kolya?"

"Grigory does nothing without a reason," I said. "A selfish reason. He saw potential in Kolya—someone he could mentor and bring up through the ranks. Kolya would be in his debt, and Grigory can always make use of people in his debt. As you've already said, he wanted me. I assume he was kind to my cousin in order to get to me." I paused. "Had I known then what kind of man my husband is I wouldn't have let him come within a million kilometers of Kolya."

"And now you know what kind of man Grigory is?" she asked.

"Babushka was right all along," I said. "But I didn't want to listen."

"You should have taken heed. We would all be better off."

"I was young," I said, "but I should have known better. I think—I think some part of me did know better, even then."

She nodded her head as if to acknowledge my confusion, but the expression on her face told me any apology or sense of regret was too little, too late.

"Kolya was young, too," she muttered under her breath. "So tell me," she continued, "don't you think your husband would have wanted to let you know how useful he was being to Kolya?"

"I stayed out of it, Juliana," I said. "It was Kolya's business, not mine."

"Doesn't it seem strange to you," she persisted, "that Grigory didn't tell you much about how helpful he was being to your cousin, whom you loved?"

"No," I said, beginning to feel uncomfortable. What had I missed? "What are you trying to say, Juliana? Grigory has never been one to share much with me."

She shook her head in agreement.

"Once Grigory came on the scene, Kolya didn't tell us much either. In fact, he seemed to be avoiding us."

"He was a university student, Juliana. He had his own life. What are you suggesting—that Grigory somehow cut Kolya off from you?"

"No, child—but once he got his claws into Kolya he made it impossible for Kolya to come back to us."

"What are you talking about?"

She took a deep breath. "Kolya was sixteen," she said, "just finishing high school. Grigory invited him to a lecture, and introduced him to one of the officials in charge of admissions at the Officer's Training College. This person was in Grigory's debt, and it was understood that if Grigory wanted Kolya accepted, then it was as good as done. Afterwards he took Kolya back to his apartment." She spat the words out. "To celebrate, he said. In the same apartment where he charmed the pants off you."

She stopped and looked steadily across the table at me.

"Now do you understand what happened?"

"No," I whispered. "It can't have."

"Oh, yes. He seduced my boy. In his apartment. On the same bed where he seduced you. Maybe on the same sheets. He had you both, perhaps within days of each other."

"What are you saying, Juliana? He couldn't have done this. How do you know?" and then, as an afterthought, "I didn't sleep with him until I was twenty."

"So, he took my son before you gave yourself to him." She halted, choked back a sob, swallowed hard. "Kolya was still a child."

I asked again how she could be sure of what she was telling me. It horrified me, filled me with fury. And I was terrified, by my own blindness, and by what this man, the father of my infant daughter, was capable of. Once again I had underestimated how controlled he was by his appetites. Perhaps this was evil, plain and simple. But whatever I might call it, for the second time that day, what surprised me most is that I was not surprised at all.

"Kolya told us everything once he was arrested. He was ashamed—couldn't look us in the eye. When he was sixteen he disappeared from our lives, yours and ours, although we were none of us aware that he disappeared from his own life, too. Grigory created him, used him. Refused to step in and help him when he was in trouble. Now he is a broken man. Nowhere to go, no protection, no work, no place to live, no status. He's even more vulnerable—and Grigory still uses him to do the dirty work he can't delegate to his own people."

Before she left the restaurant, Juliana finally reached across the table and took my hand in hers. The sadness in her eyes, the weariness, were like bottomless wells in her face. I was witness to pain far too intimate to share and I tried to look away, but she locked her eyes on mine, allowed the invasion, maybe even welcomed it. We held on to each other, our fingers intertwined, drowning women clinging together for life.

"Aiee," she said softly as she exhaled, a long keening sound.

"What do we do now?" I asked.

"We live our lives," she said, "such as they are. We do what we can for our children." She paused, grasped my hand even more firmly, and a tentative smile formed on her lips. "So," she said, "you don't wish me dead?"

Slowly, I shook my head.

"I'm ashamed I let this distance grow between us. I wasn't there for you when all this happened. I only wish my eyes had been opened before now. We have to find some way to help Kolya."

"As long as Maxim and I live, he has a place to sleep, and he won't starve." She looked down, resignation in her drooping shoulders. "But we can't make him come to us. He's afraid he will lead the KGB to our door, so he stays away."

"I want to talk to him," I said. "Do you think he'll meet with me?"

"I don't know where he is. Haven't seen him in months. For our own safety, he says." She shrugged. "They can't make me tell what I don't know, right? But I can get a message to him, let him know you want to meet. Then it's out of my hands." She looked at her watch. "I have to go," she said, rising.

I stood up and hugged her.

"This endangers us all," she said softly. "You, especially."

"Me?" I asked, surprised.

I tried to pull away from her and look into her eyes as she answered, but she held me in her embrace with surprising strength and put her mouth to my ear.

"You have bound yourself to a viper," she whispered. "I hope you have strength enough to withstand his poison."

❧

After Juliana left I sat numbly at the table, pushing Larisa back and forth in her stroller. My mind was like a deserted train speeding down a track to nowhere, blurred images of the countryside flying by me. Only the train was out of control, and the inescapable images were the landscape of my life. Kolya, fourteen when I was sixteen, standing at the side of the room in conversation with another boy as couples writhed on the couch, embraced in corners, hands all over each other. Grigory, preening at his first meeting with Kolya in his parents' apartment, and I, too blind to see a pedophile starting the seduction of a young, hapless victim. Kolya at sixteen, with his long legs, a Greek god lying on that bed, his sandy-blond hair spread out against those grey satin sheets. Grigory's breath heavy with desire as his hands explored my young cousin's body, the arch of his chest and his wide shoulders, belly flat with layers of muscle curving around lean hips, down the front of coiled thighs, twitching, pale, never warmed by sunlight, and pure, having yet to feel the touch of hands other than his own. Did he know, I wondered, as he lay there, how beautiful he was?

What Kolya was thinking and feeling, what expression was visible in his grey eyes and on his inflamed lips, I cannot allow myself to imagine. Nor can I imagine particular parts of Kolya's body, the parts where his hips and his thighs conjoin, the triangle of hair below his navel, widening as it descends to his groin, the hardened muscles of his buttocks and the tender parts below, the parts I envied as a little girl because I lacked them.

As those calculating fingers approach parts of Kolya where I deny myself the liberty of imagination, Kolya's beauty morphs into my own. The gentle savannah of his body transforms into the lush hills and valleys of my own, and I feel Grigory's hands move like summer wind across the contours of my hips and my thighs as I lay on the familiar sheets where I so frequently spread my body for him, in combinations so contorted that I can neither remember nor count them all.

All along, I think, I had held out a vain hope, a wish perhaps, that some part of our marriage was salvageable. But Juliana's revelations showed there was nothing between us that was not a sham, a mockery. I ask myself how a woman as intelligent, determined and headstrong as I, finds herself trapped in a marriage—a loveless cage—to a man with all the hallmarks of a psychopath, but no answer comes.

Grigory would never let me go. Aside from losing access to the information I provided, it would be an assault to his ego. He had already shown that he could hurt me with impunity, and that shamed me. But if he hurt me again, if I thought he posed any danger to Larisa, I would do whatever was necessary to protect myself and my child.

I stop the runaway train, realize that I am holding my breath, sit alone and look around me. At a table by the window sits a young family, husband and wife and a little boy of about three, with shiny brown curls covering his ears and his forehead. He has big, laughing eyes, and he stands on a chair beside his mother, a plain woman with eyes too wide apart, and a little flattened nose. Her best feature is her perfect skin. The little boy kisses her face, peers deep into her eyes. She looks from her son to her husband, who watches this little scene with amusement. Mother and father exchange a glance and a smile. I watch as the boy's fingers gently stroke her smooth, full cheeks, a gesture of love so tender and innocent, it makes my heart burst. I mourn that my life will never contain such a moment—I will never have a son to show me such delicate and absolute love or a husband who would appreciate such intimacy.

But as in so many areas of my life, my certainty on that occasion about what I would never have was an illusion. In the coming weeks I discovered that I was already pregnant with Anton, the result of Grigory's last and final foray into my body.

❁

Juliana called to say that we should go shopping. Rumor had it that a shipment of fresh produce had just been delivered to a local vegetable market. When I arrived I stood off to the side, appearing to look into the shop-front window. I was actually watching my own reflection, waiting for Juliana to arrive. When I saw her coming I walked slowly to the end of the line, arriving just before she did. At first we didn't acknowledge each other, but after a few moments I turned and smiled at her, two strangers meeting in a food line. She returned my smile and we talked briefly to the women in front of me. We lapsed into silence, and in whispers she told me that Kolya had agreed to meet with me. He agreed to talk to me only if he was convinced I hadn't been followed, and his instructions were painfully detailed.

I was to take the Metro three stops in one direction, wait for the second train and take it back again. I was to repeat this twice—during which time I assumed he would have me watched from a distance to see if I was being followed. Once I exited the Metro and climbed the steps to the street, Juliana went through the route I was to take towards the museum, stopping at specific points to look into a shop window, or to stand and check my watch as if waiting for someone. Then I was to enter the museum and stand beneath Lena's painting, where a man would signal me. I was to follow him at a distance, and under no circumstances to acknowledge or speak to him.

❦

An hour later I found myself in an ancient, faded light blue Lada being driven on one of the ring roads around Moscow, heading north through factory towns and farmland. I had been jolted from my reverie before Ivanov's masterpiece by a bearded man in a quilted work coat, who bumped into me.

"Sorry," he said gruffly, and then whispered, "follow me, but keep your distance."

He walked back through the atrium and when he reached the entranceway I followed, keeping a hundred meters between us. He moved fast, and I struggled not to lose him. We took a circuitous route, retracing our steps and weaving between buildings, and finally he led me into an apartment building and out the back to an alley. There were two cars waiting—one was the Lada, the other was a black nondescript vehicle behind us. There was a driver at the wheel in both cars. My guide opened the back door for me and got into the front.

"Please lie down," he said. "We need to be sure you're not visible."

"Where are we going?" I asked as I lay down across the seat.

"We're taking you to see your cousin," he answered. "The car behind follows at a distance to see if anyone's tracking us."

"Can I ask who you are?"

"Friends," he said.

"I'm glad Kolya has such careful friends," I answered, and I saw from my prone position that the two men exchanged glances.

"Not that many," said the driver, speaking for the first time. "Few enough that we can't afford to be careless. We may have *glasnost* and less State security, but the KGB still has people everywhere—enough to keep an eye on all of us who pose a threat. Your husband is even more dangerous—he plays by no rules, and he has people where even the KGB can't gain access."

"Are you ex-military?" I asked.

There was no answer, and I decided not to speak further. If they wanted to talk to me they could initiate conversation. They clearly knew the details of my life, but it was probably better that I knew nothing more about them. I doubted whether all their precautions were warranted. Could Grigory's reach possibly be as deep and widespread as they imagined? But they were there to protect Kolya, and if they felt this level of caution was necessary, I was happy to go along with it.

Fifty minutes later we turned off the main highway onto a narrow road that traveled straight to the horizon.

"No one here," said the driver. "You can sit up now."

"Thank you."

I rose and stretched, looked out the window. There were many such roads, and it was common knowledge that they all led to small villages or isolated factories. I don't remember ever seeing anyone turn off the highway onto one of them. The villagers outside Moscow were a world apart—they lived the same way their parents had half a century earlier. For the world to discover that people lived in such backward squalor so close to our modern, sophisticated capital, would have been a blow to our international image. As a result, foreign visitors were prohibited from traveling outside the city.

The other car halted at the turnoff and waited to see if anyone was behind us. Apparently the road was empty. There was no one following, and we slowed and turned onto a dirt road, two tire tracks with grass growing thickly in the middle. In spring this road would most certainly turn to mud, and it would be completely impassable. We drove slowly through the forest, trees on either side of us meeting in the sky and blotting out the sun. Eventually we stopped at the side of the track. The man in the passenger seat got out of the car and opened my door, and pointed to a footpath that led from the road into the trees.

"Come," he said. "I'll take you to Kolya."

"What about you?" I asked the driver.

"We can't leave the car here," he said. "Too visible. I'm going to drive around, make sure you remain alone. When you're ready I'll take you back."

I followed my guide along the narrow path. It was dark and overgrown, birch trees and pine on both sides, and the smell of pine tar thickened the air. The only thing thicker than the smell was the absence of civilization. No city sounds—just pine tar mixed with birdsong.

The path opened onto a small clearing around which were seven or eight well-worn military tents, faded and stretched. Rips and tears had been roughly mended or patched. At first glance it was indistinguishable from an encampment for vagrants, people who had nowhere else to go, the kind of shelter criminals and addicts sought when their families finally had enough of them. A perfect place for the dispossessed—for the lost, and for those who couldn't afford to be found. But the residents of this camp were not vagrants. The whole camp was protected from view above by carefully draped camouflage netting. It was a temporary encampment, easily dismantled and reestablished elsewhere. Now I understood why Maxim didn't know where it was—it kept changing location. That's why the KGB hadn't found and destroyed it. It lived under the State Organs' radar.

My guide led the way behind the tents, where several men sat on tree

222 Neville D. Frankel

stumps around a smoky fire. A few wore military greatcoats. Others were dressed in workmen's clothes similar to those Kolya had been wearing when we met on the street. They talked quietly, glancing intently at each other through the smoke. These were men to be respected. Perhaps, like Kolya, some were ex-military. These were not academicians or political theorists who talked about inequities and demanded change. They were thoughtful men who had already been sufficiently injured by the State, and by the look of them, were ready to do more than talk. It struck me that perhaps this was one of the faces of the dissident movement—a face very different from the one I had initially imagined.

While I was trying to decide whether this new face pleased me, a man from the far side of the fire rose and came around to me. Kolya. Straight and muscular, much taller than I was, and still handsome. I wondered why he had seemed so diminished on the street. Perhaps he had been trying to make himself smaller and less conspicuous. As he came towards me I went to throw my arms about him, but his expression was grim and unsmiling, so I simply grasped his arms and kissed him on both cheeks. He put a hand on each of my shoulders, more to keep me at a distance than to welcome me.

"I'm so happy to see you," I said.

"Come," he responded. "Let's talk."

He led the way to one of the tents, held back the flap and stood aside to usher me in. It was dark, the air was much colder than outdoors. He motioned me to a canvas chair, sat down across from me on a folding military cot.

"It gets cold here in the afternoon," he said, reaching down to ignite a paraffin heater on the small collapsible aluminum table in the middle of the floor. "The trees are great protection—they hide us from view—but they also keep the sun out."

"Thank you," I said, holding my hands out to the heater.

He looked at me without expression, arms straight and shoulders hunched to his ears as he supported his weight with his palms on the frame of the cot.

"I agreed to see you because I need to know what's going on," he said.

"What do you want, Darya? Why were you at the meeting? Why were you following me?"

"I wasn't following you," I said hotly. "I wanted to talk to Dmitry. I had no idea you'd be along until you appeared out of nowhere. And you're not the only one with questions. Why did you run from me, with such fear on your face? Why are you avoiding me? What are you afraid of?"

He smiled, amusement and derision present in equal measure on his lips. But it was derision and mockery of both himself and of me.

"I've learned about your husband the way a patient learns about a flesh-eating disease," he said. "What I know makes me quake in my boots. Not for myself—he's already taken most of what he can from me. But I'm afraid for my parents. And for you too, Dasha. I care about you like the sister you've been to me. At the same time, I'd be a fool to trust you."

"You think I'm in danger from my husband, but you can't trust me because I'm married to him? That makes no sense."

"It's complicated," he said, still smiling. "You pretend to have no clue why I might want to avoid you. My mother was convinced—but do you expect me to believe you didn't know what happened to me? Come on, Darya, how is that possible? You live with the man. Are you telling me he said nothing to you? And if he didn't mention me, why didn't you ask? Didn't you wonder why my mother never came to see you when your baby was born? Did it never occur to you to wonder why I didn't come?" He bit his lip. "I would have liked to come and see your child. But it was impossible."

"I know," I said. "I mean, now I understand why."

There was silence between us.

"I can give you tea," he said quietly.

"I didn't come to drink tea, Kolya."

He nodded.

"He told you nothing about me? What happened? What I did?"

"Not a single word. But there's nothing unusual in that. He has no interest in anyone outside himself. Including our daughter."

"I'm sorry."

"Perhaps he was silent because he thought if I knew what happened, I would have pushed him to help you retain your position."

"Would you?"

"What a question," I said. "I would have done anything in my power to help you."

"Anything in your power," he mused. "Yet you want me to accept that you never tried to find out—from him or from anyone else—where I was."

"You're like a dog with a bone," I said angrily. "What do you want me to say?"

I remembered from our adolescence that Kolya had an instinctive sense for what would push my buttons, and he would push them with a gentle assurance guaranteed to make me furious. And here he was, honing in on the one issue where I was vulnerable.

I want to know," he said with infuriating calm, "why it makes you so angry."

"Because you're right, as usual. I should have been concerned. I should have wondered where you were." I stood up and walked the three paces to the end of the tent and back. "But first I was pregnant, and then I had Larisa to take care of. Grigory only wanted me around to make him look good. Now that I've had a child, in his twisted mind, I can't even do that. So perhaps I've become useless to him. I don't tell him anything—but whatever information I have, he could get out of me. You're wise to fear him, and if I were you, I probably wouldn't trust me, either." I sat down again. "I hate him," I said vehemently. "I hate what he's turned me into, and what he's done to you. But I haven't known where you were—or who you are—for years. So perhaps I got used to your absence. That's something else we need to talk about. But first I'll have that drink, if you're still offering it. Something stronger than tea."

He rose and walked out, leaving the flap open. The cold, fresh air and the silence permeated the space and made me realize how effective the paraffin heater was. When he came back he carried a bottle of vodka and two glasses. Setting them on the table he poured two fingers of clear liquid into each glass and handed me one. I took a small sip and felt it burn down my throat. I seldom drank vodka. He downed his glass in one gulp.

"So now what?" he asked. "Accusations? Recriminations?"

"What could I possibly accuse you of? You were the victim," I said. "But I do have questions."

"Ask."

"You disappeared so completely from my life. Why?"

"Isn't it obvious?" he asked, irritated. "I was ashamed. I thought if you knew, you would want nothing to do with me."

"You were like my brother, Kolya," I said. "I thought we could share everything. But you never trusted me enough to tell me that you were gay. Did you think I would love you any less?"

He tried to continue looking at me with his clear open expression, but he faltered, and finally looked down at the heater. Lifting his hands from the cot frame, he put his elbows on his knees and interlocked his fingers.

"I'm not talking about being gay. That I would have shared with you, had I known," he said.

"You didn't know you were gay?" I asked. "That's hard to believe."

"I was an adolescent. What the hell did we know? We never discussed it. I didn't even know what it was, and back then no one could risk being openly gay. If I had shared it with you, all I would have been able to say is that I felt different from my friends. Would you have known what I was talking about?"

"Probably not. But I would have tried to understand. At least you wouldn't have had to struggle all by yourself with such terrible confusion."

"Nonsense," he said. "You would have ridiculed my bourgeois sentiments. Get out of your head, you would have told me. Stop thinking about yourself and become a more committed Socialist." He smiled wryly. "You've forgotten how much you believed in the power of the State to solve all the world's problems."

I didn't respond. Of course, he was right, just as Juliana had said. It would have been impossible for him to come to me.

"Don't feel bad, Dasha," he said softly. "We were children. Life rubs all the sharp edges off us, right?"

"Right," I mumbled. "Even so, I'm ashamed. I had no idea I was so inaccessible."

"Well, now you're accessible," he said, "so I can tell you what happened. I was sixteen, too young and naïve to understand. I was so confused, and the way I discovered just how I was different made it absurdly difficult. On the one hand, I was proud that a man as powerful and respected as Grigory was interested in me, in my career. And if such a man wanted me, and he wanted to do what we did together, how could it be wrong? At the same time, how could I face you? Even if what we were doing together was not a bad thing in itself, it was a betrayal of you."

"So you disappeared from our lives?"

"What was I to do?" he asked. "How could I face you, having had sex with your husband?"

"You didn't have sex with my husband," I said angrily. "He raped a sixteen-year-old boy who worshipped him. That's what happened. You were a child, Kolya, and he raped you," I repeated softly. "That was a crime. Would you feel the same way about what he did to you if you were a sixteen-year-old girl? Or is what he did only acceptable in your mind because you're gay? Or perhaps," I said, "you have to be gay. If you're not, you would have had to believe what happened was rape—and then how could you continue to respect him and accept his help?"

"I see," he said sarcastically. "So it was the rape that turned me into a queer. I'm not really gay—-Grigory's responsible. Is that what you want to believe?"

"Don't be ridiculous," I said. "Whether or not you're gay makes no difference to me, as long as it makes no difference to you. But the bastard robbed you of your childhood, took your family from you, and you from us. What he did is unforgivable."

Kolya was silent, but the pained look on his face was response enough. The enormity of what Grigory had taken from him was numbing. His innocence gone at sixteen; his career established under false pretenses, so that he always doubted whether he deserved the advancement he received. Now he found himself alone, without support. My husband had irreparably hurt and weakened this strong, upright man, whom I knew was good and kind to his core.

"He destroys everyone he comes into contact with," Kolya said finally. "Just look what he's done to you. That's why I couldn't face you—I was ashamed." He looked at his watch. "We only have a few minutes, Darya. Before you go I need to know what's going on. What were you doing at the meeting? You've never been interested in the dissidents, and Grigory has no interest in us, other than to crush the movement to a pulp. Is that why you're involved? And what's your interest in Dmitry?"

Just how much could I tell him, this man whom I still thought of as a brother? I was unconvinced that it was safe to reveal what I was doing— and even if it were safe for me, there was no way of knowing what danger I placed him in by speaking openly.

"What you're asking tells me how little we know of each other," I said. "Before I can answer your questions, you need to put some of my concerns to rest."

"I'll try, Dasha. But be quick. What concerns?"

"I can't tell whether you're working with the dissident movement, or whether you're just pretending to be involved so that you can feed Grigory information. I know he has some hold over you—but he's already taken your life from you, so what more harm can he do? Then there's Dmitry—what were you doing with him? And what made you run when you saw me?"

"Right to the point, as usual," he said with a humorless, unflinching smile. There was a grim expression on his face.

"Don't look at me like that," I said. "It makes me wonder whether I really want my questions answered."

"You always want answers," he said softly. "No matter how difficult they might be to hear."

"So go ahead."

"I know what your politics used to be—and I doubt they've changed. It's difficult for me to believe you're working with Grigory, especially if you're as angry with him as you sound. But you work in the propaganda office—he has access to all your work reports. So your presence at dissident meetings is as puzzling to me as mine is to you. I think you started going to dissident meetings on your own," he continued, "out of curiosity, and perhaps to remain informed about political currents in the country. But I know how the Ministry works—it's treason to be seen attending anti-government meetings without telling your bosses. So you request permission for an undercover assignment to gather intelligence for your own communications with Communists abroad." He looked at me, and the smile I was used to took shape on his mouth. "How am I doing so far?"

"Not too bad," I said. "You would have done well in military intelligence."

"Before I'm through," he muttered, "the generals who gave me a dishonorable discharge will wish they hadn't. And your shit of a husband will curse himself for not getting rid of me sooner."

"You're not going up against him, Kolya?" I was aghast. "Do you have enough people behind you?"

I didn't say what I thought—that I feared he wasn't sufficiently devious to bring Grigory down. Nor did I tell him that his words gave me a surge of optimism and hope. Perhaps, I thought, there really might be enough people willing and powerful enough to defeat my husband. But I underestimated Kolya's ambition.

"This is more than personal, Dasha. Grigory's only a tiny cog, but we're going up against the whole corrupt bureaucracy. They've been skimming the fat for decades, and now we've finally woken up to the fact that the country's bankrupt. They have to go. It's only a matter of time. They all know it, and they're terrified. This is as big as the overthrow of the tsars, the start of the Communist Revolution. That's what my friends and I are doing. Let Grigory think I'm doing his bidding. By the time he realizes I'm not, it will be too late. We're going to get rid of them. All of them."

I said nothing. I was horrified at the danger he was in, unwilling to be a party to what he had told me. Somewhere in the mix of my extreme emotions was a sense of guilt. I was a beneficiary of the corruption, a recipient of the fat being skimmed. If they threw Grigory out, I would receive the same treatment. I knew what it was to be afraid of my husband, but now I was suddenly afraid as I had never been before, of something immensely more powerful than he was. The Soviet people slept, dreaming their boring dream of Mother Russia and her red earth. But I knew from history the implacable force of the Russian people once they were awakened from their dreams of the soil, and what they were capable of was not pretty. But, I reasoned, Kolya was only one man, a man deeply troubled, who had every incentive to hate the authorities who ruined his life. Beyond a few dissident meetings and his very dangerous words, there was no proof that anything he predicted was even remotely possible.

"Don't look so surprised," he said. "You must have had some idea."

"Kolya, you're talking about treason." I found myself whispering. "You're planning to go up against the whole security apparatus. It's madness."

He shrugged his shoulders contemptuously.

"The dissident movement you know is made up of academics, writers and university students. I don't know what they think they're after. Maybe they're the canary in the coal mine. But there are others, and many thousands more will join us. Our goal is real." He rose from the cot, keeping his head bowed to avoid hitting the roof of the tent. "I've already said too much," he said. "I don't want to put you in danger."

"That's funny," I said, smiling. "I was afraid that I was endangering you."

"We're taking different routes, Darya," he said, "but we're headed in the same direction. You'd like to see an end to corruption and repression as much as I would." He reached into his pocket and took out a small notepad and a pen. "There's someone I want you to meet," he said, bending to rest the paper on the table. He wrote something quickly and as he rose, tore the page out and handed it to me.

"General Shaposhnikov. Here's his address and his phone. Don't say anything inside his apartment—it's bugged. He'll take you to the street outside his building to talk. I'll let him know you're coming—when you call tell him you're the granddaughter of his wife's dear friend, Yelena."

"At least that's partly true," I said.

"Always better to have a little truth in the lie," he said over his shoulder as he led me outside. I followed him down the narrow path to the road, where the car waited, hidden from sight by the branches of a massive oak tree. Before we reached the road he turned to me and placed a hand on my shoulder. We stood together in the shadows, and around us birds chirped at each other in the trees.

"One more thing," he said quietly. "You asked what Grigory holds over me, what he threatens if I don't do as he wishes." He paused. "He knows instinctively where everyone's weak points are—that's his success. And he holds hostage all the people I love—my parents, your grandmother Lena. You."

"Me?"

"He is a monster, Darya. He would cause harm to his own wife and child to keep me in line. That should erase any doubts about whether you can trust me." He threw his arms about me and hugged me. "I will give him whatever I need to keep him quiet, just as you will," he said into my ear. "I can't protect you from him, but I'm watching. If you need anything, ask my father to get in touch with me. I know how to find you if we need to talk. You can feel free to talk to Dmitry, if you need to. He's a friend."

"Is he your lover?"

He smiled.

"Just because I'm gay doesn't mean every man I know is my lover." Quickly he turned serious again. "Don't forget General Shaposhnikov—but give me a few days to get a message to him. He's a fine man—you can trust him down to his fingernails. Once you meet him, let him know we're related. But remember—-don't talk to him inside his apartment. The walls have ears." He hugged me again. "Kiss your baby for me," he said. "Katya, right?"

"Larisa."

"Larisa. I'll look forward to better times, when I can kiss her myself."

As he turned back down the path, I wondered how our world could have spiraled downward to the point where Kolya didn't know my baby's name; where he had to ask me to kiss Larisa for him because there was danger in bringing them together. I watched until his dark coat merged into the shadow of the trees, trying to calculate just how bad life would become before better times arrived.

On the silent ride back to Moscow, I thought about Larisa. When she was born I had no idea what life I was bringing her into. I tried with all my energy to summon a vision of what better times might look like. Perhaps it was a failure of imagination; perhaps what passed between us had shocked me into a stupor. Whatever it was, I could imagine nothing worse than the present—but neither could I conjure up a vision of anything better. It was life without possibility or hope.

But I was pregnant again, about to give birth to a second child. Only this time, I had an idea of just how toxic our world could be.

I felt choked by the very air in Moscow. It was thick and moist, smelling of rot and decay. It required a conscious effort to breathe. The idea of sleeping beside Grigory filled me with loathing, and I moved with relief into one of the other bedrooms, where I snorted and choked my way through the darkness. I had nightmares of my new baby being born a monster, and realized just how fearful I was that this child might inherit his father's character. I fantasized about traveling to Europe with Larisa, finding my way to the US Embassy and claiming political asylum. Ballet dancers did it. Writers and poets and opera singers did it—why not me? But Grigory would never let me travel outside the country with Larisa, and I would never leave her behind. At my worst moments, I cried myself to sleep, wondering how, after all Babushka's work and effort to make me into a strong and independent woman, I found myself in a marriage worse than any Grimm's fairy tale, to a husband whose manipulations were a match for Rasputin, and whose motivations were beyond my understanding. At moments I thought I was suffering from some kind of pregnant depression. I kept revisiting my conversations with Juliana, and then with Kolya, when I first knew with certainty that my world was coming apart, and wondered whether I was on a descent into madness.

I was considering signing myself into a rehabilitation spa for the overstressed elite—a place I would have shunned like the plague had I been in my right mind—when I recalled an event that occurred in 1986, around the time of Larisa's birth. It reminded me that not only was I not mad, but that I was absolutely accurate.

It was the nuclear explosion at Chernobyl—a national disaster. But the tragedy was far worse than it needed to be, the nuclear fallout far more widespread. The absence of safety procedures, fumbled recovery, and the clumsy, shortsighted desire to minimize the political fallout was a metaphor for how corrupt, inefficient and careless of people's lives our government was. The cement sarcophagus around the reactor would mark the epicenter of death and disease a thousand kilometers wide, and within a short period it became clear that the consequences down the generations would be catastrophic. No one remained immune. It catapulted me back into sanity and outrage, and I felt a renewed determination to bring my child into a world that had at least the possibility of improvement.

I decided to start by finding out who the General was, and why Kolya wanted us to meet. It didn't take long to discover that Matvei Kuzmich Shaposhnikov was an unsung hero, stripped of his rank years earlier for disobeying orders. In 1962, at the electric locomotive works in Novocherkassk, about 1,200 kilometers from Moscow, the authorities simultaneously cut wages by thirty percent, and bumped up the price of meat and dairy products. It was the kind of disastrous decision that could be made in our centralized economy, where the Ministry of Pricing set prices without taking into account the impact on the population. It was even possible that the two decisions were made independent of each other, the left hand not knowing what the right was doing. The decisions resulted in a spontaneous workers' strike—the first one ever acknowledged in the USSR. Seven thousand workers marched peacefully towards the center of the city, where they intended to demonstrate—and General Shaposhnikov was commanded to stop them, using whatever means he found necessary.

Instead, he ordered his soldiers to remove the ammunition from their guns, and for the tank brigades to do the same. Ordered to fire, his response was that he saw only Russian citizens, not an enemy dangerous enough to attack with tanks or artillery. As the peaceful demonstrators passed by, carrying posters of Lenin, the General asked where they were going. They intended to assemble in the town center, at the police station and Communist Party headquarters. He commandeered a car and sped into town to head the demonstrators off, but before he arrived, the forces in town, headed by other military commanders, had obeyed orders and opened fire. Many were killed or wounded, including young boys who had climbed into the trees to watch the demonstration. Several strikers were executed, and others sent to prison camps in Siberia. The event was barely reported. Within months it was as if nothing had occurred.

For years General Shaposhnikov sent anonymous letters to the Writers' Union in Moscow in the simple hope that the truth would be revealed. His letters were shared with the KGB, and in 1966 he was taken into the KGB offices, where they tried to convince him to admit to anti-Soviet activities. He wrote a letter to then KGB chief Yuri Andropov and managed to avoid going to prison—but he was stripped of his army rank and his membership in the Communist Party, forced into early retirement, and forgotten.

I could see that he and Kolya had something in common—both had been dishonorably discharged from the military, both of them unfairly. Beyond that, I didn't understand what purpose Kolya saw in my meeting this old man, who was already in his eighties, disgraced and invisible, without power or influence. He was obviously able to get around despite his age, but I understood why he might want to meet on the street outside his building—he would not have to travel far.

He sounded elderly on the phone, but he had a deep, commanding voice, and he agreed to meet me for tea the day after I called. He lived on the first floor of a small apartment in a shabby concrete slab building. It was clear that he had been deprived of the luxurious accommodations and privileges granted to those who retired from the military in good favor. When I knocked on the door it was opened by a woman in her fifties, who turned out to be his daughter. She took me into his study, a small, book-lined room, and I was struck at once by how easily he rose from his chair to greet me, and how he seemed to expand to fill the space around him.

"Perhaps," he said, "before we have tea together you would accompany me to the park to walk my dog."

I was wrong about him on every count. General Shaposhnikov was in his eighties, but there was nothing old about him except the lines on his face, and the loose skin around his deep brown eyes. They smoldered within their fleshy cage, and they were bright and full of mischief. He was a big man, still muscular, vigorous and unbowed, and I felt in him, rather than saw, the stability of an ancient, gnarled black walnut tree. His thick and roughened forearms would have been a perfect support for a children's tire swing.

I put out my hand but he stepped close and kissed me on both cheeks.

"Wonderful to meet you, my dear," he murmured. "I didn't know until you called that my wife's old friend—Yelena, is it?—even had a granddaughter."

He winked at me. His eyes showed that he had experienced both the richness and the poverty of the human spirit. He knew what it was to be wounded, and what it takes to heal. In the way he carried himself there was gentleness and courtesy—but he was wary. Not a man to be trifled with. I had no doubt that if he could make a difference, he would step into danger again without a second thought.

"My grandmother has spoken of your wife often," I lied. "It's wonderful to meet you, too, General Shaposhnikov."

"Please, I used to be General—but I lost my rank when you were still a little girl. Today I am a civilian, as you are. I am Matvei Kuzmich. Please, call me Matvei. Come," he said. "Let's take Sasha for a walk."

He ushered me out and we walked along the path, trying unsuccessfully to avoid the worst of the mud that was a normal part of Moscow spring. Sasha appeared suddenly at my side, an ancient, rough-haired wolfhound with a chestnut coat and a steely-silver muzzle, and poked her nose into my hand. Her head was at the level of my hip, and she probably weighed as much as I did. Sasha had no collar, but she stayed at his side as if they were connected by an invisible leash. When he stopped, she stopped immediately—sometimes even before he did.

"You see how she limps on the right," he said. "Her arthritis is painful, and she tires easily. It's very convenient to be able to walk her just outside my door."

He wore a green and brown wool plaid Scottish cap to protect himself from both the sun and the spring wind, and he stopped periodically, removed his cap and wiped the perspiration from his bald head with a large, checkered cloth.

"Thank you for making time to see me," I said.

"I happened to have an opening," he said with a wry grin, "in my very busy schedule. Besides, I was curious to meet the cousin of my good friend Kolya, who also happens to be the wife of Grigory Yanov."

I found myself standing still, as if posing for a photograph, watching his eyes as they wandered across my face with the open admiration old men can get away with because they no longer pose a threat. I was drawn to him, and I liked him immensely—and when he spoke again, I liked him even more.

"Rumor had it that Yanov married a most beautiful woman—but the rumors don't do you justice. You're not what I expected, though."

"Really?" I asked. "What did you expect?"

He shrugged.

"Perhaps, being an old man, I think in too linear a fashion," he said. "I thought you would be more like him —cold as ice, hard as diamonds, perhaps beautiful in the way cut glass is beautiful. And lethal, like a razor."

"You describe my husband accurately," I said, "but you don't know him at all. Neither did I, at first. He is far too insecure to have married a woman like himself. He would only have selected someone he thought he could control. And—" I looked at the ground, unable to meet his glance as I continued "—unfortunately for me, when we met I was young, and very impressionable."

I looked up to find him peering silently at me.

"Not anymore," he said, a grave expression on his face. "At least to me," he said, "you are still young, but you are no longer impressionable. And I have the sense that you are beyond being controlled by anyone. Pardon me for speaking openly, but knowing what I know of your husband, that doesn't bode well for your safety."

"I allow him to think that control still lies with him," I said, feeling a thrill of fear as I spoke the words. But I was not ready to have this discussion with a man I had only met, and I attempted to steer the conversation to a lighter topic. "Perhaps," I said with a smile, "what you see is just camouflage for the harshness you expected."

"I'm a pretty good judge of people, my dear," he responded gently, "and I don't think so. Actually your husband and I have never met, but he's made it a point to ensure that I know who he is. If we did know each other there would be little love lost between us. I understand from those who do know him that it's wise to be cautious when dealing with him."

"I've found that caution is always wise," I said, trying yet again to change the subject. "Kolya said I could be open with you. I assume you know what happened to him?"

"As much as he's been willing to share with me," he said. "I know all I need to know about your husband. Enough to know that I feel great sympathy for you. It is hard to imagine what it must be like, being both wife to Grigory, and Kolya's cousin."

"Matvei Kuzmich," I said gently, "I didn't come here to discuss my husband or my marriage."

"Of course not," he said, smiling. "I understand completely. So tell me, what can I do for you? Do you have any idea why Kolya suggested we meet?"

"I don't know. He said you were a good friend. Perhaps he thought I would be able to help you."

He smiled again, this time humorlessly.

"What help do you think I might need, my dear, that your husband—about whom we are not speaking—would permit?"

"I may not be the hard woman you expected," I said quietly. "But you don't know me. My grandmother raised me to be very determined, and my husband no longer dictates what I do or how I live my life."

He nodded agreement.

"I understand what you say. But if you will look over my shoulder, without being obvious, you will see behind me a dark car of some sort—I can never keep them straight—and at least two men whose hats and overcoats mark them as KGB. They're friendly enough at a distance, but they have me at all times under surveillance. They'll no doubt report back to their bosses that you were here, and I wouldn't want you to endanger yourself on my behalf." He looked down at my belly. "You are after all responsible for lives beyond your own."

"I'm well aware of my responsibilities," I said stiffly. I knew it was likely that our meeting would not go unnoticed, but seeing the KGB out in the open brought home my own vulnerability. And it rattled me that he so easily recognized how going against Grigory's wishes might endanger my children.

"I intend no offense," he said gently.

"None taken," I replied. "When I said Kolya thought I might be able to help you, I was referring to your efforts over the years to be reinstated. To get your reputation back, and to tell the true story of what happened in Novocherkassk in 1962. I could interview you and write an article exposing the truth. With the new openness in the country, perhaps it's time."

"That's a very generous offer," he said, speaking slowly. "But it's one whose time has come and gone, at least for now." He was not whispering, but his voice was low, a rumble from deep within his chest. "The work Kolya and I are involved in is very delicate, and I prefer not to draw attention to myself. Besides, history will give me back my reputation."

He rose from the bench we were sitting on, and I watched as Sasha slowly followed his lead. We returned to his apartment and drank tea together, and he showed me his most recent correspondence from the Supreme Court denying his plea for reinstatement. There were ample grounds for bringing charges of anti-Soviet propaganda against him, the final letter read, but it was impossible to find him innocent because "it is only in the context of *perestroika*... that it has become possible to find you not guilty." He laughed wryly at the tortured legalistic rationale.

"One day after I'm gone," he said, "when there is true openness and this kind of nonsense becomes public, it will be clear who was innocent and who was guilty."

We walked out into the darkened lobby of the building, and he accompanied me through the front door and onto the street. I thought, how courteous he is, and how sad that he's outlived his time. We walked halfway down the block, and then he stopped and put his huge arms about me. It was like being embraced by a bear, and for a brief moment I wished it would go on forever.

"Darya," he whispered, "listen carefully. Your visit this afternoon to a harmless old man will undoubtedly come to Grigory's attention. You will need to explain what you were doing here. When he asks, tell him the following. He knows this already—but he will be surprised to hear it from you. Tell him you understand from your sources that I'm the honorary chair of an organization of disgruntled military officers—men who in his mind fall into the category of dissidents."

"Is this true?" I asked, still in his embrace.

He shrugged his huge shoulders.

"What matters is that he believes it—and he thinks it's known to only a privileged few. The fact that you know of it will give your sources great credibility."

"He's going to ask why I wanted to talk to you in the first place, and why you were willing to see me. What do I tell him?"

"You think the KGB is the only organization with surveillance capabilities?" His voice was an irritable growl. "We also know who attends meetings, and which government employees have an interest in us. He won't be surprised that I was curious to meet you, a woman investigating the dissident movement. Tell him this: when you heard that I was honorary chair of a military dissident organization, you felt you needed to investigate. Tell him the truth—you offered to write an article exposing what happened in 1962, but I declined. And you learned nothing from me other than that I was charming. And by the way, I assume you know at all costs to avoid mentioning Kolya's name."

"I would never mention Kolya's name to Grigory. It would put us both in danger."

He stepped back and looked at me, his hands still on my shoulders.

"If you were my daughter, I would tell you, go home, take care of yourself, and bring the child you're carrying to a healthy birth. Leave the heavy lifting to others until your children can take care of themselves. You're more important to them than you are to any movement." He paused. "But that's much longer than you're willing to wait, and unfortunately you're not my daughter."

"So I should take care of my children while they're young, and leave them to live in this cesspool after I'm gone? What kind of mother would do that?"

"I had no illusions that you would listen to me. You're a courageous woman, my dear, but the line between courage and foolishness is very thin. If I were a younger man," he said, smiling wistfully, "I would tell you to go home and bring your child here with you, so that I can protect you both. But that time is gone. You're the only one who can protect her. Be very careful, Darya."

He smiled and kissed my cheeks, his lips resting for a long moment on my skin. There was nothing improper in what he did, but I felt myself suddenly in the embrace of a vigorous man who made no secret of his desire for me, and I was shocked to discover how easy it would have been to turn my head towards him and respond to his kiss. Instead I broke from him, and it came to me suddenly that General Shaposhnikov was far from harmless. He may be old, I thought, but perhaps it was premature to assume he had outlived his time.

❧

The months between my meeting with the General and the birth of my son, Anton, passed like a whirlwind. Grigory avoided looking at my body and when his eye did light on my growing belly, he made no attempt to hide a scowl of distaste. Carrying a child made me fiercely protective, and I managed to get through each day with my head held high. But it also made me deeply vulnerable, and I spent much of my pregnancy on the verge of tears.

I didn't want Anna to be alone with Larisa for days at a time. The only condition under which I would continue traveling was if Babushka would come and stay in the apartment to help take care of Larisa when I was away. Grigory initially objected, but he was far more interested in the intelligence I could gather than he was in who stayed with Larisa. It certainly wasn't going to be him, and he spent little enough time in the apartment as it was.

❦

Anna was the oldest of twelve children. Before arriving in Moscow to work for us, the only indoor toilet she had seen had been recently installed at the school in her village. She was overwhelmed by the variety of food in our kitchen. She had never seen a chicken served whole; she had never eaten an entire orange, and I watched her eat her first peach, delighted by its sweet tartness. I had to remind myself that we were beneficiaries of Grigory's position, and that what had become commonplace for me was unheard-of luxury for most Russians.

She was eighteen, with straw-colored curls at her neck, smooth cheeks, and a thin, shy mouth. Her small breasts, little more than swollen nipples, were visible through her clothes until I took her shopping to buy appropriate underwear. She had narrow hips and a tiny waist, and I thought that her growth must have been stunted by a poor diet. But she was agile, and the skin at her temples was translucent; she had big, clear long-lashed blue eyes, and the sound of her laughter as she played with Larisa or talked with Babushka in the kitchen was open and joyful.

So far Grigory had not shown the slightest interest in her, but I knew by then that nothing was beyond the bounds of his appetite, and I thought he would be far more circumspect with another adult in the house. It was the least I could do to keep Anna safe, and I knew that Babushka would protect Larisa with her life.

❦

And so I continued to travel, and before the doctor forbade me to fly at the end of my seventh month, I had made several trips—to Prague, Lisbon, Rio, Warsaw, and Manchester. I spoke as always to members of the International Communist Party, distilling the gristle of Soviet life into a tasty stew, stirring up enthusiasm in the uninformed for the false ideals of our broken State. I dreaded the guilt I felt following these talks, which inevitably ended with pointed questions from those who were more perceptive, or more concerned about how much reality differed from the pablum we were feeding them. But I was no longer a believer, and I could not ask others to swallow a brew laced with strychnine.

My lack of conviction must have been obvious, because the skeptical began to approach me with increasing ease. Previously, they had sidled up to me nervously and whispered their questions about government crackdowns in my ear. Now they came boldly; called me from the lobby of my hotel asking for private meetings; requested that I talk to a small group in someone's living room before I returned to Moscow. Whenever these meetings took place, my list of those for whom the bloom was off the Soviet rose, grew. They believed as strongly as before in the principles of communism, but they understood, finally, that the story was much different from the reality of Soviet life.

As the opposition continued to grow in strength and in numbers, the right wing of the power elite felt themselves more and more threatened. Grigory must have been watching this intently, waiting for the moment when he could capitalize on their fear, using my list of names to boost his value.

At the same time, for his own survival, Grigory had to find a way to prove to the powerful kleptocrats he served that they couldn't do without him. He had worked hard at making himself indispensable, insulated them from the reality of their own dirty hands. They must have had a moment of fear when they realized how much he knew about each of them. That knowledge, combined with his volatile and unpredictable personality, ultimately turned him into a liability. Out of favor, he needed to do something to redeem himself.

With the full knowledge I now have of him, I imagine him watching me through hooded eyes, a cobra waiting for the perfect time to strike, his forked tongue slithering silently in and out of an expressionless, scaly mouth.

✿

Other than disobeying Babushka, I think the first time in my life I stood up to authority was my absolute refusal to have my second child in the hospital. Once was enough. This time I would not cede control of when I saw or fed my baby to the wardens—kind and well-meaning, but wardens nonetheless—in an institution for birthing. Instead I would have a midwife at home. But my resolution was no match for my son's eagerness to leave the womb early, and he arrived three weeks before he was due.

In my fantasies I imagined Anton kicking determinedly through the birth sac until it broke, and then swimming breaststroke through my water down through the birth canal to emerge gasping in the world. He cared not at all whether we were ready for him, and we were not. He didn't know it, but he wasn't quite ready to be born yet, either. He spat himself out twenty minutes after my water broke. I called the midwife.

"Please come quickly," I said. "The baby's coming early."

"I don't do births this premature," she said. "If I'd known I would never have agreed to come to you."

Even in my frantic state I recognized the absurdity of her comment, and I heard myself giggling. "How was I to know it would be premature?" I said. "Of course you'll come. I still need you."

"No," she said firmly. "There's nothing I can do. This is far too early and too dangerous."

"So how do you expect me to manage?"

"Call an ambulance and get to the hospital," she said. "It's what every other mother facing a premature birth does. Why should you be different?"

I called Anna, who came running, and then the ambulance. Anton had already taken his first cry, and was lying on my belly, when the medic arrived. She examined him carefully.

"A fine little boy," she said. "Very small, but he seems healthy. And this young woman could be a midwife herself." She turned to Anna, who blushed at the compliment. "How did you know what to do?"

"My family lived far from hospitals," she said shyly. "By age fifteen I had already helped birth three brothers and sisters."

"Your mother taught you well," she said, beginning to take Anton from me.

"What are you doing?" I asked.

"Taking you to the hospital."

"Why? You said he seems healthy. Why do we have to go to the hospital?"

"Because you need to rest, and we want to make sure your boy gets enough nourishment."

"No," I said firmly. "We stay here. I can rest better in my own bed, and Anton knows already where to get nourishment. Besides, I have Anna, and now we know he's healthy, she's as good as any midwife."

We argued, but I would not be swayed. The medic left reluctantly only after I'd promised to call and see my obstetrician and the pediatrician within a week.

Anton was small, and far more vulnerable than Larisa had been, but he retained the determination that had propelled him into life. He slept with his face screwed into a tiny, obstinate knot, and when he fed he attached himself to me with a ferocity that made me laugh, his jaws moving up and down, his swollen lips holding onto my nipple like a miniature vacuum. Perhaps because he was a boy, perhaps because he was so fragile, I loved him even more fiercely than I loved Larisa as a newborn. But there was a desperation in my attachment to Anton. He was after all Grigory's son, too, and a part of me dreaded the possibility that he might be anything like his father. I found myself watching him like a hawk in search of behavior that might indicate a tendency to violence or sadism, both impossibly difficult to identify in an infant. What would I have done, I wondered, had I seen him glaring balefully at a stuffed bear, or trying in a focused and methodical way to tear his swaddling cloth into strips? I would have been terrified, I suppose, and continued to watch and worry. I smothered him with the love I feared Grigory was denied as a boy, and I would show him that not every woman is too weak to defend herself and her children from an abusive man.

When I gave birth to Anton, Grigory was in Lithuania, carrying out some unspecified task for his bosses. He could just as easily have been in Kyrgyzstan or in Vietnam, but I didn't want to know his whereabouts or what he was engaged in.

I found myself wondering now, whenever he was away, what kind of reprehensible work he was doing, and whether he chose his destinations based on how easy it would be to buy long-lashed young boys with smooth, tight little buttocks, or pubescent girls with incipient breasts like Anna's. Today I am mortified to think that I could have imagined such things and still been willing to live with him. But my life seemed both impossibly difficult, and horribly normal. I was convinced that wherever I went, he would find me. Without recognizing it, I had begun to think like a victim, abused by a man with superhuman perception and power. I felt that all I could do was to wait for something to happen, something outside us, to change the balance and make it possible for me to disappear.

Before Anton's birth, whenever I found myself thinking like this, I attributed it to hormonal imbalance. After his birth, I was convinced that I was suffering from post-partum depression. It will pass, I thought. I had suffered some adjustment after Larisa's birth. This, I thought, would be just the same.

Anton was a month old before Grigory showed any interest in his son. It was the mid-afternoon feeding and I was in our living room, sitting in the cushioned rocker with Anton at my breast. I looked down at his face, eyes closed tight as he pulled hard at my nipple. I smiled at him, thinking how much force that little mouth was capable of. Larisa sat on the carpet scribbling in a coloring book with a purple crayon. Babushka sat opposite me, knitting a baby blanket in bright blue and yellow wool. The rhythmic clicking of her needles was constant, but at a much slower pace than I remembered. Her eyesight was no longer sharp, and she moved a little more tentatively, but in her eighties she was still vibrant and energetic, and she insisted upon coming each day on the Metro. I had offered to have one of Grigory's drivers pick her up, but she refused.

"I'll let you know when you need to cart me around like a wobbly old table," she said impatiently. "But by that point I won't be any use to you and the children, will I? In the meantime I can manage perfectly well without help from Grigory's goons. The last thing I need," she whispered, "is to be indebted to your husband."

Grigory came in the front door. At the sound of his feet approaching from down the hall, the warm, light energy in the room suddenly darkened, became cool and thick, as warm syrup does when refrigerated. He removed his jacket as he came in, watched us with unblinking eyes. With a graceful pivot he draped his jacket over an end table and lowered himself into the armchair beside it. Facing me, still staring as Anton suckled, he rolled up the sleeves of his starched white shirt, loosened his red and grey striped tie, and undid the top button of his shirt with one hand. The crease in his blue pinstriped suit pants was as sharp as it had been when they were delivered from the laundry. He looked down at Larisa.

"Come," he said, beckoning. "Show me what you're doing."

She looked at me out of the side of her face, anxious, and I nodded, smiling at her. She rose from the floor.

"You don't need permission," he said softly, glaring at me, "to come to your father."

"She's not used to you being here," I said. "You're not often here during the day."

I watched as she slowly toddled over to him, head lowered, holding the coloring book against her chest. Her fine, light brown hair was cut short in back, and fell across her forehead in a little fringe. He opened his legs and pulled her onto his lap.

"What's this, Lara?" he asked, pointing at the scribble.

"Anton," she said quietly.

"So this is how you see your brother," he said, losing interest. "Very nice."

He put her down on the floor again, leaning forward toward me, his eyes on my exposed breast, and the little mouth pulling at me.

"Lena," he said without turning to her, "Leave us. Take the child with you."

"By child I assume you mean Larisa," she said without looking at him. She rose more slowly than necessary from her chair, tucking her knitting under one arm. "Your son will make a big hue and cry if we disturb him before he's finished suckling. Come, Lara," she said. "Let's go help Anna. She's making meatballs for supper."

Larisa took her great-grandmother's proffered hand. I watched them walk out together, and then turned to Grigory. He wore his physical grace effortlessly, perhaps without awareness. He sat with one ankle over his thigh, leaning far forward so that his elbows were resting on his calf. The muscles of his chest and shoulders were outlined through the shirt, and I found myself examining my own response to his physicality. He was now in his forties, and the features that made him so handsome as a young man were starting to work against him. His fair coloring showed the creases in his skin, and the blondness of his hair had softened the lines of his face. His blue eyes, once so startling, were now pastel, almost watery blue. He was not nearly as magnetic as he seemed when I first met him as a girl of nineteen. There was something thin, almost insubstantial, about the surface he displayed. It was as if all the play had gone out of his skin, as if it had dried out and draped tightly over the framework of his face. His cheekbones brought to mind pictures I had seen of a starving cow, hide hanging from the structure of her hips. The person I saw was unclean. While I was repelled, it was a relief to discover that I no longer had to monitor my own attraction to him.

"What are you doing home so early in the day?" I asked quietly.

"This is my home," he replied evenly, still looking at Anton's mouth firmly affixed to my breast. "I come and go as I please."

"That you come and go as you please is not in question," I answered. "It's just unusual for you to be here midafternoon."

He nodded, his lips pursed.

"The boy knows how to suck, doesn't he?"

"He and Lara both," I said. I removed Anton's mouth from the nipple and covered my breast. "He needs a break. You want to burp your son?"

He shook his head briefly and I raised Anton to my shoulder, gently rubbing his back, waiting for the air to come up. Grigory continued to look at me, silent and pensive.

"Shaposhnikov," he said eventually.

As he said the word, Anton burped, and I turned my head to see whether I needed to wipe his mouth. It was a convenient cover for my jumping heart.

"The poet Shaposhnikov? " I asked casually. "Or do you mean the disgraced general?"

He ignored me.

"Some time ago it came to my attention that you went to see him at his home," he said. "I waited for you to share this fact with me, but apparently you didn't think it important enough. Why were you keeping this from me?"

"Keeping what from you, Grisha?" I asked, sufficiently emboldened to show the contempt in my voice. "That I'd been to see an old man who was discredited and lost his rank and his pension twenty-five years ago for refusing to fire on unarmed civilians? If I didn't tell you perhaps it's because you haven't been around much," I said. "I may still be your wife, but other than making it clear that you wanted me to continue traveling into the seventh month of my pregnancy, you've shown no interest at all in what I do or what I discover. Besides, I assume that whatever I discover, you make it your business to know already."

I wasn't going to offer the information I had without putting up at least the appearance of resistance. That would have been out of character.

Besides, there was still something in me that relished the cat and mouse game.

"He's an old man, a recluse. He lives in disgrace, embarrassed by his poverty." Grigory spoke quietly, as if we were in the midst of a rational discussion, and he was simply explaining something I didn't fully grasp. This was the closest he came to using the voice of reason with me, and he used it only at specific times—when we both knew precisely what he wanted, and that I would eventually give in—but that I would first put up a struggle. He used the same voice, whether he wanted information from me, or a particular kind of sex. But that was over.

"I want to know how you convinced this hermit to open his doors to you, and what you discussed with him. Why did you want to meet with him in the first place?"

"I had my reasons for seeing him," I said. "Tell me why he's so important to you?"

"That's not for you to ask," he said clenching his jaws and glowering at me. "But I will tell you that there's more to him than appears at first glance."

"I agree," I said. "He's much more than an old hermit."

Grigory looked surprised at my response.

"In what way?" he asked.

"He carries himself like a much younger man," I said, looking at him brightly. "He's funny and charming, and I enjoyed spending time with him."

"I'm hardly interested in the old man's sense of humor," he said sharply, jumping from the chair. The color had risen quickly to his face. "Tell me why you went to see him."

Anton had fallen asleep on my shoulder. Grigory's raised voice startled him, and his whole little body convulsed briefly.

"Sit down," I said in a whisper, glaring at him as I rocked softly back and forth. "If you wake your son this conversation is at an end."

He was taken aback, but he turned and lowered himself into the chair. I don't think I had ever given him an ultimatum before, and I was hardly aware that this was new behavior for me. If it was a change, it was one I had grown into naturally. I smiled at him. It was a perfect time to surprise him further.

"I heard rumors about Shaposhnikov," I said, "rumors that he was, as you say, far more than he appeared. I wanted to find out whether there was any truth to what I was hearing. So I called him."

"What did you say?"

"I told him the country was in need of new heroes, people to look up to. With the new openness, we felt it was time to go public with his story, let people know the truth about how he was unfairly deprived of all that was important to him. With that line, how could he refuse to talk to me?"

"No one ever accused you of lacking balls," he said. "So you had tea with him, and you walked his ancient mutt in the park. What did he say to your offer?"

"Not interested. He said it was the distant past, and he had no intention of dredging up all that dirt. Besides, he's sure history will vindicate him."

"All history will do," muttered Grigory, "is bury him, the old fool."

"I didn't think he was foolish."

"Yes," he said with a nasty sneer, "you thought he was charming. What rumors did you hear that made you want to talk to him?"

"Sometimes I don't understand how this works," I said. "The Ministry of Foreign Affairs expects me to go abroad and talk about what's happening in the country. But when I arrive, I discover that foreign communists know more about what's going in on our backyard than I do. It's embarrassing, and it doesn't make it easy to recruit people."

"What exactly are you referring to?"

"I'm referring to the dismal intelligence I get from my own Ministry. I have to hear from sources outside the country how widespread opposition to the government really is. Apparently it extends beyond academics and artists, and the number of disaffected people in every sphere of Soviet life is growing rapidly, people who won't rest until there are major changes. And some of them are in positions to make those changes happen. Powerful positions."

"What kind of positions?" he asked.

Anton began suckling in his sleep, and I shifted him from my shoulder to the other breast, always amazed that he could feed while sleeping.

"It feels," I said quietly, looking across the room at him, "as if you're milking me for information."

"Very funny," he said, staring uncomfortably as Anton pulled ferociously at my nipple. "Answer my question. What kind of positions?"

"Military positions," I whispered.

"So you hear rumors about dissension within our armed forces," he said. "What of it?"

"It's more than just rumors," I said. "My sources tell me that mid-level officers have come together to form a powerful dissident organization. I don't know what their grievances are—I assume some are personal, like those who've been denied advancement, and some are purely ideological. Whatever it is, they're intent on change."

He waved his hand dismissively. "It means nothing," he said. "It's inevitable that in a military as vast as ours there will be some dissatisfaction— and a few among the troublemakers will be officers."

"If you're so sure," I said, "I'll discard the rumors I hear."

"What rumors?"

"About Shaposhnikov."

He tensed as he leaned towards me. "Precisely what are these rumors?"

It was clear that he didn't want to appear too eager for my response, and I took pleasure in knowing that for once I was a few steps ahead of him. I held my breath for a moment, pretended to adjust Anton's position.

"One rumor is that they've asked him to be their honorary chairman," I said. "Another is that he's accepted."

He leaned back, brushed the lank, blond hair from his eyes, and carefully draped his forearms on the armrests. Most men would have shown some wrist, but my husband's elegant hands hung loosely over the ends, emerging from his starched cuffs just where his wrists ended. It was a carefully cultivated series of movements intended to appear simple and relaxed. I knew he was anything but.

"It is of interest to me," he said, looking down at the floor and speaking in a low, controlled voice, "that your contacts have access to this rumor.

Where do they get their information?"

"I assume your interest in the source," I said, "means the information is accurate?"

He looked up from the carpet and I shivered at the ice in his blue eyes. "Whether or not the information is accurate," he said levelly, "it's my job to know where it originates. Do you have any idea?"

"None."

"You ask me to believe that you never questioned your sources about the origin of their information."

I had rehearsed in my mind so frequently the story General Shaposhnikov told me that I had begun to believe it was true—but I had to remind myself that although I had contacts, I had no data to back up my story. There were no rumors. There were no sources of information. Grigory was a skilled interrogator. If he suspected me of lying, he would phrase his questions so that I would eventually trip myself up. My breathing quickened and I fussed with Anton on my shoulder to hide how flustered I was. My agitation awoke him, and he began to whimper. I put him to my breast again and he began to suckle.

"Of course I question my contacts," I said. "My job is to foster relationships—not to endanger them by questioning the source of information. I don't have to tell you how jealously informers guard the well."

He nodded as he considered my explanation. There was no uncertainty in him—he was either convinced by my words, or he was sure I was lying. He rose from his chair, and the intensity seemed to drain from him. As I thought about it afterwards, I had to remind myself what this was all about. Grigory was predisposed to believe me. The more accurate my informers outside the country were, and the more detailed and classified their information, the greater likelihood that their sources were officials with access to the Kremlin. When the time came to expose them all, the corruption he would bring to light at the highest levels would leave no room for doubt in his bosses' minds about the value of keeping Grigory Yanov around.

"This is good work," he said. "I don't want you to jeopardize your contacts, but the next time you travel, it would be wise to let them know you're curious about their sources."

He did up the button at his collar, straightened his tie, and walked towards the door. It seemed he was about to leave, and I prepared to take a sigh of relief. But that's not what happened. Instead he quietly closed the door, turned around and came back to stand at my side. He looked down at our son, suckling hungrily, his perfect lips around my nipple, red cheeks drawing in and out, eyes squeezed shut. When I glanced up at Grigory's face and saw him musing, a quizzical look on his face, I thought for a moment that he was about to do something tender. His hand came up, and I expected that he would stroke his son's cheek. Instead he lowered his hand to Anton's head and rested it for a moment on the little crown covered with fine, light brown hair. Then he moved his hand to my breast and with two fingers on Anton's cheeks he flicked the nipple from his son's mouth. Taking my nipple between thumb and forefinger, he rolled it roughly against the side of his finger, and without warning he squeezed. Hard. I gasped in pain and tears came to my eyes as I looked down and saw my milk leaking across his fingers and down his wrist. Anton, surprised to be pulled so suddenly from the breast, opened his eyes wide, found his voice and began to squeal.

"You're hurting me," I said through gritted teeth, outraged that he could see the tears welling in my eyes. "Stop it."

I looked up to see him staring down at me, as if I were an experiment.

"Let me go," I said.

He ignored me, continued to squeeze even harder. Both my hands were busy comforting Anton, and I knew that anything I might do to end the pain would put him between Grigory and me. I felt violated and embarrassed, but more than anything I was in shock. I couldn't imagine what he was trying to accomplish other than to cause me pain. An image came to me of the young boy he had been, watching unmoved as his stepfather tore open his own throat. He squeezed harder than I thought possible, and I had to do something to stop the pain. I moved Anton to one side, bent my head and clamped my teeth on the soft part of Grigory's hand, the part between his thumb and forefinger. Very quickly he grabbed the underside of my jaw, his grip like a steel claw, and forced me to release my bite. He leaned down and we looked at each other. I assume he saw hatred and fear in my eyes. What I saw in his eyes was emptiness and calculation, which were far more frightening.

"Be very careful, Dasha," he said. He spoke softly against the background of Anton's cries. "You would be foolish to bite the hand that feeds you."

Then he rose to his full height, licked my milk from his fingers, turned and walked out. I heard his steps going down the hallway, heard the front door open and then close behind him.

I breathed a shuddering sigh of relief. With one hand I put Anton's mouth to my uninjured nipple while with the other hand I cradled my bruised and inflamed breast. Both my hands were shaking.

Grigory had dramatically changed the dynamic between us, and there was no going back. I went over in my head the events of the last few minutes. He never praised me. He usually gave me orders, and I had become used to taking instructions from him as if I were a simpleton. But I stood up to him. I refused to simply give him what he wanted and argued for my position. And he had decided to hear me. For years he had been grooming me to develop my own international network, but there was never any doubt in his mind that whatever I developed he would ultimately own and control. The rumor about General Shaposhnikov, and what it implied about the value of my contacts, was some indication to him that I had finally made the grade.

That didn't mean he could trust me any more than he had previously. What it meant is that I had suddenly become far more valuable. At first I thought that was a good thing—anything of value must be worthy of protection and nurture. But protection is confining, and being an object of value might subject my movements to greater scrutiny. It must have been clear that being of value to him was no longer my primary goal—and he wanted to show me that my goals were unimportant.

His last action proved to me without a doubt that if he ever felt betrayed or threatened by my potential defection, he was capable of anything to prevent me from getting in his way. Only if I continued to do the work he deemed valuable, would my children and I be safe. If he discovered that

I was against all he stood for, or became unwilling to share with him the knowledge I gained, I would become less than useless.

❦

Anton came out of the womb hungry, like Larisa, and with her wide-eyed curiosity, but without her natural sweetness. He also emerged with his right foot flexed, ready to kick the first ball that came his way. And within six months, he made it clear that he no longer needed my milk. He weaned himself from the breast, making it abundantly clear that he was ready to try solid food. His independence left me without purpose. My body was no longer a source of sustenance for my child, and not a source of pleasure to me, or to anyone else. Grigory kept himself at arm's length, and although I was relieved not to have to deal with his sexual demands, his lack of interest, his unconcealed disgust with my physical being, didn't do much for my self-esteem. I went back to work, unhappily, and when he suggested that I pull myself together, get rid of my fat belly, and begin traveling again, I was almost relieved. In a fury I began going to early morning fitness classes at the gymnasium, working myself so hard that by noon I was exhausted. My milk quickly dried up, and my breasts shrunk to their pre-pregnancy size. And again, I was away from home for days on end.

❦

This time was different. My isolation was complete. I had lost all the things that defined me. I felt useless to my children, my marriage was dead, and whatever belief I once had in the USSR or in communism was in shreds. I was desperate for something, some light, some meaning or purpose, in my life. And then I was sent to Italy, for a conference with the Italian Marxist-Leninist Party in Florence.

The conference took place at Party headquarters, and following the first day, I returned to my hotel, a shabby old place called Il Granduca. As I was about to enter the tiny elevator to my room, a young Italian woman wearing a press badge around her neck approached me.

"I am Valeria Bassani," she said. "I listened to you all day at the conference." She spoke in English, frequently the common denominator when I was unfamiliar with the local language.

Her face was flushed, she held her hands together at her waist, and her knuckles were white. She reached for the press card at her chest, but it was wound around the shoulder strap of her bag, and she fumbled, red-faced, as I watched.

"Please relax," I said, smiling. "You're tying yourself up in knots."

"I am embarrassed to be so nervous," she replied, smiling back. Quickly she detached the clip from its knot of cords, and pulled herself together. She showed me the card. "I produce the Marxist-Leninist Party newsletter, and I wonder if you would give me a few moments."

"So, you want to interview me?"

"Yes," she said.

The Ministry frowned on unscripted interviews. Although I could represent my country, I could not be a mouthpiece, and my personal story was out of bounds. So far I had complied with the regulation. I didn't mind talking to reporters, but it wasn't worth the risk of having something misrepresented in print. But I was tired of being alone. Valeria had followed me from the conference and worked up the courage to speak to me, and the effort it took showed on her flushed cheeks. She was a fresh-faced young woman with a brunette wave over her forehead, big dark eyes, and I could see that despite her nervousness, she had a nice sense of herself. She was clearly new to the job, and she lacked the hard edge of most reporters I knew. I liked her enthusiasm, and something in her manner—and perhaps in my mood—encouraged me to do something different. I agreed to talk to her, because although she was five or eight years younger than I was, I felt decades older, and she reminded me of whom I had once been.

"I am so grateful," she said, eyes wide with surprise. I realized that for her this had been a long shot—she had expected me to refuse. "Please, tell me what your schedule is, and when would you like to meet?"

It was early evening, and I had missed lunch, answering questions as all the attendees sat and ate. I was hungry, and tired of eating hotel meals alone.

"How about now?" I asked.

"Yes," she said, "that would be wonderful! If you have no plans, perhaps I could—" she hesitated "—perhaps I could invite you for dinner. We could talk and have a glass of wine."

"What a good idea," I said, raising a cautionary finger. "But we understand that nothing gets printed without my approval."

"Of course," she said.

"Good. I'm tired of talking politics—perhaps you'll tell me about yourself first, and then you can interview me."

"Me?" She laughed, surprised that I might be interested in hearing about her. "If you're writing an article about me it will be very short."

"No articles," I said. "I'm just interested in finding out how a young woman in Florence becomes interested in a Marxist-Leninist organization."

"Well, there's not much to know, but I will tell you anything you want to know."

As she led me out of the hotel, I wondered when the last time was that I could have made such an offer, and known that it was true.

"Where would you like to eat?" she asked.

"This is my first time in Florence," I said. "You're the expert—why don't you suggest a place."

"Well," she said, "it would be easier if I know what kind of foods you prefer."

"Fresh pasta," I said without hesitation.

It was a warm evening, and she led the way through ancient cobbled streets to a small courtyard, where we sat beneath an umbrella, drank a bottle of Sangiovese. I ordered the pasta specialty of the house; she had grilled fish. The wine was rich and earthy, and the aroma alone was enough to relax me.

"You know the origin of the word," she asked, "Sangiovese?"

I sipped from my glass, shaking my head.

"It's from the Latin," she said. "It means the Blood of Jove."

It was easy to be with her, and for the first time in a long while, I felt myself reclining into a sense of comfortable inactivity. True to her word, Valeria answered all my questions without hesitation. She had been born in Florence, as had her parents. She and her husband lived in a small apartment upstairs from her parents. Her father was a pharmacist, and owned several stores in the city. Her paternal grandparents—both Jewish communists— were murdered in a night raid during the war, victims of Mussolini's fascist brigades. That brought me up short—and I realized that if Grigory or anyone else was setting me up, this was the perfect way to do it. I had let down my guard. This woman might be nothing more than a wonderful actor with an excellent cover story, an undercover agent from any one of a number of organizations within the USSR or without. I slowly raised my glass and took a sip, cradled the stem in my fist, and looked across the table at her.

"What is it?" she asked, alarm in her dark eyes.

"I was just wondering," I said slowly, "what the chances are that you've been sent to spy on me."

She looked at me with astonishment and began to laugh. I am being ridiculous, I thought.

"It must be very hard," she said thoughtfully, "to live like that."

"Like what?" I asked.

"To be always on the lookout. Waiting. Expecting betrayal. I imagined your life to be very meaningful and exciting, but perhaps it is also full of stress and conflict."

"That's probably true of all our lives," I said. "Do you have children?"

"Yes," she said. "I have a little boy. And you?"

"Two," I said. "Two years old, and nine months."

"My goodness," she said, "how hard it must be to travel and leave them."

I nodded, not wanting to reveal my feelings, but apparently I had already done so. Valeria stretched out a hand and lay it on mine.

"I am sorry," she said softly, "I didn't mean to pry."

As she leaned forward, the chain around her neck came out of her neckline. On it was a six-pointed star. She saw me staring at it.

"Is something wrong?" she asked.

"Is that a Star of David on your necklace?" I asked.

Her shoulders stiffened. "Yes," she said. "Remember, I told you about my grandparents?"

"Of course," I said. "But I'm curious. Are you—" I had to think of the word "—an observant Jew?"

"Yes."

"You practice the ceremonies, and you keep the holy days?"

"Yes."

"And your—your place of worship—requires that you go there to pray?"

"I go to my place of worship—my synagogue—because I want to," she said defiantly, and pointed to her chest. "It is *my* choice. Why these questions? You think something wrong with my belief?"

"Not at all," I answered. "I don't mean to pry, either. I just wonder whether you see any contradiction between being a communist and practicing Judaism, or any religion."

Her body seemed to relax, as if she understood the thrust of my questions, and was no longer worried that I was heading in a threatening direction.

"I belong to the Marxist-Leninist Party," she said. "Our goal is economic equity. No one asks us to announce our religion at the door." She paused and looked at me as she decided whether or not to speak her mind. "I know in the perfect Socialist State there is no place for God. You would like communism to replace religion—but we are not so naïve as to believe it has, or ever will. This is not the USSR, Darya. Jews have been a part of Italy for two thousand years. We are as embedded in this culture as the Catholic Church."

I wanted to say that tsarist Russia was also a God-ridden place, and that the nobility used God to keep the peasants in poverty and ignorance. But that would have been dogma speaking through me, and I was silent. It wasn't what I wanted to say, or where I wanted the conversation to go. I had no interest in debating doctrine with this delightful young woman—but I couldn't quite get my arms around what I *did* want.

"I am wondering," I said, "what it must be like to be you. How does it feel, to live your life?"

"What a strange question," she said. "I've never thought about being anyone else. What are you asking me?"

"You're not much younger than I am, but you seem so much freer than I ever was at your age—unlimited by doctrine and politics, able to speak your mind and your heart. I find myself," I said, "jealous of that freedom."

"I would not have believed that possible," she said slowly. "But perhaps I am more fortunate than I know. How do you live if you can't speak what's in your heart?"

I managed to smile at her, all the while wondering how I could become her, give up my life and the lies I was married to, and become someone for whom life wasn't worth living if I couldn't speak what was in my heart. She had no idea, this lovely young woman, how fortunate she was. Even as I thought it, I felt disloyal to Babushka, who gave me everything, including my sense of self, and the knowledge that I was loved, unconditionally. But we struggled. There was never enough money, and we were essentially alone. Valeria, on the other hand, was brought up with a loving mother and father in a financially comfortable family, and with life experience that led her to believe speaking her heart was a right.

I wondered, what kind of man was her husband? Did he resemble her father? I wished I had had a better sense of how to judge a man. But with my own history, how could I have chosen well? I had no role models other than my older cousin, Maxim, who had been more like an uncle to me. Was it any wonder that my choice of a husband was so dreadfully bad? The truth was, I did no choosing—he selected me, and I was ripe for the taking. I didn't know it then but in Grigory I saw both the father I never had, and the accomplished man who would complete me, be my lover, and provide the security that I had never known. Could I possibly have been any more mistaken? My nurturer became my jailer, my abuser. The security he provided, my prison. Our children, his hostages. We pay a price for everything. I was so enmeshed in the lies that prevented me from being honest with myself, I had no idea what to do or how to begin.

"You are unhappy in your work," she said quietly. "Aren't you, Darya?" She looked at me intently across the table. "And in your life, too."

I shook my head, astonished at the tears that suddenly filled my eyes.

"I don't think this is the interview you wanted, Valeria," I said, rising. "It's late—perhaps we should call it a night."

"You're right," she said, leaning back. "I don't want to interview you. I'll find someone else to use for the newsletter. Don't leave. You need a friend tonight." She gestured at the chair I had just vacated. "Please, let me be that friend."

Friend? I thought. Do I need a friend? Of course I did. I had no friends— they were all gone, unable to deal with the threat my husband posed, or with my passive acceptance of his temper, his arrogance, his ruthlessness.

I turned to look at her, wondering how this could possibly be a serious offer, and whether she had an alternative agenda. Her cheeks were smooth, her eyes clear, and as she met my glance she flicked a strand of hair from her forehead. She wore an expectant, hopeful expression, and I couldn't believe that she was anything but genuine.

"We can all use a friend," I said with a forced smile. "Now and then."

"Thank you," she said breathlessly, gesturing again to the chair, "for trusting me."

I slowly lowered myself to the chair I had just vacated. We sat in silence for several minutes, glancing at each other, taking small sips of water, listening to the night sounds of Florence—music, laughter, the clinking of glasses, mopeds humming through the winding streets. The awkwardness I felt gradually dissipated.

"I can't tell you much about myself that would not be dangerous to us both," I said.

"You don't need to tell me anything," she responded.

"Yes, I do," I answered. "You know, we all have a story we tell about ourselves—it may or may not be true, but it's what makes us what we are, and determines how we respond to what happens in our lives. My story has led me in some very wrong directions."

"No one would ever know that," said Valeria. "You carry yourself with such strength and determination. You're a powerful speaker, and you seemed so—so unapproachable. That's why I was nervous at first, talking to you."

"I'm glad you did," I said. "I've never had that problem—talking to people has always been easy for me, no matter how many stripes on their shoulders, or what their titles. I always knew, even from my childhood, that I would be a leader, someone people would look up to and depend on. But in my personal life, my difficulties are the result of bad judgment." I paused. "I have made some huge mistakes."

"You don't have to tell me this," she said, but I waved her words away.

"Before I was old enough, against the advice of the wisest woman I know, I married my husband. Even then he was a powerful man. It was a bad mistake from the start, but over the years he's become someone I fear and despise. He would never let me leave him, and he holds our two children as leverage over me. So you're right. I am not happy in my life. But perhaps," I shrugged, "we all make some kind of deal with the devil."

"I don't believe that," she said, shaking her head, "any more than I believe we can't change the stories we tell ourselves about our lives."

"Perhaps you're right," I answered. "I certainly hope so, but I think it's too late for me."

"It may be too late to change your life," she said, "but it's never too late to change your story. Not as long as you're alive. And just think how different you will be with your children if you change the story that drives your life, and how that might change theirs. Is there some way I can help you to do that?"

I thought for a moment, not about what she could do to help me—but whether I would have the courage to utter the words in my throat.

"There is something you can do for me," I said, feeling the thud of my heart. "You can arrange a meeting for me. I need to be sure no one knows, no one follows, no one ever finds out—if this meeting is discovered, Valeria, my children's future will be damaged, and my career—my life, maybe—will be over. I place tremendous trust in you for this. Can you help me?"

"I have no access to the kind of people who could harm you," she said. "What does this person do—or know about you—that puts you in such danger?"

"It's not what he knows that endangers me," I replied, "but what he represents."

"Who is he?"

"Valeria," I said, swallowing hard. Something massive squeezed my chest and for a moment it was impossible to breathe, impossible to make a sound. One part of me, horrified by what I was doing, followed a lifelong pattern, trying to keep me safe by keeping me silent, preventing me from uttering words that might reveal anything that might raise a question about my background, my activities, my inner life. But Valeria was right. I didn't want to live my life in fear of speaking my heart.

"I have questions that only one person can answer." The words came out as a hoarse whisper. "Valeria, I want you to arrange a meeting for me with your Rabbi."

She looked confused—he was the last person she could have imagined me wanting to meet.

"My Rabbi?" she whispered.

"Yes, the Rabbi who serves in your synagogue."

"But why?" and then the light dawned in her eyes. "Darya," she began, "are you..."

"Please," I said quickly, "I'm just at the beginning of this, and I have no answers. I don't even know the questions. Do you think he will talk to me?"

"If he's going to be here," she said, "I'm sure he'll want to talk to you. When is your next trip back?"

I would be returning in three weeks for another meeting, and true to her word, Valeria spoke to her Rabbi. He agreed to see me, and together they made plans for our meeting. I would be staying at the same shabby hotel, and on the night I was to have dinner with Valeria and her family, she and her husband would drop me at my hotel. An hour later, when it was reasonable to believe I had gone to bed, I would slip out the back door of the hotel and meet a friend of theirs who would guide me to the Tempio Maggiore, the Great Synagogue.

When I returned home and told Babushka what I was planning, she was shocked and fearful, and then, excited. We were in Anton's bedroom, dressing him together before I went off to work.

"Do you remember where you hid the teapot?" I whispered. "In your room?"

"How could I forget such a thing?" she said, reaching up to pinch my cheek. "It's been under the floorboard since I showed it to you when you were thirteen. Unless he's had my room searched. But I think if they'd found it he would have used it as blackmail against you. Or he would have made me disappear. Like Kolya."

I ignored the reference to Kolya, wondering how much she knew about what happened to him. I had told her nothing, not wanting to provide knowledge that might enrage her. She was quite capable of saying something to Grigory without imagining what the consequences might be.

"Tell me what you want me to do. Dashinka," she whispered, "are you sure you can trust this young woman?"

"She's young and enthusiastic," I said, "and honest. She's not motivated by political gain. She has a good heart and she did this because she wants to be my friend. Of these things I can be sure. Beyond that—" I shrugged my shoulders "—the only thing I know for sure is that I don't want to live the rest of my life in ignorance because I'm afraid."

I saw her back stiffen. "This is how you think I've lived?" she said reproachfully, "in fear and ignorance?"

"No," I said gently. "You've lived with determination; you've shown me that it's always right to be brave, and that sometimes the most courageous thing is to do nothing. But the challenges we face are very different now. As a child you were given a secret—-and you've kept it all your life in order to ensure our safety. The way you've lived shows me that there is power in the truth—and now it falls to me to begin unwrapping the secret. I'll do it carefully, but I want to know." I picked Anton up in one arm and embraced her with the other. "Whatever strength I have to do this, comes from you."

"Well, I've done the best I could with the life I was given. I only wish," she said wistfully, "that I could make this journey with you. When you return you'll have to tell me everything that happens."

A few days before I returned to Florence, I had Viktor drive me to Babushka's apartment. I told him that she wasn't feeling well, and I was taking her some medicine and hot vegetable soup in a pot. He remained in the car while I went upstairs with my bag. I didn't want her moving chairs and kneeling down on the floor, and I wasn't sure that she could pry the floorboard up on her own. But when I arrived she was sitting calmly on the edge of her bed, the floorboard replaced. Beside her, resting on an ancient sheet, was the old Matryoshka doll containing the teapot.

"What are you doing?" I asked. "I didn't want you to...."

"I'll be the one to decide what I can and can't do on my own. Let's go."

"Go?"

"If I stay here all day sick, Viktor will think I'm at death's door, and Anna will worry. Besides, the children will miss me if I'm not there. They all think I'm a stubborn old woman, so let me be one." As she spoke she leaned over the bed, wrapped the teapot in an old sheet, and carefully stuffed it in the bottom of the bag. "Masha next door is crippled with arthritis, and she can't get out easily. I've already told her to take the soup. We can leave it on the counter in the kitchen. Viktor will drop you off at your office and then take me to your apartment on the way to work. When I get there I'll hide the bundle in the closet in Anton's bedroom. Come on, Darya." She rose, beckoned impatiently. "You make me nervous. Let's get this done."

Viktor smiled at her as he exited the car and held open the door for her. A small, wiry man in his late forties, hair chopped at the sides, a scar at one temple. I was never sure where he came from, but he was the least objectionable of the men Grigory chose to drive us around. At least he had a sense of humor, and he was capable of conversation.

"Babushka," he said, "I'm glad to see you feeling better." He had a deep, resonant voice that always surprised me coming from such a small man, and when he smiled he showed heavy gold inlays on either side of two missing teeth. "I knew if hot soup could fix what ails you, you'd be coming back with us. Takes a lot more than that to keep you away from the children. I should have put money on you."

"You'll not bet on me," she muttered as she sat down and looked up at him from inside the car, "as if I were some horse in a race. You keep your money in your pocket. If you get to my age, Viktor, you'll need every coin you have."

Viktor grinned.

"With respect," he said, "there's not much chance of my reaching your age."

She continued to glare up at him for a long moment.

"Not if you continue in this line of work," she said.

"I'm just the driver," he said, leaning down to her, still grinning, "for Grigory Yanov and his family."

She looked at the pistol in his shoulder holster, visible under his khaki jacket.

"Yes, you're just a driver," she said, "and I'm the chestnut mare you should have bet on."

As he strode around the front of the car and took his place at the wheel, he was laughing out loud, his mouth open and his golden teeth visible.

A few days later I was in Florence sitting across a battered desk in the Rabbi's study at Tempio Maggiore, the Great Synagogue in Florence. The Rabbi was in his fifties, wearing a dark suit, the jacket buttoned. A black skullcap perched atop his bald head, and he had a white beard trimmed close to his face, prominent cheekbones, and pale skin. His forehead was creased into permanent furrows, and there were bags under his eyes. He looked like a man who spent very little time sleeping, and much time in thought.

"So," he said. He steepled his hands on the desk before him and looked across at me, the trace of a smile crinkling his eyes. "To what do I owe the honor of this visit, arranged in such secrecy, and with such caution? And from a member of the Soviet Communist Party, no less?"

I looked back at him, wondering why I felt so nervous before this religious functionary, a man who believed in stories of gods and prophets no more real or meaningful to me than dragons or fairies.

"Thank you for agreeing to see me," I said, "so late at night. I'm very grateful."

"I haven't done anything yet that warrants your gratitude," he said slowly, his eyes glued to my face. "But the way Valeria described you, I would have wanted to meet you under any circumstances. I'm most curious."

Neither one of us looked at the object, wrapped in a white hotel towel, which I had removed from my canvas shoulder satchel and placed on the corner of his desk when I came in. Before I left, Babushka asked me what I would do if security opened my suitcase and found the teapot.

"If they open my suitcase, they'll see an antique Matryoshka doll that I'm taking as a gift to the head of the Communist Party in Italy," I said. "I don't think they'll open the doll."

There was no security problem. Valeria and her family were wonderful. Everything went according to plan, all for this—to find out the meaning and significance of an object made by my grandmother's great-grandfather nearly a hundred and fifty years earlier, and perhaps to reclaim a part of my history, cast-off and lost. When I planned it, I didn't realize that when the moment came, it would feel quite so momentous.

We stared at each other across the desk, he patient, and I, suddenly tongue-tied. "Would it help you to know," he said gently, "that you are not the first person to sit uncomfortably in that chair, not quite knowing how to ask the questions that brought you to me?"

"Not really," I said, and I tried to smile. "I think you'll find my questions somewhat unusual."

"Let me be more specific, then." He leaned forward as if to confide in me. "You are not the first young woman from Moscow to land up in my study with an object wrapped in cloth, wondering what it means. And if past experience is any indication, the object you brought in with you was inherited from one of your forebears, whom the authorities believe was a son of Mother Russia. But you have reason to believe otherwise."

I must have looked startled, because he sat back again. The expression on his face was not smug, but he was not displeased to have surprised me.

"So you believe there are others in Russia in similar situations?"

"I know there are," he said. "I've met several over the years. But you're the only one who is a member in good standing of the Communist Party." He rose from his chair, a tall, skeletal man with rounded shoulders. "It must be important to you, this visit. You've put yourself at great risk in coming to see me."

He came around the desk and sat in an armchair closer to me. On the corner of his desk, which was now between us, rested the wrapped bundle.

"Since the thaw in the USSR, many *Refuseniks* who were allowed to leave the country came through Italy, and some ended up here in Florence on their way to Israel or the United States. I've met with many, here in this office. It seems to me they fall into three groups. Some are practicing Jews. Others are not, but know their families gave up being Jewish in order to survive. Then there is the third group, who have a suspicion based on an old family tradition, or something a grandparent said, or the presence in the family of some venerated object." He paused. "Which are you, Darya?"

In answer I reached over and picked up the bundle. I set it on my lap and silently unwrapped first the towel and then my great-grandmother's ancient threadbare shawl, laying bare the faded red and yellow paint on the Matryoshka. I untwisted it and the top part came off, revealing the teapot. Holding it by the open top, I lifted it out. It felt foreign in my hands. Not just unfamiliar, but alien, and I had no idea what to do with it. I set it back on the corner of the desk.

I hadn't seen it since Babushka showed it to me briefly over twenty years earlier, when she introduced me to our heritage, and in the process tore down the scaffolding on which I had built my life. I had hidden my experience of that evening from her—it would have broken her heart to know how badly she had injured me, although perhaps she knew, and would have done it, anyway. Over the years I also managed to hide the experience from myself in some small, closed cave of memory. Now, as I looked at the teapot, the memory I had so long managed to bury came flooding back. I was again thirteen, the sense of personhood I had worked so hard to cultivate, destroyed. I felt ripped open and dismembered, pieces of my carefully dovetailed self lying still and unmoving on some cold stone floor. And I had lost whatever tools I needed to reassemble my separate parts into a cohesive whole.

The elongated teapot was smaller than I remembered—small enough to be cradled easily within a large man's cupped hands. The Rabbi had pale, long fingers with soft, immaculately cut nails that might have been carved from alabaster. His hands moved lovingly about the round pot belly and fondled the narrow spout that rose up from the base. Entranced, I watched as he unscrewed, unhinged, separated and lay the discrete parts on the desk in an organization that eluded me. Even to my untutored eye, the parts were exquisitely made.

"I have seen pieces like this," the Rabbi breathed softly, "but never one crafted so well, or so lovingly."

"How can you tell it was made lovingly?" I asked. It was a silly question. I was curious, but I lacked the vocabulary to form intelligent questions.

"Look here," he said, pointing to where the spout was soldered to the body. It was smooth and even, almost invisible. "See how carefully this has been joined together? Only a highly trained artisan, with a sense of the importance of his work, would have taken the time to do this so carefully. This join alone could have taken days. And look at the blue stones. I doubt these are sapphires, but they may be lapis lazuli, or tourmaline. See where they're set into the silver leaves? With such delicacy? There's no evidence that these stones are affixed to the silver leaves, or to the brass beneath, yet they've remained firmly attached since—-" he looked at me "—since whoever made this." The whole device now laid out on the desk, he leaned back in his chair.

"I assume you're here because you want to know what all these parts are for," he said. "At least, that's the reason you tell yourself you're here."

"You think there's another reason?"

"In my business, there are generally hidden reasons behind the stated one." He smiled. "You belong to the scientific age. Only what can be measured, explained, untangled, is of value. You are here, curious about an old teapot. Nothing more. And so you can forgive yourself for this inquiry."

He leaned back in his chair, interlaced his fingers across his buttoned jacket. "Am I right?"

"I don't know," I said. I had never considered what actions I might or might not be able to forgive in myself, but his question made me feel uncomfortably exposed. "Perhaps."

"But you still hold fast to a basic tenet of communism—that there is no room for any God in your system. That belief and faith are tools of an oppressive economic system. That biblical history is only myth, without relevance today."

He paused and leaned forward to rearrange some of the pieces. I could see that there was a system in his ordering of the little cups, saucers, containers, scrolls and other objects that had been detached from beneath and within the belly of the teapot. With delicate, knowing fingers, he was finding ways to reunite some of the pieces.

"And even though you believe this," he said, slowly, still intent on rearranging, "your system continues to penalize and disenfranchise a whole people because of what happened two thousand years ago. Your communism discourages religion and denies the divinity of Jesus Christ, yet it is a commonplace among Soviet people that Jews killed the son of God. So how much more danger do you put yourself in—danger of betraying what you believe most fervently—by coming here and asking me what it means to be a Jew?"

"No," I objected. "That's not what I came here to ask."

Again he smiled.

"Is it not?" he asked, his eyes still lowered to the desk, where he was fiddling with a pile of tiny, painted saucers. "In my work, I often find the most important questions remain unasked. Haven't you discovered the same thing as you travel the world talking about communism? That what people ask is not always what they want answered? Like your teapot, which seems to be one thing, but is in fact another." He lifted up the thing he had created, a delicate filigree made of six tiny saucers attached around the edge of a slightly larger plate. "These little plates, for example, hidden in the body. When shown the light of day, they combine to form a Seder plate, which we use to celebrate the Passover, the expulsion of the Jews from Egypt." He put the plates down again. "Which, by the way," he said dryly, "is not some mystic make- believe passed down through the ages from one ignorant, impressionable generation to another. It's a historically documented event. A part of our culture. Come," he said, rising from his chair. "Before I answer whatever questions you think you've come to ask me, I want to show you something."

On the way to meet the Rabbi, I had been too intent on secrecy, and on getting to my destination, to notice the building we were in. Now, as I followed him down the stairs, I realized that we were in a new addition to the building, in which his study and the administrative offices were housed. He led the way through a short corridor and into what looked like a vestibule, and pushed open a massive walnut door. My impressions of the synagogue were first of the smell—lemon-scented wood polish, lamp oil, the must of damp, ancient, closed-in spaces. I remember white travertine and pink limestone; huge Spanish-looking, almost Arabic arches; alcoves and closed pews with family names on them. There was a massive dome high above us, lit from above just enough to allow a sense of the richness of the place. The walls were decorated with arabesques in gold, and painted in a geometric pattern. The overall impression was one of wealth, stability and beauty.

Even I was aware that this building married elements of Christian cathedrals to Spanish and Moorish architecture. The dimly-lit beauty, the magnificent design and the heavy, spirit-filled silence in this huge space, all took my breath away. But even as I was awed by it, I felt the old sense of contempt for the magnificence and show. This, I told myself, like any other religious building, was intended to impress the congregation. It was a trap to convince them that this world was of less significance than the next, and so to lull them into acceptance of their lives.

"We Jews are called the People of The Book—but I think we are also the people of the half-full glass," said the Rabbi, his voice hushed beside me. "Who else but a people who always expect an optimistic outcome, despite their history, would have imagined building such a structure? This synagogue—" he gestured around us with one hand, pale in the distant light from the dome "—is thought of as one of the most beautiful architectural achievements of the nineteenth century in Italy. It would be funny, if it weren't so ironic or sad."

"I don't know what you mean," I said, realizing as I spoke that I was whispering.

"I know," he said, turning to look at me in the half-light. "That is why I've brought you down here. To see this through my eyes, so that you can perhaps come to understand something about the blood that runs through your veins. And so that, if the time comes, you can make an informed decision about whether you want any part of it."

He stepped forward, walked further into the interior until I could barely see him, and turned to face me. We were separated now by about twenty paces, and he was visible in the semi-darkness only as a darker shadow. But when he started speaking, the acoustics gave his whispered voice a startling clarity. It was an echo that suffused the entire sanctuary. The sound seemed to have no source of origin. It might have been a voice from the lectern, or from some source high above us.

"In the last five centuries, Jews have been expelled from Florence at least five times. During most periods when we were permitted to live here, we were confined to a Jewish area—a ghetto—and at times forced to wear clothing that identified us as Jews. When the various city-states united as the Kingdom of Italy in 1861, the Jews were emancipated—allowed to live freely. And we thought, finally, we have arrived. Within twenty years we felt safe enough to undertake the construction of this building. It was a symbol of our belonging; a tribute to the cultures and religions with which we lived side by side. At its height there were three thousand proud members of this community. Then came World War II. Everyone in Europe suffered—the Jews were not alone. The Nazis used this building as a garage, and at the end tried to destroy it as they retreated. Thankfully, they failed. We fared better than many communities—by the end of the war, a third of the population still survived. But throughout Europe and the USSR, Jewish communities like this one were wiped out. Only a few old people were left. Synagogues were empty, cemeteries untended. And even here, there was an insufficient number of members to support this building. And so we thank God for tourists from the New World, whose curiosity leads them here. And whose generosity makes it possible for us to maintain this ancient, beautiful hulk as a memorial to the better days that, if they came at all, came and went in the flash of an eye."

He walked further into the gloom until he disappeared, and his voice continued in the darkness.

"Why do I tell you this? Because I understand why, faced with the choice to remake themselves, those born as Jews might choose to be something else. Anything else, in fact, that might make their children's lives less subject to a repeated history of rejection and then tolerance and then again denunciation. Never real acceptance. These patterns will continue to repeat themselves in coming centuries, as they have in the past. My grandfather knew this. He used to tell me, we Jews have learned to live with our suitcases packed and ready to go."

He paused briefly, and his voice echoed and faded into the silence as I tried to imagine how it might have been had my own grandfather, Vasily, lived with his suitcase packed. But his disappearance had nothing to do with whether or not he had been a Jew.

"I don't have to tell you how this has played itself out in the USSR. We are destined to go down through the centuries shadowed by this black cloud from which we never seem able to escape. So why would anyone in her right mind choose to be identified with us, history's scapegoat? I can think of no good reason to be identified as a religious Jew, unless you believe in the Jewish version of God."

He reappeared from out of the shadows, and walked slowly towards me.

"But we are also a culture that spans the globe, with a very specific place in history. Our friends point to the influence of Maimonides and Spinoza and Disraeli, and to the many Jewish philosophers, scientists, artists and philanthropists; our enemies point to Karl Marx, and Trotsky, and to those scientists who had a hand in the discovery of nuclear weapons. As with every people, there are those among us who've influenced the world for both good and for evil. But it's undeniable that our influence, from the ancient world through to modern times, is way out of proportion to our numbers. Once you understand that history, you may decide for the sake of expediency to keep your identity to yourself. But you might perhaps begin to acknowledge it, to be curious about your heritage, and to be proud of it."

I followed him back to his study, our echoing footsteps on the stone floor the only interruption to our silence. We resumed our chairs on either side of the desk corner. Between us lay the parts of the teapot.

"Do you know who made this, Darya?"

"My grandmother's great-grandfather," I said.

"So it has been in your family for six generations, hidden for at least three, at some risk. It must have seemed important to them."

I nodded.

"Do you know why he made it?"

"If I knew why he made it, I would understand what it meant. There would have been no need to meet with you."

"You're right—there would have been no need to meet with me, at least, no need to ask about the teapot. But as I've suggested, the teapot may simply be the vehicle you're using to ask other, deeper questions."

He leaned forward and made minute adjustments to the arrangement of pieces on the desk.

"I told you earlier that I've seen such things before. In parts of Eastern Europe, where Jews were always about to be kicked out, it became fashionable among skilled tinkers to design such things, embodying as many as possible of the rituals and traditions that Jews practice. This teapot is really a compendium," he said, "of Jewish religious ceremony. Let me show you."

First he explained the Seder plate, surrounded by the six little saucers. Each one contained something symbolizing the expulsion from Egypt— bitter herbs, for the years of slavery; greens, to be dipped in salt water, for the tears shed; an egg which for some reason was a sign of mourning and rebirth; a mix of chopped apples and nuts, representing the mortar with which the Hebrews built the pyramids. And lastly, the shank bone, representing the paschal lamb cooked and eaten on the last night before the exodus, whose blood, daubed on every Hebrew's doorpost, was a sign to the Angel of Death to leave the house untouched.

When the spout was detached and folded back on itself, it became two small candlesticks, which represented the candles lit each Sabbath evening, along with the Sabbath blessing, which he recited for me. There was a spice box, and place to light an eternal flame, and on the oil vessel were written the Hebrew words, "Man's soul is the light of God." There was a tiny scroll, written in miniature Hebrew letters on parchment, that the Rabbi said contained the biblical narrative of the Book of Esther, traditionally read at the festival of Purim. When the base was detached and unlatched, out folded a menorah, a small candelabrum lit during the eight-day holiday of Hanukkah. When he was through, he upended the teapot and looked at the underside through a magnifying glass, and he pointed out that there was a small Jewish Star engraved to one side, with lettering at its center.

"When your grandmother gave you the teapot, did she tell you her great-grandfather's name?"

I thought back to that evening in our room, when Babushka first told me everything, and I remembered looking with her at the unfamiliar star on the base, and searching for the letters of her great-grandfather's name, which she was convinced were somewhere engraved. And from some recess, I pulled up the memory of his name.

"Shtein," I said hoarsely. It was the first time the name had passed my lips, and it sounded terribly foreign. But at the same time, it felt deeply intimate. "Our family name was Shtein," I repeated, taking ownership. "And my great-great-great-grandfather's first name was Asher. Asher Shtein."

"Now," he said, "through the glass, look carefully at the middle of the star. What do you see?"

"Two letters," I said. "In a script I don't know. What do they say?"

"They are your great-great-great-grandfather's initials," He said softly. "The letters are A, and S." Again he leaned back in his chair. This time, I did so, too.

"So now we know Asher was the craftsman. He signed it using a

Germanic script, which tells me that your people may have spoken other languages, but that German or Yiddish was their main tongue. They probably came from somewhere in Latvia, perhaps an area called Courland. We know that he was a Jew, and that somewhere between his being a Jew in Courland and your grandmother receiving this icon, their Jewishness lapsed. Do you know the story?"

I nodded.

"Would you tell me how it happened?"

And so, for the first time in my life, I shared the story about how Babushka's mother received the teapot, and how her father carried it back with him to Illuxt. I told him about Esther's decision to change their names and their identities, and how, through her stepsister, meeting for twenty minutes at a deserted rail stop in Siberia, the teapot came into Babushka's hands.

"That's some tale," he said. "A heavy burden for a girl of thirteen. And you've carried it for many years. Alone."

"Yes," I said.

"I hope you feel lighter, having shared it with me."

I was numb. "I don't know what to feel," I answered. "Perhaps I will know better tomorrow."

Do you know what happened to the top?" he asked.

"What top?"

In answer he slowly reassembled the pieces, looking at me periodically to see if I was watching. Having shown me how to disassemble the teapot, he was now showing me how to put it together again, should I ever wish to. When he was through, he held it up and pointed to the top. For the first time, I realized that he was right. Something was missing.

"It's the lid," I said, looking closer. "Why would the lid be missing?"

"We don't know what purpose the lid served," he said, turning the teapot around carefully in his hands as if searching for the answer, "other than to close off the top. But I believe such an artifact would not be complete without a cup to drink wine on the Sabbath, and we have found no wine cup hidden within the teapot. So it must be found elsewhere, and there is only one possibility—the lid was also the wine cup. It could be lost. Or perhaps someone in the family kept it so that they would be always connected. You'll probably never know, but maybe your grandmother remembers."

And that was it. We talked a little more, I thanked him for his explanation and his wisdom, and he invited me to return if I ever needed his help. I wrapped up the teapot, and Valeria's husband came to pick me up. Using a different car, and taking a circuitous route, he drove me back to my hotel. I don't remember the short trip, nor do I remember going up in the elevator to my room. But as I climbed into bed and turned out the light, the thought came to me that I had no idea who I was, or who I wanted to be.

For reasons I could not articulate, I found myself sobbing into my pillow with a sadness so profound that even in its midst I was surprised at the intensity of my grief. I understood for the first time that a heart really could break. For the life of me, I couldn't understand why I was weeping as if mine had already shattered.

PART THREE

Steven's Story

My father dragged me away from South Africa—he would say rescued me—when I was seven. It was 1962, a year after my mother was killed by the apartheid government's security forces. After her murder, many who had been my parents' friends dropped my father like a hot rock. We were under constant surveillance by the Special Forces, and he felt it impossible for us to remain in the country. When he was offered a job in the Engineering Department at Boston University, he jumped at the opportunity to leave a bitter past behind us, and start a new life.

As an adult, I understand how impossibly challenging it must have been for him. He had been reared with servants—doing laundry, preparing food, caring for a child, were foreign concepts. He is a solitary man, non-communicative, probably depressed. But he was determined, and stubborn, and the only thing he hated more than emotional confrontation was asking for help. Alone, without a community or a network of support, he managed to adjust to being the single father of a seven-year-old boy mourning the loss of his mother.

We rented an apartment in Cambridge, and he learned quickly how to be an American. When we first arrived, he didn't know how to boil an egg. In later years, he joked that he wouldn't have known how to make a sandwich if you gave him a can of tuna, a jar of mayonnaise, and two slices of bread. Even a can opener wouldn't have given him much of a clue. But in our new life, he realized that being able to cook was a survival skill. So we learned to cook, and he involved me in the learning. We made a game of it, experimenting first with simple meals.

We started with cheese sandwiches grilled in a frying pan, using white bread and processed cheese. Graduated to multigrain bread with Gouda, cheddar, and Jarlsburg. For breakfast we started with plain fried eggs, and added bacon. Moved on to scrambles, with cheese, onion, red peppers. As his confidence grew, he decided to make spaghetti sauce from scratch, and I recall laughing with him as we cleaned up chopped tomatoes, onions and garlic that had slopped all over the stovetop, the counter and the backsplash. I stood on a stool with him behind me, stirring a steaming pot of pungent tomato sauce, into which he ladled the hamburger he had cooked in a pan with garlic and spices. He liked his spaghetti al dente; I didn't. We agreed that we preferred our meat sauce with more meat and less tomato, but he liked oregano on his, while I liked grated parmesan. He made me feel that it was a joint effort; that my likes and dislikes were as valid as his, and so we took his spaghetti off the stove before mine.

By the time I reached the age of ten, I was competent to handle the gas stove. I knew how to ladle pasta out of the pot and onto a plate without burning myself or making a mess. Pretty soon we advanced to lasagna, and when he bought a little house in the town of Dennis on Cape Cod, he added fresh fish to the menu. We experimented with bluefish, salmon, and cod at the local fish market. His preference was salmon; I was perhaps the only child on Cape Cod who actually liked the rich, oily taste of bluefish. We baked potatoes on the grill, made salads with fresh radishes and cucumbers. Went clamming on the beach, and learned to make clam sauce with our pasta. And in winter we made soups and stews, which we froze. Chicken noodle soup, beef and barley soup, rich beef stew with carrots and potatoes.

Cooking and eating together became our primary means of communication. As an adult, I recognize that talking made my father uncomfortable. He was far happier engaging with me in an activity that required no revelation or exposure.

Weekends on the Cape, when we weren't on the beach swimming or throwing a ball, we spent hours in silence. He wrote and graded papers, while I discovered gradually that I was meant to be an artist, and began spending afternoons drawing and painting. I sat on the beach with my drawing pad, trying to capture the dance of the gulls as they swooped to the sand, running themselves to a stop and then turning into the wind, like an audience anticipating the start of a show. I began to draw—and then to see—the living exhalation of clouds over the ocean shifting shape, and how the water mirrored their movement. I learned how the wind played with the surface of the sea, brushing it gently and raising ripples, like goosebumps. And when it stormed, how the character of ocean and sky darkened, each loosing fury on the other, so that instead of playing together they were opposed in a dramatic struggle as the sea lashed out wildly, while the sky roiled and smoked. The wind, invisible by itself, was the evil force that pulled ocean and sky into raging battle.

For me, the challenge in painting storms was to capture the power of the invisible wind, so that watching ocean and sky colliding, it was clear in my paintings that there was a power behind them both, forcing them into conflict. That became one of the themes in my work, and I struggle with it still, finding ways to show the resentful participation of ocean and sky, forced into battle by the wind.

As I describe my childhood, I'm surprised at how well-rounded and normal it sounds. I don't think about it that way. In retrospect, I didn't have a bad childhood, but if my father was good in many ways, his preference for non-engagement made it easy for him to withhold information. He told me nothing about our family. His father, my Papa Mischa, died soon after we left South Africa, and all I knew about him was that he had been born in Latvia and brought to South Africa as a boy. When he and his brother were in their teens, just before World War I, their father returned to Latvia, leaving them to fend for themselves. I tried to pull more information from my father, but he refused to be drawn out.

He also refused to discuss the details of what happened to my mother. My own experience of her disappearance is that one day she was there, and the next she was gone, murdered. There was no funeral; he never shared with me where she was buried. Neither of my parents had siblings, and my father never spoke of other family. I grew up believing that we were alone in the world.

My father was never one for celebration, and most of the time that was fine with me. But during holidays, when my friends were with their families,

I felt a sense of bereavement, loneliness and perhaps anger. Another father might have recognized that I needed more in the way of family. Perhaps if he'd been less comfortable in such isolation he might have remarried, and life would have been very different for us. But I learned to accept that we were alone. I had friends, their parents liked me, and I was often included in their family events. As a result I had people around me who became family by choice. And I convinced myself that I was fortunate to be able to choose, and not to have family imposed on me by blood.

❧

I have a crystal clear memory of how I discovered that we were not alone. It was a Saturday night, and I had just turned sixteen. I had a shiny new laminated driver's license in my wallet, next to a ten dollar bill and five ones. Nestled beside the bills was a single condom. Top of the line. Lambskin. Lubricated. I didn't know at the time that all condoms were individually sealed, and took pride in the fact that I had been thoughtful enough to splurge on one that was. I had no realistic prospect of ever unrolling it, but hope springs eternal, and I was confident that one day my dreams would come true. Even if the dream was premature, I didn't want to be caught unprepared.

My first act when my driver's license arrived was to call the most unattainable girl in my high school class and invite her to Harvard Square to see an old classic—*The African Queen.* Her long shining hair draped over one shoulder, and she had a Mediterranean complexion that set off her angular face, dark eyes and lips that I can draw by memory several decades later. In my wildest adolescent dreams I could never have hoped to see her naked, but my eyes undressed her with an expertise my hands could only have longed for, and to me her body looked unclothed no matter what she wore. To top it off, she was unpretentious, smart, and soft-spoken.

I was surprised when she accepted my invitation—and even more surprised by a deeply desired but wholly unexpected goodnight kiss that seemed to go on forever in the front seat of my father's car. Eventually she pulled away from me, both of us panting and unbuttoned, her hair wild and sweet over her face. With her forearm across her forehead, she gathered her hair, hooked her hand behind it, and tossed it carelessly across her shoulder. It was a particularly masterful gesture, showing that she was in full control of her unruly hair when she wanted to be—but it raised her breasts in a way that made her seem exposed and vulnerable. The combination may not have intended to inflame, but it did, and I moved towards her mouth again, her lips swollen and her eyes wide and moist.

"No," she said, her hand on my chest. "Stop, Steve. Not here. This is really uncomfortable."

"How about the back seat?"

It was all I could come up with on short notice, and if she was disappointed by my suggestion she didn't show it. I quickly discovered that she knew a great deal more than I did about what felt good, and where, and why. Had I known what might have been possible I would have suggested a more comfortable venue—the basement of her house, the park, even the mystery and excitement of a hotel room—but I was young and tongue-tied, I wasn't thinking clearly, and I hadn't yet learned that timing is everything.

When I arrived home I was still tingling with elation at what I had discovered, and I stumbled uncomfortably into the apartment hoping that my father was asleep, and that I could go directly to my room and relieve myself. But my father was bent over the kitchen table, a tall, gaunt man with greying hair, and his shoulders were shaking. I had no memory of ever having seen him cry, not even when my mother died, but here he was, sobbing. My first thought was that someone had seen us in the car, but I quickly realized that even if they had, my father would hardly have responded with tears. My second thought was to wonder what I had done wrong, but I could imagine nothing that might elicit such grief.

He was holding a letter in his hand, one of those blue, single-page, lightweight airmail letters that you seldom see any more. It had gaudy, unfamiliar stamps that I recognized—I was not sure how—as coming from the USSR, the Union of Socialist Soviet Republics. Perhaps the Cyrillic print stenciled over the stamps was my clue. It was not an unfamiliar letter, and it struck me that as far back as I could remember, such letters had periodically been delivered to the apartment. I had never asked, and my father had never volunteered, any information about them. They belonged to the adult part of his life, which, I had learned, had nothing to do with me.

It was the kind of scene that I knew from books and movies occurred when someone close died—but that could hardly apply to us. My father had few friends, and we had no family left to die.

"What happened, Dad?" I asked. "Who's the letter from?"

Surprised to see me, he removed his glasses hastily and wiped his shirtsleeve across his eyes and cheeks, as if he could simply erase the evidence of his grief. It was the clumsy action of a man so unfamiliar with his own emotions that any expression of them, even to the person closest to him, was shameful.

"I didn't expect you back so early," he said. Still trying to distract himself, he used his shirtsleeve to polish his glasses, and put them on. "I wouldn't have bothered you with this, but now that you're here, I suppose I must." He sighed. "I suppose I should have told you a long time ago."

"Told me what?"

"A lot of things," he said, gesturing to the chair across from his.

I sat down, and he gently pushed the letter across the table. I picked it up and unfolded it. It was written in black ink, in laboriously printed capital letters, and as I read the halting English to myself, the hair on the back of my neck rose and I experienced jolts of anger, disorientation and excitement. Above all, I was bewildered. The letter was assurance that, through no fault of my own, at least some of the assumptions on which I had based my sense of myself were flawed.

Dear Leonard,

This is first letter in many months, to share with you a new sadness in our life. My mother, Nina, was ill with cancers of the stomach last winter. She has been dying all through the spring, and last week we said to her good-bye. She was sixty-three years, only. She had not much pain in her death, although life for her was very hard. Now with your father, Mischa, gone, all left from that generation is our Aunt Lena, and she lives alone, raising her granddaughter, Darya, who is now just younger than your Steven. And so, we are all together almost all orphans.

Your packages come still —the last one only two weeks ago. The suit cloth is beautiful, especially the navy blue. The shoes and raincoats also are good to send—for these we can get more, as you know. From your letters we know what you send, but you know packages are opened, and then closed again, a little smaller. We pay a price to the ones who stand at the gate.

We are of good health mostly, the children too, and we think often of you in Boston. We send to you and your Steven our love and wishes for best of health.

Your Cousin, Juliana

I read the letter over twice, gathering all I could from it before I put it down. Here was a cousin I had never heard of sending love to me through my father. Here was family I was unaware of, in the Soviet Union, a country of which I knew only what we had studied in school, to whom my father was apparently in the habit of sending parcels of cloth and clothing. I smiled with delight even as I was filled with a furious anger—delight at the discovery of family, fury at the tissue of lies and deception that had kept from me any knowledge of them until now.

"You have a cousin named Juliana?" I asked, pointing to the letter. "In Russia?"

"Moscow," he said.

I wanted to shout at him, and the effort it took to speak calmly sent the blood racing to my face.

"All this time you said it was just us," I said accusingly. "You and me. Alone." I pushed the letter calmly back across the table; knew that he heard the ice in my voice. "She knows about me, but I've never even heard her name. Great, Dad. Let's hear you explain this one away. Another crappy example of how you never communicate with me about anything."

In silence my father looked at me, a quizzical expression on his face, and I was surprised to see how much green there was in his mostly grey eyes. He shrugged and rose, walked over to his potted ornamental fig tree. Some people, when nervous, chew their nails, bite their lips, or pace the floor—my father's habit was to check his *Ficus lyrata* for insects.

"We all handle what life serves us up as best we can," he said slowly, laying a sheet of newspaper on the floor as he lowered himself to one knee. "It's easy for you to stand in judgment on what I have or haven't done—but that doesn't make it fair, or wise." Carefully turning each scalloped leaf, he examined the undersides, using a fingernail to scrape any insects and larvae onto the newspaper at his feet. "Perhaps I should have handled certain things differently. In your own life I hope your decision-making is better than mine. I certainly wish you an easier path." He paused. "You'll discover that time changes the past, Stevie. You were a small child, and I was a young man. Now you're sixteen, and I've become different from who I was when we left South Africa. Perhaps I should have shared some things about my family with you, but when you were younger, we had other concerns."

Many years would pass before I discovered what decisions he thought he might have handled differently. At the time, his statement didn't even register. I was too angry to ask, or even to wonder, what he meant.

"*Your* family?" I said, punching my chest with a finger. "You forget that this is my family, too."

He said nothing, just kept on checking the leaves. Finally he looked up at me.

"I don't know what to say, Steven," he said simply. "But I'll answer any questions you want to ask."

His response confused me, but it was typical of his passive reaction to whatever occurred in our lives. It allowed him to distance himself from events, and at the same time retain an illusion of control over them. But I had learned from him, and I could be as stoic as he was. I would get what I wanted—as soon as I discovered what it was.

"Who are they?" I asked. "How come they live in Russia?"

"Papa Mischa lived most of his life not knowing whether his family in the Soviet Union was alive or dead. He only discovered his sisters alive in Moscow a few years before he died, and he went to visit them."

"I don't remember him going anywhere," I said. "How come he never told me?"

"You were still reeling from losing Mom," he said. "We all were. He went to Moscow to see the family he hadn't seen since he was separated from them in his teens. He had two sisters living, the one who just died, and the other, Lena, who was raising her granddaughter, Darya. She was just a little girl when he visited, around your age."

"What's with the packages—the coats and shoes and cloth? Why do we send them clothes? Are they poor?"

"They live in the Soviet Union," he said wearily. "You wrote a paper about communism last year. Remember what Karl Marx said, 'from each according to his ability, to each according to his need?' In theory, it's a great system. In practice, it doesn't work. We send them clothes because they need our help."

"Didn't it cross your mind when we discussed my paper last year that this was a textbook example of why their system doesn't work? Here we are, capitalists, helping our family in a communist country. It would have been a perfect opportunity to tell me about them."

"I should have. If I had to do it over again, I would have. I'm sorry I didn't."

"Right," I said. Like most sixteen-year-olds, I was a master of sarcasm.

"Can we move on now?" he asked gently.

I ignored the question—but I was impressed by his refusal to become involved in a petty argument.

"What did Papa Mischa find when he went to Moscow?"

"He found his sisters living in very shabby circumstances. They have a roof over their heads and enough to eat, but beyond that, life is tough for the average Russian. What he saw upset him so badly that his doctors thought it ultimately brought on the coronary that killed him. He promised to help, and when he arrived home we started sending them a package each month. They sell what we send them on the black market, or they exchange it for whatever they need. The underground economy is how things work there—it's how people survive. He made me promise that if something happened to him, I would continue sending the packages. The woman who just died, Nina, was his sister.   Her daughter, Juliana, who wrote the letter, is my first cousin."

"Why have you never visited them? And why don't you visit them now?"

He was checking the lowest leaves, his tall, gaunt frame bent double. After a moment of hesitation, he answered without looking up at me.

"We are alone, Steven. It's delusional to think that having distant family in Moscow—family we've never met—makes us less alone. I didn't visit them before because going to the Soviet Union was dangerous. I wasn't about to take you with me, and I certainly wasn't about to leave you behind. I may not be much, but I was all you had. If something happened to me, you would have had no one. Why do you think I never left you when you were a child? Traveling to the Soviet Union is still dangerous, and I'm still all you have. So I'm not about to leave you here and go visiting." He rose to his knees, crushing a few dead leaves in his fist. "I would have liked to visit Moscow and see my aunts, but we had no extra money, and I was too busy making a living."

"It never crossed your mind that we might go to Moscow together?"

"No."

"Why?"

"Because I've had enough excitement for one life," he said. "You may not understand or appreciate it, but that's how I feel."

"I don't like it. I guess I have to accept it, though. It's who you are." I thought for a moment. "But you have to start including me. I'm not a child. Even if the closest family we have is in the USSR, I want to know about them. You can start by telling me how we come to have relatives in Moscow."

My father stood up slowly, awkwardly, dusted off the knees of his trousers. "Very well," he said. "I'll tell you what I know."

He sat down opposite me again with his elbows on the table and absently rolled the letter between his fingers. I remembered, as a young boy, how Papa Mischa had pulled me onto his lap and told me the fairytale version of the story. He was an inveterate pipe smoker, and whenever I think of being on his lap, I am enveloped in the safe warmth of his acrid-fruity pipe tobacco. But now, for the first time, I heard the real story. My father told me what it was like to be raised by a man whose most basic belief in the world had been shattered, and who spent his life waiting for his own father to come home, unable to accept that it would never happen.

I thought about my grandfather, left alone in a boarding house, a year younger than I was, and began to feel a little less angry at my father. I looked at this tall, unkempt, rangy man with grey hair growing over his ears, and wrists that extended beyond his shirtsleeves. I looked at his lean, long face and his reddened eyes. He was not a perfect father, but he loved me, and he demonstrated his love in every way he was capable of. The parallels in our lives—my father and his grandfather, widowed and left with young children; my grandfather and I, left motherless with fathers who, in their own ways, had a hard time being wifeless.

"So your grandfather was widowed, just as you were. But he was wise enough to realize he needed a new wife, and he must have seen that his kids needed a new mother." I smiled at him. "It's a little late to get me a new mother, but perhaps we can still send you somewhere to find a new wife. What do you think, Dad?"

"We're not talking about me," he said.

"No," I said quietly. "We never talk about you. So tell me, what happened?"

My father looked at me from across the table, his face expressionless, as if he were far away.

"World War I happened," he said absently. "And then The Russian

Revolution." He sat with his hands clasped before him.

"What do you mean?"

"You think my grandfather was wise and thoughtful," he said, "to venture back to Latvia to find a new wife and mother. You should have heard Papa Mischa on that subject."

"Why?"

"Because Papa Mischa's father never came back. He and his new wife and all their children—some of whom he took back with him from South Africa—were all trapped in the Soviet Union. I grew up with a father who knew that somewhere in the USSR he probably had a family, but he had no idea where they were, or how to find them."

I remembered Papa Mischa as a warm, loving grandfather. But even when he was still relatively young and in good health, I felt protective of him. He always seemed sad to me, as if he were carrying a weight on his shoulders. No wonder.

"So how did he find them?"

"In the late 1950s, through the Red Cross, Papa Mischa discovered that he had two sisters still living. They were in Moscow. He couldn't wait to go visit them—and he never recovered from that trip."

"I bet it never crossed your mind to include me in buying stuff for them and sending it off together."

He sighed and looked up. He seldom seemed to me like a happy man, but at that moment there was grief in his eyes and lines of sadness around his mouth that I hadn't noticed before.

"When I started buying things and packing them up to send to Russia, I was still dealing with my own grief. My father was gone. The packages felt more like a burden to me than anything else, and I didn't want to impose it on you," he said. "I'll leave it to you to travel to the Soviet Union when you're ready. In fact, when you graduate from college, if you still want to go, I'll send you to Moscow. I can't change the past, but you're right—they're your family, too. And when you get back, you can turn the tables and tell me about them."

At sixteen, my college graduation seemed light years away, and promising me a trip to Moscow in the distant future didn't feel like much of a concession. But it was his way of making amends, and at least it opened the door.

"Since they already seem to know who I am," I said, "I think I'll write to them. I've never had family to write letters to before."

"That's fine," he said. "I'll give you all the names and addresses I have."

I was the only child of two only children, and the idea of having a living, multi-generational family had always been foreign to me. After reading the letter from Juliana, I lay in bed with a new feeling of fullness, of being whole, a sense of belonging to something bigger than myself.

On many nights in the years that followed, I went to sleep salivating over images of the colorful, steaming platters of succulent food that would be on Juliana's table in celebration of my arrival in Moscow. I imagined the laughter and the heavy Russian accents of my new family, and the warmth of loving arms around me as I was embraced in welcome. I had just discovered their existence, but I knew that, whoever they were, I belonged to them, and I missed them already.

I asked my father no more questions, but I started writing letters. Anything I learned about the Moscow family came from my correspondence with Juliana. Suddenly, my closed world exploded into a new universe. I had been alone, a part of nothing bigger than my father and myself, and in the instant of reading Juliana's letter I was thrust into the warm, throbbing, messy life of an extended family.

I approached my letter-writing believing that our connection was absolute and unbreakable. Either they had a sense of the inviolability of family and accepted my introduction without question, or there was something in my spontaneous enthusiasm that touched them and made them want to reach out to me. I was flattered to discover that they were as interested in the details of my life as I was in the details of theirs, and so our correspondence was never just about family history.

Juliana attempted to educate me about family lines—who was related to whom and how, and what each person's relationship was to me. I wrote about my likes and dislikes, the weather, what I did during vacations, my favorite foods, how I spent my free time. Juliana responded by sharing the same information about her extended family. So I learned about her husband Maxim and their son Kolya, who dreamed of becoming an officer in the military; I learned about Lena and Darya, the brilliant, staunchly communist granddaughter she was raising.

I entered Boston University, studying art, and at the beginning of my second term signed up for a course in Russian. I had never enjoyed or done well at foreign languages—but then, I had no burning desire to talk to anyone in French or Spanish. Russian was a different story. I aced my courses, and was soon corresponding with my family in Russian. Unfortunately, they responded in Russian, and I often needed translation assistance from my Russian professor.

Professor Primak was an overweight émigré in her sixties, given to colorful wool jackets and excessive hair spray, but she turned out to be warm and approachable. She had been a professor of literature in Ukraine, and was able to help me understand more about my family than simply translating their words. I appreciated her expertise, and the fact that she could be helpful made her warmly inclined to me. That was something else I discovered—if I allowed people to help me, they became my friends. It was a lesson my father never taught me, and one he still hasn't learned. How different his life—and my childhood—might have been had he been open to such a lesson.

What I learned in my Russian classes was not only a new language. It was also a course in self-discovery. Until then, I had been a mediocre student. I had no particular interests outside painting, and was filled with doubt about my ability to make a living as either an artist or a teacher of art. My academic record was good enough to get me into Boston University, but I thought I had pulled the wool over the eyes of the admissions department. Yet here I was, enjoying my Russian course, memorizing grammar and vocabulary with ease, picking up the accent without difficulty. I found that

I couldn't wait to get back to my dormitory room and start my assignments. It became clear to me that I was smarter, more adept, and more driven than I or my teachers had imagined. All I needed was sufficient motivation. That lesson has stood me in good stead. Unfortunately, I seem to be hard-wired to forget it on a regular basis, so I've needed to relearn it over and over again.

I wrote several letters to Darya. Because we shared the experience of having lost a parent—in her case, both parents—I thought perhaps we had a basis for communication. She never responded. I did get some indication from Juliana, who seemed to be the central clearing house for family information and gossip, that Darya was a leader in Komsomol, the youth division of the Communist Party, and that she wanted nothing to do with capitalist cousins in the West. Juliana sent me family photographs, but Darya was never present, and I soon forgot about her.

Almost seventeen years passed before I went to Moscow, much longer than I thought it would be. But my correspondence gave me such a sense of kinship with my Moscow family that I no longer felt the urgency to visit. I began to fear that meeting in person might jeopardize the connection we had made through the passage of our words on paper. I had come to love them, and, I hoped, they had come to love me. But what if, in meeting face-to-face, we discovered that we didn't like each other?

Whenever I began planning my trip, I imagined myself returning to Boston bitterly unhappy, the loving relationships built through years of writing letters wiped out in a week. They didn't like the sound of my laugh or they found my slightly crooked smile insincere. I was too soft, or not well-versed enough in their history; or they were simply disappointed in me, because in person I was neither as interesting nor substantial as I was on paper. What if I had unknowingly misrepresented myself?

On the other hand, it was possible that I had inflated expectations, and that I would be terribly disappointed in them. How would I react if I found that there were petty jealousies among them, or that in reality they were stingy and selfish? What if I found their food unpalatable, or their living conditions as distressing as Papa Mischa had? What if, after all my fantasies, I simply didn't like them in person, or found the closeness of family life suffocating?

It was easier not to face these possibilities. I hoped that we would eventually meet, and in the meantime I would get on with my life and maintain the fantasy, if that was all it turned out to be.

❦

I graduated from Boston University in 1977 and spent several years working and traveling. I painted wherever I went—the southwestern United States, Peru, Chile, and Mexico. Those years are filled with memories of days spent hiking and painting in the desert, along the crests of mountains or on the beaches. I camped for days in unpeopled reserves, trying again and again to capture the magic of sunrise over Chilean snow-covered mountaintops. I stood at my easel on the shore of a silent mountain lake at sunset, as the still air shimmered with pastel light, and the sky, filled with indescribably mauve, pink, orange and yellow clouds, seemed to repeat itself both on the surface of the water, and on the lake bottom beneath.

During those years I produced many paintings, and wherever I traveled I seemed to find lovely women. Or they seemed to find me. I met them on the dance floors of clubs in Argentina and Chile, hiking through the Grand Canyon or camped out in the Painted Desert, or swimming in hot springs in New Mexico. We made love in my tent or under the stars, in motels and hotel rooms and in women's apartments in Albuquerque, Taos and Bogota.

It was a new experience for me—until then I didn't think I was particularly desirable, but women seemed to find me both charming and good-looking. I went to Spain, intending to see all the Picassos and El Grecos I could fit in. I went to Andalusia, and spent a week in Ronda, painting the hanging white cliffs. In the evenings I wandered about the city, and ended up meeting a language student at the University of Madrid. Her name was Mariela. Glossy black hair surrounded her head in soft curls. She had flawless, milk-chocolate skin, big dark eyes and a smile that made me light up inside. We spent three nights together, and on the third night, after a session of passionate lovemaking beneath the moon on the veranda outside my room, I went inside to the bathroom. I remember vividly standing before the full-length mirror, trying to understand what she saw in me. I suppose I was not bad-looking. I was a soccer player and a runner, and unlike my father, who was tall and lanky, I had a broad chest, a flat stomach, and muscular thighs. My light brown hair was cut short in front, but hung down at the sides to mask overly prominent ears.

But the first thing I saw when I looked at my face in the mirror was my nose. A collision with someone's knee during a soccer game in high school had knocked me out, broken my nose and shifted it to one side of my face. It had been reset, but I refused plastic surgery, and as a consequence it was thickened across the ridge, and slightly askew. I didn't mind it, even liked the idea of having a visible sports injury. But I was acutely aware that it was not the perfect nose of my childhood. I had my mother's clear greenish-brown eyes, my best feature, according to my father. My mouth was too broad, my chin too small for my elongated face above a very knobby Adam's apple.

I was convinced that I didn't have much to be vain about. If anything, I was overly critical of myself. Then an event occurred that was a revelation. Mariela came into the bathroom and stood behind me, draping herself over my shoulder so that all I saw of her was her face in the mirror. She looked at me, and in her shining eyes there was only pleasure in what she saw. I had the sudden transformative experience of seeing myself, not through my own eyes, but through hers. I didn't see my eyes or my mouth or my physique. What I saw through her eyes was how I made her feel—safe, feminine, attractive, funny, sexy, and playful. It was only a momentary awareness, and then it faded. But whenever I doubt myself or hesitate to approach a woman, I recall that short moment. It helps to remind me that what a woman sees in me is deeply influenced by how I make her feel.

❁

Eventually I came back to Boston to finish my Master's Degree and found a job teaching art at the Boston Museum School. And when, after several years of teaching, I was ready to travel again, I also realized that I had reached a point in my life where I was confident enough to risk meeting my family in Moscow. By then I had collected several shoe-boxes full of letters and photographs, and I knew all the names and faces. At the age of thirty-three, I wrote to Juliana and asked her to set the table. I was coming to visit.

❁

My life has become an onion, and writing about it, an act of peeling the layers away one by one. My first visit to Moscow turned out to be an onion all its own, with layers that I couldn't even perceive, let alone understand. It's only in retrospect that I realize how uninformed I was, and how lacking in guile.

In 1988, when I made my first visit to Moscow, the Soviet Union felt to me as solid and invulnerable as it would have liked to be viewed by the outside world. But the Kremlin was fearful of western influence, and even more fearful of the internal vulnerabilities of the Iron Curtain. People walked sullenly through the frozen streets of Moscow, always vigilant, always aware that the KGB was watching. They were afraid of being seen speaking to strangers, especially to those from the West.

I should have realized from the nature of our correspondence over the years—from what was left unsaid, from which of my questions they ignored, from what personal information I had to guess at—that in many ways they lived circumscribed lives. They were in constant fear of the government security apparatus, and they had a built-in sense of suspicion. But I couldn't have imagined until I began to plan my trip just how fearful—and cautious—they were.

My first inkling that the trip would be other than how I imagined it was a three-line letter from Juliana. It was forwarded from Rome, and simply said that someone named Robert would be calling me with suggestions regarding my forthcoming trip. When he did call, he had a thick Russian accent, and began by saying that he would not tell me where he was calling from, and that he would not mention the names of any of my family during our call. He cautioned that if I was concerned at all about their safety, I, too, would avoid mentioning names, and that I would further take his suggestions regarding my trip.

I was to apply for a visitor's visa as an art teacher interested in learning about modern Russian art, and to view the collections held in the many museums in Moscow. I was to make no mention of family, and to give no indication that I knew anyone in the city. When I had received permission to visit, my flight was booked, and my hotel arrangements made, I should send the information to a post office box in New York, and I would be contacted once I arrived in Moscow. Robert made sure that I had written down the address, and then he hung up. The call left one half of me wondering whether I should go at all, and the other half more curious than ever. I had the sensation of being a character caught in the middle of a story—with no idea where the plot would take me, and no way to avoid the outcome, whatever it might be.

I landed in Moscow in January, having booked my trip through the Russian tourist agency, Intourist. The customs agents emptied my suitcase, cut open the lining, and searched every crevice for contraband. Three dour officials in succession asked me whether I had brought with me any books on politics, any books banned in Russia, any bibles. Each time I said no, each time with less conviction. I had none of the items they asked about—but I had withheld information about my family. It was my first experience of feeling guilty simply because I was being questioned by figures of authority. Eventually they allowed me into the country—by which time I would just as happily have turned around and gone home. As I walked out through the restricted door and into the airport, two people holding a welcome bouquet detached themselves from the crowd and came towards me. I tried to walk around them as I searched for my driver, but they seemed to follow me. One of them called out my name, and when I looked at her, I recognized Juliana. And the man beside her was her husband, Maxim.

I was surprised to see them. After all the secrecy and after avoiding any mention of family in Moscow on my visa, I had assumed that they would contact me at the hotel. It was a disconnect I experienced over and over in Moscow, this absolute fear of the authorities, precautions taken to avoid being noticed, and then an inexplicable act that threw into question the whole need for precaution in the first place. I learned that the fear was real, and the precautions necessary—everyone was always under surveillance by neighbors and acquaintances, and everyone was a potential informer. The irony was that if every Soviet citizen was spying on every other, no one was safe, and it was reasonable to assume that everyone knew everything. In which case, there was really no purpose in hiding anything. As a result, while there was a real danger, there was also room for spontaneous gestures.

"Steven!" cried Juliana. "How wonderful to see you!" She threw her arms about me. "We've been so excited for your arrival. And now, here you are!"

When she released me Maxim threw his arms about me in a great bear hug, pounding me on the back.

"Welcome, my boy," he said. "Your Grandfather Mischa is smiling down now, so happy to see us all together."

"I'm glad to be here," I said, over and over, in English and then in Russian. It's difficult to describe now, but as Juliana put her arms around me and I hugged her in response, I felt as if I had come home after a long absence.

As we left the airport building, Maxim went off in one direction, and Juliana pulled me to a stop.

"We wait here while Maxim finds someone to take us home," she said, taking my arm and pulling me close to her. She whispered into my ear. "Steven, one thing I must warn you. For all our sakes, talk nothing to anyone about you are a Jew. We left our history behind a long time ago, when it was more unsafe to be Jewish, and yet no one knows our history here. Even some family members don't know. Better we keep it that way. Safer. You understand?"

I was stunned, but I nodded agreement. "What about Maxim?" I asked. "Have you told him?"

She laughed as if it were a ridiculous question. "Between Maxim and me there are no secrets," she said.

I need to be careful, I thought. It was rapidly becoming clear that very little in the next few weeks would be predictable.

Maxim returned a few minutes later sitting in the front seat of a dull green Lada, driven by a middle-aged woman. A friend of theirs, I thought. But I learned quickly that this was a stranger, and that people got around Moscow by holding a handful of rubles in the air and waiting for someone to offer a ride. For those fortunate enough to have a car, it was a way to earn a little extra money. We piled into the backseat with my luggage. Maxim had already told the driver where I was staying.

Juliana was a little younger than my father, with his eyes and his facial structure—but she was an animated, talkative woman, warm and smiling.

"My English speaking not too bad," she said with a warm smile, "but I think your Russian better, no?"

There was something unnerving in hearing the heavy Russian sounds emanating from a face that might have been my father's.

"Between my Russian and your English," I said in Russian, "I think we'll do just fine."

Maxim laughed. "That's the true meaning of *glasnost*," he said.

"So tell us, how is your father?" she asked. "So strange, that we have never met him, and now we meet you first."

"He's fine," I answered. "Still working hard, and he sends his love."

"Why he doesn't come to visit us? Difficult for us to visit United States, but he could come to see us here. Moscow is such beautiful city! You'll see. We have wonderful architecture, great ballet, and you will love our museums."

"The boy's had a long flight," Maxim interrupted. "Let's give him time to relax. There will be plenty of time for museums."

She nodded vigorously.

"Of course," Juliana said. "We go straight to your hotel now. We can talk after you rest." She turned to her husband. "But Maxim, he is a young man with energy, and curious about our city. We should let him decide how much rest he needs."

She looked often at Maxim for confirmation—but then did or said exactly what she wanted. He was patient, but when she was overly enthusiastic or invasive, he knew how to get her attention. He was a thick, shortish man in middle age, his slate-grey hair roughly clipped, with a warm smile, deep blue eyes, and an open face. He looked like a wrestler who had stopped taking care of himself—still powerful arms and a deep chest, but more attention now being paid to his appetite than to his body. I liked him immediately. And I was aware that although he carried himself with confidence, he was also cautious, in a way that I came to recognize was characteristic of most people I met in Russia.

"How is your son, Kolya?" I asked. "Is he still..."

"Tell me," Maxim interrupted. "How was your trip? Where did you put down?"

"Yes, and how was the airline food? You must be starving." She looked at him. "Perhaps we should go first..."

"No, Juliana," Maxim shook his head. "First we get him settled in the hotel," he said, "just as we agreed." He looked at her, eyebrows raised, with a slight nod towards the driver. She nodded in agreement.

"Of course," she said. "So, how is your teaching? And are you finding yourself a wife yet? Such a handsome young man, and unmarried." She smacked my leg with the back of her hand. "What are you waiting for?"

"You think he came here to get marriage advice from his cousin?" said Maxim dryly. "Watch out you don't scare him away. He'll go right back to the airport."

"Nonsense," she retorted. "I have thirty years of advice I have to give him, and only two weeks to give it. We don't have time to waste."

We all laughed, including the driver.

"Once you're settled at the hotel," said Maxim, "you'll have a sleep, then we can collect you and arrange to have some supper. Okay?"

"That sounds great," I said. I realized how uncomfortable they were talking about themselves in the car, and decided to hold my questions until later.

Hotel Rossiya was right on Red Square, a colossal building that advertised itself as the largest hotel in the world. It was ornate in a drab and washed out way, and all I remember is corridors that seemed to extend forever. The unsmiling clerk registered me and took my passport, pointing at the elevator. I picked up my bag, expecting that Maxim and Juliana would accompany me to my room. Maxim took my arm and embraced me.

"We cannot come with you to your room," he said into my ear. "It is not wise. You rest now—I will come and get you this afternoon and take you to our home for supper." He looked at me. "Remember," he whispered, "be very careful who you talk to, and please speak nothing of us to anyone. Okay?"

I nodded, kissed Juliana, and they left. I made my way to my room. In the corridors, every few hundred feet, was a small rectangular desk at which sat a succession of large, serious and unexpressive women whose sole job it was to keep an eye on the comings and goings of each guest—to see who went into which rooms, and when, and if possible, to hear why.

I looked around my room—dusty curtains, discolored walls, a bathroom done entirely in black tiles—and quickly realized how tired I was. But before I lay down to rest, I opened the curtains to see what direction I faced, and to get my bearings, and was pleasantly surprised to find that I had a clear view of the Kremlin.

In the late afternoon Maxim came to the hotel to escort me to their home. It was cold, and the car had no heat. The sun had already set, and the roads were terrible. We drove in silence through the wide, almost empty boulevards, swerving to avoid potholes, into a neighborhood of apartment buildings.

I didn't understand why I couldn't have simply taken a taxi to their home on my own, until I realized that things worked differently in Moscow. Maxim stepped into the street outside the hotel with his arm raised and a ruble note in his hand. Before long a grey Lada stopped, the driver asked where we were going, and said he'd take us to our destination. Maxim asked him to drop us off in front of what I assumed was their apartment building. But as we stood on the sidewalk and watched the car drive off, Maxim beckoned for me to follow him. He led the way through the dusk into and out of one building, onto the street and around the corner, through several other buildings and interior yards until he stood in the entranceway to a fourth apartment building. He opened the door, gestured with his open arm, and smiled.

"Welcome," he said.

As we entered the darkened hallway, Maxim pulled on the light cord hanging from the ceiling, and a single bulb came on, lighting one flight of the undecorated concrete stairwell. It was dark. It smelled of fried onions. As we climbed from floor to floor, he turned off the light bulb behind us and pulled on the next string to light the stairs ahead. Their apartment was on the fifth floor. I followed, increasingly apprehensive about the conditions in which I would find them living.

I needn't have worried. Their apartment was small, but it was brightly lit and warm, filled with overstuffed bookshelves, the walls covered in bright, watercolor landscapes. There was a cramped living space that served as both dining room and sitting room, a crowded kitchen, and two other tiny rooms. One was Maxim's office; the other had space for little more than a single bed. I must have looked puzzled, because Maxim explained to me that when Kolya was growing up, he slept in one bedroom. The other served as a tiny study, and he and Juliana slept on the couch in the living room, which opened into a double bed. Often, when Lena was working nights, Darya slept over, and she and Kolya had grown up like brother and sister.

"Much better than our first place, where we lived when Kolya was little," he said, grinning. "We had one room in a six-bedroom apartment, and we shared a bathroom and kitchen with five other families. But when I qualified in medicine, I began to teach in medical school. My salary doubled, and we applied for a bigger apartment."

"Maxim," said Juliana from the kitchen, "you make it sound as if when your pay was increased, all you had to do was apply for apartment with more space. Explain him how it works, otherwise how can he understand?"

He winked at me as he asked her a question in rapid Russian.

"Henpecked," she said, laughing as she came in to set a bowl of salad on the table. She pinched his cheek as she returned to the kitchen.

"Yes, that's it. You see how henpecked I am? So. The way it works here is that to apply for a bigger apartment, you have to prove you don't have enough living space."

"How do they decide what's enough living space?"

"Each person is allowed nine square meters," he said. "But our son was born already, and between the three of us we had less than nine square meters each, so our application was granted." He took a step into the kitchen and stood with his arm about Juliana's waist. "It helped that we had enough money to oil the way." He grinned, rubbing his thumb against the tops of his first two fingers. "I remember in the beginning, when we first moved here, I would see Juliana pinch herself before we went to sleep, and one night I asked her, 'Juliana, what are you doing?' So she told me, 'I'm pinching myself to make sure that it's not a dream that we sleep together with no one else in the room.'"

Juliana laughed, and came out of the kitchen with a bowl of thick borscht. We had chicken stew, and there was salad, bread, and a bowl of stewed fruit. I was relieved to see that food was plentiful—but as I visited other members of the family, I realized that how they lived depended upon who they were in the hierarchy. As physicians, Juliana and Maxim were comparatively well paid. Others lived in less comfortable, even smaller, more crowded conditions, and their tables were less well stocked.

Sitting around their own table after supper, drinking vodka from little glasses, Juliana and Maxim were more relaxed, although, like almost everyone else, they always seemed somewhat guarded. We talked about the family I would meet over the next few days, and they mentioned that their son Kolya was in the military, stationed at some distance from Moscow, and that he was unable to get leave while I was visiting. They were reluctant to discuss him, and I attributed their reluctance to his military status. Juliana was sitting next to me, and after a brief lull in the conversation, she reached over and put her hand on my forearm.

Our life here is difficult," she said. "More than your life in Boston. But thinking too much about what might have been is not good." She shook her head as she stroked my arm.

"Juliana, look at his face," interrupted Maxim. "He doesn't understand what you mean. You need to explain."

She did as he suggested, looking up from where she sat beside me.

"When I speak of what might have been," she whispered, "I mean the terrible decision your great-grandfather Isaak made, to bring the children back to Latvia when his wife died. But for that, we might all be living together. We would not be strangers to each other, and there would be no need for your father to spend his money sending us goods to sell here on the black market."

"Juliana and I have been through this many times," said Maxim, mildly irritated, I thought. But he seemed resigned to the conversation. "Isaak thought at the time it was a good decision—how could he predict the consequences to his children and grandchildren?"

"And to all the generations after him," said Juliana. But she rose from the table with a smile, and stood behind Maxim, her arms about his neck. "There is a bright side to this story, Steven. If he hadn't come back here I would never have found Maxim."

"No," he said with a smile, reaching up to caress her hair. "Instead you would have married a prince. You'd be living like a princess in a mansion with an enormous dining table and a big round bed."

"I'm enough happy with the bed we have," she said, kissing the top of his head. "If we have a round bed you're falling on the floor every night."

The next day Juliana took me to meet her aunt, Lena. All I knew was that she was a widow, now in her eighties. She had one bedroom in a communal apartment shared with several other families, and had lived there for over three decades. It was where she had raised her granddaughter, Darya. The room was colorfully decorated with handmade curtains and knickknacks, and she entertained us there, serving us strong tea made on a hotplate, and a dish of little pastries.

Lena was a tiny woman with temples and forehead crosshatched in wrinkles. When I looked at her, I had the uncanny experience of seeing my grandfather, Papa Mischa, staring out at me. Lena had a similar experience. When she saw me, she caught her breath and gasped.

She stood before me and placed her hands on my cheeks. Tears threaded their way down through the fine crevices about her eyes and down her face. She had seen her brother, Papa Mischa, only once since their separation as children, when he came to visit after discovering that his sisters were still alive. But that's not what brought her to tears. Once she recovered herself, she went to the little table at her bedside, and carried over to me an old framed photograph. I looked at the yellowing print and saw a formal, family portrait. A serious young man with a dark beard, his wife, a buxom, formidable young woman in a dark dress buttoned up to the neck, and several children. Lena pointed to one of the little girls.

"This is me," she said. "The older boys are your grandfather, Mischa, and his brother, Yossel. The man in the middle is our father, Isaak, your great-grandfather."

She shook her head, shrugging her shoulders in disbelief, and pointed with a gnarled finger from the photograph of her father to me and back again, and I looked carefully at the image of my great-grandfather. It was like looking in a mirror.

He must have been in his late thirties when the photograph was taken. Dressed in a shabby, tight-fitting suit, he sat uncomfortably in a formal chair, trying hard and failing to look like the confident head of the family. He was already balding, with a sparse beard and mustache that covered part of his lip, and he looked bewildered. He was smaller than I am, but we shared the same face. I understood why Lena had reacted with such shock at seeing me—it must have been like having her father walk through the door.

"You have his face," she said. "And his eyes."

"And you also," I said.

The first thing I had noticed about her was the intensity of her blue eyes. They gleamed as if backlit, and when she looked at me I felt the aquamarine warmth of her recognition. She looked at me quizzically, squinting over the thick reading glasses perched on her nose. Then she did something no one else has ever done. She raised a hand and gently stroked the bridge of my nose, where it had been broken and reset. "Once you had his nose. But no more. This one is your own. From boxing?"

"From soccer," I said.

"Still a good nose," she said smiling, "on a handsome face."

We sat in silence and drank our tea. We looked at each other. She shook her head, the disbelief on her face changing from moment to moment, and I could see that she was thinking, as I was, how sad it was to have been so cleanly severed from each other, how joyful to finally meet, and how impossible to bridge the years, the generations, and the differences in our lives. But we both wanted to connect, to know each other. She tried first.

"So you are an artist," she said. "A painter."

"Yes."

"But what work do you do? How do you earn money?"

"I'm fortunate," I said. "People like my paintings. I sell them."

"And from this," she said, surprise evident on her face, "you are paid enough to live?"

"I am a teacher, too," I said. "At an art school."

"Ah, a teacher. Good. So the State pays you a salary."

I nodded. It was too complicated to explain that, unlike the USSR, the State was not the only entity that paid salaries.

"These paintings that people want to buy, what kind of pictures are they?"

"Oil paintings," I said. "And acrylic."

"No," she said. "I mean, what are the pictures of?"

"I paint landscapes," I said. "Mountains and rivers and trees and sunsets and the sea."

"No one tells you what you should be painting?" she asked.

"I paint what I like. No one tells us what to paint."

"Yes, it would have been like that before the Revolution," she said. "When Ivanov was painting."

"Alexander Ivanov?" I asked.

"You know Ivanov?" she asked, looking up as she sat beside me, one small hand tightening on my wrist like a vise. "You know his big painting here in the Tretyakov Gallery?"

"You mean the painting of *The Appearance of Christ Before the People?*" I asked, and she nodded. "Of course I know it," I said, hiding my surprise that there had been time and energy in her life to be interested in painting. "It's very famous. One of the paintings I want to see while I'm here."

"It makes me happy that our Ivanov is known outside Russia," she said. "That painting has been my favorite, since I was a child," she said. "We will go together to see it. Yes?"

The old lady turned to me again.

"When your grandfather Mischa was here," she said slowly, "many years ago, I took him to see that painting, too. I want you to see the picture that saved my life when I was a child, new to Moscow." She turned to Juliana and spoke rapidly, but I understood. "Just make sure it's not when I'm taking care of Larisa and Anton," she said.

She began to speak, slowly, sitting ramrod straight on her meticulously made bed, her hips sunk into the thick feather-filled comforter. She enunciated clearly, careful that I would understand every word, and she spoke with dignity and pride that made her seem far bigger than her tiny frame.

"You know I was born in South Africa," she said, "like your father was, and you."

I nodded. I thought she was going to talk about the return to Latvia, and the journey to Moscow, which Juliana had warned me not to discuss. But she skipped over all the tiered layers of hidden history, as if there were no secrets.

"My father brought us back, to our little village in Latvia. It was before the Revolution. We had nothing. There was no schooling. I worked hard, always. I rose to be a conductor on the railway between Moscow and Siberia. When my daughter died, I took in my baby granddaughter, Darya, and raised her. I felt like an old woman back then, but I know now I was still young. She has been my life, here in this room, where we lived together until she married."

She had been looking into the distance as she spoke, but now she turned her glowing eyes on me.

"No one knows this history. I tell you because I want you to remember it when you go back to Boston. Our lives have been hard. Very hard. But we have survived. Day by day, we put one foot before the other. I want you to know, with enough hope, and something to believe in, you can get through the worst of times. For me, it was Ivanov's painting. That's why I want to show it to you." She waved a finger at me. "So, don't even think about going to see that painting without me."

Juliana rose from her chair and walked the two steps across the room to place a hand gently on Lena's shoulder.

"Don't worry, Aunt," she said quietly. "I know how important this is to you. I will make sure we don't visit your Ivanov without you."

"Good. Before you go, I want to show you something." Lena hopped off the bed and went to a drawer, where she pulled out a pair of delicate black leather gloves that looked as if they had never been worn. Supporting them in both hands as if they were made of porcelain, she brought them to me and sat beside me.

"From your grandfather, Mischa," she said proudly. "When he came to see me."

❦

"I never heard her talk so much," said Juliana as we walked out of the apartment and down the stairs. "Or tell her life story to anyone."

"I didn't know what to say," I said.

"You did fine," she said. "Lena just wanted to know you heard her."

"What was all that about the gloves before we left?"

"Those gloves," she said tenderly, "came in the first package from your grandfather. He sent one pair to each of his sisters—my mother, and Aunt Lena. Both came as part of a much bigger shipment, but separate from everything else, and wrapped up in beautiful paper. Lena kept the paper—she might have it still."

"But that was almost thirty years ago," I said. "The gloves look as if they've never been worn."

"Where would she wear them?" she asked. "My mother and Lena could never be seen wearing such gloves. They were soft leather. They were luxury, not meant for us. To wear such gloves in public would have meant trouble—jealousy and suspicion. Sometimes, when there was no heat, they would wear the gloves in the apartment. My mother kept them until she died, and Lena treasures hers still."

What an awful story, I thought as we reached the ground floor. I held the door open for Juliana, and we walked out into the frozen street. It was late afternoon and the sun had already set. There were no street lights. It was cold, we were buffeted by the wind, and snow was beginning to fall. I hunched my shoulders and we started walking down the curb just as a long black car pulled up outside Lena's building. It was a Zil limo, the kind I had noticed ignoring traffic signals, being waved through by traffic police, and being given a wide berth by other drivers. It belonged to a high government official, and this one was as clean and shiny as any I had seen. When Juliana saw the car she took a sharp breath and stopped in front of me so suddenly that I bumped into her. She reached back and took my elbow, pulling me to her side. When I turned to her there was a forced smile on her face.

"Be very careful what you say," whispered Juliana.

The driver was a small, ferret-like man with a big smile that showed a strange mixture of missing teeth and gold replacements. He ran around the car to open the back door. The boots that stepped out of the car belonged to a woman, and they were followed by a black leather coat with a hood of dark fur. She walked towards us, head bowed against the cold, heading to the door from which we had just exited. When she was five paces away she looked up and saw us.

"Juliana!" she said, smiling.

"Hello, Darya," replied Juliana.

"How nice to see you." She looked at me, and then back to Juliana. "You've been to see Babushka?"

"Yes." She turned to me. "Steven, this is your cousin Darya."

She stepped forward, a head shorter than I was, and reached up to kiss me on both cheeks. Before I saw her face, I smelled her scent, as subtle and simple as to be almost invisible—rose, the cleanness of lemon, a hint of vanilla. I knew enough about women and fragrances to recognize a very expensive perfume.

"So this is the cousin I've heard so much about," she said. "I'm so happy to meet you, Stevie."

Her English was heavily accented, with drawn out Russian vowels and throaty consonants, but her voice was smooth and honeyed. As she said my name I felt myself flushing, and the hair at the back of my neck rise. Stevie was my childhood name, and she enunciated it with an intimacy that felt like an invasion of privacy. She looked at me in the dusk, curious, welcoming, and a little distant. She had high, elegant cheekbones that magnified her dark eyes and made her look just a little exotic, almost Asian, and smooth, barely rounded cheeks that reminded me of women I'd known who were long-distance runners, fit and athletic, but too lean for my taste. I thought the smile she gave me was both amused and slightly mocking, and the contours of her mouth had the shape that made women jealous and mesmerized men. I had to tear my eyes from her lips.

"I'm so glad you came to see my grandmother. I'm sure she told you that you remind her of her father, yes? Sorry to rush—I have to get her ready to come to my house, and then I have a meeting this evening. We can talk more tomorrow." Then she waved, smiled at Juliana, and left us.

Juliana was more reserved than usual as we continued on our way. When I turned toward her I saw that she wore a worried expression, and was shaking her head.

"What's the matter?" I asked.

"Tomorrow you will meet other family. Darya will be there, too."

She paused and continued in a low voice so that I had to walk in step with her, my head bent towards her so that I could see her lips. When I stumbled because I couldn't see the ground, she took my arm and pulled me along as we continued to walk, and she spoke into my ear.

"Steven, even inside family, we need to be very careful who we speak to, and what we say. Darya's husband, Grigory, has a very important position in government security. He is in a very high place, but not a good man. Not at all. In fact, I think a very bad man. It may not be the same in America, but here, because Darya is his wife, she must be with him in what he does. What you say to her, you say to him. You understand? This is important—it is not just words. Not being careful here can lead the way to labor camp in Siberia, or worse."

She looked up at me for confirmation, glancing around for anyone who might overhear us. I nodded, but she sensed my skepticism.

"So, you don't believe me," she said.

"It's hard to imagine how the girl we just met could be dangerous."

Her left arm was through mine. Juliana's handbag hung from her right forearm, and she brought her right hand across her body, handbag banging against her thighs as we walked, and wagged her finger in my face.

"You listen to me," she said. "When Darya was a girl, she needed someone younger than her grandmother to confide in. She was like a daughter, and she shared with me most things in her life. But not anymore. When she married she cut off most contact with the family—I don't know whether that was her decision or his instructions. But he is a cold man. One moment he works for Komsomol, the next he has an office in the Ministry

310 Neville D. Frankel

of Communications. It's all a lie. He is KGB. If he wants to make trouble for us, we would never know where it came from. We didn't want her to know that you were coming, but she would find out anyway. So we invited her to come tomorrow and meet you."

"And him?"

"He will not come," she said. "He knows I will not have him in my home."

She stopped in the darkness and stood before me, and in the waning light her expression was fierce.

"She is a most charming and lovely young woman, but we do not know what he asks, or what she answers, or how he hears. You must tell her nothing about where you go in Moscow, or who you see. You understand how important is what I tell you, Steven?"

"I understand," I said, "and I'll be very careful. You don't have to worry about me."

But apparently I understood nothing. She stood before me and gripped my coat lapels with her fists, pulling my face down to hers. She looked up at me, frowning, shaking her head, her cheeks wet from the falling snow, flakes on her eyelashes and brows.

"It's not you I worry about. You go back to United States in two weeks. But we—" she paused, struggling for words "—we are here still." She sighed deeply, and we were enveloped in the mist of her breath. "Writing letters to us, I think it was a game for you. But this? No. This is not playing. Here, what you say to her can hurt us. If you are in KGB, you learn how to make a meal from crumbs. If you are not in KGB, you learn to leave no crumbs." She shook me by my lapels. "You understand?"

I thought I did. But Juliana was still worried.

The next night, Darya was already there when Maxim and I arrived at their apartment. I recognized her voice, and as we entered she was standing with her back to us. She wore a light green sweater and jeans, and she was surprisingly different from the roundish, bundled figure of the previous day. I had no idea what to expect. But when she turned around to greet us, I realized that there were grounds for Juliana's concerns.

What the dusk had revealed of her face the previous afternoon was only a vague outline of what made her attractive. Her hair was cut short, a rich, auburn chestnut, with golden-reddish highlights. The wide mouth I recognized was only the beginning of looking at her. Each time I glanced in her direction, I noticed something else. Her big eyes, clear and girlish; wide lips full, naturally upturned at the corners, so that she seemed always to be smiling; the smoothness of her forehead; her pale neck, the delicacy of the V above her breastbone.

She offered me her hand. It was small in mine, her handshake warm and firm, the touch electric. We kissed each other's cheeks, and again I was aware of her perfume. It took all of fifteen seconds, but there was too much intimacy in our brief greeting. There was nowhere else to take the conversation, and I made it a point to ignore her for the remainder of the evening. I reminded myself that I had not come to Moscow in search of women. She was a cousin, albeit a distant one, the mother of two young children, married to a dangerous man, and I had been warned against her. I would simply make no attempt to see her again. It was disappointing, but not too difficult. I was in Russia for only two weeks, and my schedule was full.

It was an evening of conversation, of family jokes and teasing, and they all tried hard to make it accessible to me. I understood some, but not all, of what was said. We drank wine and vodka, ate dinner together around a table piled with salad and cheese, sausage and boiled potatoes, olives and pickles. Despite myself, I watched Darya. She laughed easily, turned from one member of the family to another, participated in the conversation as if unaware of the slight unease focused in her direction. As the evening progressed, the unease lessened, and even Juliana began to warm up to her. It was as if they suddenly remembered who she was, or who she had been, and wanted it all to be the way it had once been.

And then the evening ended. As we prepared to rise and leave, in the confusion of Russian being spoken all around me I must have missed something, because once all our coats were on, I turned to say good-bye to Darya, and she laughed.

"Your Russian is not so good as you would like to think, is it?" She looked flustered for a second. "No, I'm sorry—I wasn't making fun. But my driver waits outside, and we just agreed that I would drop some cousins of Maxim at their home, and then take you back to your hotel. So, not yet good-bye."

As we left the apartment, Juliana kissed my cheeks, squeezed my hand, and gave me a meaningful look. Then we were in the car with an elderly couple, Darya and I sitting in the back seat. Between us sat the woman, Maxim's cousin; her husband sat in front with the driver. It was the same car we had seen the previous day, with the same driver, whom Darya called Viktor. It was spacious, and it was warm, and I knew that soon there would be no one sitting between us.

We maneuvered through the streets of Moscow, making strained conversation, and eventually the passenger in the front seat told Viktor to pull over to the side of the road. It was at a point between two buildings, and as was customary, there was no indication of which building was theirs. I stepped out of the car to make way for the cousin whose name I didn't remember, she kissed me goodnight, and I shook her husband's hand. When the car took off again, swerving wildly to avoid potholes, I was sitting beside Darya, alone in the back seat of her husband's luxurious limo, being chauffeured around through the freezing Moscow night by Viktor, whose revolver I had seen in a shoulder holster as he opened the door. If Grigory had connections to the KGB, then so did his driver. And for all I knew, Darya was as connected as he was.

"Now," she said softly, in English, "for the benefit of Viktor, we speak Russian. Watch my fingers." I glanced down, to see her waving one finger from left to right. "This is no; and this—" now she waved the same finger up and down "—is yes. Okay?"

I nodded, my mind racing. What was she doing?

She looked at me quizzically.

"So," she said, raising her voice over the noise of the engine, "you are enjoying Moscow?" She waved her fingers up and down.

I stared at her from across the car.

"I've enjoyed what I've seen so far."

She smiled at me, nodding. This was a game we were playing, and my first answer had been right.

"Good. Babushka tells me she invited you to go with her to the Tretyakov Gallery the day after tomorrow." She waved the finger for yes.

"She seemed excited to go," I said. "Yes."

"Wonderful. Would you mind if I come along? It's been a long time since I was there, and I know it's her favorite museum." This time she opened her hand in a question, as if asking me whether I really wanted her to join us.

"That would be fine," I said.

"Did she tell you about Ivanov's painting? How it brought her back from the brink of death as a child?"

"A little," I said. "Sounds as if she's had a difficult life."

She shrugged her shoulders, a gesture barely visible within the confines of her fur coat.

"Life was difficult for everyone in that generation. I don't know how much you're taught about our history, but we've been through much hardship in this country—a lot of it caused by the West. Everybody from that generation had difficult lives." She leaned forward and spoke to the driver. "Right, Viktor?"

"Not just that generation," he nodded, turning his head slightly towards Darya. "We love her, but sometimes Mother Russia forgets we are her children." He grinned as we passed a streetlight and it glinted briefly off his gold teeth. "I wouldn't feel too sorry for your Babushka. She may be an old woman, but she has a steel spine. If you cross her she's likely to pull it out of her back and beat you over the head with it."

Darya laughed.

"Viktor is secretly in love with my grandmother," she said.

He laughed, and from deep in his throat emerged a heavy smoker's harsh bark. The sound made me want to clear my throat.

"At twice my age," he said, "she's still more woman than I could handle."

We all laughed, and then there was silence in the car. I wondered whether it would be acceptable to ask her into the hotel for a drink, whether there was even a bar at the hotel, and since it was almost midnight, what chance there was that it would be open this late. In the darkness I felt heat behind my eyes, as if her profile were burning into my retina. The infrequent streetlights passed across the smooth curve of her cheek, silhouetting her eyelashes, her hair, the lines of her mouth as she smiled at me. I wondered whether I was in any danger, and whether I was jeopardizing Juliana or any of the other members of my family by even thinking this way.

"I'm so glad," she said loudly, "that you're interested in seeing the photographic exhibition at Moscow University tomorrow. I think you'll really enjoy it."

This was the first I had heard of any photography exhibit, and I thought perhaps I had misunderstood, or misread something in the activities I'd scheduled. I looked at her quickly, to see her hand in her lap, hidden from the driver, shaking her finger up and down.

"Yes," I said. "I'm looking forward to it."

"Remember, it opens at 11:00 am," she said. "I would travel there with you but I have to arrive very early. You can take the Metro, and when you get to the University you just go to the Arts Center. The Metro comes right by your hotel. You know where it is?" Her finger moved from side to side.

"I've seen the station," I said, "but I have no idea how to get to the Arts Center at the University."

"Don't worry—it's easy. When we get to your hotel I'll come in and show you on the map," she said, "I won't take a minute. You have to transfer from the Circular to the Red Line, and then take a bus. You know, we take great pride in our public buildings, and we have the most beautiful subway stations. You will enjoy the Metro."

Apparently I was going to see some photographs the following day, and despite my resolve, we were going to see each other again. I didn't know quite what to make of it, but I was hardly disappointed. We passed the remaining journey to my hotel in silence, sitting at opposite sides of the car. By common consent, we left the center of the seat empty and looked out of our respective windows. Several times, against my will, I turned to look at her, only to find her turning simultaneously in my direction. Her wide eyes were luminous, her pupils molten, and her face was filled with surprise, even shock, as if what she was experiencing was wholly unexpected. It must have appeared to the driver, as it probably did to the family through the entire evening, that we were unaware of each other. But I couldn't have been more aware of her physical presence had we been breathing into each other's mouths, our limbs intertwined. We might have been connected by an electrical pulse that jumped the space between us with torrential force. The intimacy in the back seat of the car was so intense that it felt inappropriate in a public place. I was embarrassed, and Darya's cheeks, when next I looked at her, showed that she was, too.

Until then, all my relationships with women began and ended with sex, and anything of consequence that occurred in between almost certainly happened in bed. There were many things I didn't yet know, and one was that everything between Darya and me would be of consequence, whether it was in bed or out. One thing I was sure of, however, was that Darya looked like someone I had always known, and I felt as though something missing from my life had been suddenly retrieved. I imagined us together, my lips on the side of her pale neck, my hand tracing the curve of her naked hip. I found myself wondering what would happen between us, and realized that I knew. And with a shock, that she knew, too. What I didn't know was how we would make it happen.

When we reached the hotel, Darya told Viktor that she would only be a moment. I thanked him for the ride, and he nodded silently.

"I apologize for putting you on the spot," she said, smiling at me as we walked towards the hotel entrance. "You're not used to this, are you?"

"I guess not," I answered, wondering whether she was talking about the need to deceive the driver, or about her efforts to arrange a meeting between us. Or perhaps she was referring to something that I wasn't even aware of.

"Well," she said, "Just so you know, I don't make a habit of doing this.

In fact, I've never done it. But—"

"You've never done what?" I interrupted.

She looked at me, and the frankness in her eyes told me more than any words could have said. Unless my imagination was working overtime, which it well might have been.

"I've never covered a photography exhibit." She smiled, again playfully. "But that doesn't matter. Here in the USSR, all high-ranking government employees are capable of anything. So, for example, although I have no experience with photography, apparently I do the students a great honor by going through the exhibit with them." She paused. "I'm also not in the habit," she said quietly, "of arranging to meet with men I've only just met, even if they are cousins, and even if the event is a photography exhibit. But I think you will enjoy it. If you come, we can perhaps have a coffee afterwards."

"Coffee sounds wonderful," I said, "and I'm sure I'll find a student photography exhibit interesting." I smiled at her. "After all, I am a painter, and one of my objectives in coming here is to learn about Soviet art. So if I'm asked, my story holds up."

She picked up a map of Moscow and the Metro stations off the deserted counter, and we sat in the cavernous lobby. "So," she said softly, "you're willing to spend time together with me despite Juliana's warning?" She must have seen the surprise on my face. "Don't worry—I know what the family thinks. I don't blame them. When I married, I took on my husband's status. You know, people in power are always suspect. We've come to believe, under our system, that you have to be corrupt to rise. And so I lost the trust and confidence of those closest to me. It's only natural that they think this way, but it doesn't make me happy. Being married to a powerful man in the security service is not easy. The family perceives me as dangerous, even if I don't always agree with my husband's politics."

I must have looked shocked again, and I was—she had admitted what even Juliana had seemed unsure of, that Grigory was with the KGB; and she had revealed that she was not always in agreement with him. Was this her way of manipulating me, or was she showing me who she really was? At that moment, it didn't matter. I looked at her for a long time—her forehead, her eyes, the line of her neck, her mouth. She flushed, dropped her head, and began drawing on the map.

"I don't think you would do me any harm," I said, "even if you could. Besides, if you want to have coffee with me in order to find out whether I'm hiding anything, you'll be very disappointed."

She was bent over the coffee table, marking the map. Now she looked up.

"I am already not disappointed," she said in a low voice, almost a whisper. "Because of my work, I have been allowed to travel to the West. I know how different it is here in Soviet Union. This separates me from our family, because I have seen another way to be. Here, we need to be cautious, because we don't know who we will harm, or from what source harm will come to us." She rose, came around the table and sat beside me. I had to concentrate on keeping a distance between us in order to focus on the directions she gave me.

"I must go now," she said, standing.

I stood beside her, and we kissed first right cheeks, and then left. As we moved from one side to the other I had a powerful inclination to stop at her mouth. Our lips may have brushed in passing; I don't remember. It may have been wishful thinking.

"Until tomorrow," she said. I walked her outside, closed the car door for her, and watched as the limo pulled from the curb and drove away.

❦

In the light of day, as I thought about what I was planning to do, I remembered Juliana's warning. It made me wary, but not enough to dampen the enthusiasm I felt at the prospect of spending part of the day with Darya. I would go, but I would be cautious. I wondered, if her intentions were really as underhanded as Juliana thought, what she might want from me. It was possible that she had access to my itinerary, that there was no coincidence in the selection of a day on which I had no plans. But to what end? As I ate breakfast in the hotel dining room and drank a cup of weak, stale coffee, I found myself grinning at the idea that the Soviet government might think I had anything of value to them. Could they possibly think I was something other than an artist visiting his family?

Despite my misgivings, nothing could have prevented me from going, even though every step of the way I was completely out of my element. The Department of Tourism apparently kept track of tourists by knowing at all times where their passports were, and the front desk at the hotel had mine. It would have been madness to leave the hotel without it, but I had no idea whether the clerk at the desk would return it to me without asking where I was going. I didn't know whether I would be questioned as I entered the Metro, or how I would know when to get off the train.

The clerk gave me my passport without question. No one that I could see followed me, and entering the Metro was easy. Waiting for my train, I was bowled over by the elegance and beauty of the station, and by how clean it was. In comparison, the subway system at home in Boston was dismal and filthy. I was struck by the contrast between the grandeur of the station and the appearance of the people. With the exception of the young—mostly high school and university students, who were like students everywhere— the adults were mostly silent. To me they appeared unhappy, sullen, and drab. Beaten.

I negotiated the transfer from one Metro line to another, and then to an above-ground bus, and finally arrived at the University, where I was directed to the photography exhibition. Very little about it remains with me. Industry and agriculture. Romantic shots of factory buildings casting long shadows at dawn and at dusk. Portraits of farm and factory workers with lined faces. Small children playing. There was only one group in the room, who turned out to be the student exhibitors and a woman who was their teacher. Darya was with them, going from one grouping of photographs to the next, and taking notes on a pad. She looked at me as I entered, and then ignored me. I went around on my own, several stations behind them, listening. She was charming, asked questions about the photos, stood back and commented seriously on several shots, laughed openly with the students. I found myself admiring her grace, the natural, unencumbered way she moved, watching and feeling proud of her, as if she were somehow mine to be proud of.

When it was over she thanked the students, who left, and then she beckoned to me. She introduced me to the teacher, Marta, as a visiting American artist. We exchanged pleasantries, and I followed her outside. The temperature was below freezing, but the sun was out, and it wasn't uncomfortable. She began walking, and I fell in step with her.

She looked up at me with her wide smile. "You came," she said. I took in the lines and planes of her face, and in the cold winter light, when I realized that she was genuinely happy to see me, my heart expanded to fill my chest.

"I told you I'd be here," I said. "Why do you sound so surprised?"

"I hoped that you would find the courage to come," she said. "It makes me happy that you did."

"Oh, it took great courage," I joked, "to walk past the dragons in the hotel corridors."

"They're always watching." She laughed. "Be careful what you say as you walk by them. They miss nothing."

"So I'm told," I said. "I thought you were wonderful with the students."

"They work hard," she said simply. "They're good students, and I even liked some of their photographs." She looked up at me. "I notice you spent time looking at the photography of industrial buildings. You liked them?"

"Yes, some of the ones taken at night are good."

"She uses the moonlight well. Her pictures are stronger because of deep shadows. And how she composes her elements in the frame is excellent."

I laughed.

"You are laughing at my English?" she asked, ready to be offended.

"No, but I assumed that whoever took those pictures was a boy, not a girl—and I thought you were a journalist, not an art critic."

"Can a journalist not have aesthetic sensibility?" She looked at me out of the corner of her eye. "Perhaps in Boston you are allowed only one skill. You are an artist, so you cannot also have educated opinion about politics or world events?"

"You're right, of course," I said. "But what you have to say about art is far more interesting than my ideas about the world."

She was setting the pace, and although it felt good to walk fast, I had no idea where we were going. We had been on the path for at least ten minutes, long enough for her to have shared our destination with me; long enough for me to acknowledge that I was beginning to have misgivings.

"I like how you laugh," she said, looking up at me as we walked. "So quick, and natural. Do you always show so easily your feelings?"

I took her arm and stopped, turning her toward me.

"It's not that complicated," I said. "Most of the time I don't have any reason to hide what I feel. I'm very happy to be here with you, perhaps happier than I have a right to be. But I begin to wonder whether this is a mistake." I stopped speaking, still holding her arm, her face very close to mine. "I can't help wondering whether Juliana was right in warning me to be careful. Is this really about our having coffee together? Or are you following instructions to take me somewhere?"

Her eyes opened in shock and her mouth tightened. She swiped at my hand and pulled her arm away.

"You think I'm taking you somewhere? For what? Interrogation? Such ridiculous American stereotype. You have very low opinion of me," she said angrily, "and you show me just how big your ego is. What information could you possibly have that the KGB would want? Forget coffee. I put you back on the Metro, and you can go to your dark little hotel room."

"I have another feeling you should know about."

"You go to hell, with such easy feelings and judgments. What is it?" she said, mocking. "You want to go back home to America, where everything is safe and predictable?"

"No," I said, taking her arm again, this time more gently. "I don't want to go home. I want you to stop breathing fire at me. The only sure way I know to do that is to kiss your beautiful mouth."

She shook her head vigorously, eyes wide.

"No," she whispered, with an involuntary intake of breath. "Not here." She continued walking, pulling me along. "Come. I was going to tell you where we go to, but now I am glad I didn't, because now you know me better—I am not all sweet and light. And I know you, too. I am glad you spoke as you did," she said breathlessly. "So I am not sorry. The photography teacher, Marta, I introduced you? She is my friend. We go to her apartment to have coffee with her. Her building is there." She pointed at a complex of towers ahead of us. "She lives on the university campus, close to where she teaches. So it is very convenient." She paused, turned quickly to me, and our eyes met. "For us."

"Oh," I said. "That's good."

I was deeply disappointed. It would be a strenuous discussion with Marta about art and photography, in Russian, and Darya and I would have no further opportunity to be alone. But when we arrived at the apartment, there was no one home. The door was unlocked. We walked in to the smell of fresh-brewed coffee. Darya closed and locked the door behind us. She took off her coat. I did the same, and watched her as she turned slowly in the studio apartment and lay both coats over the back of a small, red armchair. We stood facing each other in the enclosed space, crowded bookshelves against one wall, and a large black and white photograph on the other. We moved towards each other, and as she lifted her arms her sweater rose across her breasts and I saw a pale sliver of her waist. I put my hands against her naked skin, and gently pulled her towards me. Her arms were around my neck, her fingers in my hair, the length of her body against mine. She sighed deeply as I passed my lips across her cheek, down her neck, over her eyes. Her breath was warm and sweet against my face, and her skin smelled of roses and lavender, of toasted sesame, and coffee. I took the lobe of her ear between my teeth, and she pulled away, shuddering.

"You smell wonderful," I murmured into her hair.

"No talking," she whispered. "Time to do what you said before."

She opened her lips to me. Our kiss was measured, gentle and controlled, as I tasted her mouth and the warmth of her tongue. Her fingers in my hair as she held my head between her hands was the most intimate sensation I could remember.

For the first time in my life I felt that I had found my center. The sensation shocked me—both because I had not been aware that my center was missing, and by the realization that it was directly linked to this woman. And in the midst of the most joyous kiss of my life, there was a wash of anguish at the knowledge that she belonged in Moscow, to another man, and that I would be leaving in a week. Without her.

Then it was over. There was a knock at the door, we separated, looked at each other and smiled. She went to unlock the front door as I went into the bathroom, took a deep breath and made myself presentable, and then we exchanged places, and I greeted Marta. When Darya came out of the bathroom, her hair smoothed, her skin glowing, we sat together and drank Russian coffee, and discussed art and photography as if it were the most natural thing in the world.

We said our farewells to Marta and took the bus and then the Metro together, sitting beside each other in silence, thighs touching. I was desolate. She turned from the waist towards me so that we could look at each other, and I had a visceral memory of the way her body moved beneath her clothes, how the soft curve of her waist submitted and flexed to the broadness of her hips. The remembering was at once natural and thrilling, ecstatic and excruciating. We spoke quietly, just above a whisper.

"You are sad that we had coffee with Marta?" she asked.

"Is my sadness so obvious?" I reached out and touched the soft curl at her cheekbone.

"You told truth when you said you didn't hide your feelings. But I am also not happy."

"Because?"

She gave me a sad smile.

"Even if we could spend every moment together until you go, we would not have enough time." She brightened. "But tomorrow we go together with Babushka to the Tretyakov, and the next day you go to Saint Petersburg, yes?"

I straightened, and moved my thigh away from hers.

"How did you know that, Darya? I didn't tell you where I was going."

"So," she said slowly, "it's true. You really don't trust me."

I took her hand, but she gently pulled it away. I wanted to take her in my arms and tell her I did trust her, but it wouldn't have been totally true. In my heart I trusted her completely, but in my head Juliana's warning was still present, a small bell of caution, tolling distantly.

"You told Juliana your plans, and I overheard her telling Maxim. But the truth is that I have your itinerary in my office. Even before I heard anything, I knew where you would be going."

"Is this supposed to make me trust you? How could you know my schedule?"

"In USSR, everything is hidden, but everything can be found, if you know how. Nothing is private." She shrugged. "Because of my work, I know how. We have international visitors from the press, and often it is my job to meet them at airport and show them the city." She turned away from me. "But if you prefer, I will forget where you're going."

I laughed, and she turned back to me. "You can't just forget what you know," I said, "even if I want you to. And I don't want you to. I'm sorry to doubt you. But I really don't know what to think."

"Well, then," she said sadly. "Perhaps we should not see each other again."

"Can we see each other again?" I whispered, suddenly excited by the possibility of another meeting.

"So," she said, smiling happily, "you would like it if I could come to Saint Petersburg?"

Suddenly the possibility of seeing her again existed, in another city where the constraints of family were absent. Until then I hadn't allowed my mind to wander much beyond lying beside her and running my hands over her body, but now I was flooded with images of making love to her, of standing before paintings in a museum and talking about them, of eating a meal together.

"It would be wonderful," I whispered. "But what about your work? And your family?" It was the first time either of us had mentioned her husband or children.

"The children will be fine—they have a wonderful nanny, and Babushka comes most days to be with them. She stays at the apartment when I am away. Grigory," she said carelessly, "does not care if I am here or not. For him I am only to show off, like a doll. And work—well, I am sometimes away overnight for work. I have friends in Saint Petersburg, and also journalist colleagues. Work is not a problem. We have a saying here, Steven." Her voice faltered as she tried out my name, and then she smiled at me again. "You will hear it often if you lived here. We say that in Soviet Union, we only pretend to work—and they only pretend to pay us."

We agreed that she would meet me in Saint Petersburg in two days—if she was able to change some appointments in Moscow, arrange a meeting with colleagues to justify a trip, and ensure that her children were taken care of. If it turned out that she could arrange to come, she would have to make preparations, and would not be able to meet me the next day at the Tretyakov Gallery.

Her stop was two before mine. We shook hands politely for the benefit of any who might be watching, and before she released my hand she leaned toward me. Her dark eyes were full of secrets, and I almost kissed the upturned corners of her mouth, where she was hiding a smile.

"I hope not to see you tomorrow," I said.

"Me, too. Maybe in Saint Petersburg you leave hotel door unlocked. If all works out well, perhaps," she smiled, "you will receive a visitor in the night."

Then she turned and walked towards the door of the slowing train. I spent the time after she left reliving our moment alone in Marta's living room, and wondering whether, after tomorrow, I would ever see her again.

❦

The next afternoon I took a taxi to Lena's apartment, and we went together to the Tretyakov Gallery. She explained that, regretfully, Darya would be unable to join us. My heart leapt.

"I'm sorry to hear that," I said. "But I'm happy to have this time alone with you."

"Yes," she said. "It will be just like it was when I took your grandfather Mischa to see Ivanov's painting."

When we reached the museum, I understood even better what the Metro had taught me about the pride Russians take in their public places. It was a magnificent building, an elaborate statement about the public ownership of national treasures. The art in the main galleries was as extraordinary as I had been led to believe. In anticipation of my trip, which was supposed to be about Russian art, I had prepared myself for questions from customs and immigration at the airport, and I knew what to look for.

Lena was as energetic as I was, which was remarkable for this tiny, old woman. She wanted me to see whatever I needed to see, and then, just before we left, she would take me to her favorite painting. I didn't want to tire her out, but there were several paintings I would have regretted not seeing. One was a painting of the Crucifixion by Dionisii. It was painted in 1500, in a Byzantine manner, the figures slender and elongated, with a yellow background, bright colors so different from Renaissance versions of the Crucifixion. For the first time since arriving in Moscow, I remembered that I was an artist. Looking at the depth of color in Dionisii's painting, it was difficult to believe he could achieve such a range from the materials available to him. I struggled to find the words in Russian to explain to Lena how he made his paints, from colored pebbles of soft stone, which he ground up and mixed with egg yolk and thinned with Kvass, a drink made of fermented rye bread—and it lasted for five hundred years.

She had been unusually silent as we stood before the painting, and I thought perhaps she was as taken by the colors as I was. But finally she came close to me and beckoned me down to her level so that she could whisper in my ear.

"Are you ready?" she asked. "Time to introduce you to Ivanov." She took my elbow and with surprising strength she pulled me along beside her. "You know he painted over three hundred years after Dionisii?" she asked, peering up at me.

"I did know that," I answered.

"Good."

When finally she drew to a stop, there were twenty or thirty people standing before the massive painting, but Lena was undaunted. She squeezed her slight frame between the observers, still holding on to my elbow, dragging me in embarrassed apology behind her.

Here," she said. She was breathless, pointing to the beatific figure in the middle ground. "Very different from Dionisii's crucified, mutilated Christ, eh? Ivanov's Christ is a man to admire, calm and peaceful. The color of his robe, that blue, it's an important color. These men, and the boy, are being baptized in the Jordan River by the man in the fur. That's John the Baptist. And that man there, with the stick, and the hat? Ivanov. He painted himself into the picture, a wanderer from the future." She glanced at me. "Now I will be quiet. We can view together. It takes time to see this painting. Longer to know it."

Afterwards, she took me to see the character sketches Ivanov had made in preparation for the work. She knew them all, whether they were included in the painting or not, and the reasons why. Her husband, Vasily, had told her about the sketches, and she had never forgotten what he taught her. I had no idea at the time just how much the painting meant to her, but for sixty years it had been a touchstone that gave her life meaning and beauty. Not a bad legacy for a painter.

The train to Saint Petersburg was delayed by unscheduled stops. By the time we pulled into the station it was evening, the city was darkened, and all I wanted was to sleep. I registered at the Hotel Moscova, where Intourist had booked me, ate in the dining room and then went to the desk to check for messages. There was nothing, so I went up to bed. I left the door unlocked, lay wide awake and filled with excitement, but that night there were no visitors. We had arranged that if Darya was unable to get a message to me, we would meet in the sculpture garden on the first floor of the Menshikov Palace the day after my arrival in the city. The Palace opened at 10:00 am, and we agreed that I should wait there for her until noon.

The next day was cold and overcast, threatening snow that didn't arrive. There were no messages at the desk, and after breakfast I returned to my room to see whether a note might have been stuffed under my door. There was nothing.

I made my way past the famous Tikhvin Cemetery, stopping to see Dostoevsky's tomb, and then into the sculpture garden at the Menshikov Palace, a magnificent building on the bank of the Neva River. Under other circumstances I would have been spellbound by the sculpture.   In my memory they were all large nudes. Maillol's *Standing Woman*, and several nude women by Henri Matisse, but most were statues of nude pairs—Bartholomé's *Adam and Eve*, and several by Rodin, including *Romeo and Juliet*, and *Eternal Spring*, all in various states of amorous embrace. I stood before each sculpture and pretended to examine it, but what I was really doing was using the peerlessly beautiful stone images to camouflage my search for Darya. Each young woman who walked into the garden energetically, or stood graceful and athletic before one of the statues, was potentially she, and by the end of my two-hour wait I was exhausted by the number of false alarms, of excited surges that I had to catch before they escaped me in a shout of welcome to someone who wasn't Darya.

I spent the afternoon wandering about the city, and the day seemed to drag on without end. By evening the desk clerk knew me well, and when he saw me approaching he shook his head apologetically: still no messages. I had an unremarkable dinner alone, drank a gin and tonic, went to bed. After about an hour of lying awake, I rose to recheck that the door was unlocked. I climbed back into bed convinced that Darya had been unable to arrange the trip, and I would end up returning to Boston without seeing her again.

But just before midnight my melancholy thoughts of unrequited love were interrupted when the doorknob turned and the door cracked open, letting in a sliver of light from the hallway. A figure materialized, slipped through the opening, and closed and locked the door silently behind her, shutting out the light and muffling the sounds. She turned on the bathroom light and left the bathroom door open enough to cut the darkness, and she walked toward the bed. She was smiling, and she put her finger over her lips. I had no need to speak; I was happy to simply have her there, and to watch as she undressed slowly, placing her clothes neatly on the armchair. She stood naked beside me, only the silhouette of her shoulders and hips visible in the darkness, I lifted the sheet for her, and she entered my bed. She had walked to the hotel and she was chilled, and as our bodies touched I felt that she was shivering. I held her quietly. We said nothing, and it took a long time for her to stop quivering with cold. When she did finally warm up, there was still something in her that made her uncomfortable. Several things, it turned out.

"Steven." And then she quickly whispered, "Stevie."

"Yes?"

"It makes you happy that I am being here?"

"Very happy," I said. "Can't you tell?"

I noticed that when she was in the grip of strong emotion, her perfect English syntax reverted to some confused mix of English and Russian.

"When I was a girl," she whispered into my neck, "they said I was very beautiful." We lay shoulder to shoulder, hip to hip down the length of her, and I was acutely aware of her cool hand at my waist. "I didn't believe, didn't understand that this was a great gift, also that it could bring great hardship. How I looked and smiled and walked—that was the attraction for my husband. Nothing else. If I had been less, he would have put his eye on another girl, and I would have waited to be older and choose my own husband, instead of being chosen so early, when I had not the wisdom to refuse. But now, with two children, I am in a trap without a door. I would prefer to bring you who I was before children, but that body is gone with my youth. It makes me sad to come to you all used up."

I rose to one elbow and looked down at her, thinking at first that she must be joking. But there was only misery on her face.

"You're talking crazy," I said. "When you walk into a room every man turns to look at you, and every woman is green with envy. How is it possible you don't see that?"

Slowly I ran my hand over her shoulder down her hip and along the length of her thigh, long and muscled. She was supple and smooth, the curve of her hip dramatic, her belly taut as if she'd never had children. Her breasts were rounded, firm, like oranges, her nipples full and responsive to my touch. She was lovely. I wondered what her husband could have said or done to make her feel so damaged.

"Girlish beauty is very thin," I whispered, "one dimensional, like a photograph. When I saw you at Juliana's apartment, you took my breath away."

She put her hand up to my cheek. "Thank you for your kind little lies," she said.

"These are not lies," I said. "You need to keep me around. I can be the magic mirror on the wall, reminding you that you're the fairest of the fair." She smiled. "What happened to you that you have such a poor opinion of yourself?" I asked.

She looked up at me, her face framed by short, dark curls. I lowered my mouth to hers, but she put two fingers on my lips and pushed me away. For a moment her eyes glazed over, and she was far away.

"Where are you?" I whispered.

"I'm here," she said. "Your question is very complicated. Perhaps one day we have enough time to tell the whole story, but what happened to me is Grigory. He keeps me like the bird in a golden cage, and he hopes that I will sing for him. But he likes only young, perfect bodies, and he does not hide from me the disgust on his face. When he looks at me, I feel used up. Ugly."

"But you said he wants you to be an ornament on his arm. How can he feel both things?"

"He is complicated. Devious. He has contempt for the men who still think I am a prize, and it gives him pleasure to see the envy in their eyes when we walk into a room together. But he knows better—he has seen me with my clothes off. He makes very clear to me that this body will not win any prizes in his competition."

Grigory's deranged opinion clearly had an impact on her—and the vast disparity between the ugliness he made her feel about herself, and the beauty I saw when I looked at her, made her even more desirable to me.

"He's crazy," I whispered, kissing her neck. "And he's wrong. And in this room he has no power to influence what I see, or to make you feel bad."

She rose up onto her knees, and the silvered light from the bathroom washed over her shoulders and lit the tips of her swaying breasts. "I will try and believe you. They say feeling is believing." Her hand moved cautiously across the front of my hip and she gently closed her fingers around me. I took an involuntary breath. "Maybe," she said with a wicked smile, "this is the only feeling I need to believe you think me beautiful."

She shrugged her shoulders and raised one hand, throwing the blanket off me. "I want to look at you," she said.

I watched her face as her eyes slowly panned across my body.

"Under your clothes you are still just like a beautiful boy," she whispered.

I reached for her, one arm around her waist as I rolled over, wanting to hear sounds of pleasure in her throat, to feel her mouth on mine, to taste her and breathe in her smell. But she turned her head to the side, her fists against my chest, and she pushed me away.

"Stop," she said. "Stop it. Please."

She was panting, there was something close to hysteria in her voice and when I rose to my knees and looked at her, there was panic in her eyes. I pulled the sheet up over us, took her gently in my arms. She shivered, as she had when she first arrived and came to me out of the cold. I realized quickly this had nothing to do with me.

"What is it?" I whispered.

"I can't." she said. "Can't do this. Not yet." She snuggled into me, and I held her. Gradually she calmed, stopped shaking, and her breathing slowed.

"Better?"

"I'm so sorry," she said, her face buried in my neck. "This makes me so red-faced."

"Red-faced?"

"You know," she said. "That word. Embraced. No. Embarrassed."

"He doesn't just have contempt for you," I said. And then without knowing what I was going to say, or what it meant, I asked a question. "He's hurt you, too, hasn't he? You want to tell me what he did?"

For a second she froze, her breathing stopped.

"Is it so obvious?"

"I don't know. I'm not sure where the question came from. I'm sorry."

I kissed her eyes, and her mouth, very gently, and she opened her lips to me for just a moment before she pulled away.

"No. I need to tell you."

"Tell me what?"

"To answer your question. What he did to me."

"I don't need to know," I said. "Being here with you is answer enough."

"But I want you to know."

When I said I didn't need to know, perhaps what I meant was that I didn't want to know. It might just be too much information too soon. If the intimate difficulties of her life were sufficiently traumatic, I might be put off enough to lose interest or be scared away. It could overlay the excitement and purity of what we were experiencing with a darkness I would be unable to get beyond. But I had no choice.

"Then tell me," I said.

"Not the whole story," she said. "But enough so you can understand. All right?"

"Yes."

She looked at me gratefully.

"I was not yet twenty when my husband first set eyes on me. I was little more than a girl, full of idealism, and I knew nothing of the world. Already he was in his thirties, well on the way in his career. At first I had no idea what his work was, and he hid very well that he was sick in his mind, sick with evil and rage, and a terrible fear of being without power. I was so shocked and pleased that he showed interest in me. I had never been with a man, and I was happy to give myself to him. But he didn't want that."

"He didn't want you?"

"Oh, he wanted me—but he didn't want that I give myself. He knows only to take. I became used to his patterns. At first, it was only a little rough.

It felt like a game, so I enjoyed it sometimes. Today it shames me to say that. But after we married, it became violent, and it was painful. He was cruel, and it became worse and worse. So I decided, enough is enough—I would never let him touch me again. But it only made him angrier. He forced me—and this time it was not just cruel. He raped me. But in a marriage here, especially to a powerful man, there is no such thing as rape. People would only laugh. Our son Anton was born from that. Since his birth Grigory lets me know that I disgust him. So far he leaves me alone."

She stopped to take a breath, leaned down and rested her cheek on my shoulder.

"Why don't you take your children and leave him?"

"Not possible," she said. Her lips pursed, she shook her head. "He would not allow it, and he would find me. Wherever I went."

"Even the United States?"

"There would be no place to hide from him. But for now this is not important. We can do nothing to solve it. What I want you to know is, I have been in my life with only one man, and since then, I have not been with anyone. And now you know a little of my story, you realize, being here is very dangerous for me."

"That's a long time," I said. "So why me? Why now?"

"I ask myself the same question. I wonder, is it because you leave in a few days and I will never see you again? But I have had many opportunities in other countries to sleep with strangers, and I never wanted to. I think, when I first saw you, you were the first man since many years that made me want you. There was in you a kind of gentleness, and ease. Perhaps because you are from United States. But there is also science. I mean, there is chemistry between us. Very strong."

"Yes."

She moved slightly, her thighs parted, and she threw one leg over my hip.

"Very strong chemistry," I said. My hand at her waist found its way to her belly and as she adjusted herself my fingers felt the hot wetness between her legs.

"Now you know I want you, too," she said. "I would like to be able to tell you, take me, Steven, I want to give myself to you, but for now, that is too frightening for me. I can't say that, or feel it. When I even think it, my throat closes up."

"What do you need me to do?"

"You do nothing," she whispered, rolling her thigh all the way over me so that I was on my back and she kneeling above me. I ran my hands up her sides, brushing the flanks of her breasts where they extended beyond her torso, and down to the narrowest part of her waist, where it curved in from the round fullness of her hips. "I do everything. Can you let me take from you what I need, and give to you only what I want? Let me be in charge of what happens?"

"What you want to do, most men fantasize about. And most of them complain that they never get it. " I grinned up at her. "And you make it sound as if I'm making a sacrifice."

In response she rolled her hips back and forth, rubbing herself against the underside of my erection, and her wetness sent a breathless frisson of excitement through my belly and up my spine so that I involuntarily arched my back, raising my hips to her. She leaned forward and lowered the underside of her breast to my face. I kissed her, pulling at her nipple. It grew taut and hard between my lips.

"Softly," she murmured, "pull it softly."

I did, and she pulled back, breathing deeply. After a moment she raised her hips and with one hand she positioned herself over me, rocking back and forth, and slowly she took me inside her, lowering her hips until she was lying flat on top of me, one leg on either side.

"Now you kiss my mouth," she whispered, "Show me how you wanted to kiss me at the university."

I took her upper lip in my mouth, and then her lower lip, showed her with my tongue just what my body wanted to do to hers, and as we traded tongues she moved her hips in miniscule circles, first in one direction and then the other. She wanted control, and I was glad to give it to her, but there were some things over which I had only partial control, and I was reaching my limit.

"I can only hold on for so long," I whispered, burying my face in her hair. "What do you want me to do?"

"I don't want you to hold back at all," she replied.

"Not without you," I said hoarsely. "Come with me."

"Next time," she whispered, looking down at me with a smile. "This time I watch your face."

I took the round tightness of her buttocks in my hands and I heard the groans in my chest as I pulled her down onto me, and she gave me access to the deepest, most hidden and secret parts of her body. Finally she began to arch against my movements, raising her back and shoulders. I took both nipples in my mouth and pulled gently, and together we let go, thrusting and shuddering, enveloped in each other, until I couldn't tell whether the breathless gasps and sobbing, or the high pitched keening, was coming from me or from her. We came together, and when the last fluid left my body in an ecstatic rush she came again, and this time I watched her face, and she watched me watching. She let me see in her expression the emergence of the girl she had once been, full of idealism, innocent and excited and taken by surprise. When finally it was over she rolled off me and into my arms, both of us wet and the smell of sex on us. She turned her head to my underarm and breathed in deeply, and when she came up for air she was laughing.

"You laughing at how bad I smell?" I asked.

"I'm laughing because without your clothes you look like a boy, and you come how I think a boy comes, hungry and sweet and without stopping. And even you smell like a boy." She ran both hands through my hair. "I'm laughing because you delight me."

Until then I had slept with girls who might have liked me or my body as much as I liked them, and with a few women where we had some mutual admiration or affection. But no woman ever spoke such words to me, and as we lay in each other's arms, I thought, so this is what it feels like, to be loved.

She grew up without a father, and I without a mother, and somehow in our coming together we fulfilled some absence in each other. I was sure, as I fell into the wishful, sometimes euphoric state that precedes sleep, that I would find a way to spirit her away, to take her and her children home with me, and to keep her safe.

I awoke at dawn to find her kneeling above me, kissing my mouth, and I pretended sleep for as long as I could restrain myself. When at last I opened my eyes and looked at her, she smiled sleepily. I reached up and stroked the short curls at her forehead. She rolled off me onto her back and opened her arms to me.

"Come," she whispered, "make love to me."

Our legs were intertwined, and with the clumsy adjustments that we necessarily forgive or laugh at in our love partners, I raised myself on one knee and crawled over her and between the spread of her thighs, and carefully, softly, lowered myself to the heat of her hips.

Later that morning she left for a conference, but we met after lunch and spent several hours back at the Menshikov Palace, where she showed me around as if I were one of her international guests from the press, and I looked at the sculpture garden with different eyes. We had dinner together in a darkened restaurant on the outskirts of the city, where no one was likely to recognize her, and later she came to my room as she had the previous night. It was to be our last night together, and we made love with slow deliberation. I wanted to commit to memory every inch of her, her perfume, her sounds, and every movement of her body as she explored mine. I watched and felt the way she stretched and tensed in passion, knowing that it was all I would have to subsist on once I returned to Boston.

On our last morning, we lay together, full of sleep and content to be quiet in each other's arms. We talked softly about our common roots. I told her about my Papa Mischa, who had waited his whole life for his father Isaak. I had no way of knowing whether Darya knew anything about our history, and I was mindful of Juliana's warning not to reveal anything about our being Jewish. But there was no need for concern, or for secrecy. She shared with me the stories Babushka had told her over the years as granddaughter and grandmother snuggled at night in their little bedroom, whispering. And before we rose I knew the touching way Babushka had welcomed her into the sorority of Jewish women, the devastating impact it had on her life, and how curious she was to discover more about the meaning of our shared past.

But while we were peaceful and sated on the surface, we were each living our own versions of tumult below. We had made the inevitable discovery that we keep making throughout our lives—that the satisfaction of one desire gives birth to the next. In whispered voices, like children oblivious of practical constraints, we talked about whether there was a way to continue seeing each other. Using the particular measures of our own lives, we tried to gauge what each of us had to gain or lose by doing so. But even as we talked, the idea unraveled like so much fantasy. Because of her children, she felt no option but to return to Grigory's abuse. I had to return to my life in Boston. The beginning of our relationship was over, and it seemed clear that we were headed straight for the end. There was no possibility of a middle.

She was returning on the train that day, and I had only one day left. Still speaking in whispers, I suggested changing my ticket so that we could travel together, and she told me gently that too many people who frequently traveled the route knew her, and that it would be unwise to travel together. I gave her my address, and she gave me a safe address where I could write to her. She told me where I should spend my last day in the city, and then she dressed, and we embraced each other, and she walked out.

I have no memory of where I went or what I saw that last day. Had I suggested a reasonable way to get her out of the USSR, with the children and with Babushka, would she have changed her mind and been willing to rely on me?

But I had no such plan. Such a thing was so far beyond my experience as to be laughable. Rescuing Darya was a job for a man, and she had made very clear that, although she liked me, in her eyes I was a boy. She may have had little or no experience in her life with good men—but apparently she knew enough not to send a boy to do a man's job. She couldn't rely on me. No wonder I spent the rest of my stay in Russia filled with shame, unable to meet my eyes in the peeling, black-edged mirror in my hotel room.

❦

I saw Darya again briefly at Juliana's apartment the day before I left Moscow. She had Viktor bring her by on the way to some evening presentation. It was the first time I had seen her wearing makeup, and it accented the delicacy of her face and the width of her mouth. Her dark hair had been trimmed even shorter, and it was a frame for her cheekbones and for her fair skin. Above a black evening dress her shoulders were bare, and she was gorgeous. When she took off her coat and looked at me from across the room I knew that her visit—and her appearance—were a parting gift to me. She made the visit in order to say good-bye to me, and when I walked her out and we embraced, it was all I could do not to press her against me and crush my mouth against hers. But I was careful, and in the darkened lobby she turned her head to the side as I kissed her neck.

"You cannot kiss my mouth," she whispered. "It will spoil my lipstick. And if you make me cry," she continued, choking on her sobs as I greedily kissed her cheeks, tasting the warm salt of her tears, "my makeup will be ruined."

I walked her to the door and she went out, alone. It was early evening. Through the grimy window I watched as Viktor held open the back door for her. She entered, and he closed it again. Then, before he got into the driver's seat and drove off, he offered a clownish bow, a big shining grin, and an exaggerated wave. Was it for me? Was he playing the part of Grigory's loyal retainer, signaling that he knew she had come to bid me farewell? I had no idea. And anyway, it didn't matter. What happened between us was over.

The window was darkened and once the door closed, she was gone. I watched the car drive off, and then made my way through the gloom and up the darkened stairwells to the light and warmth of Juliana and Maxim's apartment. I recall feeling in the back of my throat the oily, metallic taste of my sadness at the certainty that I would never see her again.

❀

I left Moscow the following day. In Boston I picked up my life—resumed teaching classes and painting in my studio as if nothing had changed. I had simply been on a trip out of the country, and now I was back. I drove to Cape Cod to take photos in preparation for what I imagined would be a new series of paintings: seagulls arrayed on the snow-covered dunes in Truro; the bleak tidal-flats in Brewster, buffeted by howling winter winds; the sun setting in early afternoon over the water, with snow-crusted sand in the foreground.

Wherever I went, I carried my sadness with me. It felt like a heated weight in my chest, but as the days passed and I became accustomed to that heavy presence, I began to take comfort from it. As long as it was there, I had proof that what I had experienced with Darya was real. Soon, I thought, it would lessen, and the sadness would dissipate, as it had in the past when other relationships with women ended.

But I was wrong. Instead of dissipating, my sadness fermented. Instead of being suffused by an emotion warm and smooth, I was now enveloped in grief with the lumpy thickness of milk soured in the sun. I didn't paint. I couldn't sleep. Had to force myself to eat. Every waking moment was filled with thoughts of the time Darya and I had spent in our hotel room in Saint Petersburg; of her body, and her mouth and her eyes and how she looked at me and how she smelled, and of the conversations we had as we walked, sat together, lay wrapped in each other's arms.

I dreamed of her, and when I woke in the morning and discovered myself alone—or with a woman I had taken home as a way to get Darya out of my mind—I found myself distraught and bereft in a way I had never experienced. It was frightening. Was this love? Perhaps it was that we came from two branches of the same family and that we shared familial memories, and were somehow bound together in a way neither of us expected. And I wondered, was she experiencing the same dislocation I was, or simply getting along with her life, having forgotten that she ever met me?

I was reluctant to share this with any of my friends. They would have laughed at me, I thought, the only one of us unmarried, happily playing the field, snared finally by a woman I couldn't have and who might not even want me. Eventually I sat down with my father, told him what I was going through, and shared with him the sense that I was going mad. He didn't laugh, but he was dismissive.

"You're not going mad, Steven," he said. "But it can't be love. Love comes with time. You've known this woman for two weeks, and you tell me you only spent two days with her. You're infatuated. It'll pass."

But it didn't pass. And in March, when I received a letter from Italy, I knew it wasn't going to pass. Before we parted, Darya had given me the address of a woman in Florence, Valeria Bassani.

"Valeria," she had said, "is my good friend. She can get letters to me, and through her we can write to each other. She cares about me, and she has helped me already. Whenever I am in Italy, I will be seeing her."

I ripped open the envelope. Inside was a smaller envelope, sealed, my initials printed carefully on the front. And within, a postcard, on the face of which was a watercolor reproduction of the old synagogue in Florence, Il Tempio Maggiore. I remember thinking that it was a strange choice of postcard. Based on what we talked about, she would have been reluctant to have it known that she had any interest in the old synagogue. She must have picked up the first card she found the last time she was in Italy.

————◆————

Steven—I have meetings in Florence next month. Someone in Moscow in very high position, I cannot refuse him, asks me to find him in Italy a secluded resort for him to entertain his friend. I have found right place. After my meetings I go to see if it serves his purpose. You and I have similar purpose.

There is, in Umbria, ancient monastery of 12th century, La Badia di Orvieto, being converted now to luxury hotel. No one knows yet of this place; it is still very private. Only a few rooms ready for guests. This is I think two maybe three hours by car from Florence. Come direct yourself to La Badia.

We have each separate life to live—I am understanding if you cannot be able to meet me. But I am missing you, and if I see you, Stevie, my whole self will be filled with smiling.

Darya

If there was a man in his right mind who could refuse such an invitation, it wasn't me.

She could have written in perfect Russian, and I would have understood. But from the start, without my being aware of it, the medium of our communication had been English. I found myself repeating the last sentence in her note. It was a mantra that both calmed me and filled me with excitement at the prospect of seeing her. I imagined how she would look, her whole self, filled with smiling. Did she have any idea how her imperfect English would impact me? She probably had no idea that her particular errors of syntax and grammar added a softness to her communications. Adults speaking inexpertly in a tongue not their own often seem more artless and spontaneous than they might sound in their native language, where they know how to manipulate the subtleties of speech. Even though I knew this, I was completely captivated by what sounded like the naïve, innocent quality in Darya's speech.

I told my department head that I had an opportunity to visit Orvieto, where Signorelli painted his frescoes. Michelangelo had been inspired by Signorelli's work, and although I had seen slides, I had never viewed the original work. I figured that if Darya didn't arrive, I would at least have accomplished something. I arranged for a colleague to take my classes while I was away, and I booked my plane ticket.

High above the clouds, trapped in a plane on the way to reunite with this woman I had pined for, I allowed the creep of doubt to dull my euphoria. Could she possibly be as obliging and sweet, as wide-eyed and unguarded, as her language would have me believe? I imagined that her job required clarity of purpose, that it allowed no room for ambivalence or indecision. Then I realized with surprise that if asked, I would have been hard-pressed to describe the work she did. I wasn't sure why I was surprised—I never asked her about her work, and she didn't volunteer much detail. Which led me to wonder whether my father might be correct in his certainty that I knew nothing about her.

We had spent two days together. I could reproduce on paper a likeness of her face accurate to the length and density of the hair on the back of her neck; the delicate indentations at her temples; the microscopic downturn at the very corners of her mouth, and the way I knew, by the imperceptible crinkle at her eyes, that her face was about to break into a smile. *My whole self will be filled with smiling.* I knew the dark brown of her eyes, and how, looking into their depths, in a certain light, her irises appeared backlit by a luminescent, grey-green glow. I knew this because, since returning from Moscow, she was all I had painted. Darya, nude, posing like a dancer, arms at her sides, one leg raised, exposing the pale inside of the other thigh. Darya, spread against an ivory-colored wall, head uplifted. Darya, reclining Manet-like, looking over her shoulder at me with seduction in her eyes.

I had painted the few fading, silvery striations from childbirth on her taut belly; the long line of her thighs, rising out from just above the knees into dense muscle that had tightened with surprising strength about my waist. I had visualized again and again the delicate slope of her shoulders, and below and between them, her breasts, heavy, yet pointed up and outward at angles that differed by a few degrees. In only two days, I knew her down to the length of the joints in her fingers, and the shape and color of her nails. It made sense to me. I was a painter—I understood visually.

But I had learned that there were ways in which I lacked understanding. Perhaps it was beyond me to know her in any way other than through my senses.

I had no idea how other people perceived her. Her Russian colleagues, for example. Did they feel she took advantage of her position as Grigory's wife, lording her privileged life over them? And what about her subordinates? It never crossed my mind that anything less than legions of people reported to her. Did they find her flexible or rigid? Did she tend to kindness and good humor, or bad-tempered arrogance? I imagined and hoped for the former; nothing I had seen would suggest the latter. But I had to admit that I didn't know her well enough to guess one way or the other. She seemed willing to travel far more than I would have thought a new mother might want to be away, and she hadn't said much about her children. Was she an absentee mother, and if so, did she have a choice? What would I think of the way she mothered her children?

As I considered the possibility that my father's assessment might be right, I had to admit that he was not alone in his caution. I recalled Juliana's warnings, which, once I met Darya, I had been all too ready to dismiss. I wondered whether, as Juliana feared, I had now placed myself in a compromising position, and in addition, endangered the whole family.

This was a time, my father would say, for a clear-headed, dispassionate evaluation, and I knew he was right. Even if she was in every detail the woman I imagined, what, in the real world, was possible for us? Whatever the answer, I would not allow myself to fall back into the emotional limbo of the previous months. If that was all there was, I would have to end it completely. I warned myself to be careful, reminded myself that this was a life-changing event, and needed to be carefully thought through. Yet even as I framed it, I was outside the frame, my arms tight about Darya's waist and hers about my neck. I longed for the feel of her fingers in my hair, recalled the warmth of her arms, and the smell of her skin. I promised myself to ask all the hard questions of her, but any hope of making a rational, well thought-out decision was far beyond my grasp. There were moments, on that flight to Italy, during which I would have turned the plane around and headed back to Boston. But I was in control of neither the plane, nor of myself. I was an indecisive passenger, a boy who couldn't make up his mind whether the woman he thought he loved was the best thing that ever happened to him, or the worst. I recognized that some of what I felt for myself was contempt, and, I thought, it was well-deserved.

❦

Umbria, where rolling hills extended beyond the horizon, formed a patchwork of improbable slopes and irregularly shaped fields. It looked as if a giant had taken the rolling hillsides of New England and squeezed them together, creating a compressed landscape with rougher terrain, hills that were higher and steeper, and deeper, narrower, canyon-like valleys. And dotted across the landscape, instead of the plain white steeples of New England churches, loomed the hulking masses of medieval and renaissance cities built on towering tufa cliffs, surmounted by church towers and elaborate steeples, each intended to be a fortress impregnable to invaders.

La Badia di Orvieto was a 12th century monastery in the process of being converted into a hotel. When I pulled my rented Fiat into the courtyard parking lot, it was one of only three cars, surrounded by what appeared to be the ruins of a massive stone abbey. It was cleverly done—while they had reconstructed the interior, parts of the structure remained in disrepair, intended to be seen in their ruined form. Across a half-fallen stone arch lay a huge, blackened wooden beam. Where the beam rested on the ground an ancient trumpet vine had taken root, and it coiled around the old hardwood like an ever-tightening noose. From across the courtyard I could see where the vine, covered in early summer orange trumpet flowers, had actually compressed the beam and twisted it out of true. Beyond the beam were the remains of a toppled tower, fire-darkened stones rising starkly into the blue sky. In the distance, visible between two leaning pillars, was the city of Orvieto, up on the cliff, so high that I had to look up, tilting my head back to see it. The sensation was disorienting—my mind would not easily accept that so massive a structure could exist at such a height.

There was no note waiting for me at the front desk, as we had agreed, so I left one for her, saying that I had driven up to the Cathedral in Orvieto, to see Signorelli's frescoes. I was not about to wait at the hotel—that would have been too much like my experience in Saint Petersburg, where I had waited for her, stopping at the front desk every few hours in desperate hope of a message.

I took the road from the monastery to the base of the cliff and then drove up the steep, narrow lane leading to the top. From the base, the Cathedral appeared to have a small footprint, but it was a massive, imposing structure. From across the immense paved courtyard, the spires and crenellations soared upward, a massive tribute to the architect's belief in God—and as I approached I saw how that tribute was equally reflected in the ornate and detailed work of the stone masons who crafted and decorated the face of the building.

In the Chapel of San Brizio, I stood before Signorelli's frescoes of *The End of The World*, and *The Last Judgment*. Extending up the curved walls and into the domed ceiling, they depict both humans and devils, beauty and ugliness painted with almost photographic accuracy and detail. The colors had been restored to a brilliant richness, far grander and more moving than the reproductions I had seen, or the art slides I used to teach my classes. I found myself wishing I could share this experience with Darya and, if not her, then perhaps with my art history students.

I lost myself in Signorelli's figures for hours, moving from one fresco to another, awed at the way his bodies intertwined to create a dense crush of humanity. When the bell rang announcing the Cathedral's daily closing, I moved toward the exit with the crowd. As I approached the main door, I felt a sudden, surprising surge of delight, almost euphoria. I couldn't figure out what it was—until it registered that the familiar figure standing to one side, smiling softly in my direction, was Darya.

She walked out before I reached her, and I followed, realizing that even though this was Italy and not the Soviet Union, we needed to be careful in public. It was dusk, and the courtyard was full of people, but I held back, wanting to follow whatever example she set. As I tracked her across the courtyard, she slowed and allowed me to catch up with her, and when I did, she put her arm through mine.

"I have been watching," she said, "as you stared at the frescoes. When you turned to leave, I saw on your face that you saw me with your body, even before your mind recognized that it was me."

When she turned to me and I saw the joy in her eyes, my father's caution and all my doubts were eclipsed by the fullness in my chest. He was wrong—it was possible to love someone after only two days. Not particularly wise, perhaps, but possible.

"I see that you're smiling," I said, "with your whole self."

"And you?" she asked. "What is your whole self doing?"

"It's laughing at me," I said.

"You laugh at yourself? Why?"

"Because sometimes I'm an idiot," I said, lowering my head to kiss her. "And because there's nowhere I'd rather be right now than here."

We decided to have dinner in the town, where we would be less conspicuous than at the hotel. There were several places just off the cliff top and we found a little *ristorante* on Corso Cavour, and we ordered Chianti, and salad, and pasta made with black truffles. We looked at each other over the candle on the little table between us, fingers touching, and she asked me again, why I thought I was an idiot.

"I thought perhaps when I arrived, you might not be here."

"That's not being an idiot," she said, "that's caution. I was afraid, too, that you would not come. And then I was afraid you would come—but that we discover what we feel for each other is gone, like a magic spell. And how sad I would be, if you didn't any more want to be with me, and I would have to go back to Moscow without hope of seeing you ever again."

"There is something like magic between us," I said, "but that's the easy part. Making the magic work in the real world—that's what's difficult. I don't want to go back to Boston and worry about you, wondering where they'll send you next, and whether it's safe enough for you to have me join you in Mexico or Turkey. Or will it be Cuba, or some other country where I can't get a visa?" I cradled her hands in mine. "I want to be where you're not afraid, and where I can see your eyes across the table every day."

"I would like that, too. But I can only want what is possible today, to enjoy what we have here, right now. That has to be enough."

I didn't respond immediately, and she pulled one hand away, raised it to my face, and gently traced my lips with her finger.

"Now I've made you sad," she said. "I'm sorry."

"No," I replied. "You're only saying what we both know. If it's all we can have, it will have to be enough."

❦

We had three sun-filled days, and we spent them exploring the countryside. There was an Olympic-sized pool at the hotel, the water pristine and chilly, and completely deserted. We played together like river otters, touching gently and publicly so that when we returned to shower and change before dinner we needed no foreplay, and fell into each other on the bed, or on the floor, to make love as if there were no tomorrow. We were both acutely aware that our tomorrows might exist only in fantasy.

On our fourth day, the weather turned wet and chilly. We awoke to lightning and thunder, and at dawn we stepped out onto our porch overlooking Orvieto. For the first time since we arrived, the city was invisible, shrouded in fog. And then, as we watched, the fog slowly lifted. The mountain was still veiled in mist, but the city at its summit was visible, an apparition floating in the sky. For a moment it hovered, ethereal and beautiful, and then it disappeared again into the clouds, and the rain began.

It stormed so heavily at times that the roads were impassable. We spent the time wandering about the monastery buildings and found ourselves one afternoon in the small, ancient stone chapel, its walls three feet thick. We entered, the wind blowing a chilly rain at our backs. I forced closed the massive wooden door, fourteen feet high and six inches thick, shutting out the storm, and with it the outside world. The space was muffled and darkened, and the only light shone from a spotlight aimed at the front wall, illuminating an ancient fresco of Christ on the cross. The floor was uneven and worn smooth, and in front of the few benches, depressions were worn into the stone. I thought of the thousands of devout knees it took, kneeling daily, for so many centuries, to wear away the stone.

We sat on a bench facing the fresco, and stared at its faded and half-ruined surface. It was strikingly graphic, so much so that, beyond the obvious anguish of nailed flesh, it captured and seemed to transfer to my body the agonies of the crucified Jesus—the excruciating pull on the shoulders; the stretched and constricted diaphragm that made breathing a cruel labor; the awkward and unnatural attitude of the legs, forced into a bend as the body relaxed downward into a final exhaustion.

Something about the silence in this cramped, medieval chapel, with Christ's pain frozen in time on the front wall, made this a safe, contemplative place. I understood how it might have become a refuge from the secular world, and remained that way for so long.

"So, what now?" she said.

The space magnified her voice and threw it across the room, echoing from one wall to the next like a living thing. She quickly put her hand to her mouth, her lips visible through the separations between her slim fingers.

"This place, I think it is holy," she continued, her voice hushed. "It remembers our voices. I think in here, truth speaks in whispers. There must be many secrets hidden in cracks between these broken old stones."

"Perhaps it's no accident that we find ourselves here, together," I said. "Do you think this is an easy place to speak the truth?"

"I have no trouble speaking truth to you, Steven, wherever we are," she said sadly. "You are the one who doubts me."

I was about to disagree, to defend myself, to deny her accusation. But—and perhaps it was the place—I didn't. If I wanted her truth, I had to give her mine.

"I don't doubt you," I said. "But it's hard to believe this is all real."

"You were ready to trust me," she said, still wearing that sad smile. It made me want to take her in my arms and kiss the sadness away. "And then when we were on the train, coming back from art exhibit, I admitted I knew your itinerary even before you told me. And now you are still not trusting me, even though I put so much at risk to be here with you. So," she said wearily, "ask. If it doesn't endanger my children, or you, I'll tell you whatever you want."

"You go first," I said. "You must have as many questions as I do."

"I wonder many things. About your parents—why did your father never come to visit us? What happened to your mother? How was it, losing her and being raised alone by a father? I imagine how you came to painting, but I would like to know your story. Why you are not married? Can it be you never found love with anyone? Or maybe you don't want children?" She hesitated briefly, coming to an end—and to a beginning. "As a father, how would you be? If we could have children I wonder, would they be as lovely as I imagine? And I dream. If it could ever happen, would you be a good father to my children, to Larisa and Anton?"

I breathed out slowly, feeling the weight fall from my shoulders as she itemized her curiosities. I wasn't sure I wanted to reveal how much relief I felt at the nature of the things she asked about me.

"That's a lot of questions," I said. "Where do you want me to begin?"

But apparently I was an easy study.

"Why do you feel such relief from my questions? What terrible, private things you expected me to ask?" She smiled, reached out and stroked my cheek. "I tell you one thing about you I love," she said. "You show me all what's in your mind. I think you cannot hide anything from me. But I need no answers now—all my questions will be answered in time. I know already what kind of man you are." She rose from the bench and stretched, arms above her head. "Maybe love is like looking through a window covered with ice," she said, "and as the sun rises it melts and we can see through to the other side. Everything else is details."

Slowly she walked to the front of the chapel, where she stood before the fresco of Jesus, peering from up close at his tortured and twisted torso.

"How many long centuries he has been holding himself in this terrible position," she said, "all alone in this dark little chapel." She turned and came slowly back to me. "They say, Christian believers, that he is the son of God, and he died for our sins. How is it possible for people to believe such nonsense? I don't even understand what it means, that word, to believe in something."

"Yes you do," I said. "You believe in communism. Isn't that what you lecture about all over the world? Communism as the best hope of the masses?"

"So that's what you think—that I buy the doctrine, hook and sinker, and I parrot it like a robot?"

Her anger was impressive. Her brow furrowed, her eyes seemed to blaze, and her movements and speech increased in power and intensity, even though she was whispering.

"If that's what you believe," she said, spitting the words out with soft precision, "then you're right—you don't know me at all. Perhaps all what I think about you is wrong, too."

"I doubt that you do anything like a robot," I said, "but how would I know what you think about the work you do? I don't really care—I just want to make sure that whatever the answer is, it leaves room for our differences." I took her hand and pulled her down beside me, wrapped my arms about her and put my lips against her neck. "Do you prefer ice hockey or soccer? Jazz or classical music?" Very gently, I took the soft skin below her ear between my teeth. "How do you like your steak? Which endangered species do you care more about—the green-toed frog or the bottle-nosed dolphin?" I paused, kissed her mouth. "Pepsi or Coke? Chocolate or vanilla? Polar bears or Kodiak? Kandinsky or Klee?"

She pulled away impatiently.

"You make jokes," she said, "but this is not a game. I told you already—I know you well enough to trust, to see what kind of man you are. Either you feel certainty about me—" she shrugged "—or you don't. If no, I will be sad, but there's nothing I can do to change it. My politics are complicated, too dangerous to discuss with you. And not really important. When I was younger, the Party and my politics defined me. Not anymore. Everything is changing." Her voice suddenly brightened. "But there is something else I want to share with you," she continued, "that I discovered recently. Something very important to me. You want to hear it?"

"I want to hear everything you want to tell me."

"This will give you more understanding of me," she said as she snuggled into my shoulder. "I talked a little about it when we were together in Saint

Petersburg. Remember I told you how Babushka pushed my head under the water when I had my first period?"

"That's a hard story to forget," I said.

"And then she told me the history of her family, and how we were Jews. That part I told you. But I didn't tell you how at first I refused to believe her. How could I? I thought I had the soil of Mother Russia in my blood. Jews were outcasts, less pure, less Russian. Not trustworthy. Sometimes I felt sorry for them. They seemed not so different from us, but somehow unworthy. At first I thought Babushka had lost her mind, but she only laughed at me. She locked our door, and pulled up from under the floorboards an old teapot. It only looked like a teapot—but also it was a puzzle, made up of hidden parts for all Jewish rituals."

"Really," I said, as I tightened my arm about her. "How did she come to have this strange teapot?"

"It was family treasure, made by her great-grandfather, a tinsmith in Latvia. I don't remember details, but I think their father gave it to one of her sisters who was sent to Siberia, and she got it back during the war."

"So what did you do with it?"

"Nothing. It went back under the floorboards. We didn't speak of it again for years. I was poster girl for the Communist Party—I believed the world would be better if all countries became socialist, like ours. But now I had Jewish blood. Even though I was pure in my heart and my intentions, suddenly I was not good enough to serve at my country's highest levels. Because of Babushka, I had strength enough to know there was nothing wrong with me. So what I believed—what I had been taught—must be wrong. Outside, nothing changed. But inside, I was never the same."

Darya told me about her first visit to Florence, her chance meeting with Valeria Bassani, the young journalist who turned into a friend, and her recognition that she wanted to know more about her own history. She described in detail her meeting with the Rabbi at Tempio Maggiore.

"That's why your note to me was on the back of a Tempio Maggiore postcard."

She nodded.

"The Rabbi talked a long time to me about history of the Jews, and what it means. He did it all through the teapot, showed me how to take it into pieces, explained all the different parts for the ceremonies and festivals, and when he put it together again he said that there was a part missing. It was very confusing for me, but I felt as if there was a part of me missing, too, and when I went back to my hotel I cried myself to sleeping on my bed."

"The missing part of the teapot," I said, "was it the top, where the lid was supposed to be?"

She looked at me with astonishment.

"And it could only have been used as one thing. For drinking wine. Right?"

"How can you know this?"

"I have the other side of your story," I said.

I told her the other side of the story, which I heard over and over from Papa Mischa when I was a little boy in South Africa. He told it on Friday nights, when we welcomed the Sabbath and said the blessings over wine, drinking from his treasured little wine cup with the strange hinge attached at one point on the rim.

"You know what this little thing is, Stevie?" he would ask me.

"Yes, Papa. It's where the cup was joined as the lid of the teapot."

"And you know the story of how I came to have the cup? Come, let me tell you," Papa Mischa would say, pulling me up onto his lap, "even though I have told you before. I was fifteen when my father left me and my brother Yossel, and returned to Latvia with my little brother Avrom, and my sisters Mirjam and Lena."

"Why, Papa?" I would ask. "Why did he leave you behind?"

"He didn't have enough money to buy us tickets on the boat. He planned to be gone for only a little while, but he knew we would miss him. At the station, as we said good-bye, my brother Yossel began to cry."

"But you didn't cry, Papa, right? You were older, and you had to be brave."

"That's right, my Stevie," he would say. "I had to take care of my younger brother, Yossel. But our father knew he needed to do something to make Yossel feel better. You know what he did—he removed from his bag the teapot his grandfather made, and he took out the pin that connected the top to the base. He turned it over in his hand so that now it was a cup, and placed it into my brother Yossel's hand. 'Until we meet again,' he said, 'we can drink wine together on the Sabbath, you, my sons, from the cup, and I from the teapot, and so we will be together, even though we are at opposite ends of the earth.'"

❧

"All those years they were drinking from the cup," she said, "wondering if any one of us was still alive. And the teapot waited, wrapped up beneath the floor." Her voice broke for a brief second. I held her in my arms and I felt her throat quiver as she swallowed her sobs. Her eyes filled, but there were no tears. "Do you know where the cup is now?" she asked.

"When we left South Africa for Boston, my father brought the cup with us. All through my childhood he drank wine from that little cup every Friday night, and when I was old enough, we drank together. He still uses it every Friday, I think as a tribute to his father, who waited all his life for his own father to come back. It never occurred to me," I said, "that the teapot might still exist, or that you might know about it."

"I could have gone anytime to see the Rabbi in Florence," she said slowly. "But I never did. I went only after I became curious, when I thought of using the teapot as my reason for a meeting. Wouldn't it be wonderful to join the parts back together?" She smiled up at me. "I think our ancestor who made it, Isaak's grandfather, would be very pleased."

"Come home with me to Boston," I said, "and we can bring the pieces together. I'm sure we can find a way to get Larisa and Anton out of the country."

"Grigory would make it impossible. And what about Babushka? I can't move her, at her age. No," she said sadly, "this is a dream."

"And it ends tomorrow," I said.

"Yes," she said. "Come. It's time to go."

We left the chapel hand in hand, walked slowly along the corridor paved with ancient red tile rescued from the original structure. It was uneven, lower in some places than others. Every footstep echoed. We didn't speak. The storm had passed, but it was still raining softly, and the air was cool. When we reached our room I unlocked the door. We entered, and I turned on the light. Darya closed and locked it behind us, rested her back against it, her hips thrust slightly forward. She reached to one side and flicked the light switch off. The soft, early evening light coming through the window reflected on her face, gleamed from the angle of her cheekbones. I walked back to her, and as I leaned down and brushed my lips against her rounded cheek, I smelled the perfumed soap from our morning shower on her skin.

"Do you have answers enough to your questions about me?" she asked.

She was wearing a loose cotton jacket, and when I put my arms about her I felt her warmth through the fabric.

"I have more answers than I expected," I said. "More information than I know what to do with." I ran the tips of my fingers down her sides, where her waist narrowed in anticipation of the outward swell of her hips, where I rested my hands. "Now I'm ready to study other subjects."

"Like what?" she asked, looking up at me. Her eyes shone in the gloom.

"Like how finely you're made," I answered.

"Is it possible," she asked in a breathless voice, gently kissing one corner of my mouth and then the other, "for you to study while you make love to me?"

We never made it to the bed. Our clothes seemed to peel from us without our doing anything, and we were suddenly lying on a bed of garments carpeting the floor, our thighs joined and our hips, the swell of her breasts full against my chest as she arched her back, my fingers running down the indentations of her spine to find the rounds of her pelvis as it tilted up and back again like an unstoppable wave, breaking on my shore. We were joined, too, at the mouth, her lips in mine, speaking in tongues, and there was very little that wasn't clearly communicated between us. It was a burning, joyous coupling, a searing celebration, a ritual in which I understood for the first time why it was called making love, because in the act of intertwining our bodies and surrendering to each other we were creating love, so that when we were done, lying in each other's arms, panting and stroking, there was no doubt what the thing was between us.

Darya gave me the gift of her whole self, and I gladly returned the favor. I did love her, and my love overrode whatever doubts I might otherwise have recognized playing in my head. I would do anything to have her be with me. All I had to do was wait for her to recognize that she could no more live happily without me, than I could without her. When she said the word, I thought, I would be ready.

I danced on air for several weeks after returning from Italy, and then, gradually, the real world insinuated itself back into my life. It was one thing to be ready at a moment's notice to drop what I was doing and join Darya anywhere on earth; it was something else to wait impatiently for her next invitation, holding my breath as I opened the mail, exhaling in disappointment when there was no word from her. Eventually, I managed to locate a space somewhere between the two extremes. I made it a point to exhale as I opened the mail. I made plans with friends. I taught my classes, made sure I spent several hours each day in the studio, working on my own canvases. I exercised. Shopped. Spoke to my father. Went out with other women, all of them disappointing. Life went on as usual. Until it changed.

My father's calm, reasoned advice to me as a teenager used to drive me wild. Whenever I expressed a wish for something—that he would remarry so that we could have a real family, that we could go on vacation together like other people, that we might live in a house instead of an apartment—he would pretend to consider for a moment what I had wished for, and then he would dismiss it.

"Be careful what you ask for," he would say. "Once you put your money where your mouth is, your decision's been made for you. But remember, there's no decision to make as long as you're clear about what you want. Decisions only have to be made when you're not sure what to do."

"That's such nonsense, Dad," I would say irritably. "You're just avoiding the subject. I don't even know what it means."

His response was always the same.

"Give it time. You will."

He was right. When the request came, I wasn't prepared for it—not for the form it came in, nor for what it asked of me.

One Saturday morning in the middle of May, I was in my studio working on an abstract seascape that covered two large canvases, five feet square. I was using broad strokes of titanium white, lightly tinted with trace amounts of magenta, purples and yellows, to create the impression of space and openness, and I was deeply involved in the process when the phone rang.

I ignored it. It rang again. I answered the third call.

It was a man, with a strong French accent. He identified himself as a freelance art journalist, Bernard Robinaux, doing an article about Cape Cod painters. He was interested in featuring my work, and wanted a preliminary interview. I wondered what his real intent was. What would a French art journalist want with me?

"I really don't have much time right now," I said.

"I'm sure you're extremely busy," he said smoothly. "But this won't take long. Perhaps it would help if I said I'd also like to discuss a trip you took to Italy recently, where you stayed in an ancient monastery?"

Suddenly I was on guard. An art journalist would know nothing about my trip to Italy. This had nothing to do with me—it was all about Darya.

"I don't think I have much to say to you, sir," I said.

"I disagree. Let me remind you about another trip, this one to Saint Petersburg, where you stayed at the Hotel Moscova for two nights? You waited at the sculpture garden in the Menshikov Palace for your—" he paused "—your Russian guide. For three hours, I believe. She was delayed, and didn't arrive until shortly after midnight, when she came to your room."

No one knew about our little detour to Saint Petersburg. Unless we had been watched. My chest tightened, and I felt my heart racing. Only she would have known that I waited at the Menshikov Palace for hours, but that she was delayed, and only she would have known that she came to my room after midnight.

"Very well," I said. "I'll meet with you. Do you want to come to my studio?"

"Not a good idea," he said. "I prefer a public place, and so should you. I have a very short publication deadline. Can you be available in an hour?"

"Where?"

"The Arlington Street subway stop. We can find a coffee shop and talk a little."

"I'll be there. How will I recognize you?"

"You won't. But don't worry—I know you."

Bernard didn't look much like a journalist—more like a middle-aged, off-duty investment banker in expensive jeans, shiny cordovan loafers, and a collared yellow T-shirt. He was taller than I was, lean and solid, and he had a three-day beard and salt-and-pepper hair swept back. As I emerged from the T station he approached me, smiling, arm outstretched. We shook hands and then this stranger put an arm around me like a long lost brother and steered me quickly down Boylston Street to Starbucks, where he ordered espresso and I a double cappuccino, and we sat down at a small table towards the back. He walked around the table to take the chair facing the door. We looked at each other. I had the sense that he was appraising me, and it made me angry.

"You can start by telling me who the hell you are," I said.

"Fair enough," he said. "I'm a journalist. I edit what you would call a left-wing political rag in Paris. Darya got a message to me, saying that if I needed to contact you, I should mention how you waited for her at the Menshikov Palace. No one else would know about that." He smiled. "I guess it worked."

"How do you know Darya? And why would she tell you anything so personal?"

"We met several times, first when she was in Paris representing the Soviet press at a conference. You must be aware that she's had doubts about the Communist Party line for a long time. At our last meeting about a month ago, she wouldn't say anything, but she was on edge, looking over her shoulder. She seemed scared. I told her if she was in trouble she should get a message to me through the Russian Embassy in Paris, where I know she has a good friend. She just laughed, as if she thought I was joking. I wasn't convinced. And then yesterday morning I received this." He reached into his shirt pocket and withdrew a folded envelope. "Darya addressed it to me. I apologize. I opened and read part of it before I realized it was intended for you."

He handed me the envelope, looking over the top of the espresso cup as he tipped and emptied it.

"She discovered a few weeks ago that her husband knew about you. He had the letters you sent to each other. She's in deep trouble, but the letters are only a part of it."

"We were so careful," I said as I opened the envelope and withdrew a sheet of folded letter paper. "They must have been intercepting my letters before she got them. And she had no idea."

"No, she didn't. When she found out, she was ready to pick up and bring her family to Boston. But she didn't have time to arrange it. He was too quick."

I opened the sheet of paper and recognized Darya's hurried script.

Steven—

Grigory has taken children to dacha, and Babushka also. Viktor comes now to take me, also. I must go or he hurts them. If I give what he wants—names of contacts outside Russia, and dissidents inside—

many will die. Good people, friends. If I refuse, he can do terrible things to us. He is like trapped bear with no escape. Very dangerous. We also have no escape.

Grigory thinks the children are not his. Even though he watches me every moment, he cannot believe I was never with another man, until you. This terrifies me—if he will threaten to harm children, I will not be able to keep silence.

He never loved Larisa and Anton—this is excuse to do what he wants with them. Already he makes threats to send them to institute for orphans. He will hurt Babushka —to him she is useless old woman, a nuisance. Me, he sends to worst prison camp in Siberia, where I must certainly die. When he has from me what he wants he sends me, anyway. I feed him bits of information slowly. Perhaps that way we have more time.

First in Moscow, then in Italy, you told me, come away with you. Both times I have said no because of children—but now they are in danger. I have no more choices.

I have nowhere to turn. Come now to Moscow. Please.

You will need help. Talk to our cousin Kolya, son of Juliana and Maxim. You did not meet—he was in prison when you came. Grigory has destroyed him. Kolya is rough, a hard man. But a good heart. We were children together. He loves me. He will bring you to General Shaposhnikov; together they will help. His parents know to find him. Be careful—they are afraid, and Grigory watches.

I send you all myself.

Darya

———◆———

I sat in disbelief, staring across the table at the stranger who had delivered this awful message. My tongue was stuck to the roof of my mouth, and my heart beat so fast I was convinced the vibrations were rippling the surface of every cup of coffee in the shop.

What was she thinking? She needed saving, but there was no way I could deliver what she asked. Not knowing what else to do, I raised the cappuccino to my lips, my hand trembled, and coffee sloshed over the rim, splashed into the saucer and left a symmetrical spatter on the letter. I lowered the cup noisily back to the saucer.

"Come to Moscow?" I croaked, my hands shaking as I blotted the damp letter with a napkin. "Me? Go up against the KGB? Come on. It's lunacy. There has to be another way."

"Get a grip, Steven," said Bernard, reaching across the table and placing a large hand firmly on my wrist. "Let me give you a few pieces of information before you make a decision. You want to walk?"

I nodded and we rose together. On the way out Bernard bought two bottled waters. It was overcast and cool. He opened one of the bottles and handed it to me, and I drank it as we walked across to Commonwealth Avenue and between the trees on the wide, grassy divider.

"I'm a fucking artist," I said angrily. "I paint pictures. Damsels in distress are above my pay grade. What makes her think I can suddenly become her rescuer?" I looked at him, suddenly struck by the obvious. "She thinks the artist is just a cover. She thinks I'm with the CIA, right?"

"Nonsense, Steven. She's at her wit's end—she has nowhere else to turn."

"And if you're right, what difference does it make? I can't compel him to release her—he'll laugh in my face. Then he'll shoot me, and we'll all disappear."

"He won't release her, no matter what you do," said Bernard. "Which means we have to force his hand. But remember, you won't be doing this alone. There's a whole network of people working under the radar to help dissidents leave the USSR. We have organizations implicitly sanctioned by the US government, assisted by several others—Great Britain, France, Germany, Israel and Italy. And in this case, they all have an incentive to help. If Darya is forced to give up the names he wants, she will compromise networks built up over decades—and she's right. Many will die."

"So you think I should go."

Bernard shrugged.

"Do you love her? Do you want to be responsible for what might happen to her—and her children —if you don't go?"

"I can't go without a plan. How do I get there without being seen, and what do I do when I arrive? I'm a single American in Moscow. I don't know where she is, or how to get around. And what do I do when I find her? Knock on the door and ask if she can come out and play?"

"I'm glad you found your sense of humor." Bernard smiled. "It's a necessary ingredient."

"This is gallows humor," I said. "I've never been so scared in my life."

"Great. Fear will keep you on your toes. And as long as you're on your toes, you're alive."

"If you have people in place to help dissidents leave the country, and they have an incentive to help Darya, why do you need me? Why doesn't the network just do what it does, and get her out?"

"It's not that simple. Moscow is in a political uproar—the left hand doesn't know what the right hand is doing. Darya's right. The USSR is about to blow up. The people in power are all terrified of a revolution. They all want to hang onto their privileged positions and access to the good life. Truth is they're petrified of having to live like the average Russian. Every one of the people in our network is doing the work of ten people. They can show you what's possible and steer you in the right direction—but someone has to be there to spearhead this. That's you."

"I'm not a project director," I said. "I don't manage people—I manage a paintbrush. What makes you think I can do this?"

"I don't know what you can or can't do," said Bernard, looking up as we passed the statue of Alexander Hamilton. "All I can tell you is what needs to be done. Darya apparently thinks you can do it."

"I'm glad she has such confidence in me. That and a few rubles will buy her a glass of vodka."

"We can get you into the country, set you up with false papers, find out where Darya is being held, and get them all away from her husband. We have safe houses around Moscow. We'll help you get in touch with her cousin Kolya. Sounds as if he has his own reasons to oppose Grigory, aside from his love for her. From that point we have to get them out of the country, and there are ways to do that. But you need to know this, Steven: if something goes wrong, you're on your own. There's no appeal to the US government for help. If you screw up, you'll find yourselves transplanted permanently to some shack on Siberian permafrost."

"You make it sound so appealing. I love the encouragement."

"I'm just telling it like it is. If you do nothing, she ends up dead—or worse."

"I can't make a decision like this on the spur of the moment. I need to think. When do you need to know?"

"It's not what I need," he said. "I'm just delivering the message. So here it is, in its simplest form." He pulled me to a stop and stared down at me. In place of his friendly smile he wore a determined scowl, and his eyes were clear and cold. He wasn't about to release the grip on my upper arm until he had delivered his message.

"You're no more the editor of some left-wing rag than I am," I said. "So what are you? At least tell me the truth. Is the note even genuine?"

"I'm a friend of Darya's. The note is hers. I am the editor of that left-wing rag." He managed a grim smile. "Among other things. And here's another truth. The USSR is bankrupt. It can't survive. What she describes is only the tip of the iceberg. There's a revolution coming, and when it's over no one knows what the country will look like. CIA analysts predict the end of the Soviet regime. I wouldn't be surprised to see tanks rolling through Moscow. That's why Soviet bosses are so paranoid, and why her husband will do whatever he can to preserve his skin. There's no knowing how long she can keep him on hold. It may sound cold, but you need to know that she's only one in a long line of people in trouble. If you're in, I'm authorized to make arrangements to get you there. If you're out, I need to move on to the next project. So," he said, "you in or out?"

I took a deep breath, not quite knowing what would come out of my mouth once I exhaled.

"Well," I heard myself say. "What do I have to do?"

❦

Bernard said within a day or two he would provide me with a false identity that Grigory would be unable to trace, and book me on a flight to London. Part of me hoped he would disappear, and I would never hear from him again. When I reached into my pocket to retrieve Darya's letter, I would discover it gone, dematerialized, having never been. I had imagined it all. Bernard was an apparition; Darya was not in trouble, and had never called for my help. I was terrified. Every nerve in my body was like an alarm screaming at me not to go. Regardless of the assistance Bernard promised, I was hardly equipped to survive any encounter with Grigory and his men, and I couldn't imagine far enough into the future to see myself returning unharmed. Far more likely that I would end up—with or without Darya— in some grisly Soviet prison. But I also knew that if I didn't go, my life would not be worth living. I had no choice.

Bernard didn't disappear. He came through with his promises. Before I left, I'd gone directly to see my father at his condo in Cambridge. He knew something was up the moment I walked in the door.

"What's happened? Are you ill?"

"No, Dad. I'm fine. But I'm going away for a while."

"Another painting trip?"

"Not quite. I'm going back to Moscow."

"Darya," he said flatly.

"Yes."

"Not a good idea."

"I know you don't believe it, but I love her."

"Doesn't matter what I believe. Why now?"

"She's not safe there."

"What a surprise. Married to a fellow in the KGB, and having an affair with an American. Of course she's not safe—thanks to you."

I wasn't about to give him the details of Darya's life, or to tell him that I was the least of her problems. He glared at me.

"You're digging yourself a hole you can't climb out of, Steven."

"I can handle it."

"That doesn't sound convincing," he said dryly. "I might be more inclined to believe you if you didn't sound so damn scared yourself. What are you planning—to bring her back here with her children?"

"That's the plan," I answered.

My father was a tall, bony man in his sixties, with a long face, sallow skin, and a shock of white hair. His eyelids took wing and disappeared into his thick eyebrows as his grey eyes widened and he rose from his chair.

"Have you been reading the news?" He picked up *The New York Times* from the dining room table. "Moscow is the last place in the world you want to be right now. Their treasury is empty. They've stolen the country blind. Even *The Times* is predicting a coup. That means mayhem. The Russians don't give up power without violence."

"I think you're overreacting," I said.

"Really? You're a student of Russian history now?" He threw the paper down, where it unsectioned and spread across the table. "Steven," he hissed, "you can't do this. I—" he searched for the words "—I won't permit it."

I managed a weak smile. "That's a new one, Dad. What am I, sixteen?"

He stood unsteady but straight in his small living room, arms spread in mockery. "My son, the white knight, comes to the rescue of his fair lady," he said.

"Very funny."

"Don't you dare make light of this, dammit. I didn't pull you out of South Africa to start a new life for us here, only to have you throw it away under a Russian tank."

"You're shouting."

"You bet I'm shouting! What else should I do when my son tells me he wants to give away his life for a woman he barely knows?"

"All I'm doing is going to Moscow to see if I can help. I'm not about to do anything stupid."

"It's a little late to claim that," he said. What the hell do you know —" he flapped his long arms in exasperation "—about rescuing people? From

364 Neville D. Frankel

the bloody KGB, no less? You've never even fired a rifle. For Christ's sake, how are you going to defend yourself—let alone a woman and her children? I'm sorry for her, but I think you've lost your mind. You're so infatuated you're not thinking straight."

"I'm not asking for permission—I came to tell you what I'm doing. I can't not go, Dad. I don't want to live the rest of my life wondering whether I could have done something to help her."

"You'll never get out of there alive." His voice came from deep in his chest, where he held his grief. "Darya's only there today because my grandfather was trapped in the last Russian Revolution. He went back to Latvia at the worst possible time. Now the Soviet Union is falling apart— again. You're so involved you can't even see the pattern you're following." He sat down heavily in his chair. "What makes you think your fate will be any different?"

"You'd be the first to agree that we don't always get to choose our time," I said. "This has been thrust on me. I can't just walk away."

The last thing my father did when I left him was to jam a couple of magazines into my hands.

"You'll have plenty of time on the plane. Do yourself a favor and read these on the way."

I looked down at the previous month's issue of *The Atlantic Monthly* and *Foreign Affairs*.

"Read the article on current events in the Soviet Union," he said. "It's what you're diving into. Nothing's changed much since the Russian Revolution. That was over seventy years ago—and the next one is about to happen. This is why I never visited my family. If you decide to go after reading these, you're either much braver than I am, or a bigger fool than I thought possible." He threw his arms about me. "Either way," he said, kissing my cheek for the first time since I could remember, "make sure you come home safely."

Within twenty-four hours I was on a plane to London, the magazines he'd given me in my suitcase. Was he right? Was I out of my mind? Partly, perhaps. But as I thought about our conversation, I knew why I had to go back. I couldn't have told my father the truth even if I'd recognized it at the time. It would have been too painful for him, and we had a long pattern of protecting each other from painful truths. I did love Darya—but there was another reason why I felt compelled to return to Moscow.

My father had never been able to talk to me about my mother's death, and I'd never been able to share with him the fear and guilt I had carried with me into adulthood.

My mother, Michaela Green, had been deeply involved in the anti-apartheid movement. When I was seven, the Special Branch—a division of South Africa's security forces—murdered her. Although I knew in my head it was completely irrational, I had lived my life believing that both my father and I should have done something to save her. It was a massive burden for a small boy to carry into adulthood. Now here I was again, faced with what felt like a similar choice. If I did nothing, I would live the rest of my life knowing that even as an adult with the power to choose, I elected to do nothing. Had I been willing to wound my father beyond healing, I would have told him that I had no choice; that I would rather die than, like him, live with the knowledge that I was a passive spectator to the destruction of the woman I loved.

When we landed in London I took a taxi from Heathrow to West Finchley. Bernard had made a reservation for me at a nondescript bed and breakfast, and we arranged that in the morning I would take a twenty-minute ride on the Underground to the London hotel where I was to meet up with a British tour group about to leave on an art tour of Moscow. It made sense—the Underground was the most inconspicuous way to travel, and if anyone followed me or tried to recreate my steps, the most untraceable.

Before we parted in Boston, Bernard took a photograph of me. It was a given, he said, that my name had been flagged, and Grigory would know the moment I arrived in Moscow. That evening in West Finchley, again according to plan, I sat at a corner table in a local pub, and was joined by a young couple who identified themselves as Bernard's friends. They slipped me an envelope. In it were Russian banknotes which they said were worth about $5,000, and a forged British passport. Under the picture Bernard had taken of me was the name Manfred Parks. I went back to my room, practiced signing my new name and signed the passport. The next morning Manfred Parks took the Underground to London and registered at the Mayfair Hotel near Trafalgar Square. After lunch I followed the signs marked "Baltic Europe Tours—-Moscow Art Trip" to a small conference room where I registered, had a glass of wine, and made myself known to the tour guide.

I was reluctant to talk much. I could hide my American identity beneath the South African accent that still lurked in the back of my throat, but I was sure that in any conversation with others on the trip, I would reveal that Manfred Parks lacked substance. Pleading weariness, I went to my room, and the next morning, surly and silent, I embarked with the tour group on a plane for Moscow. I spent the journey hunched in my seat, staring out the window. Under normal circumstances, I would have been looking at the reflected light, the texture of the clouds, the colors of the fields, imagining the topography of the mountains beneath. But all I could see was the 30,000 feet of gaping emptiness between me and the earth, and it only made me feel less grounded. Perhaps I recognized that I needed to find a way to immerse myself in reality before I landed. Perhaps it was just a way to pass the time. Whatever the reason, an hour into the flight, I withdrew the magazines my father had given me and began reading.

❦

Before my first trip to Moscow I had little interest in global affairs.

I knew nothing about Russian politics. That changed once I returned to Boston, when I could think of nothing but Darya, and when anything Russian made me feel closer to her. I wanted to know more about anything that might have an impact on her life. I suppose I was looking for something—anything—I could use to convince her to leave Grigory and come to Boston. I knew only that there was instability in Russia—it was difficult to avoid having a basic sense that the Soviet Union was crumbling. But I didn't understand why, or what it really meant, and it certainly never struck me that I was traveling halfway across the globe to put myself directly in the path of what might become a civil war.

The magazines I read as my plane flew across the Atlantic explained that by the early 1980s, the USSR faced economic ruin. The inefficiency of their centrally controlled economy, where barter had become a preferred method of exchange, and where prices were set arbitrarily, had finally depleted their treasury. In 1986, two years before my first trip, Premier Mikhail Gorbachev instituted his policy of *perestroika*. It was intended to restructure the country, and to liberalize strict communist policies. It included the first multi-candidate elections, and took steps to encourage individual economic opportunity, for which people were previously punished by long sentences in Siberian prison camps.

These changes were beginning to have an effect when I was there. I didn't realize it at the time, but people were already happier, more open and friendlier than they had been a few years earlier. I remembered my own sense of the man in the street, who seemed dour and paranoid. Hard to believe this was an improvement. But shortly after my trip, the second step of Gorbachev's program, *glasnost*, took effect, giving Soviet citizens more freedom of speech than they had ever had.

Unfortunately, Gorbachev's economic policies, at least in the short term, led to even worse shortages of basic supplies like meat, flour and sugar. To avoid riots, the government reinstituted the food distribution system used during the war—food cards and rationing.

One might have hoped—Gorbachev clearly did—that his political changes would bring about increased freedom and prosperity in the country, but the opposite was true. It was like drilling an outflow pipe in the massive walls of the Hoover Dam, in the hope that releasing a little pressure would be helpful—only to discover that the pressure behind the wall was so intense that the outflow pipe became a flood and the massive dam was in danger of complete destruction. But major change always brings with it unintended consequences.

The Union of Soviet Socialist Republics was just that—a union of Republics, some of which had been absorbed unwillingly into the Soviet Union by Stalin in 1940. There was strong nationalist feeling in the Baltic republics—Lithuania, Latvia, and Estonia, as well as in Georgia, Ukraine, Armenia, and Azerbaijan, but expressions of anti-Soviet sentiment were prohibited. It made sense that in a system where censorship had been cruelly imposed for so long, the sudden freedom of speech released long-repressed anti-Soviet feelings, with increasing demands for independence from Moscow. The floodgates opened, and there was no closing them. But the USSR was dependent on the Republics for its economic survival, and without them it had no claim to superpower status.

Hardliners in the Kremlin, multiple layers of bureaucrats, appointees who receive privileges from their membership in the Communist Party—all were terrified. Gorbachev's policies would bring an end to the whole basis of the Soviet economy. The big offices, vacation homes, travel, access to stores containing the best and most expensive products in the world, inaccessible to ordinary Russians, would not survive multi-party elections and the defection of the wealth of the Republics. Many of those with access to material pleasures and privilege were not about to give it all up without a fight.

It wasn't public knowledge at the time, but as I was boarding the plane in London, Gorbachev, along with a core of loyal followers, was at his *dacha* in the Crimea, drafting a document to give greater political and economic independence to the Baltic States. The country might have been moving towards more enlightened politics, and the doors to free enterprise were being opened, but the old guard were not about to stand by as the Baltic States were given their freedom. Gorbachev was about to discover that he was no longer the General Secretary, the titular head of the Communist Party. Instead, he was being held prisoner under orders of powerful Kremlin hardliners, some of whom he had known and worked with for forty years. They were a small, badly organized band, who within twenty-four hours would be mostly drunk and frightened by what they had unleashed. But at the time they were sending news over the wire that Gorbachev had been taken ill, and that the Soviet government was under threat. The right wing was about to stage a coup in Moscow.

It was in this chaos that Grigory Yanov felt his fortunes sinking, and made a brutal effort to intimidate Darya into revealing information that he thought would allow him to leverage his way back into the good favor of those at the top. It was fortunate that I didn't have the time or head space to read the articles my father gave me before I boarded the plane. I would most likely have taken his advice and stayed home.

It seemed for a moment laughable to worry about whether I might repeat my great-grandfather's mistake. So what if I were trapped in the USSR for whatever span of time I had left? My life—Darya's life—would pass in the blink of an eye. Far better to take the long view. For the first time I wondered what that really meant. Was it the belief in karma and reincarnation? I fell asleep on the plane thinking that perhaps I would come back as a shooting star or a black hole, or as a dollop of cerulean blue paint on an artist's palate, destined for that blink of an eye to grace a canvas as someone's vision of a blue sky on a planet in this or some other solar system.

❀

We arrived at Sheremetyevo International Airport in Moscow in mid-afternoon. The very practical need to function—to put one foot before the other, and to follow the directions I'd been given—quickly took over, and I made my way down the gangway to the waiting bus, trying to ignore the Soviet soldiers standing with legs widely planted, Kalashnikov rifles over shoulders and forearms, carefully observing the disembarking passengers. I concentrated on taking one step at a time, not wanting to draw attention to myself by tripping over my own feet.

Once we emerged from customs and immigration, the tour guide herded us all onto a bus and we made the trip to the Hotel Rossiya—the same hotel I had stayed at on my first trip. Other than short moments of sleep from which I awoke startled and uneasy, I rolled around the bed all night, playing in my head over and over again the instructions I had been given in London. By the time morning came, I had rehearsed what I had to do so many times that it felt over and done with.

I left my room and went down to breakfast. All I had in the small shoulder bag I carried was my toiletries and a change of underwear. No identification; my passport had been taken by the registration desk. As instructed, everything else I left in my suitcase. During breakfast, the English guide was sitting with our Russian minder, a big, smiling man in his forties with full, ruddy cheeks, a narrow grey mustache and a military haircut. He had accompanied us on the bus from the airport, been a fixture the night before at dinner, and here he was again. At 8:05 am sharp I stopped at their table and announced that I needed to go back to my room, having forgotten my pills. The tour guide was unconcerned, but our minder watched me carefully through slit eyes as I walked out, wiping egg yolk with meticulous care from his mustache. Instead of going up the stairs, I went down two levels and found myself in the bowels of the massive old building, where the pipes were uncovered. Unlike the public areas, nothing had been done to make the place palatable to foreigners. There were puddles on the concrete floors, the metal banister was rusted, and the walls were cracked. As I came down the final stairway there was a young man waiting for me. He must have recognized me from my picture, because as soon as he saw me he unfolded and offered me a worn black raincoat, holding it by the shoulders like a valet so that I could quickly slip it on.

"Do up the belt," he said in Russian, as he jammed a hat on my head. "Be quick. Someone goes upstairs to check on you in a minute. You left your suitcase open, right? As if you were coming right back?" I nodded. "Good. Come."

He turned and I followed him down corridors past several bolted exit doors until we came to a loading dock. There were guards—soldiers carrying rifles—everywhere. My guide took me by the elbow and stopped me before we stepped out of the passageway. He pulled a blue pack of cigarettes from his pocket and tapped it against his index finger. Despite the situation, I was able to read the name upside-down and in Russian, which surprised me. Belomorkanal. Two popped out and he put one in his mouth, offering the other to me. I shook my head. I hadn't smoked cigarettes since I was in college.

"Take it," he said quietly, tapping the cigarette against my fingers. "In Moscow everyone smokes. So do you."

I took it and placed it in my mouth. It was only half tobacco—where the filter should have been was a hollow cardboard tube. My fingers were shaking. He struck a match against his roughened thumbnail and lit us both. I dragged at it, careful not to inhale deeply. The smoke was hot and acrid, and almost immediately my fingers stopped shaking. I must have seemed surprised.

"Better, eh?" he said, grinning. "Religion used to be the opium of the masses. Turns out cigarettes are a cheaper substitute." He slapped my shoulder. "You ready to go?"

"Where to?" I asked.

He pointed past the loading dock to where the truck door opened onto the street. "See the old grey car? Engine running? I get in the front seat—you get in the back. You don't talk to the driver—all he needs to know is where to take us. You and I will talk later. Let's go."

The loading dock bustled with activity. Several large delivery trucks were being unloaded, men and women in overalls smoking and talking loudly, laughter harsh in the echoing basement garage, the air thick with the smell of gasoline and truck exhaust. Workers pushed carts and two wheelers down the truck ramps and along the cracked and puddled concrete walkway.

As we walked out he murmured into my ear. "Bend your head to me. We're talking very important stuff. Ignore the soldiers—they don't even see us. They're watching for foreigners. We're both dressed like KGB—and KGB never talk to them. And none of them care that hotel workers are stealing toilet paper from the State to sell on the black market. This is what the great Soviet experiment has come to. By the way, you call me Pyotr. Don't tell me your name. I already know why you're here, and that's all I need. Safer that way."

The soldiers did ignore us—they were more concerned with watching the workers, and I was never so happy to know that there was rampant pilfering in the Russian hospitality industry. We walked out the exit to a grey Lada idling on the street, trailing exhaust fumes. He got into the front seat as I got into the rear, and before the doors were closed the driver had pulled away from the hotel. Now there was no going back. According to official records, Steven Green was somewhere in London, and the person I had become, Manfred Parks, had disappeared from his tour group. They would have no idea where I was, or what had happened to me. Perhaps they would assume I had been kidnapped. Either way, I was off the grid. I knew what loneliness felt like, but I'd never felt such isolation. I had about $5,000 in rubles, but no resources and no contacts. If I were injured or arrested or lost, there was nowhere to turn.

The car had no suspension, and exhaust fumes crept in from the trunk or from a hole in the floor. The smell of stale cigarettes, along with the fresh cigarette smoke from the front seat, made me nauseous. I tried opening the window but it was stuck closed. We drove for an hour, through busy traffic on major thoroughfares and onto deserted side streets and back again, and the driver spent as much time peering into the rear-view mirror as he did looking out the front windshield. Eventually the tension in his shoulders seemed to relax, he slowed down, and the velocity with which he took each turn decreased.

I gathered from the change that he was confident he had lost any tail. Just as I began to relax enough to look out the window at our surroundings, he pulled up at the entrance to a concrete slab building, one of many in a vast apartment complex. We exited the car, which drove off rapidly, and my companion led the way through two more buildings before we ended up in a darkened corridor, on the third floor. He unlocked the door to a corner apartment and motioned me in.

It was an old two-bedroom apartment, and it looked as if it came straight from the 1950s. There were two mattresses on bedframes in each bedroom, a battered folding card table in the alcove that passed for a dining room, and a tiny kitchenette with an electric plate, a half-refrigerator, and a small sink. The apartment had a bathroom, containing a miniature bathtub, a toilet and a sink behind the bathroom door. It wasn't much, but I was relieved—it meant I wouldn't need to share a bathroom with other apartments on the floor.

Pyotr removed his hat to reveal short sandy hair, an open, serious face, and blue eyes. He was about thirty, shorter than I was, but solidly built. He moved around the apartment with practiced ease, checking lamps and vents and electric outlets for signs of surveillance. When he was satisfied, he removed his raincoat to reveal a pair of black jeans and an orange T-shirt. He took off his black shoes, and from a closet in one of the bedrooms he retrieved a pair of worn sneakers and a soccer cap. Now he looked more like a college kid than a member of the KGB.

"Welcome to Moscow," he said.

"So what happens now? What's the plan?"

"Plan?" He laughed harshly. "The plan is, we wait to see what happens. This may be the best possible time for you to be here—the military and the KGB are too worried about their own asses to waste any time on you. But I don't have enough men to do what needs to be done, so everything is on hold. I have to leave you here tonight. I'll be back tomorrow. You'll be safe here. They'll never find this place."

"How can you be so sure?"

"This used to be a safe house, until one of their London agents defected. He revealed this location, so now it's useless to them. But safe houses are never registered. When they wiped it from their list, it ceased to exist. No one knows or cares about it." He spread out his arms to take in the whole apartment. "It's not much, but it's all yours for as long as you need it."

"Not for long, I hope."

"We'll see," he said. "After a while you might come to like it." He grinned unevenly, and quickly lowered his upper lip—but not before I noticed ragged spaces in his mouth, and several teeth broken and chipped. I looked away.

"They do good work, don't they?" he asked.

"Who?"

He pointed to his mouth. "The KGB," he said. "Those fuckers would just as soon tear your head off as wring a chicken's neck, and they'd enjoy it more. I know—I've had a close relationship with them. No one is safe here with these people in power. They make life for the average person unbearable. I'm an engineer. I have a good job. Why do you think I risk it all to do this? We have to get rid of them." He pulled the soccer cap lower on his head, fitted it carefully at just the right angle. "Now I have to go—but first let me show you the kitchen."

There were cans of sardines and black bread, coffee and milk and sugar, canned peaches, and eggs. The freezer contained a bar of Swiss chocolate and a bottle of vodka. He showed me how to use the propane stove, warned me to keep the volume on the television low, and not to answer any knocks at the door, and then he left.

I had inserted myself right into the midst of chaos. Now I was stuck, with no way forward, and no way out. It sounded as if Bernard's vast organization of dissidents was otherwise occupied. Bernard and his people had their own reasons for being willing to arrange and foot the cost of my trip—but I didn't care much about protecting Darya's sources from discovery. The idea that I had come all this way, and that I might fail because I was helpless without the network, filled me with despair. Where was she in this massive city, which I had come to think of as her husband's? Was she still at the *dacha*, or had he taken her someplace else? Was she safe? Did she know I had come, as she asked, to save her? And, I wondered, did she have any idea yet how absurd her request was?

When Pyotr did return, it was close to midnight. He smelled of cigarette smoke and sweat, and he was wasted, his face drawn and his eyes glassy and red-rimmed. He said he had been going nonstop since leaving me the previous day.

"I need to sleep," he croaked, as he lay down on one of the mattresses, taking off his sneakers and removing the soccer cap, his hair plastered to his scalp. "Just a few hours. Then we have coffee and decide what to do next."

He pulled a blanket over his shoulders, and he was asleep in seconds, snoring softly. I lowered myself quietly to the other mattress, certain that I would never fall asleep, but the anxiety and uncertainty of the previous day had been exhausting. I fell asleep immediately, only to be awakened what seemed like seconds later, to the smell of coffee. It was after dawn—I had been asleep for at least six hours. Pyotr had showered and put on a clean T-shirt and jeans, and again he looked like a college student. I went to the bathroom, splashed water on my face and brushed my teeth. Pyotr was sitting at the folding table, his hands cupped around a coffee mug.

"Sit," he said, taking a sip of coffee and pointing to the other chair, where a second cup was steaming. He had opened a can of sardines, cut slices of bread, and fried eggs in a pan on the hot plate.

"What's going on?" I asked as I joined him at the table. "Where do we go from here?"

He shrugged. "I have no answers, my friend," he said. "All I can do is tell you what I hear and what I see. In this business, I know from experience, when what I see matches what I hear—" he held his arms out and pointed his fingers at each other, moving them together until his fingertips touched, "—then we have truth."

"So what are you hearing?"

"Limos with black windows speed out of Moscow, like rats. They have reason to run—there are rumors that a coup is about to happen."

"Who has the power to stage a coup?" I asked.

"The right wing," he said. "It makes me shudder to think what they're capable of, but if they can drum up support and make up enough believable lies, it could happen. There are enough dissatisfied military officers, enough civilians fed up with shortages, anything is possible. Troops are moving into Moscow. I know at least one tank battalion is on alert. Good news for us is that security resources are focused on the real danger—those within their own ranks and in the Politburo who threaten mutiny. So there's less manpower to keep us under surveillance. No one is interested in chasing after a missing tourist. The bad news is that the people supposed to be helping you are stretched thin protecting their own."

He took a bite of fried egg on toast with sardines and chewed slowly, looking across the table at me, eyes now clear and frank.

"There is another rumor going around. Grigory Yanov has taken his wife and children and an old lady to his *dacha* outside the city. He has a half-dozen of his private torture squad there for protection. We know a couple of his men, and I hear it's not his usual pattern to surround the *dacha* with his own guards. Either he's concerned about his KGB colleagues coming for him, or he's worried that someone will try and rescue his wife. The question is, what do you want to do about it?"

"You can't be serious," I said. "You want me to make this decision without knowing what I'm doing, and without any help from you?"

"I don't have a choice, my friend. This is all way beyond our control. That's why I tell you, if there's anyone in Moscow you haven't thought of contacting, there will never be a better time than now."

Darya must have anticipated that I would need help, which is why she asked me to contact Juliana and Maxim to find our cousin, Kolya. She may have had no idea that Bernard and his people would offer any assistance. If so, she wouldn't have been dismayed, as I was, to discover that no help was forthcoming. I had no choice but to follow her direction, unless I was willing to abandon my search for her and return to the tour group with my tail between my legs.

I didn't remember whether Juliana and Maxim had a phone, and even if they did, calling them would have been a bad idea. But I did have their address. Pyotr and I went down the stairs, in and out of several apartment buildings to an alley where another car was waiting, as ancient and dented as the first. The same man sat in the driver's seat, as silent as he had been before. Pyotr gave him the address, and he eased into traffic.

"If you're being trailed, follow protocol," said Pyotr.

"What protocol is he following?" I asked.

"This late in the game we have no room for mistakes," he answered. "I speak English now to be sure you understand my answer."

"I didn't know you spoke any English," I said.

"Everyone in Moscow with education speaks some English," he said. "Protocol for emergencies is for the driver to lead his tail to a place where we have friends waiting. It changes each day—sometimes a garage, sometimes a deserted street or a road through a forest. He signals with flashing lights so our friends know to stop the tail. We find out who they are."

"Then what?"

Pyotr glanced at me from the side of his face. "Then we make sure they don't ever follow anyone else. You understand?"

"You kill them? Just like that?"

"Sometimes. Sometimes not." He shrugged carelessly. "Depends who they are," he said. "I just wanted you to know, this is not a game of cops and robbers. This is a revolution."

I was silent, taking in the message. Juliana's warnings were suddenly far more sinister, and I understood that her fear for the family's safety was more real than I could have imagined. As if he had been reading my mind, Pyotr turned to me.

"So, who are these people you think can help you? You mentioned a letter Darya sent you. You have it with you?"

I reached into my inside jacket pocket and withdrew the letter, handing it to him. It was a personal appeal, and revealed more than I would have wanted Pyotr to know, but he was already in a position to hurt us both. If I couldn't trust him there was no one else to turn to. He opened the letter and read it, and he was sporting a wide grin as he folded it up.

"There's nothing to laugh at," I said angrily, snatching the letter from his hand and burying it again in my inside pocket.

"You misunderstand," he said, still grinning, this time at my discomfort. "I'm not laughing at the letter. What I mean is, the letter is not what I expected. I knew Darya was married to Grigory Yanov, but I had no idea she and Kolya were cousins."

"You know Kolya?"

"She says Kolya will bring you to General Shaposhnikov. If he has access to the General, he must be the Kolya I know." He stopped. "And I know what Grigory has done to him."

"If you know him," I said, "why involve his parents? There's no reason to risk being followed to their apartment. Let's leave them out of it and go directly to him."

"I know who he is, not where. He moves around a lot. Right now he's not likely to be in any of the obvious places. There's too much going on, it would take too long to find him, and we don't know how much time Darya has. I'm sorry, but we have no choice. We have to go to his parents."

We drove in silence on a circuitous route out of Moscow, and then retraced it back into the city again, the driver's eyes in the rear-view mirror. Eventually he slowed down and Pyotr looked out carefully at the buildings on each side of us.

"Here is good," he said.

The driver pulled over, and we exited the car. Pyotr told him to drive by every hour on the half-hour. He nodded assent, and the car stayed in place, the driver silently watching as we walked swiftly along the face of the building.

"I wouldn't burden these people with questions about what Grigory did to their son," said Pyotr. "They'll find this visit troubling enough. If you want more answers, you'll have to get them directly from Kolya." He smiled at me as he opened the door to the first apartment building. "Or from Darya once we get her out."

I led Pyotr the same route that Maxim had taken me on my first trip, through one apartment building, down the steps and out the back into another, through a third, and finally into the stairwell that led up to their apartment. The six floors with light cords at each floor, to be turned on at each floor and off at the next, and the smell of fried onions at each landing, came back to me as if I had been there yesterday.

I knocked at the door gently, trying not to think about how they would react to my sudden appearance, or to my request for help. Juliana opened the door, shock on her face when she recognized me, and fear when she saw that I was not alone. Quickly she peered out of her doorway and glanced down the corridor to see if any of her neighbors were watching, and then she ushered us in and quickly shut the door. She put a finger to her lips in warning, switched on the radio, and turned back to us.

"Juliana," I said, "It's so good to see you."

I put my arms about her and she returned my hug, but she quickly pulled away and she held me at arm's length, looking first at my face and then at Pyotr's. She had lost weight since my last visit, and she appeared to be in ill health. She looked older, her face gaunt, her bright eyes sunken. There was something unkempt about her, as if she no longer cared how she looked.

"Steven, what's happened? Who is this you bring into my home without warning?"

"This is my friend, Pyotr," I said. "He's driving me around Moscow. Juliana, we need your help."

"We?" she asked, sitting down with her arms tightly crossed, pulling her stretched and worn green sweater across her breasts. "Who is this man? How do you know him? And who is 'we'?"

Her hair fell in a dull wave over her forehead, her cheeks flat and pallid, unlike the plump, pink cheeks I remembered. She was all grey and pale, like a faded painting. Either she was ill, or something dramatic had happened in her life since my last visit.

"I can leave, if you wish," said Pyotr softly, "but I think we should first tell you why we are here. If you still want me to leave, I will go, and take

Steven with me."

"There's nothing we can help you with," she said, looking with hostility at Pyotr. "We don't know anything beyond our own lives, and all we want is to be left alone." She turned back to me. "How can you be so stupid, Steven," she said angrily. "Do you even know who he is?" She rose from her chair and walked to the kitchen. "I can only imagine what terrible things bring you here. Maxim will be home from work soon. You can tell us both. I make tea."

We drank tea in silence until the key turned in the lock and Maxim walked in. The blood left his face when he saw me, and there was panic in his eyes when he realized that I was not alone. He, too, had changed. The old wrestler I remembered had become an old man, his sturdiness dissipated, his straight back bent. He lowered himself to a chair as Juliana took his raincoat and briefcase from him, and went to pour him a cup of tea.

"Hello, Steven," he said in a monotone as he took the cup from her. "What a surprise. Then again, perhaps not."

"What do you mean, Maxim?" I asked. "Do you know why we're here?"

"Can I know who your friend is?" he asked, ignoring my question.

I repeated what I had told Juliana.

"They need our help," said Juliana. "I told them we have no help to give."

"That's true," he said quietly. "We know nothing that would be useful to you, and we know no one you would be interested in meeting. The best thing would be for you both to leave, now." He rose from his chair. "Go," he said, pleading. "Please. There is nothing we can do for you."

In rapid Russian, almost whispering, Pyotr began to speak. I understood only a few words of what he said, but he was talking about the brewing political crisis, the possibility of a coup, and the power vacuum that would be created. Maxim and Juliana looked at each other, and I thought I saw in their eyes a glimmer of hope that had not been there a moment earlier. Maxim lowered himself again to the chair. Juliana stood behind him, her arms still tightly crossed over her breasts.

"Interesting," said Maxim, "but not altogether unexpected."

"If it will really happen," added Juliana, standing behind him.

Pyotr shrugged. "What I tell you is based on the intelligence we have. What I observe in the streets confirms it. But only time will tell."

"But these events are not what brought you here," said Maxim. "You'd better tell us what did."

"Darya," I answered.

"Always Darya," spat Juliana. "What does she want?"

"She's in trouble," I said. "She asked me to contact you."

"Why?"

"She said you would know how to find Kolya."

"No," said Maxim, his voice rising. "No more. Leave him in peace. He's had already enough trouble from Darya and that psychopath she married. Enough pain. Enough."

Pyotr explained that Grigory was holding the family under guard at the *dacha*.

"He's holding Lena? And his children, too?"

"He doesn't believe they're his children," I said.

"Whose does he think they are?" asked Juliana, glaring at me. "Yours?"

"If that's what he thinks, he's crazy," I said. "Darya already had both children when we met."

"I warned you he was a danger to us," continued Juliana. "Didn't I tell you she was trouble? Leave her alone, I said. If you had listened to me, we might have avoided all this."

"You would have avoided nothing," said Pyotr. "Grigory was always dangerous. He thought he was too smart to make mistakes—but now he's afraid he allied himself with the wrong people. I think that's driven him over the edge. If Steven had listened to you, Darya would have had no one to turn to."

"Why should we believe what you say?" asked Maxim.

"He knows Kolya," I said. "They've worked together."

"Plenty of people have worked with Kolya," said Juliana sourly. "Because of this you brought him here?"

"I had no choice," I said. "There's nowhere else for me to turn."

Pyotr raised a hand. "Wait," he said. "I asked Steven who you were and why he thought you could help us. As soon as he told me, I knew we would have no problem."

"Why?"

"Because you are Kolya's parents," he said softly, "and I know him well enough that he would want you to do this. You know it, too, even though it goes against your deepest wish to protect your son from further harm." He stopped for a moment, looked from Maxim to Juliana and back again, as if he were trying to decide how much more to reveal. "Darya said that Kolya would be able to contact someone who could help us."

"Who is this someone?" asked Maxim.

"General Shaposhnikov," said Pyotr, in a whisper. "One of the few men left who has no personal agenda. No designs on power. All he wants is to make sure that our military understand their jobs—to protect the people, and never again fire on Soviet citizens."

"I remember him," said Maxim, puzzled. "But I thought he was long dead."

"It's convenient for him that people believe him dead. He's old, but I assure you, very much alive."

"Alive or dead, what does an old Soviet hero have to do with all this?" asked Juliana. "I don't understand."

"I work with him," said Pyotr.

"How do you know our son?"

"He works with us." He smiled. "I didn't make the connection until we were in the car on the way here," he said. "I can't tell you more." He looked at them again, frowns at the corner of his eyes, his mouth a thin line. Suddenly he didn't look anything like a college student. "Our goals are to get Darya and her children, and your Aunt Lena, out of Grigory's hands. You know, as I do, that Kolya thinks of her as a sister. You may blame her even today for what her husband did to Kolya—but he doesn't. He would do anything for her." He paused. "And for Lena. Will you?"

Maxim looked down at his feet, then up, to meet Juliana's eyes. There was pain in his face, and resignation. Her face revealed only defiance. But they nodded in agreement.

"I'll let him know you want to see him," said Maxim heavily. "He'll get word to you. If you've worked with him as you say you have, you'll know where."

"I know the place," said Pyotr. "We'll wait there this afternoon."

"If he doesn't send word, there's nothing more we can do." Maxim raised his arms in a gesture of impotence and as he spoke he lowered them, shaking his head in defeat. "I'm an old man who happens to be his father. I stopped being able to take care of him a long time ago." He looked down at the floor, and I was relieved that I couldn't see his eyes. "Grigory made sure of that."

We drove around aimlessly, hoping that Maxim had been able to deliver his message. Finally we stopped at a little kiosk on a bridge over the Moscow River.

"This is Kolya's favorite eating place," said Pyotr. "Here we wait."

We sat on grimy, plastic-covered stools, eating dumplings and fish stew. We drank black tea. The afternoon passed with interminable slowness. Darya, Lena and the children had been held captive for a week, and as we waited helplessly, Grigory was pulling up outside the *dacha*.

PART FOUR

Darya

It was clear that something was in the wind. There were disturbed rumblings from the Kremlin and from Party leaders. Grigory was manic and short-tempered. He stormed about the apartment, muttering, shattered plates against the wall when his breakfast was late. We all stayed out of his way, and Anna kept the children at a distance. When he left the apartment we all breathed with relief.

I thought I would know when he was about to make his move, that I would have time to get the children and Babushka out of harm's way first. As usual he was ahead of me. He called my office, something he seldom did. I was the last person he wanted to talk to in the middle of a workday.

"I'm at the *dacha*," he said brusquely. "Viktor is on the way to pick you up and bring you here. Make sure you're ready."

"Why?" I asked. "I have meetings this afternoon."

"The old woman and the children are here with me," he said, ignoring my question. "Viktor will be there in an hour."

He hung up. It was understood that if I didn't comply, those I loved would bear the consequences. I was not surprised that he was willing to use the children against me. I feared for us all, but mostly for Babushka. He would relish the opportunity to silence her.

Before I got into the car with Viktor, I had to cry out for help, let someone know that we were about to disappear. I had few options. There was no one to call, and anything I sent out within Moscow would be intercepted. The only choice I had was to use diplomatic channels, going around the usual delivery mechanisms to avoid scrutiny. I had a trusted friend at the French Embassy in Moscow, and we had found a way of communicating with each other that worked in the past.

Quickly I wrote a letter to Steven, asking him to come to Moscow, and to get in touch with Kolya. He had pleaded many times for me to join him in Boston with the children, but I had been too frightened to make that decision. Now I was ready, but there was no guarantee that he would still want us. I hoped he would do as I asked. But even if he couldn't find in himself the courage or the wish to come, there were others who would read the note on its way, understanding the implications both for me and for the dissident movement. They might have the resources that could be put to use, with or without Steven.

From my desk drawer I withdrew and opened a box of Belgian chocolates, carefully removing the contents. Under the chocolates was a protective cardboard sheet, and below that, the bottom of the box. But the bottom itself was two-ply, and the layers had been meticulously separated. I inserted my letter between the two layers, pressed them together so that the pre-applied glue sealed the base, and replaced the chocolates. I called in my secretary and asked her to have the package delivered to the French Embassy. While she waited, I wrote a card to be attached to the box. It was a note of thanks, on behalf of the head of my Ministry, for his help in securing tickets to a performance in Paris. It would be opened and read before it arrived, but the Minister's name in the card made it unlikely that anyone would check further. I smiled at her as I pushed the box and the card across the desk. She picked them up and left, without knowing that in her hands she held our only possibility of rescue.

Grigory kept us prisoner for over a week. Larisa asked constantly why she couldn't go outside, and Anton was afraid of the strange men in the house with us. They were not unpleasant—they even seemed uncomfortable in their role as our guards. But Grigory had never had his men in the house with us before, and their presence was an unspoken threat.

Grigory came and went, mostly ignoring us. One afternoon he arrived without warning, and Anton rushed towards him as he came in. Grigory reached out to brush our son's blond hair, but he stopped himself in mid-gesture, thinking better of it, and waved Anton away. At best, he tolerated the children. It was as close as he could come to loving them. But now I was consumed with fear, wondering what he might be willing to do to them to get what he wanted from me. And his refusal to ruffle Anton's hair did not make me any less worried.

He motioned me into his office, followed me in and closed the door behind us. I stood with my back to the windows. He was calm, a cold smile on his mouth. He had fine soft lips, and I remembered, as if in a different life, that I had once taken pleasure in kissing them.

"My men in the house," he said curtly. "They make you uncomfortable?"

"Why would strange men in my house make me uncomfortable?" I replied, unable to hide my anger. "What do you hope to accomplish by this?"

"I hope to keep you from leaving, and to prevent you from sending messages to anyone outside." He spoke quietly, his voice devoid of emotion, and I knew already that in this mode he was far more dangerous than when in a rage. "And you already know what I want from you."

"But Grisha," I pleaded, "I don't—"

"There's no point in lying to me," he said, holding up his hand. "Did you think you could take my words to dissident cell meetings, and that I wouldn't find out you were one of them? I've got enough evidence to put you away for life in the most godforsaken place on earth. And I know all about your affair with the American—but I don't know how long it's been going on, or whether he was the first."

"He was the first and only affair I ever had," I said. "But you're going to make me the unfaithful one, right? Despite the multitude of your affairs over the years. How long has it been since you were a husband to me? I don't think we've been together since Anton was conceived."

"And how do I know that?"

"How do you know what?" I asked, not understanding the point he was making.

"How do I know," he said, "that I had anything to do with Anton's conception? Or Larisa's? Perhaps your American is their father."

"Anyone who looks at the children can see that they're yours," I said, glancing around wildly. Had there been a heavy ashtray or a paperweight within reach I would have heaved it at him. "You're the only one who refuses to see it."

"I see plenty," he said. "I see your American asked you to come to Boston to live with him—with the children. What kind of man would want children that weren't his own?"

"The kind of man who loved the children's mother. But that's beyond your understanding, isn't it? The children are yours," I said wearily. "If we were to test them you would find you share the same blood. Everyone but you looks at them and knows they have your genes.   But none of that's the point, is it? You've said what you want—and you know I'm not going to give you the names of innocent people so that you can ruin their lives. These are not anti-Soviet agents—they're ordinary people, Russians and foreigners, working to make a better country. So why do you want them now?"

He walked behind his desk and sat down, looking up at me over the expanse of wood, as if I were a supplicant.

"Life in Moscow has become very uncertain. It will become even more uncertain as the next few weeks unfold. Gorbachev is on the plane as we speak, flying to his *dacha* in the Crimea. Hardliners in the Kremlin—far more conservative than I am—are afraid of what the people will do to them if *perestroika* becomes as powerful a force as they fear. If they are not stupid enough to ruin the opportunity for themselves, they may actually succeed in toppling Gorbachev." He examined his fingernails. "If they succeed, order will be restored in the country, and it's my belief that *perestroika* will go the way of the tsars."

"What does all this have to do with me? And the children?" I asked. "And do you really want this coup to take place? It will be a disaster for the country."

He leaned back in the chair and stretched out his legs. He was still athletic, slender and muscular, but now I was aware that he radiated something malign and ugly, the threat of unpredictable violence that might show itself and then disappear in an instant. Was this the quality I once found so attractive, without even recognizing it? Or had he changed? And then suddenly he frowned and sat straight.

"You're smiling," he said. "You think this is a joke?"

"I wasn't smiling in humor," I said. "I was remembering what I once found so attractive about you. You still have it, but now I know you better, and perhaps I'm wiser. Funny what happens with the passage of time."

"You will remember," he replied, "that I once found you beautiful, too, until children took your shape from you and turned you into a shapeless bag."

"That's the kind of comment I've learned to expect from you," I said. "You want women who look like teenage boys with tight little asses and hard, pointy tits. Do you wonder why I went elsewhere for affection?"

In two steps he crossed the space between us and before I could take a breath he had a hand around my throat. He glared at me with hate-filled eyes as he squeezed, cutting off the blood to my head. My vision blurred. I must have gagged or begun to lose consciousness because he loosened his grip, holding me up by the neck as I gasped for air.

"I would be very careful," he warned, the hatred still burning in his eyes, "how you address me. It is of no consequence to me that you are my wife." He enunciated carefully, each word filled with menace.

"You bastard," I said. It came out as a whisper.

He ignored me.

"You asked whether I thought this coup would be good for the country." He shrugged his shoulders. "What I think doesn't matter. It's already underway. Within a day or two phone lines to Gorbachev's *dacha* in Foros will be cut and the country will be told he's taken ill. The old guard at the Kremlin will announce a state of emergency, tanks will surround the White House and Yeltsin and his people will be taken down. They'll appoint a provisional government to restore order and the deal will be done." He rose and walked over to me.

"Sit," he said, pointing to the closest straight-backed chair as he took me by the arm and maneuvered me into a sitting position. He stepped behind me, rested his hands on my shoulders and placed his fingertips below my clavicles. As he spoke he leaned over me and slowly closed his fists, compressing the fleshy part of my shoulders and pulling the clavicles upward. At first it was bearable and I refused to cry out, but he kept squeezing. I knew from those who had experienced pain at his hands that he had mastered the art of causing agony without leaving bruises, and that he was not anywhere near the limit of how tightly he could close his fists.

"Stop," I said. "What do you want?"

"Much better," he said. He released pressure on my shoulders and moved around to stand in front of me. "I've already told you what I want. Now I'll tell you why. It served my purpose to let you believe that because of your proximity to me, you know what the men in the Kremlin are thinking. But you have no idea." He paced the length of the room, and then back again, his hands held before him, fingers clenched, rubbing his thumbs against his forefingers as if to release energy. "I have enemies in the highest places—men whose power will increase if the coup is successful, men who feel betrayed by the associations I've made, threatened by how rapidly I've advanced. Unless I make myself indispensable, they will do all they can to get rid of me. They'll send me to the furthest, most miserable outpost we have." He smiled thinly. "I will do anything to avoid that. Fortunately, their first priority will be to reestablish order—and that means rounding up those responsible for anti-government activities. I intend to produce these people, one by one, until my contribution is recognized and my position secure. That's where you come in."

If I had known this earlier, I might have acted in time to protect those in danger. I could have ensured their disappearance before Grigory managed to pry the information from me. I knew he would, eventually. I was not all that strong, and I knew he was right—he would do anything to avoid being sent into exile. Despite myself I glanced at the phone.

He stood before me with his hands in the pocket of his custom-tailored suit, an amused expression on his face.

"Don't even think about it," he said. "There is no way for you to alert your friends."

"You're going to turn your own wife in as a dissident organizer? Don't be ridiculous. You'll make yourself a laughing stock. The KGB will mock you into obscurity."

"I'm not interested in you—I want the names of your contacts in the country, and the names of the foreign agents you've been communicating with for the last decade. You are going to provide me with the list I need to make myself indispensable."

"You think they'll keep you around once you give them this supposed list?"

"You're not listening. I'm not going to give them a list. I'm going to give them your friends. One, by one, by one, until there are none left."

"I see," I said. "And what do I get for handing these supposed friends to you for execution? How do I know you won't put me on the list, too?"

The skin around his forehead seemed to tighten, his cheekbones became more prominent, and his eyes radiated cold. I would almost have sworn that his pupils became vertical slits. His voice was silken, with the sharpness of frozen gravel.

"You are in no position to negotiate," he said. "If you refuse to give me what I know you have, there will be consequences. To you, to your children, and to the old hag."

"Yes," I responded. "I know the threats. You will send our children—hardly more than babies—to an orphan home. Me, you will ship off to the worst prison camp in the Gulag to rot until I die, and no one will ever find out what happened to me. I will just have disappeared. You have the power to do this, I know. But I wonder—even now—whether you are really capable of such depravity."

He looked carefully at his coat and brushed at his lapels and sleeves, and I was sure he was searching for strands of my hair that might have remained on him. Then he pulled his shirtsleeves out so that they were visible from the end of his coat sleeves, straightened, and strode to the door.

"More to the point, I'm counting on the fact that you would do anything to avoid such a fate, for yourself and for them. As for your children, after all your lies, how do I know what to believe?" He opened the door and turned back to me. From my chair I could see two of his men in the entrance hall. "In the meantime, why do you think I had Lena brought here? Instead of protecting your friends, perhaps you should be thinking about the old woman."

He walked out of the room and closed the door, and through the window I watched him leave the house. He exchanged a few words with his man at the front door, walked down the path as if this were just another day. Viktor held open the back door of the limo, closed it behind him and then ran around to the driver's door, settled himself in the seat, and drove off.

Lena

There are times now when I have flashes of remembering the distant past that lay so long buried.

I remember when Avrom was murdered in the shadow of trees that watched with ancient wisdom, branches spread like fingers reaching out in helpless pity, their songs offered in comfort, silent whispers in the wind. I remember running breathless after Papa as he stumbled sobbing through the forest, Avrom cradled in his arms, head lolling in one elbow, little shoes bouncing at the other. He stopped on the bank of a small stream, and I see the little girl I was, hiding behind a massive tree trunk, my hands on the rough bark, watching as Papa gently lowered my twin brother to the ground. After removing his shoes and his clothes, Papa took him into the stream and allowed the water to wash away all the blood from his body, and then with the help of a stick, in a frenzy of anger and grief, he dug a shallow grave and like a priest—a rabbi—he lowered the other half of me into the dirt. With his hands he gathered up the soil he had removed and carefully, so carefully, covered Avrom's pale little body whose heart could no longer keep pace with mine. I knew when his heart stopped beating—it felt as if mine had been ripped from my chest. As Papa covered him with soil, I tasted the dark, moist earth as it packed my mouth, and it was all that prevented me from crying out.

Memory or imagination? I don't know. We never discussed it. When Papa was alive the memory was hidden from me. And even if I had remembered, would I have put him through the anguish of retelling his version of that afternoon?

The luxury of the *dacha*, where Grigory has held us now for a week, is a far cry from the isolation and terror of that forest, but for me it is the same place. It has the same icy coldness, the same stink of death. Who could forget that stink? It has remained with me all these years. I remember now, as we made our way night after night through the woods we came upon abandoned mongrel dogs dead of starvation, and birds who died and fell from perches overhead. We trod on rotting skunk and fox and half-eaten deer alive with maggots. And occasionally we stumbled on a human corpse. They were all the same and they all smelled alike, and the older they were the worse they stank, until they were no longer bodies but became again a part of the earth they lay on.

Death has a particular stink, and violent death, even more so. As an old woman I have come face to face with enough evil men to know that they, too, have a distinctive stench. Truly evil men with blood on their hands carry their victims' pain, and they smell worse than death itself. Grigory is one such. I knew it when Darya first brought him to our rooms. Like a corpse, the stench on him has intensified with time. He sprays expensive French cologne on his cheeks and behind his ears and up his bum, but nothing can hide the putrefaction surrounding him like a foul mist, and it brings the burn of vomit to my throat.

I have known a long time something like this would happen. Men like Grigory have no friends. They use and are used, and when their time is up they land on the dung heap with those they've tossed away like old kitchen rags, and often they receive their dismissal with a boyish surprise that's charming in the way a crocodile's surprise would be charming. But there is nothing peaceful or resigned in their going. They struggle and strain in decline like old men trying to shit, and as they get flushed down the drainpipe, would drag the whole world with them. Wives and children. Suckling infants and their nurses. Ancient grandmothers.

But not this one. I have pretended long enough to be of Russian soil. I've played the game and lived the lies necessary to draw breath under the Soviet system, which all my adult life I have known is as alien to my soul as the blind monsters lurking beneath the frozen Siberian tundra. Mother Russia devours her young without choice. To do what I must, I have no choice, either.

Steven

It had the feel of an encampment set up by vagrants. There were several dark khaki military tents, the canvas stained or faded in patches, some torn, and roughly repaired with needle and thick thread. They looked like tents discarded by the Soviet military.

We were ushered down a narrow path worn into the undergrowth, followed by two men in fatigues, semi-automatics slung from their shoulders. The weapons looked ugly and brutal, designs cut out of their grey metal stocks to reduce weight. I found them more frightening than the rifles carried by guards and police in Moscow.

It was the end of the day. Everything was in shadow. The sun was low on the invisible horizon and the foliage around us thick enough so that although we could see, there was very little illumination. The tents were set up in a semi-circle beneath towering trees, invisible from the sky. We waited, sitting on upturned logs, watched by the guards, until three men emerged from the other side of the clearing, one in front, flanked by a man at each elbow. They approached us and I recognized the one in front from the photo in Juliana's apartment. It was Kolya. After hearing some of what he had been through, I expected him to be beaten down, resentful, physically diminished. He was none of those things—in fact I was struck by how much the opposite he was. A large man, a head taller than I was, in grubby fatigues that only exaggerated his physical grace. He moved with the ease and flow of a natural athlete. From the moment we met, the artist in me was drawn to him. He had an imposing presence, and being around him was daunting.

I rose as he approached and looked up into warm grey eyes, broad cheekbones, a generous mouth. His military haircut had grown out and filled in, and the thick hair falling over his forehead was an almost amber color. That, and his welcoming smile, gave him a boyish appearance. It was only when I looked carefully at him that I saw the dark creases beneath his eyes, saw how cautiously he looked around him, and from up close, how weary he was. It made me all the more aware of what a beautiful boy he must have been, and of the price he had paid for his beauty.

He and Pyotr shook hands and spoke briefly, and then he turned to me, placed his hands on my shoulders and kissed me on both cheeks.

"So this is the Steven I've been hearing about for so many years," he said. "Not the kind of welcome I would have liked to give my American cousin. But we're shaped by forces outside ourselves, no? Come."

He led the way into one of the tents, and turned on a propane lamp. Pyotr and I followed him in, and the three of us sat down in the camp chairs around the light. Kolya examined me silently.

"How did you find my parents?" he asked.

I must have looked at him blankly, trying to understand the question. He grinned.

"I'm sorry," he said. "My English. I mean, how are they? We talk sometimes, but it's dangerous for us to be seen together. It is hard for them."

I wondered whether he actually wanted to hear what I thought, or whether he was trying to gauge how honest I would be with him. Or perhaps he was fishing to see how connected I felt to his parents.

"When I saw them two years ago they seemed much happier," I said. "They didn't expect to see me this afternoon. But I found them anxious, worried about you. Frightened, I think. They seem—diminished. At first they were reluctant to involve you at all."

"Diminished," he said grimly. "Made smaller in size, right? Yes. They're dried up with fear, for themselves and for me." He paused to light a cigarette. "And for Darya." He inhaled, and spoke as the smoke spiraled from his mouth and nose. "Which is why we're here. You tell me that bastard holds Darya and Lena and the children at the *dacha*," Kolya said, looking at Pyotr. "How can you be so certain they're in danger?"

"When has she not been in danger from him?" asked Pyotr. "Besides, there is the letter. Steven, show him what she sent you."

I pulled it from my pocket and handed it across the propane light. Kolya squinted at the letter through the smoke as it entered and then passed across the cone of yellow light cast by the lamp. There was silence in the tent as he read it slowly and handed it back, eyes half closed.

"Quite a letter," he said.

"We also have word from some of Grigory's hand-picked guards. You know them, Kolya. They're not all as loyal to him as he'd like to think."

"Yes," he said in a dry voice, "I know his hand-picked gang of ex-convicts. He still thinks I'm one of his boys." He stamped the remnant of his cigarette on the mud floor of the tent. "You know, Darya and I used to be like brother and sister. But this—this business—drove us apart. One day she saw me on the street, and I tried to dodge her. It would have been dangerous if Grigory found out she had been talking to me." He smiled affectionately. "But she's always been as stubborn as a mule. She went to my parents and insisted she needed to see me. So my parents made the arrangements and we met. They've never been able to say no to her. Apparently they're not alone." He pointed at me. "You couldn't refuse her request either, could you?"

He didn't wait for me to reply.

"I won't embarrass you by asking whether you love her—you wouldn't be here if you didn't. I know her well, and based on her letter, she loves you, too. I don't know whether to offer you congratulations or condolences." He laughed, at the same time shaking his head, waving his hand as if disavowing his own words. "No," he said, "you know I'm joking, and in very bad taste. Darya is wonderful. If you deserve her love, you must be something special.   But what the hell are you doing here? You go up against Grigory he'll destroy you all. You don't have any military training, do you?"

"I'm a painter, Kolya. I don't know the first thing about combat."

"No self-defense training?" he asked.

I shook my head.

"Martial arts?"

"No."

"Weapons?"

"I'm a painter," I said again. "Just a painter." I paused, feeling stupid. Some additional explanation was called for—I just didn't know what it was. Kolya just stared at me.

"That's rich," he said. His voice was bland. I had the sense that if he had shown any expression at all, it would have been disdain, or laughter. "A painter, come to rescue the woman he loves. From her husband, a brute who has behind him a small army, not to mention a band of ex-convicts who owe him their freedom. And you plan to use what tools to rescue her? Paintbrushes and turpentine? Perhaps you'll squeeze red paint on them? Wrap them in canvas? Either you're a great lover or a brave fool."

I glared at him angrily. He had deftly described my predicament, and despite Darya's love for him, I didn't much like him at that moment.

"Perhaps I'm both," I said. "I didn't intend to fall for her. It just happened. All I want is to find her and take her home with me. You're right. I'm not equipped to do any of this. Darya knows more about what's happening than the people who got me here. She realized there would be no help once I arrived. That's why she asked me to contact you." I shrugged. "I love her, so I came. What kind of person would I be if I refused? But it seems you're more interested in mocking me than helping her." I pushed myself up from the chair. "Let's go, Pyotr," I said. "You'll have to help me find another way to get to General Shaposhnikov."

Pyotr glanced at Kolya, eyebrows raised as if asking what to do now. Kolya grinned in amusement.

"Well, it's good to see the painter has balls. You think there's another way?" He laughed loudly, his mouth open and his head thrown back. "Until I introduced them, she didn't even know who the General was. She wanted you to meet me because that's the only way he'll talk to you. Even Pyotr here couldn't get you to him."

I looked at Pyotr for confirmation, and he nodded.

"Cousin, please, sit again." Kolya rose to stand beside me, and gently steered me back towards my chair. When I resisted, he shrugged his shoulders and returned to his own seat. "I've been told if I were a little smoother, a little less direct, I might have gone further in life. Apparently it wasn't something I could manage. But I'm not quite as unsympathetic as I seem. Darya sent you here because she was certain I would do whatever I can to help." He grinned. "I like the idea of reuniting two lovers. You must

398 Neville D. Frankel

admit, the idea of a peaceful painter, a single man—someone who's not an assassin or a marksman—coming to Moscow in this political climate to rescue his lover is a little laughable. The situation cries out for comic relief."

"Apology accepted," I said, relieved, and sat down again.

"The writing's on the wall," said Kolya. "Her husband's lost his supporters in the Kremlin, and he doesn't know it yet, but there's nothing he can do to redeem himself. You can't imagine what pleasure it will give me to have a hand in bringing him down." He clapped me on the shoulder. "My connection to General Shaposhnikov will be helpful to you, Cousin, but we have resources that even Darya is unaware of."

Darya

The children are crying, but Grigory will not let me go to them. He keeps me in his study, with the door closed, forcing me to sit in a straight-backed chair as he asks me again and again for information. Some of his questions I have no answers for, but even those I can answer I am not yet desperate enough to reveal.

Anton calls for me, his footsteps outside the door, and then tears up as one of the men, perhaps trying to be tender but more afraid of allowing Anton to interrupt Grigory, picks him up and carries him from the door. My boy cries for me, for Anna, for Babushka, who is alone in the kitchen. Grigory has commanded that she make ice cream in his electric Italian ice cream maker. If it were not so terrifying it would be comical. Anna cannot come—she is still in the apartment in Moscow.

"You met a man in Cuba, a man close to Castro, who's been sharing security information with Washington. In Warsaw you attended a secret meeting of Russian dissidents. On every trip you've taken—to North Africa, Italy, Portugal, the Eastern bloc—you've attended unscheduled meetings, made contact with people whose only goal is to sabotage us. I want their names, and how you contact them."

"You're wrong," I said. "I have no names that would be of any use to you. If I had any unscheduled meetings in the places you sent me, they were with people dedicated to making the Soviet system better, not sabotaging it."

"I'll be the judge of whether they were patriots or saboteurs."

"That's what I'm afraid of," I said.

"So who was it you met in Florence? I know you had dinner and drank wine with a young woman, sitting together at an outdoor restaurant. I know you left your hotel that night. You went somewhere. Where did you go?"

"Your watcher lost me, did he? What did you take from him as punishment? An ear? A finger? Perhaps you removed a testicle?"

Casually he put a hand on my cheek, and I felt his fingers caress my skin. I looked up into his face and as soon as our eyes met, he grinned. Without apparent effort or change of expression he whipped his fingernails across my cheek. I flinched at the sting, refusing to give him the satisfaction of raising my hand to my face. He took a handkerchief from his pocket and gently wiped my cheek, turning it to me to show me that he had drawn blood. He handed me the reddened handkerchief.

"You seemed to have scratched yourself," he said. "Perhaps you will be more careful in the future."

"When did you start having me watched?" I asked, pressing the handkerchief to my face.

"Interesting you think there was ever a time when I didn't have you observed."

"If you've always had me watched, you know you're the only man I was with before Anton and Larisa were born. How can you claim not to know whether they're yours?"

"You've already proven that you can outsmart the men I assign to watch you." He shrugged his shoulders, self-absorbed, on show as always, evaluating his every gesture as if watching himself in the mirror permanently affixed to his heels in place of a shadow. "I have no reason to trust you. I can only assume they are not mine."

"So even at the beginning you didn't trust me, even when I believed I loved you."

"You never loved me," he said. "If you loved anything it was the luxury I could provide. What you married was my power to advance your career. And you know what you loved most? There was no limit to what I was willing to do to you in the bedroom. That sound, that moan deep in your throat, when you couldn't tell pain from pleasure, that sound I will treasure forever."

He stood two feet in front of me, one hand across his waist, cradling his elbow, the other hand stroking his chin, and I could feel his eyes on me, taking in my face. To my own disgust, I found myself aroused by his words—aroused, embarrassed and humiliated. My cheeks burned.

"I took you in every way possible," he mused. "I found deep satisfaction in possessing the kind of beauty you once had. Pity it's all gone now. You no longer have anything I want."

"Back then I still believed you were a human being." I said. "I thought you had it in you to become a good husband and a father. It was the biggest error of my life."

"So far, perhaps. But not giving me the information I want will be a much greater mistake."

There was a commotion outside the door and it burst open. Larisa ran in, outrage on her round face, and she was followed by Anton, crying. He ran to me and buried his face in my lap.

"Mama," she said breathlessly. "Anton only wanted to go in the kitchen to be with Babushka, but that man—" she pointed to the door, where one of Grigory's men stood "—that man spanked him on his bottom." She looked at my face and raised a little hand to my cheek. "What did you do to your face?" she asked accusingly. "You see what happens when you don't be careful?"

Grigory glared at the man standing in the doorway. He was tall and muscular, with an oafish face, broad shoulders and big hands, but he stood slumped like a schoolboy awaiting a reprimand, eyes lowered to the floor. I would gladly have murdered anyone who lay a hand on my children, but I felt sorry for him. Anton still had his head on my lap, trying to catch his breath from crying. His skin was warm and moist, and I ran my fingers through his silken blond hair, so much like Grigory's.

"Get them out of here," he snapped. "You think you can keep two children quiet without making them run to their mother?"

"Go, children," I said, "It's all right if you go help make ice cream. Papa's going to send Viktor in the car to get Anna, and when she arrives you can all have some ice cream together." I looked at Grigory. "Either I leave this room and go take care of them," I said softly, "or you get Anna here now. Your choice."

402 Neville D. Frankel

Lena

Grigory is mad for ice cream. Appropriate, I think, for a man with ice where his heart should be. He has to have it fresh, with whole cream, Madagascar vanilla, grated Belgian chocolate, farm fresh strawberries in summer. It has to be as cold as it can be without being crystalized. Russians eat ice cream all year round, especially in winter. This has never made sense to me, even when I sold it to passengers on the trains going to and from Siberia. Who needs to take such coldness into the body when Mother Nature gives us winters to chill the blood? I've told him this habit will be the death of him, but he laughs in my face.

"You don't have to worry about my death, old woman," he said once. "You'll be gone to your own long before me."

Not if I can help it, I thought.

Russian ice cream is not good enough—he likes it homemade. Money is no object when he wants something. He has a fancy Italian ice cream churn at the apartment in the city and he bought one for the *dacha*, too. But he prefers to have his ice cream hand-churned. There are not many who could hand churn ice cream at my age, but I don't mind. The children love it, too, although they only eat it when he is not home. Darya feared that churning by hand would kill me. So Grigory bought churns with electric motors. But at the end of the cycle, when it's important to churn with a slow, steady hand that feels the final hardening, I am able to turn off the motor and let my hands decide what the ice cream needs.

He likes it fresh from the churn, where the ice in the inner walls of the machine keep it so cold that it numbs tongue and lips, and when I taste it to make sure it's done, I can't feel the roof of my mouth. I have to make sure the children don't get to the ice cream before it warms a little, because they might bite their little tongues or the tender inside of their cheeks, and the only way they would know it was the taste of blood in their mouths. Perhaps I can make it cold enough, I thought, so that Grigory will chew off his tongue.

I have known for some time that it might eventually fall to me to protect those I love from Grigory. But I had to find a way of taking care of him that would require neither power nor speed. I can no longer move fast, and I was never strong. But I am still nimble, and what speed the years have taken from me, they have replaced with stealth and craft. When I realized that the effect of very cold ice cream was like an anesthetic to the mouth, I began to consider how I might use that when the time came.

I waited, and thought, and planned, not sure what to do or how necessary it would become for me to act. What finally pushed me over the edge was Anna, who came to me hysterically in the kitchen one morning as I arrived at the apartment. Darya was not home—she had left the previous day on a trip to Cuba. Grigory had also left the apartment early, and Anna couldn't wait until I arrived to break the news that, after being in their home for over a year, Grigory had finally done what he was bound to do sooner or later. The night before, once the children were asleep, he came to Anna's bed. Her face and neck were bruised where he had slapped her and held her down. She was a country girl, saving herself for a husband, and he forced himself on her, tearing her so that she bled all over the bed that night, and for days afterwards. She was in pain, frightened. She felt that it was somehow her fault, that she had betrayed Darya, and she didn't know what to do or how to make sure it didn't happen again.

As she wept, I rose to my full height and put my arms about her trembling shoulders. She was a slight girl without much flesh on her, and as I pulled her into my embrace I felt the smallness of her breasts against me, and she flinched, pulling away in pain. The bruises on her face and neck were only the ones I could see, but there were clearly others. It didn't take much to imagine how terrified she must have been as Grigory did his brutal work on her.

At that moment in the kitchen I felt the fire of my own fury and hatred for this man who brought us nothing but unhappiness. I knew for a certainty that it was only a matter of time before he hurt Darya badly. My first thought, from the mind of an old woman, was that I might die before

I had a chance to protect my children from him. But fast on the heels of that thought came another, this one from the fighter, the ancient warrior within me that has propelled me through every obstacle I've encountered. Yes, I thought, I might die, but I would make sure I killed him first. Warrior I might be, but ancient, slow and rheumy-eyed. I would need help. And Grigory had ensured that Anna would be my ally.

"He's already hurt Darya, and now you—and who knows what else? My child," I whispered to her, "I'm afraid he might do something unspeakable to the children, and if that happens I would never forgive myself. I have to stop him."

She pulled back and looked at me, horrified at the idea that he might be capable of harming the children she had come to love. But she knew I was right. One could not live in that apartment without seeing how cruel he was to Darya, how detached he was from the children, and how ready he was to mock and humiliate me. It didn't take long to convert her fear and humiliation into outrage. She agreed to help me in whatever way I needed, but I was cautious in what I shared with her. I didn't want to put her in danger. She was incapable of concealing what she knew, and Grigory would read her like an open book.

One day when I left Darya's apartment I took with me a glass from the kitchen, wrapped in old newspaper. When I reached my room I banged it on the floor until it cracked. With the old pestle and mortar Vasily and I bought to grind herbs and seeds and what nuts we could find when I was in my twenties, I crushed down the shards each night until after a week or so I had a cupful of fine glass powder. But when I tested the ground glass, rubbing my finger tip against it, first gently and finally as harshly as I could, it barely broke the skin. I had to start over, now with the knowledge that the glass should not be ground too fine. It needed instead to be splintered into tiny, razor sharp shards. This time I wouldn't use an ordinary kitchen glass. Though he didn't deserve it, Grigory would get only the most expensive crystal.

I wrapped three of his French Baccarat wine goblets in an old cloth, and took great satisfaction in smashing them on the stone floor in the kitchen.

The bases I discarded, being too thick, and then, closing up the cloth again, I ground my rolling pin across it. Several times I stopped and opened up the cloth to examine my work, not wanting to grind too finely. It took many rolls back and forth before I was satisfied with the consistency of the glass shards and the sound they made as I crushed them. When I opened the cloth, the morning sunlight from the window reflected from my little pile as if it were a collection of diamonds. I ran a fingertip lightly across the shards and this time the blood flowed in tiny rivulets down my finger and across my palm, to splash off my wrist onto the counter. I turned my hand over to examine the results of my work, and saw that my flesh had been sliced cleanly, as if by a thousand tiny razors. The tool I had created was good enough for the job I had to do.

There was a cupful of glass shards, fine enough so that when I leaned over to look closely, the shards swirled at the impact of my breath. I poured it into a paper bag, wrapped the bag in a clean cloth, and hid it behind the scrub soaps in the kitchen, where Grigory would never find it.

Before I put it away I showed it to Anna, and told her how I intended to use it. Again, she was horrified, this time, though, I think more by the violence and duplicity of my plan. It was not what she expected of me. Younger people never think of the very old as capable of much. Somehow, they assume time has eroded all our sharp edges, that we are incapable of scheming; that cruelty is beyond us, and that we have outlived the capacity to be creative. I would use all those misconceptions to full advantage.

Viktor was in the kitchen with me, sitting on a kitchen chair, his legs outstretched, cigarette in his mouth, watching through the smoke as I waited beside the electric churn. He grinned at me, smoke wafting from his mouth.

"I've always dreamed of returning to the Caucasus," he said. "Will you run away with me, old woman?" he asked. "We could live in a little cabin in the mountains, and you could make ice cream. People from local villages

406 Neville D. Frankel

would think they'd died and gone to heaven. They've never tasted anything like your ice cream."

I glared at him, saw his shouldered pistol visible beneath his open jacket. "Put that thing away, you fool," I said. "I don't want the children to see it."

He looked down and closed his jacket.

"Sorry," he said. "My jacket is like my mouth—sometimes it doesn't know when to stay buttoned." Grigory's raised voice echoed through the house and into the kitchen. The office door must have been open, and he was addressing one of his men. Viktor jerked his head toward the sound. "He's climbing up someone's rear end," he said.

"May he climb all the way in and drown in bile," I said. "So tell me more about this rural paradise in the mountains. I run away with you. What do you do while I churn ice cream?"

"I collect the money, of course," he said, gold teeth shining, delighted that I was willing to play his word game.

"And when I've died of boredom and you've buried me, up there in that forsaken mountain cabin, what will you do then?"

"I would miss your fire," he said, suddenly serious, "and I would mourn." Then the grin returned. "For a least a week. After that I would have my pick of all the big-breasted young village girls. They'd give their eye teeth to come churn my ice cream."

"Keep dreaming," I muttered at the churn. "That's about as close as you'll ever get to any village girls. Big tits or not, they'd all just as soon spit in your eye. You may be younger than I am, but to them you'd be just one more randy old bandit trying to get your pickle squeezed."

He laughed uproariously, and then looked at me with admiration in his eyes.

"I'm not joking, Babushka," he said. "I really will miss your fire when you're gone."

"Don't hold your breath," I said stonily.

The door swung open and one of Grigory's men stood in the doorway. I saw from his face, flushed and humiliated, that he had been the object of his boss's wrath. Anton and Larisa pushed past his knees into the kitchen.

He jerked his head at Viktor.

"She doesn't like the way we're handling the kids—Grigory wants you to take the car and go get Anna. Better make it fast. He's in a foul mood."

Both children ran to me and sat on the floor around the churn. "Mama says when Anna comes we can all have ice cream," said Larisa. Viktor rose quickly from his chair and headed to the door.

"Viktor." He stopped and turned to me. "She's a sweet girl," I said. "Be gentle with her. Give her time to collect a few things. And remind her to bring my special sugar, the stuff I use for the ice cream. She knows where it is in the kitchen."

"So that's your secret," he said. "I'll remind her—but only if you promise to bring it with us to our cabin in the Caucasus."

"When you take me away with you," I said softly, "I'll bring all the sugar you can stomach," I said. I only hoped Anna would remember what sugar I was talking about.

Steven

"I'm not quite sure what to do with you, cousin," said Kolya, dropping his arm heavily about my shoulder.

I was so taken with his good nature and his warmth, he could say almost anything without giving offense. He knew how charming he was. Perhaps that's why he felt so little hesitation about saying whatever was on his mind.

"Just keep me in the loop," I said. "I won't be in the way—but I started this. All I want is to know what's going on. I do have a vested interest in the outcome, you know."

"My interest," he said somberly, "is to keep everyone safe. Including you. I can't be worrying that you'll shoot off your foot or blow a crater in someone's skull. Under normal circumstances I'd send you home. But Grigory gets jittery when he's not in complete control, and that makes his men jittery, too. Meantime every one of our people is assigned to jobs that will minimize bloodshed when the right wing mounts its coup. I have less support than I'd like. That's the only reason I've given you a weapon. Just don't do anything stupid with it."

"Thanks for the vote of confidence."

"All I'm saying is, if you give me a paintbrush all you'll have is a mess on your canvas. But put the tools of my trade in inexperienced hands, and you end up with broken bones and dead people."

"I'll do my best not to shoot myself in the ass."

"Not your ass I'm worried about."

"When do you think they'll drop this bombshell?"

"Anytime now. They're just waiting until they've isolated Gorbachev. Once he can no longer mount any opposition to them, they'll give the word. Tanks will roll out, they'll send troops to surround government offices, and demand that Gorbachev loyalists step down. This coup is being masterminded by the worst of the right wingers. They're either power-hungry opportunists, or bureaucrats pickled in vodka. It's not going to be pretty, but it won't succeed."

"But won't it change the balance of power? I mean, isn't every major power going to be on alert?"

"You've been watching too many spy movies." Kolya grinned. "This country is run like an island dictatorship. The people in charge are a bunch of corrupt fuckers whose biggest worry is when the next bribe will land in their overseas bank accounts. They're robbing us blind. If the CIA knows anything about this coup, it's because of people like General Shaposhnikov. He's built a reputation for integrity, and he has connections to people in Washington. That's why it's so important to have him involved—because without him there's no way you'll get out of the country in one piece. Remember, even your own embassy has no record of your being here."

❦

Beside Kolya I felt like Charles Atlas's ninety-pound weakling, and it was only a matter of luck that he wasn't kicking sand in my face. But old General Shaposhnikov was another matter altogether. He was like an ancient version of Paul Bunyan. We met just after dawn on the outskirts of Moscow, at an all-night restaurant adjacent to an industrial laundry. It was the only time Kolya could arrange for us to be safely in the same place. Shaposhnikov was under constant surveillance and had to leave his apartment by taking a basement corridor to an adjoining building, where the laundry truck was waiting in the alley with its door open and the tailgate down as if stopped for a pickup. It was difficult to imagine this hulking old man climbing into a wheeled laundry cart and crouching down as it was rolled from the building up the ramp and into the truck.

"Like a load of dirty sheets," he said with a smile.

We had just been introduced and shaken hands, but he was not ready to release me. He wasn't squeezing, but his hand was broad, with thick, powerful fingers, and a heavily calloused palm. I could have pulled away from his grasp, but that would have seemed rude. Besides, I had the sense that pulling away from him might have been like scraping my hand against

410 Neville D. Frankel

a concrete post.

"I prefer to do business directly in my watchers' line of sight," he continued. "It keeps them humble, and me on my toes." He looked at me through a lacework of creases and darkened age spots around his eyes, but the eyes themselves were bright and focused. I felt their heat as he examined my face. "We all need to be reminded how important it is to remain humble, no?"

"Yes sir," I answered.

"Matvei Kuzmich," he said. "Please. So you're Darya's American. I've been hearing about you, come to rescue the beautiful maiden from a corrupt and powerful husband. Who comes, moreover, unarmed, without a strategy, having left his identity at the border. You know, in this country, perhaps more than in your own, if the authorities catch you without identity papers, you are at a high risk of disappearing. And you select an interesting time—a pivotal time—to arrive." He paused. "I've lived a long time, but I have never seen my country so close to dissolution. I think what's happening now, as we speak, will change the course of history."

"Everyone I know has already told me how unqualified I am to be here. I know all about the risks I took by coming, but I'm here because Darya's asked for my help. So please, let's just get on with what we have to do and get her to safety."

He nodded his head slowly, the loose flesh around his jawbones flowing like waves against a pier, the corners of his mouth drawn down in thought.

"It takes character to do what you're doing," he said, "especially if you know you're out of your depth." He smiled again, that wide, boyish grin in the middle of his creased and jowly face. "You probably need to be a bit of a fool, too, but then, in matters of the heart, aren't we all fools?" He released my hand, and my fingers spread wide as if to convince themselves they still could. "If I were fifty years younger I would have already rescued Darya and run off with her. Assuming she would have me. So I understand better than you can imagine why you're here—and how fortunate you are." He waved a thick finger at me. "Don't screw it up," he warned. "Come sit down, boys." He waved Kolya and Pyotr over to the table. "Time to take Grigory off the map. He's done more than enough damage for one life."

They sat together at a table in the laundry office, and Kolya withdrew from his pocket a schematic of the *dacha*. In low voices they talked over the drawing, pointing to spots in and around the property.

"Do we know where in the *dacha* he's holding her?" asked the General.

"He may have her locked up in one room," answered Pyotr. "Or perhaps he allows her the run of the place. I mean, it is the house they live in together with the children. He must have his men inside, so he probably doesn't see her as a flight risk."

"It's not easy to rescue a woman from her own home," said Kolya, "and it's even harder to prove that she's being held against her will."

"If Grigory comes to the door and says she's there voluntarily," asked Pyotr, "how many in Moscow would question his word?"

"But we know she's being held against her will," said the General. "The whole compound is protected by a military guard. Anyone coming to see Grigory would be stopped at the entrance, and he has men inside. He thinks he's safe from the possibility of a rescue. You need to come in the way he least expects you."

"If we're going to get her out, we have to make an assumption about where she is," said Kolya. "I doubt he allows her the run of the place. I'll bet he has her isolated in one room, door locked. Maybe she's even bound. Not that he needs her tied up—but it would keep her off balance."

He stopped, the unflappable military man suddenly rendered speechless, as he fought to keep his voice under control. The others waited, looking down at the table, aware and respectful of Kolya's struggle. When he did speak his voice was cloaked in fury, low and shaking.

"It's easier for him to hurt her if she's isolated. And that's exactly what he's doing." He pushed his chair back and rose quickly. "We all thought he was holding her there, waiting for the coup. But he's not waiting for anything. That's not his way—and besides, he's desperate. He needs her names, and he'll break her bones one by one until she gives him what he wants. If we wait until the coup has taken place, it'll be too late. We need to go in now."

General Shaposhnikov rose heavily to his feet. "Go then," he said. "I wish I could join you, if only to see Grigory's face, but I would be a burden."

"With respect, General," said Kolya, "You have more important things to do."

The old man turned to me. "I wanted to meet you, Steven, before I put myself at risk and call in what favors I'm owed by your consulate. Now that we've met, I'm satisfied. If Kolya and Pyotr can get Darya and the children and her grandmother out of the *dacha* safely, I'll get you into the American Embassy."

I put my hand out to shake his, but he grinned, threw his arms about me, and kissed me warmly on both cheeks.

"If you end up getting Darya home to America," he whispered, "plant these kisses on her beautiful face. Tell her they're from an old soldier. Let her know I'll miss her. And Mother Russia will be poorer for her absence."

Darya

Where was Steven? I could no longer count on his having received my letter, and I had no way of knowing whether he had sufficient love for me—or courage, or resources—to act on my request. Without him, Kolya had no way of knowing where I was, which meant there was no help coming. How, I wondered, had it happened in my life that I was so completely alone?

As I waited for Viktor to return from Moscow with Anna, these were the thoughts that went through my mind. And I wondered, what if Anna had decided to run away, and Viktor returned without her? It was clear from Grigory's actions and his mood that the tension in him was building to a climax, and that like my delaying tactics, his patience was close to an end.

Viktor was gone for over two hours. There were demonstrations in Moscow, the military was out in force, and even the darkened windows and the official plates on the limo were not enough to give him the usual special access and easy passage. By the time he arrived with Anna, I had a clear indication of where things were headed. It started when Grigory approached me with a roll of duct tape in one hand.

"Uncross your arms from your chest," he commanded. "Lay them on the arms of the chair."

"And let you tie me up?" I asked. "You can't be serious."

In response he grabbed my left arm and slammed it on the heavy wooden arm of the chair. With one elbow pressed painfully on the back of my hand he used both of his to unroll the tape, but I still had one free hand and with it I clawed at his face. He dropped the tape and raised a hand to his cheek, but not before the scratches from my three middle fingers darkened and I had the satisfaction of seeing blood rise to the surface of his skin. At the same time he raised his elbow from the back of my hand and without a sound drove it into my face.

I don't know if I actually lost consciousness or if I was merely stunned, but my first awareness was trying to touch my face and not being able to move my arms. When I looked down at them my forearms were taped tightly to the arms of the chair, and my hands were already puffy from the pressure. An aching heat radiated from my cheek, and without being able to touch my face I couldn't tell what damage he had done. My vision was blurry on the side he had hit, but I could open and close my eyes. Working the muscles of my face caused intense pain around my cheekbone, and I wondered whether he had broken it. It crossed my mind that now I would really be the saggy-faced unattractive woman he saw, and Steven—even Steven—would find me ugly and undesirable.

Grigory was sitting at his desk, paging through an open file. When there was a knock at the door he closed the file, inserted it into an envelope and taped it shut. He rose.

"Don't let the children come in," I said. My voice sounded strangely distant to me. "I don't want them to see me like this."

Grigory ignored me as he unlocked and opened the door. Viktor stepped in and Grigory closed and locked it behind him. Viktor glanced quickly at me and just as quickly averted his eyes, but not before I saw the shock on his face.

"Anna's in the kitchen," he said. And then, perhaps for my benefit, "the children are with her."

Grigory handed him the taped envelope. "Deliver this," he said. "Shouldn't take you more than a couple of hours. Before you go tell the old witch I want coffee. And tell her to bring my ice cream as soon as it's ready."

Viktor left, closing the door behind him, and I heard the lock click.

"Are you really going to eat ice cream while I sit here tied up, with a broken face? You really are a sick bastard."

"Romans drank wine as they watched lions ripping apart their gladiators. You think this is any different?" He gave a casual shrug, crueler for its indifference, and grinned. "None of this is really necessary, Dasha. Give me what I want and it will be as if this never happened."

Through my swollen, painful face I glared at him in disbelief. My vision was blurry, but I had never seen so clearly. "You have no intention—you never had any intention—of returning to our life. And after this," I said, "you think I would willingly go back to that charade? Never knowing when you would explode, or come take my body—the body you claim to despise— by force? You think I would return the children to that life?"

Grigory stood in front of the chair I was in, and he looked down at me, eyes half closed, lips pursed in thought.

"What first attracted me to you—after I saw how beautiful you were— was your spirit. I may have tamed you a little, but I'm perceptive enough to recognize that you're still impulsive, and your courage is what's made it possible for you to do your job. I've always known it would be dangerous for me to get on your bad side—that's why I've never crossed you beyond your limit. But after this—" he waved his hand casually at me "—I think I've crossed the line." He grinned. "I would never feel safe in my bed. So you're right—I never had any intention of living with you again."

A wet, guttural sound—something between a sob and a laugh—escaped my throat.

"So," I said, "all these years I've been living with the restrained, considerate version of you?"

"If you like," he said. "The point I was going to make is that my superiors in the Kremlin are mostly cabbages. They're a boring bunch— dull and conventional. You can see how it might raise some inconvenient questions if you disappeared just as I presented them with a list of your contacts. Not insurmountable questions, but sufficient to make me consider a return to our conventional little life together." He paused. "Or, at least, the appearance of that life."

"With you, everything is calculated down to the last detail, isn't it?"

"In this business, I have no choice. And at this point the only choice you have—" he held his open hands out before him, raising first one and then the other, mimicking a scale "—is between pretending to live our conventional little life with your children by your side, and the Gulag. Alone. Seems to me not a very difficult choice. In case you're unsure, here is some additional incentive."

He took two steps towards me and brought a fist down like a hammer on the outstretched fingers of my left hand. I heard the sound of bone cracking, and then the animal grunt as I closed my throat to prevent the children from hearing my scream. Then came the nausea, and I swallowed the vomit that wanted to rise up and drown me.

"I'm going out for a couple of hours," he said. "When I get back, one way or the other, you will give me what I want."

He walked out, closing the door behind him, and I heard the lock click into place. There was silence in the room, and through the door I could hear the children in the kitchen, laughing with Anna. I considered the choice he was placing before me, and I admit, without shame, that my determination began to waver. Was I really willing to risk my life and my children's future to protect people I neither knew well nor loved? Would they do the same for me?

I was capable of taking much more punishment before I had to make it stop, but for the first time, I recognized for certain that eventually, I would succumb to the pain and give him what he wanted. If that were the case, why give him the satisfaction of taking me apart piece by piece? There was no rescue coming. Unless I changed the dynamic, the path was clear.

Steven

We left the laundry and returned to Kolya's camp, where he briefed the four men coming with us. He spent a few minutes showing me how to use a pistol, in which I had no interest, but I listened carefully to him, recognizing its potential utility. I learned how to load and aim the weapon, and concealed my surprise at how heavy it was. By the time the men were armed and we'd all put on bulletproof vests, it was late afternoon, and we drove in two cars for another hour until we were within a mile of the *dacha* compound. We pulled off the road down a lane that was no more than two tire tracks and concealed the cars behind a stand of trees.

Kolya had explained that the *dacha* was in a compound of twelve houses, Grigory being the lowest-ranking resident. When all the residents were onsite, military security was tight, and guards were everywhere. But because of the crisis, Grigory was the only one present. All other residents—heads of ministries, high-ranking military officers, powerful Party members—were at their offices in Moscow. Either they were working to avert the coup, or they were helping to make it happen. As a result, there was only a skeleton security force at the main guardhouse, and a couple of guards walking the perimeter. Kolya sent three men back to the road to watch the compound wall, to see how often the guards patrolled, and to make sure we were not followed. As dusk began to fall, we walked in shadows parallel to the main road until well past the compound, and between the guards' rounds, turned left down a path to the river. Once at the river we turned left again, until we reached the point where the compound wall ended at the riverbank and converted to a fifteen-foot barbed-wire fence that declined into the river. There were scudding clouds luminous on the surface of the water, and the three-quarter moon appeared periodically. At moments the light seemed to emerge from within the broad, rolling Moscow River.

"Grigory's is the first *dacha*," whispered Kolya as we bent down and peered through the barbed-wire. "It's the one right next to the wall. The one with the lights. See? All the others beyond are in darkness." A moment later he pointed at two lights bobbing along the waterline. "Quiet—Grigory's men." He pointed down the beach. "You wait here."

He and one of the other men left my side and disappeared into the water. I could see through the barbed-wire two guards approaching, one training a flashlight on the sand before them, and the other focusing his on the water. They wore black trousers and shirts, and had Kalashnikov rifles slung across their shoulders. At the compound wall, they stopped. One reached into his pocket and came out with a pack of cigarettes; the other withdrew a bottle of vodka. They lit their cigarettes and stood on the other side of the wire, talking softly. Between puffs they took turns sipping at the bottle. When it was empty, one of the guards threw it into the middle of the river, and it turned spout over bottom slowly in the moonlight until it landed with a flat splash in the water. The guards resumed their patrol and as they walked away from us, two dark figures emerged from the water. Like shadows catching up with the figures that created them, they merged, and without even a scuffle, the guards dropped soundlessly to the sand.

From his belt pouch Pyotr withdrew a wire cutter and quickly cut a passage through the barbed-wire. We slipped through, helping Kolya and the other man to drag the two guards up away from the sand, back through the hole in the fence, and into the forest beyond. We stopped at the base of an old pine, the needled branches providing shelter from view.

"They're Grigory's men. They'll know what's going on in the *dacha*," said Kolya. "Tape their mouths—we don't want them shouting when they wake up."

As we waited in the silence I was aware of the sound of wind chimes on a porch, and in the background, the rhythmic chirps of summer insects and frogs at the riverbank. Finally one of the men groaned, and Pyotr gently slapped his face to bring him around. He opened his eyes.

"I'm going to take the tape off your mouth," whispered Pyotr. "Any sound you make will be your last. Understand?"

The man nodded his head. Pyotr placed one hand around his throat, and with the other he took one corner of the tape and quickly ripped it off.

The man grimaced and grunted softly.

"I'll be quiet," he said. "Let go my throat."

Pyotr stepped back and Kolya took his place, stepping between the two prone figures and bending down on one knee. If I had any doubt about Kolya or his reputation, or what he was capable of, the expression on the face of the man he was kneeling over erased it. Even lying down, he tried to raise his arm to salute.

"You know who I am?" he asked.

The man nodded.

"Then you know I keep my word."

"They say that about you, yes."

"Can you sit?"

Again he nodded, and Kolya helped him up to lean against the trunk of the pine tree. He looked over at his companion, still unconscious, and shook him by the shoulder. He breathed deeply, opened his eyes, and groaned as if he were in pain, bringing one knee to his stomach.

"Yuri, what is it? Be quiet—they'll take off the tape."

Yuri nodded, and the moment Pyotr removed the tape, he gasped. "My leg," he whispered, "I think it's broken. When I fell."

"Pyotr, take a look," said Kolya. "I'm sorry we had to silence you. We couldn't take the chance you would raise an alarm."

"You'd better be here to take care of Grigory Yanov," said the first man. His words were flat, but his face was hopeful.

Kolya ignored the question. "Tell me why you work for him."

"Bad judgment. I was stupid—got into a drunken barracks fight. We were all sentenced to five years in military prison. Grigory got me an early release. Afterwards he said I owed him—and there would be a penalty if I refused."

"What was the penalty?"

"He never said." The man swallowed. "He didn't need to make a particular threat—you know better than I what he's capable of."

"So you're paying back your debt. How long?"

"Until my sentence would have been up. I've been with him a year—

two more to go." He stopped. "I should have refused his offer, served out my time."

"How many men does he have in the *dacha*?"

"Four inside, and the two of us."

"Where is he keeping his wife?"

"She's in the room he uses as his office." He hesitated, looked down as if he was ashamed. "When I was inside one of the other men told me Grigory has her strapped to a chair."

Without thinking I reached forward and gripped Kolya's shoulder. He was squatting beside the man on the ground.

"We can't just stand here asking questions," I said, unable to be silent. "We have to get her out of there."

The man on the ground looked up at me, and then at Kolya, his eyes suddenly narrowed in suspicion. "You bring an American here with you?" he said. "What is this?"

Kolya turned to give me a warning glance. He had told me not to speak, to do nothing but observe unless otherwise instructed. Without thinking I had spoken in English.

"The American is with me," said Kolya brusquely. "You never saw him, understand?"

The man nodded sullenly.

"Tell me about the children. Where are they?"

"With the old lady. In the kitchen." He shook his head. "What kind of man holds an old woman and his own children captive?"

"Is he in the *dacha* now?"

"His car left a while ago, but I couldn't see who was inside."

"Come morning, he won't be a threat to you or anyone else." Kolya rose to his feet and dusted off his knees. "If you're smart, my friend, you'll wait until your companion feels better and then get out of here. It would be a bad idea for you to be in the *dacha* when we arrive."

"We'll both be happy to put the whole of Russia between us and that madman," he muttered.

"You and Yuri aren't going anywhere on your own," said Pyotr, looking up. "This guy has a broken ankle. He can't outrun the patrol—I don't think he can walk. And he's in pain. I don't trust him to think straight. If they try and get past the patrol they'll be caught, and they'll give it up like cows with swollen udders. You want to tie them up and leave them here until we're done?"

Kolya's mouth was a thin line as he considered the alternatives. It was clear that he didn't like any of them.

"Not a good idea to leave them," he said. "They're a liability as long as they're around here. We need to get them away." He turned to the two men who had come with us in the car. "You two, go with Pyotr, get these two back to the car and drive them far enough away from the compound so they can't get back. Far enough so if they're picked up by the military, they can't be associated with us. Then make your way back here. We'll go through the fence and wait at the front of the *dacha*—where we planned—until you get back. I don't like to wait, but we have no choice. At least we'll be able to see who comes and goes. If I have to I'll go in without you."

And so I found myself beside my cousin Kolya, hidden in a pine grove fifty miles outside the city, watching who came and went from the comfortable *dacha* on the banks of the Moscow River. Inside the *dacha* was what I hoped would be my future, although I hadn't really allowed myself to imagine what it might be like. Darya and the two children, living with me in Boston. That's what I had come to Moscow for; to make the fantasy a reality. I was within range of having it happen, separated by only a few walls from the woman who had asked for my help and whom I thought I loved. This was no time to be having doubts, I told myself. Sometimes you just have to close your eyes and leap, and if you're fortunate enough to land on the other side, then you're fortunate enough, and you deal with the consequences. Far better than not making it across the divide.

"You having second thoughts?" whispered Kolya.

"No," I answered, wondering how he knew. "Why do you ask?"

"Don't worry," he grinned, "you're not pissing in your pants yet, but you're shaking your head and muttering to yourself."

"That's what painters do when we're inspired," I said, returning the grin.

"So long as you don't cut off an ear," he said. "You feel comfortable with the pistol?" I nodded. "Good."

"You think I'll need to fire it?"

He shrugged in the darkness. "No idea. Until Pyotr gets back, you and I are all Darya has. If we need to go in, I have to trust that you're with me, and that means being prepared to use it."

I found myself trying to imagine how difficult it must be for this highly trained and disciplined man to have to rely on someone like me. I bridled at the thought.

Someone like me? What did that even mean? We shared the same blood, or at least some of it. We shared a love for Darya. We had experienced different lives, and his had been harder, much harder, than mine. But we were only as different as experience could make us. With enough time and training I realized suddenly that I, too, could be a soldier, capable of invading a building full of hostile men to rescue people held captive.

"I'm with you," I whispered, believing for the first time that it might even be true. "Use me however you think best. I'll do whatever is necessary."

He glanced at me and in the dusk I saw a question in his eyes. But there was also a sense of relief, the same relief I felt, that I had finally crossed some boundary. I was no more a soldier than I had been five minutes before, but there was suddenly less doubt about whether I was capable of carrying out whatever was required of me. I was no less afraid or nervous, but I was in some way more prepared.

Kolya might have been about to ask his question, but we were interrupted by the sound of a car entering the compound. We heard it stop at the entrance, heard the manual barrier being pushed aside, and the car came towards us. We looked out at the roadway that passed between where we were and the *dacha* as a limo pulled into view.

"It's Grigory's car," he whispered.

The reflections of light from the curtained *dacha* windows fell on the grass outside, elongated, softened, and draped carelessly like a black satin sheet over the bushes. A black Zil limo, recently washed and shined, pulled silently into view and stopped outside the front entrance. The driver's door opened and a small man stepped out. He was dressed in a chauffeur's uniform, with a khaki peaked hat, and I recognized him from my first visit. It was Darya's driver, Viktor, who drove us as she and I sat in the back seat of the limo on the way to my hotel. I didn't think it was possible under such circumstances to feel sexually aroused, but I was, and I shuddered, the hair at the base of my neck standing straight, at the memory of that drive. I felt again the electricity between us as Darya and I tried to avoid looking at or touching each other.   Remembering that drive made me wonder how crazy I must be to have any doubts about the wisdom of being where I was at that moment.

Viktor held open the rear door and Grigory Yanov stepped out. He looked around as he brushed the sleeves of his jacket and gave an instruction to the driver, who nodded, got into the car and started the engine. Grigory walked up the path to the front door, which opened as he approached. He disappeared within, the door closing silently behind him. Once he was inside, the car drove off. For a moment there was silence, and then the forest noises recommenced.

"Shit," said Kolya.

"What is it?"

"I didn't account for the driver."

"Viktor?"

He looked at me, startled. "You know him?"

"He was Darya's driver the first time I was here."

"He's sly as a weasel, with those shiny teeth—but he's one of the only people Grigory trusts. Perhaps the only one."

I had wondered, but was suddenly certain that Grigory knew everything there was to know about me and Darya. As she and I sat together in the back seat while Viktor drove us to my hotel, he was probably taking mental notes of what he would be reporting to his boss. He had probably seen right through our subterfuge. I didn't mention it to Kolya. There was nothing to do about it now, other than to reflect on how foolish I had been.

For about an hour we sat cross-legged in the darkness beneath pine branches swaying and rustling above us in the summer breeze. Cicadas were all around us, and the sound of the river on the other side of the *dacha*, not fifty yards away. The low croak of frogs echoed across the surface of the water. It seemed so placid and uncomplicated, and I had difficulty reconciling Darya's predicament with the peacefulness of the forest around us. I found myself composing paintings—through the fringe of pine branches, the warm lights of the *dacha* reflecting on the bushes, with a moonless, cloudless sky full of stars as a background. And then my compositions dissolved and I was back in the present, the peace of our surroundings overshadowed by menace.

Eventually the silence was broken by the sound of an approaching vehicle. It stopped at the guardhouse, and then the limo drove into view and stopped outside the *dacha*, directly in front of us. The forest noises subsided again. Viktor emerged slowly from the car, leaned back against the door, lit a cigarette. He was humming to himself, smiling when he wasn't sucking smoke. When he was finished he crushed his butt under a heel and went up to the front door, which opened at his approach. It was clear that someone was watching from inside.

"Where the hell is Pyotr?" growled Kolya. "If he doesn't come soon we'll have to go in alone." He looked at me. "Just the two of us. You've got the revolver?"

I nodded.

"Good. He said. "Just don't forget which end the bullet comes out of."

Darya

My head had fallen forward and I was asleep, perhaps the only way to deal with my discomfort and the impossibility of making a decision that might cost one or more of my contacts their lives. I awoke when I heard the sound of the limo pulling up outside, and a moment later Grigory walked into the office. He closed the door noisily behind him, and without looking at me sat down at his desk and began going through papers.

"What have you decided, Darya?" he asked.

"You'd better give me a pen and paper," I said, "while I still have a hand to write with."

Grigory rose from the desk, picked up a pen and notebook, and brought it to me. "Very wise of you," he said.

Both hands were swollen and red from the pressure of the tape, but the fingers of my left hand were twisted, badly bruised and twice their normal size. Already I was unable to move them.

"Better loosen my arms if you want me to write," I said.

He returned to the table for his scissors, and cut the tape from my right hand.

"Left hand too," I said. "Please. It's too tight."

"Prepare yourself," he said. "It's going to be painful."

I thought he was going to hurt me again, but he cut through the tape gently, and I gasped at the pain as blood pounded into my injured hand, each beat of my heart like a hammer blow. He took my wrist between two fingers, raised my hand above my head, and held it there.

"This will help," he said, and I felt a huge sense of relief—I was almost grateful to him—as the pounding subsided.

There was a knock at the door, and Babushka's voice from the other side. "Your ice cream is ready."

He lowered my arm to the chair again and re-taped it, this time more loosely.

426 Neville D. Frankel

Babushka entered, and the door closed and relocked behind her. Her eyes searched for me. I didn't know how bad I looked, but her response told me it was not pretty. Her lips trembled at the sight of my face, and then her eyes went to the arm of the chair. When she saw my injured hand her shoulders began to shake, and the vibrations rattled whatever she carried on the tray.

"I'm all right," I said. "It's not as bad as it looks."

I was concerned that the shock of seeing me so damaged would be too much for her, but her trembling was not from fear or shock. She was shaking with rage. I had seen that look in her eyes before, when she insisted that a meat vendor give her the fresh chicken reserved for the more privileged customer or, when I was at school, and she felt the need to stand up for me against children with more powerful parents. In each case, the fury in her eyes and the authority in her voice carried sufficient weight to get her opponents to retreat. There was a time when, once roused, she had been impossible to stop.

She nodded slowly, turned away from me as she lowered the tray to the desk. There were two bowls on the tray, and as Grigory sat back in his chair, she gave him one of the bowls, heaped with ice cream.

"So this is what you've been up to while I was churning." She spat the words out, her voice harsh, as if she were speaking through iron grit. "Your ice cream has the frozen bits of chocolate and nuts in it, just as you like. Choke on every mouthful."

He laughed.

"I'm going to miss you when you're gone," he said as he raised the first spoonful to his mouth.

"That's just what Viktor said," she responded.

"And what did you tell him?" Grigory asked, curiosity on his face as he anticipated one of Lena's unedited responses. I saw that he was holding the frozen ice cream on his tongue, kneading it against the top of his mouth until it was soft enough to swallow.

She ignored his question, turned her back to him and came over to me.

"Dashinka," she whispered, raising a hand to my cheekbone. She was quivering with anger.

"I'm all right," I whispered. "Promise me you won't do anything stupid."

"Nothing stupid," she said, her face expressionless. "Only what I have to." She glanced at my feet and my wrists. "You can get up if you have to?"

"Yes," I said. "But…"

"Don't argue," she said furiously. She turned to Grigory. "You can't have her sitting here looking like this. I'm going to take the tape off her and help her wash her face. Don't even think of trying to stop me."

He nodded in agreement. She leaned down and hurriedly pulled the tape from my forearm, more roughly than I would have expected. I was surprised.

"Get up slowly," she whispered, "and be ready to help me."

She took something from her apron pocket and slipped it quickly under my right hand. It had a wooden handle, the tool itself long and thin, coming to a point. It felt like an awl. "Be careful," she whispered as I pricked my finger on the needle sharp tip. As I got up slowly from the chair, hiding what she had given me behind my wrist, she turned back to Grigory.

"What I told Viktor," she said, "is that I didn't plan to go anywhere before him, or without him. And I say the same to you."

My chair was opposite his desk and to one side, and I had to cross the room to reach the door to the little bathroom we had installed when the *dacha* became ours. I moved past Babushka, surprised at how shaky my legs were. I had to hold on to the chairs I passed to keep myself upright. As I reached the edge of the desk and put my hand on the corner to steady myself, Grigory coughed. It was an unusual cough, moist and strangled, as if he were coughing underwater. I turned to look at him. He was gumming his mouth, red spittle hanging from his lips. As I watched, unsure what was happening, his cough intensified, and blood began to stream and then pour from his mouth.

He tried to speak but his words were garbled. In his eyes there was suddenly an awareness that his moment might just have passed, that he had not managed, despite all his efforts, to calculate everything down to the last detail. He looked across the desk at Babushka as he tried to control his

428   Neville D. Frankel

coughing.

"There's a special place in hell for bastards like you," she said, loudly enough so that she was audible above the sounds emerging from his throat. "And I'm going to help you get there as soon as possible."

He raised a hand to his throat, as if he had something stuck in his windpipe or his gullet. She picked up the sugar bowl from the tray, took a deep breath, and blew out across the surface of the bowl. A rain of what looked like sugar blew across the desk and into his face. His eyes were wide open as he struggled for breath. He blinked several times, rapidly, and blood began streaming down his cheeks. The more he blinked, the faster the blood flowed. Now he was shouting, roaring his anguish and frustration, and it took me a few seconds to realize that there was no sound—only the intent, strangled in his bleeding throat. At the same time, his blinded eyes pulsed blood as he tried to blink it away, his corneas shredding themselves on whatever Babushka had blown into his eyes. Whatever it was, it wasn't sugar.

With a speed and energy that astounded me, Babushka tripped around the desk, drawing from her apron pocket another tool like the one she had slipped me. I saw it in her hand as she stood behind him, a screwdriver with the tip sharpened to a chiseled edge. I was so weakened by my ordeal and my pain that all I could do was stand and watch as my ancient, tiny grandmother locked one arm about his throat. With the other she jabbed furiously at his neck, again and again, each time piercing the soft tissue around his carotid artery. She only had to hit the right place once, and he would bleed out. Even blind and choking on his own blood, Grigory must have been aware of the irony. The woman on his back was over eighty and she stood less than five feet tall. She was the one he had verbally abused at every opportunity since our marriage, whose cooking he loved, the old witch who saw through him from the first moment.

He pushed himself to his feet, kicked the chair out of his way, and stumbled to the wall behind him. Lena was still holding on, riding him, jabbing at his neck, as he stepped hard back against the wall, banging her head against the window frame. Before she allowed herself to fall to the floor she tightened her grip on his throat, scrambled up so that her tiny feet were resting on his hips, and raised her head as if in a victory shout. Then she buried the screwdriver once more into his neck, jerking it around inside the hole she had made until, slick with the gush of blood, she slipped down off his back and onto the floor.

Grigory was not far behind her. He fell forward onto the desk as blood pulsed from his neck, spraying the area around him. He was still alive and choking as I ran around him to where Babushka lay on the floor, covered in his blood. Her eyes were closed, but she was smiling.

"Babushka, are you hurt?"

She nodded.

"Yes, you're hurt?" I asked. "Or yes, you're fine?"

"I'm fine," she whispered, "as long as I killed the bastard." She smiled a crooked smile, and I could see that breathing was painful. "Let me lie still awhile."

The noise—and Lena's yell of triumph—had attracted the attention of Grigory's men. They gathered outside the door, trying to force the lock.

"Wait," I shouted as loudly as I could. "I'm coming." I went to the desk drawer and found Grigory's revolver. I made sure it was loaded, and then unlocked the door and stepped back.

"It's open," I called.

The door opened slowly and in came two of Grigory's men. I pointed the revolver at them. They walked around the desk and looked at Grigory's body. His eyes were open; blood seeped slowly from his neck. One of them was about to kneel down and feel his neck for a pulse, but thought better of it. There was no artery to feel, and he was lying in an expanding pool of blood.

"Too much blood," he said. "He's gone."

"You don't seem too upset," I answered.

"Good riddance to him," he replied. "He was an evil shit. I didn't hear a shot. How did you do it?"

"I didn't," I said, pointing to Babushka.

He turned to the floor, bent down and leaned over her. "I wouldn't have thought it possible."

"Put a finger on her and I'll kill you," I said.

He turned to me. "I am not a monster, Darya Iosifovna. None of us signed on to cause harm to you or your family." Then he looked back down at Babushka. "What did you do to him?"

"I used a screwdriver," she said.

"No one put the screws to more people than Grigory. Dostoevsky couldn't have written it better." He grinned. "A grandmother wielding a screwdriver."

"Great-grandmother," she corrected him, her pride visible even from her position on the floor. "Evil men have weaknesses. He had two. The first was ice cream." She smiled weakly. "The second was seeing in me only a used-up old woman."

"That was a bad mistake," he said, rising to his feet and shaking his head in amazement. He looked at my face. "I'm sorry we had anything to do with this."

"How many of you are there?"

"The four of us, and two outside, walking the perimeter. And Viktor. He's out with the car."

"I know what hold my husband had over you," I said, "but you'll understand if I take your apology with a grain of salt. I want you and the other men gone. Now."

"What about my money?"

I looked past him to another man standing at the door, whom I had never seen before, and raised the pistol until I was aiming at his head.

"Grigory didn't pay you for kidnapping me and my children, injuring me, and holding me here against my wishes? What a shame. We can wait until State Security arrives, and you ask them to make good on Grigory's promises. Or I can just shoot you now."

"Don't be an idiot," growled the first man, stepping past his companion. "Let's get out of here. We can give thanks he didn't have us kill the whole family. You know that's where this was headed."

I listened, revolver in hand, as they walked out the front door and their voices were lost. I heard their car start up and drive down the driveway, through the guard post and onto the main road. Then I went to Babushka and leaned over her, tried to place a cushion under her head. She wanted to sit up, so I helped her sit, and then stand, and I supported her as she made her way slowly to the couch. She was shivering, her hands cold to the touch. I put my arms about her and kissed her cheek.

"Stop," she wheezed crossly. "I'm not yet a corpse. Make sure Anna throws away the ice cream, and get me a cup of tea. But first wash your face. You'll scare the children if you go out like that."

She raised a hand to my cheek. For the first time I could remember, there were tears in her eyes. She tried to blink them away, but they found a way down through her wrinkles like an incoming tide.

"Look what he's done to your beautiful face." She wiped her cheeks with the back of her hand. "Now see what you've done," she said angrily. "You've upset me. You should have listened when I told you to stay away from him."

"You were right," I said. "You've always been right. But if I'd listened to you I would never have seen what you did today. You let the tiger out. You were wonderful." I rose from her side. "We need to get you to the hospital."

"Not until I've had my tea." She waved me away irritably. "Go to the children. Don't worry, I'm not going to die on you. Tell Anna I want it strong and black. Not that lukewarm stuff she likes. I told her, she might just as well drink Anton's piddle."

In the kitchen Viktor sat on a chair with Anton on his lap. Larisa sat across from them. Both children were eating a slice of bread and butter with fig jam. Anna stood against the kitchen counter, her face a mask of fear.

"Anna, pull yourself together," I said. "Everything's going to be fine." I opened the freezer and took out the ice cream. "Throw it away," I said quietly. "Carton and all. Make sure no one touches it."

Anna took it out the back door to where the garbage was collected. I heard the sound of the garbage container opening and closing.

"I understand your husband has been dispatched," said Viktor in a low voice, "to whatever destiny awaits him. I'm sure this loss affects you deeply."

There was the shadow of a grin hidden beneath his tight mouth. "Besides you, few will mourn him as other than a source of money. And now even they have left us. What a shame."

He tickled Anton so that he laughed and choked on his bread. Anna came back into the kitchen and stepped toward the table, arms outstretched, but Viktor slapped her hands away.

"I told you," she said quietly, fighting her instinctive fear of Viktor, "not to tickle the children when they're eating."

"Don't worry," he said jovially, "we'll be just fine, won't we, Anton?"

He rose from the chair, still carrying my little boy. Anton didn't mind, and neither did Anna, who stepped back.

"Just be careful with him," she warned.

But something was off. The slap was meant to look playful, but it contained a hidden menace. Perhaps it was not the slap itself. It was the look in his eyes, which I had never seen before. I knew Viktor was capable of violence—Grigory would never have relied on him otherwise. But I had never seen it. Now the look in his eyes as he stood there with my Anton in his arms was cold and removed.

"Anna, Babushka's not feeling well. Make her a cup of tea please, and perhaps Viktor can bring it to the study for her. Viktor," I said quietly, "as soon as she's had her tea, we need to get her to a hospital. You'll drive us."

"Of course," he said. "The car is just outside."

I went back to the study. My knees shook, and my left hand throbbed painfully. Babushka was sitting where I left her, eyes closed, unmoving. She seemed not to be breathing. For a moment I thought she was dead, and a moan of grief began to take shape in my throat. After all this, I thought, I can't lose her now. It would be unbearable. But she opened her eyes.

"Where's my tea?" she croaked.

"It's coming," I said. "Viktor's bringing it."

"Good," she said. "The children shouldn't see me like this."

I dropped onto the couch beside her. "I think we're free, finally," I said. "I can begin to live without being afraid for the children every minute. You'll come and live with me."

"You think they'll let you keep your big place after this?" she said. "I wouldn't be too sure. There's always someone just behind you with more pull, who wants your apartment. And you can say good-bye to the *dacha*."

"Good riddance to all of it," I whispered. "We're not staying here. I'm taking you and the children to Boston."

"Boston?" she snorted derisively. "You think Steven is going to come take you away? Haven't you learned yet there's no prince coming to rescue you?"

"With or without Steven," I said, "we're leaving Moscow. I've had enough."

My hip bumped against the revolver I dropped on the couch when I went into the kitchen. Now I was too tired to move it. I leaned back and closed my eyes, and in a second I was dozing. Something hard against my ankle woke me. I opened my eyes to see Viktor standing in front of us, kicking my foot. He had Anton on one arm.

"Where's my tea?" asked Babushka.

"My days of bringing you tea are over, old woman," he said grimly.

She sat up, holding one shoulder with the opposite hand. There was surprise on her face, and perhaps something else. I didn't realize until much later, thinking about her expression, that what I saw was the beginning of fear, and a dawning knowledge that things were not what they seemed. Anton was staring over Viktor's shoulder at the body of his father, lying in a pool of blood. Anton's face was hidden from me, but I saw from the tension in his body that he was not happy.

"This room is not a place for a child," said Babushka. "Viktor, take Anton back to the kitchen."

Viktor ignored her, and walked over to look more closely at Grigory. Anton tried to turn away, but I saw Viktor's grip on him tighten.

"I'll take him out," I said, and started to rise slowly from the couch.

"Sit back down," he snarled, turning around so that he was facing us again. "You go nowhere until I say. Understand?"

His face was feral, a wild animal threatened. I was about to ask him just who he thought he was talking to when he put his hand in his pocket and withdrew a black rectangle. He flicked a lever on the device and a knife emerged from one end. It was a switchblade. He placed the tip against Anton's cheek. I understood, finally, that Viktor was more—or less—than Grigory's driver, and that our ordeal was not over.

"You deprive me of my source of livelihood," he said lightly. "Am I supposed to take that lying down? I don't think so."

"What do you want?"

"That's better," he said. "What I want from you is what your husband wanted, what you refused to provide. But you will give me all the names you have, because I have the means to take from you what you most value. And I will take it slowly." He flicked the knife at Anton's cheek and drew a thin line of blood. Anton screamed. Viktor shook him, and when he continued screaming, slapped the side of his head. The shock silenced him.

"I'll give you whatever you want," I said quickly. "I'll write down all my names. Just give Anton to me."

"You think because I did your husband's bidding for twenty years I'm some mutt without a brain, like all the other dumb dogs he gathered around him? You'll discover I'm not like them. I don't care about the names—but the people I work for will know in a minute if your contacts are genuine. You can start listing them when we get back to Moscow."

"We're not going back to Moscow with you," I said evenly, hunting slowly with my right hand beneath the couch cushion. "I'm taking my children and Babushka far from Moscow."

"You think your boyfriend's going to come take you away? The American painter?" He laughed harshly. "That one couldn't rescue shit from an asshole."

"And I don't think," I continued, "that you are really capable of hurting my children."

"No?" he said. He put the knife to Anton's calf and slowly drew a line downward from just below my boy's knee. A thin line of blood began to trickle down, and again Anton screamed, more in terror than in pain. This time he struggled furiously to get away, and Viktor had to concentrate on keeping him still. In that instant I raised the revolver from my side, prayed for the first time in my life, and aimed. I pulled the trigger and immediately jumped up to catch Anton, whose face was spattered in a rain of blood and skull and brains. And I thanked the God whose existence I didn't acknowledge that my son was screaming as if his lungs would burst.

Steven

Four men hurried out of the house, arguing softly, got into a car and drove off.

"What's going on?" I whispered. Kolya shook his head.

"I think we should go in."

"We don't know who's still in there," he said. "Could be a trap. Someone inside waiting to cut us down as we approach. You saw how they were waiting for Viktor, and let him in as he approached the door."

"Look," I said, "they left the door open behind them."

A child inside began to scream wildly, and was suddenly silenced. Then a sound that could only have been a gunshot. Darya, I thought. Too late. They've killed her. We waited too long. I rose up on my knees, legs numb from kneeling, and ran as fast as I could towards the house, my revolver in my hand. Kolya was at my heels and overtook me before we reached the open door, stopping suddenly as he entered the study in front of me. He turned his head from one side of the room to the other, taking in whatever was there, muttering softly to himself.

I had to walk around him to see what he was looking at. I'd never seen anything like it. The carnage was everywhere. Grigory lying slumped over the desk, blood pooling and dripping onto the floor; Viktor dead on the floor, half his head blown away. A young woman I didn't know was holding the little boy, Anton, whose leg was bleeding. He had blood and solid human matter all over his face. All that told me he was alive was the fact that he was screaming, choking on his sobs, unable to catch his breath. Lena sat slumped on the couch, her face white, holding her shoulder. Larisa sat beside her, weeping, holding Darya's hand and stroking it gently. And Darya, wide-eyed, her face bleeding and bruised, one hand cradled against her chest. When we came in she pushed herself from the couch and stumbled towards me. I opened my arms to her but she pushed them away.

"After all that's happened," she shouted, her voice rising hysterically, "now you arrive? Now, you get here?"

For a moment she pummeled weakly at my chest with her uninjured hand. Then she collapsed into my arms, weeping.

Lena

So? I was wrong. Steven did come.

I am not ashamed for being wrong—my certainty is based on my own life experience. What I know is that little girls play at being women, who feed and nurse and take care of the people around them. Little boys, on the other hand, don't play at being men—they play at being heroes, but few are sufficiently heroic. My father would have liked to be a hero, but for most of his life—I say this with a heart full of sadness and love—at being a hero, he was a miserable failure.

The real hero was my stepmother, Esther, who held the family together and made impossible decisions. Vasily, my husband, was a kind, sweet man, but he was swept up in what he thought would be heroic actions. Like most aspiring heroes, he threatened the system, and it eradicated him from the earth. Steven tries, in all his sweetness, to be heroic, but he turns out to be as much a caregiver as any woman. Thankfully, he seems to recognize that he is not hero material, and he is a better, more loving father to Larisa and Anton than their own father could ever have been. Perhaps it is living in the freedom and surplus of America that makes this kind of man possible. That, and the deep love he feels for my Darya. He is the first such man I have known in my life. The world can do with fewer heroes, but it needs all the caregivers it can find. Darya, I think, wanted to be a hero, but she is a recovering hero, a wonderful giver of care and love to all around her. She is my hero, and, she says, I am hers. I'll take it.

❁

Kolya wanted to take us in Grigory's limo straight to the United States Embassy, but I never knew anyone who went into that building and came out again still a Russian. They go in Russian, and when they come out they speed off in an airplane to the United States. Probably better for us. With what happened in the *dacha*, Darya would be in trouble—but my trouble would be worse. For killing Grigory, they would send me to the Gulag for the rest of my life. Not a great punishment—how much time do I have left? A year? Perhaps two? I'd be sure to die on the first day, with a smile on my face. That would show them. But I'd probably find some people to take care of, and last longer than even they expected. Whatever happened, I'd make sure to smile every day left me. I wouldn't give them the satisfaction of seeing me miserable.

But that wasn't going to happen. I knew once we arrived at the Embassy, we would be safe.

"Kolya," I told him, "I'm not going to America without some things from my room. You need to take me there first, before we go to the Embassy."

"It's not safe, Babushka," he told me.

"Then leave me here," I said. "I'm not going without my things."

So first we went to my room, and I went upstairs and took what I needed from beneath the floorboards, and then we went to the Embassy. The Americans recognized General Shaposhnikov as a Soviet hero of the people. He arranged for us to go past the Russian guards, through the heavy iron gates, and into the Embassy building. Their medical people mended my shoulder. They were very professional, with knowing hands, and they put me in a little hospital room where I was the only patient. I told them I would have been happy to share my room, but I think maybe they wanted to keep the other Americans away from me. I had to fight to get up off my bed, and I made such an argument, the nurse went to get the doctor. He came, and Steven with him. We argued about pills.

"In my life," I told him, "I never took pills for pain."

"You have a separated shoulder and a broken collar bone," he said. "It will be hard for you to sleep. You move with great difficulty, and that tells us you are very uncomfortable."

"With respect, Doctor," I said, "I don't have a monkey, but if I did, it would also know I'm in pain."

I saw Steven trying to hide a grin. So, I thought, he does have some spirit in him. Then he had the bad manners to say, "The doctor's just trying to help you," he said. "There's no need to be unkind."

"Unkind?" I said, feeling angry. "What do you know about unkind? I was never unkind in my life." I turned to the doctor. "You think a broken shoulder can heal without pain? When it mends, the pain will go. In the meantime, it tells me I'm alive, while that bastard is dead. The pain won't kill me, but your pills might."

Eventually they all shrugged their shoulders and left me alone, but not before I asked them for a good hot cup of black Russian tea, with plenty of sugar.

Steven was reprimanded by Embassy officials for entering Russia without his identity card, and under a false name. Why he did this I cannot imagine, but he did it for Darya, and he meant well. They scolded him the way a loving uncle would scold his wayward nephew. In the Russian embassy in Washington, they would probably have made nice with him, and then sent him back to Moscow to be shot.

From the Embassy we watched on television as the Soviet government began to unravel. Tanks rolled through the streets of Moscow and stopped outside the White House, where Yeltsin and the forces loyal to Gorbachev took refuge. Patriots outside had built barricades, and no one knew whether young Soviet soldiers would be willing to fire on their own citizens. I saw General Shaposhnikov stand at the top of the stairs, and heard him tell our troops what he already knew back in 1962, when he lost his rank and was disgraced—that Soviet soldiers should never fire on unarmed Soviet citizens. And after that, all the people of Moscow came out and celebrated with the soldiers. They stuck flowers into tank gun barrels, and the soldiers sitting up on the tanks lowered their rifles so that young girls and old women alike could put blossoms into their rifles. It was a wonderful moment—a moment when I wished I could be out there with them. I thought perhaps I should stay in Moscow and be a part of the new Russia.

I'm stubborn, but I've never been foolish, and it would have been a shame to start so late. Going to America with Darya and the children was a far better idea. Besides, who would I take care of in Moscow?

Darya

The days we spent inside the US Embassy are a blur. With tears in my eyes I watched on television as my country imploded. I felt vindicated, and furious, aggrieved at the waste, and joyful at the possibilities a new state might offer the Russian people. At the same time I was numb, because this was no longer my country. Even in the new state that was about to be born, my children and I would not be safe. We had to leave.

Babushka and I had both become killers. I was more relieved than anything else that Grigory was dead, but while I rejoiced at the freedom from fear, still, a part of me wanted to wear mourning. Anton and Larisa were traumatized by what they had seen and wouldn't let me out of their sight. Anna begged to come with us to Boston. She could not return to her impoverished family in Ukraine, and she had come to love the children, and to see me as a mother. I could not refuse her.

Despite her injuries and mine, Babushka wanted Kolya to make a stop at her room on the way to the Embassy. Kolya was reluctant, but she insisted, and he's always had a soft spot for her. We could have been apprehended at any moment, but Kolya reasoned that no one knew yet what had happened, and only orders from the most senior level would have justified interfering with Grigory Yanov's car. Anyway, it was a foolhardy decision. I wanted to go back to our apartment, but it would have been far too dangerous. Besides, I was hurting badly, I was in shock, and most of all, we needed to get to a doctor.

The United States offered us all refugee status, in exchange for whatever intelligence I could give them. They took me to their safe room in the basement of the Embassy, soundproofed and immune to electronic surveillance. It was a small room, crowded with two serious men from the CIA, and a woman from the State Department. They told me what they wanted, and were surprised, even affronted, when I burst into hysterical laughter. What did they want? The same thing Grigory did: the names of all my contacts in the dissident movement worldwide. This time, I was happy to comply.

I may never trust another man, and I am willing to live with that possibility. What I am unwilling to do is to tie myself to anyone I'm not absolutely sure of. Which brings me to Steven. Yes, I thought I loved him, and I believed he thought he loved me. But the truth was that we barely knew one another. He had come to Moscow as I asked, but he and Kolya and the General together had been unable to rescue us. We had to be our own rescuers.

Now he wanted me to come live with him in Boston and take care of us all. Steven, who had no experience with extended family. Steven, who told me how he took off to paint for a month whenever the spirit moved him. Steven, who in his mid-thirties had never been in love. I wasn't ready to trust that he knew himself well enough to make such a commitment.

This was not an indictment of him—I had the same questions about myself. I had no idea who I might become in America. All my life I had felt the impulse to take a political stand. In a free country, would that impulse disappear? I might decide to become a real journalist, in a country with a free press, but it was equally possible that I would go in a completely different direction and open a shop, or become a farmer. I had no idea. And while I thought Steven might be the man I wanted in my life, there was no knowing how I would feel in six months. I had to protect myself. But I was equally sure I didn't want to take advantage of his help while I was vulnerable, and then hurt him by leaving when I was able to stand on my own two feet.

I had these thoughts while we were still in the Embassy, but there was a great deal going on at the time, and it was hard enough to live minute by minute. Thinking about the future was impossible, planning it even more so. All I could focus on was the fact that there were others who depended upon me, I had no means of support, and all we possessed were the clothes we wore.

Just before we left, Steven called his father, Lenny, in Boston, putting him on speaker so that I could hear.

"Dad? Are you there?"

"Steve! Where are you? The operator said she was in Washington."

"I'm calling from the US Embassy. In Moscow."

"They're holding you there? Are you in trouble? Do you need a lawyer?"

Steven laughed.

"I'm fine, Dad. Not in trouble at all. I'm calling to let you know when we'll be arriving at Logan. Can you pick us up?"

"Of course I'll pick you up. I can't tell you how relieved I'll be to have you home in one piece. What airline, and what time?" He paused for a moment. "Who is 'us'? Who am I picking up? Is there more than one of you?"

Steven laughed again, and it was the first time I heard that kind of delight in his voice.

"What's so funny? Are you sure you're all right?"

"Never been better. Dad, your Volvo won't be big enough. You're going to need to rent a van."

"A van? How much luggage do you have?"

"Hardly any."

"So why do you need a van?"

"I'm also going to need a bigger place to live."

"How much bigger?"

"Much bigger."

"You already have a big apartment with two bedrooms. And if you need an extra bedroom for a few days, there's your old room in my apartment."

Steven looked at me, smiling, saying nothing.

"Steven, are you there?"

"I'm here," he said.

There was a long silence. "Who are you bringing back with you?"

When told how many of us there were, and how many bedrooms we would need, Lenny didn't know whether to laugh or cry.

It didn't all happen as planned. We had to wait several days for the immigration paperwork to be approved, and my debriefing by the State Department and the CIA took longer than expected. After four days with them in the little safe room in the basement, I was ready to pull my hair out. At the same time, Steven had teaching commitments in Boston.

"I can get someone to cover for me," he said. "I'd much rather stay here and make sure everything goes smoothly. Besides," he smiled, "I'm looking forward to sitting beside you on the plane."

I didn't want him arranging his schedule around me, and I didn't want to be any more indebted to him than I already was. Now that I was no longer living under threat, I wondered whether I was pulling away from the safety that Steven represented. But I was injured and confused, and this was no time to make a stand one way or the other.

"It might be a good idea for you to go back a few days early," I suggested. "Perhaps you could find a place for us to live. It would make the transition a little easier for the children. And it would give your father a few days to get used to the idea that we're all descending on him at once."

To my relief, Steven saw the wisdom of trying to prepare for our arrival, and he took the next plane out of Moscow.

We followed a week later, arriving at Logan Airport in the late afternoon. The meeting between Lenny and Babushka was touching, and it contained an element of humor. Lenny is tall, and the top of her head doesn't reach his shoulder. So when each saw in the other a resemblance to Mischa, Lenny's father and Lena's brother, the tears were mixed with laughter at the physical contortions necessary to look into each other's eyes. Lenny told me that he was overcome by the courage of this tiny old woman, with her small face, lost expression, and eyes that shone like beacons and missed nothing. Even a spine of steel couldn't explain to him what she had been able to do to Grigory.

Steven found an old Victorian house in Cambridge, not far from

Lenny's apartment. It was being renovated, and had been divided into two condominiums. One of the units was big enough for us all, and it would be finished in a few weeks. Until then, the children and I stayed with Lenny, while Anna and Lena settled into Steven's apartment. It was crowded for everyone, and there was a lot of movement back and forth. Lenny wanted to be a help to us. We were family, and he insisted that as a single man with no dependents, and with a good job, he could easily help us without changing his lifestyle. Steven felt the same way, but for him, and for me, the situation was far more complex.

Steven described Lenny as rigid, emotionally withholding and inaccessible, but he was delightful from the first moment we met. I found him funny, warm, open and available. Lenny, on the other hand, once I came to know him, described Steven as emotionally immature and impulsive, and he implied that as a result, he was unlikely to be reliable. I'm not even sure he's aware of the message he gives, because he clearly loves and is proud of his son. But Steven is compassionate, generous and thoughtful. And he is strong, in his own particular way.

I have outgrown a certain kind of strength and power in men. The aggressive physicality of young men, once so attractive to me, has lost its appeal. Steven's strength, which coexists with an awareness of his own weaknesses, is far more palatable and comforting. But from the security of Boston, I was no longer so sure what I wanted. Safety was important, but at moments the idea of designing my life around safety and comfort seemed boring. And to my surprise, I discovered that I was terrified of being bored.

❁

Once we settled in, a whirlwind of activity started that feels unlikely to ever stop. We made medical appointments and spent whole days at Massachusetts General Hospital. The first priority was Babushka's shoulder—but she refused to be seen until I had taken care of myself, and she insisted upon coming with me to my appointments.

I had never thought much about my hands, but now I had two painfully crooked, swollen fingers that already looked old and arthritic. I became aware of how beautiful my hands had been.

The right side of my face was swollen and purple, my eye blood-red. My cheekbone was cracked in several places, and there was a loose bone fragment beneath the skin. A moveable lump, the surgeon called it. There would be a jagged, diagonal scar from the inner corner of my right eye, all the way across the cheekbone. We made an appointment for surgery to reset my fingers, and several others to repair the damage to my face. The first available appointments were six weeks into the future. It seemed forever.

Babushka eventually saw the doctor. He was a tall man in an open white lab coat, almost bald but for a narrow grey tonsure around the back of his head. He stood with his chin in his hand, clearly puzzled by her.

"Her clavicle is cracked and she has a torn rotator cuff," he said. "Anyone else would be rigid with pain."

"I'm not surprised," I told him. "She'll admit to discomfort, but that's about as far as it goes."

He gave her pain medication, but she would have none of it. Her shoulder did mend, but it will never heal fully. She favors one arm, holding it against her side when she walks. When she cooks, as she does every day, she avoids movements that might strain the shoulder. And she refuses to discuss with me how she feels.

The children were deeply worrying. Anton clung to me, his face a picture of terror. Larisa was so protective of Babushka that at first she wouldn't let Steven or Lenny anywhere near her. But they were both patient and understanding, and Lenny, who had more time on his hands, was ready to be a grandfather in their lives. He fell in love with them, and they with him.

We had to be outfitted with everything from toothbrushes and combs to underwear and shoes and clothing. I had only temporary identification, and no money, and Steven wouldn't let us on the Boston subway alone. He took us everywhere, and when he had to teach, Lenny was always available to drive us to stores or doctors' offices, and to show us how the city of Boston worked.

Having traveled in Western Europe, I had some idea of what the stores were like, but Anna was thunderstruck by the vast selection and the choice of clothing. She wandered about Filene's Basement at Downtown Crossing in Boston with her mouth open. She is a pretty young woman, and I was pleasantly surprised to see that she had some fashion sense. I had been uneasy about how she would adapt, but our first foray into the capitalist world showed me that she would do fine.

Babushka, on the other hand, without a frivolous bone in her body, was overwhelmed for only a moment. Then she spotted a rack of plain black dresses and walked straight to them, her mouth a grim line. It took some persuading, but when she did agree to move off the black, her favorite outfits became grey track suits with cotton drawstring sweatpants. And once she discovered how comfortable sneakers were, she wore nothing else on her feet but pink sneakers.

There were no end of issues to organize. We visited Immigration to sort out paperwork, and applied for Social Security numbers. I had to find a preschool for Larisa. Anna needed English classes so that she could master enough of the language to attend high school. And I needed a job. Lenny was sure that my experience made me an attractive catch for any Russian Studies department, but I doubted whether I would be a catch for anyone. Besides, I wanted to see first if journalism was a possibility. He put me in touch with people he knew at Boston University, where he had taught for many years. They interviewed me, vetted me through the State Department, and eventually they offered me a job.

✿

Lenny took me shopping to furnish the condo. I didn't know where to begin, but he made sure to introduce me to Linens 'n Things, Jordan Marsh and Filene's. And he prevented me from following my instincts and buying the cheapest things I could. He showed me the utensils and cooking pots in his own kitchen.

"Inexpensive pots and pans get scratched, and the handles come off.

And I never buy Teflon, although it's all the fashion. I'll bet in a few years they'll discover it's toxic. If you buy cheap," he said as we walked through the aisles of Lechmere, "you'll end up replacing everything in a couple of years. Pressed board comes apart; cheap fabrics fray and don't last."

"I have to buy cheap for now," I said, "or I'll never be able to repay what you lend me."

"Who said anything about lending you money?" he asked.

"I thought that's what we discussed," I answered, flustered. We were in the middle of the store with a cart full of kitchen and bathroom supplies, and if he wasn't going to lend me the money to pay for them, I needed to put them all back.

"I guess I wasn't clear," he said. He turned me towards him and put his hand on my shoulder. "I've worked hard all my life and saved far more money than I need. There's enough to help Steven buy a house, which he's not yet taken advantage of, and more than enough for me to furnish your condo and get you settled."

"You are very generous," I said, "but I can't accept. I don't want to be indebted to you."

"It's my pleasure to do this," he replied. "You're the closest thing I'll ever have to a daughter. Remember that my father vowed to do all he could to make Lena's life comfortable. If you have difficulty accepting what I'm doing, then accept it graciously on behalf of your grandmother and your children."

One more thing I had to learn—to accept graciously what I couldn't afford to buy. I began to realize in yet another way how insulated I was in Moscow. All my adult life I shopped at stores stocked for the Soviet elite, and there was seldom a limit to what I could spend. Now I was free of all the constrictions I had lived with, but limited by cultural ignorance. What kind of bed was best for the children? What furniture would be easiest for Babushka to manage in her bedroom? Would she need an electric blanket, and which of the ten varieties would be best for her? How many sets of sheets did we need? Carpets for the old wooden floors that would be cold in winter. Comfortable chairs for the living room. A television set. Pots and pans, cutlery and plates to eat on. A table for the kitchen, where I thought we would eat all our meals—but Lenny insisted the kitchen was too small, and that we needed a dining room table instead. What was the difference? And why was a perfectly serviceable Formica table inappropriate for the dining room?

There was no end to what I didn't know. It was exhausting. And just when I thought I had understood how something worked, I was confronted by yet another decision that showed me how culturally illiterate I was. The dishwasher alone created a host of problems. We never had a dishwasher in Moscow. When I bought a set of dishes, proud that I had made the purchase on my own, and on sale, Lenny insisted I return them because they were not dishwasher safe. I bought drinking glasses at the same sale, and took them back because they had a deep indentation in the base, and would always need to be wiped dry at the end of the dishwasher cycle.

Lenny became a fixture in our lives. He took Anna and Babushka food shopping, and showed them what to buy. He exhorted them to stay away from the packaged foods and artificial ingredients in the center of the supermarket and to stick to fresh fruits and vegetables, meat and fish and dairy around the edges. He introduced them to kohlrabi and Japanese radishes and other things I assumed were part of the American diet, until I discovered that many of my colleagues at work didn't know what these items were, or how to prepare them. Butchers' cuts were very different from what we were used to, so Lenny showed them how to recognize what part of the animal they were looking at.

He put on a white apron and demonstrated cooking, Lenny-style. Chicken stir-fry in a wok; lasagna; stuffed peppers; meat loaf and hamburgers. Kale or Brussels sprouts baked in the oven with walnut oil, seasoned with capers and sea salt. Salads with marcona almonds and dried figs. He came in the afternoon and read the picture books he bought, with one child on each knee. Larisa soon knew the words to *Goodnight Moon*, and they both came running when they heard his step at the door, shouting "It's Lenny! It's Lenny!" In a matter of months, they were speaking English as well as they spoke Russian.

Lenny and Babushka spent hours at the table together, he taking apart and putting together the pieces of the teapot, she watching and nodding as she began to recognize the individual parts. He sat with an English-Russian dictionary, trying to explain to her the significance of each vessel and to describe the Jewish rituals involved in each. When she was not cooking or taking care of the children, or sitting beside Anna and trying to learn English, she was taking the T to the Boston Museum of Fine Arts, and being the good citizen she always was. If you walked down our street to the corner and she happened to be coming home from the store with a bag on each arm, she might ask you if you needed help crossing the street. One day she came home from the museum quite angry at how ungracious Americans can be. She had offered her seat on the subway to a man with a cane, and he had glowered at her, turned red and gruffly refused her offer. There was no way to explain to her that people might be amused or offended by the idea of taking a seat from an ancient and diminutive woman, or that it was unnecessary for her to give up her seat for anyone.

When the condo was ready, we moved out of Lenny's and Steven's apartments. I signed the rental contract; Lenny vouched for me since I had no credit history. The furniture we had bought was delivered, and we spent days setting up and organizing. Anna worked like a dynamo, and nothing could slow Babushka. It was a spacious condo, with high ceilings and lots of light, but I couldn't find within myself any appreciation for its beauty. All I felt was confinement. And it had nothing to do with the condo.

We never discussed it, but Steven didn't move in with us. I was surprised and relieved that he hadn't assumed we would automatically combine households. Perhaps he was waiting for an invitation and didn't want to show his disappointment; perhaps he thought it was too soon. I didn't know what I wanted. Babushka was the only one who showed any impatience. We were in the kitchen, she sitting at the table and unwrapping individual plates, handing them to me for stacking in the dishwasher. She loved the dishwasher, although she was openly contemptuous of it.

"He won't wait forever," she said, "even for you, Dasha. Leave love hanging too long unpicked and it rots like grapes on the vine. And rotten grapes make sour wine. Choosing men in your life is not one of the things you do well. Don't make the mistake again of not listening to me. I know what I'm talking about when I say Steven is good for you."

When I next turned to her to pick up the unwrapped plates, she grasped my sleeve and pulled me towards her. "You have a chance now to settle down with the companionship of a kind man. To make a good life for your children. Forget about excitement and thrills. It's time to take him into your bed, and make sure he stays there."

❦

One evening, Lenny came for supper and helped Anna put the children to bed, and then we sat down in the living room for coffee. Babushka looked up from her strong, sweet black Russian tea and smiled at Lenny, and he smiled back. They had quickly established a warm relationship of affection and understanding that required no words. Then she turned back to the television set, where she was watching a women's golf tournament intensely, wearing an expression of incredulity on her face.

"Lenny," I said, "we need to talk. In confidence."

"Of course," he said.

"We are connected in so many different ways," I began, "and that makes this a difficult conversation."

He nodded, listening carefully.

"I know you would do anything for us, and we are all so very grateful."

"You're family, Darya. Next to Steven, the closest family I have. And you know how happy I am to have you all here. You and the children have already enriched my life. So I'm grateful, too."

"I know," I said. "And that applies also to Steven. But with him, it is also more complicated."

"It's no secret," he said, "that Steven loves you."

"I know," I said. I fumbled with the amber and silver beaded necklace Steven had given me, and I was ashamed that I could not say the words Lenny wanted to hear. "But we have been thrown together in such sudden ways, after knowing each other for only a few days all together. It is very confusing, for us both, I think. But he is so busy with his job, and taking care of us, being responsible for these new people in his life, I don't think he has energy to be confused."

Lenny smiled at me.

"You read him well," he said. "That's his way."

"And then what happens after, in his way?"

"What do you mean?"

"Well, what happens when he finds that these responsibilities were thrown on him and he doesn't want to handle them anymore?"

"You mean, will he stop loving you? I can't answer that."

"Or," I said slowly, "in a few months, when I am become a different person, I might discover that I don't love him, even after all the help he has given me. And then our hearts are broken."

"And mine."

"All of us," I said. "He is already a better father to the children than they ever had in their lives. And they never had a grandfather at all. Already they love you."

"It is complicated," he said. "But whatever happens between you and Steven, I'll always be there for you. And for Anna, if she needs me."

"I know," I said. "But that wasn't my question."

"I didn't know there was a question," he said.

"We need some help, Lenny," I said, "Steven and I. I feel we're on a runaway train. I don't know if it will crash, but we need to slow it down so we can think which track to go on. And Steven can't see that the train is gathering speed, with no direction. Maybe," I continued, "our journey will be longer if we slow down now. He listens to you. Perhaps you can talk to him. All I want is for him to see that we take big risks by going too fast."

"You're right about slowing the train," he said, laughing. "Steven tends to go full speed ahead until he crashes. I have great admiration for you,

Darya." He reached across the couch and gave my shoulder an affectionate squeeze. "What you suggest is both wise and compassionate. I can talk to Steven, but I don't know whether he'll listen."

Several nights later, Steven arranged for us to go out to dinner, just the two of us. It was the first time we had a chance to be alone for an evening since we spent a week in Italy so many months before. A lifetime, considering how much had changed.

I wore white slacks with strappy sandals and a maroon satin blouse showing a lot of clavicle and cleft. I wanted to look sexy and attractive, but I felt neither. I was an abused wife who had done nothing to stop her abuser or to protect her children, and at the end had been ready to give up the names of her friends. One of my hands was deformed, and I felt that the other was dirty. Now that my face was disfigured, I was finally able to acknowledge, after the fact, that I had once been an attractive and desirable woman. Without being aware of it, I had been willing to use my beauty to get what I wanted. The irony, of course, is that not knowing quite what I wanted, I didn't get much. Now my face was swollen and scarred, and I had no idea how much of the damage might still be visible even after the injury was repaired. I felt like used goods—weak, damaged and unlovable.

We sat at a table beside the open window of an Italian restaurant in the North End. Half of me was convinced that no man could possibly find me attractive, which made me wonder why Steven wanted to be there. The other half of me was aware, as I had been for several weeks, that I was free. I had been bowled over by the interest and enthusiasm shown me by the community of journalists in Boston, and I was beginning to think it possible that I might just become the kind of journalist I had once dreamed of being. And to top it all off, I had a job that would allow me to support the family I had brought with me. I began to wonder why I had agreed to be there with Steven, engaged in an awkward and uncomfortable verbal dance, if I was able to be self-sufficient and even successful.

My would-be rescuer sat across from me. He was an artist whose art I didn't know, and the person he was in Boston was a stranger to me. I didn't know what I wanted to say to him, and I couldn't imagine what he was about to say to me, but even before the conversation began, I wondered how could I possibly think I loved this man. I would have been relieved, I thought, to hear him say our affair had been a huge mistake.

"What would you like to drink?" he asked gently.

"White wine, please. Pinot Grigio."

He put his hand on the table, palm up and open, asking for me to take it. I left my hands in my lap, and he withdrew the offer. He was a handsome man with firm cheeks and a fine jaw, and there was kindness and understanding in his eyes. It crossed my mind that perhaps there was something wrong with me.

"Don't look at me like that," I said sharply.

"I'm looking at you because I find you beautiful," he said. "Even if you don't."

I groaned at his comment, and then the waitress came, a young college student with blond hair pulled back, and smooth pink cheeks. She looked at me and quickly averted her eye. Steven gave her our order.

"I didn't imagine this would be so awkward," he said, as he leaned back and crossed his arms over his chest.

"Neither did I, but it is. I was talking to your father about you," I said. "He told me you approach life on joyful tiptoe, as if it's a sleeping tiger, and you're about to flick its tail. You never consider that it might just turn around and rip an ear from your head."

He laughed. "Maybe he's right."

"Is that how you felt when we met? That our affair was like flicking the sleeping tiger's tail?"

"Is that what you think?" he asked. "That it was just a game, and I was playing with you?"

"I don't know what to think, Steven," I said.

"You know, since I became an adult, I've tried not to take life too seriously. That strategy was working quite well." The humor faded from his face. "Until you came along."

The waitress arrived and delivered our drinks. We ordered dinner. He raised his glass of Chianti, and I raised my white wine.

"To our first dinner alone together," he said, "free of surveillance and out of danger."

We clinked glasses, and took a sip.

"If we are safe and unwatched," he said slowly, "why are you so uncomfortable?"

We looked at each other for a moment, and it was my turn to extend an arm across the table, palm up. He rested his hand gently on mine.

"Thank you," he said.

"You asked me to leave Moscow and come live with you here, in safety. Now I am here with my whole household, and the danger is gone."

"That should be good news," he said. "Yet we both feel as if we're in mourning."

"Because we are grieving," I said, "for the dream we dreamed, when we both wanted more of each other than we could have. When we planned, packed as much as we could into short time, and made love in secret rooms. It was exciting. But now there is no limit on what we can have of each other."

"And because the urgency is gone, we don't want each other anymore?" he spoke quietly but his grip on my hand was fierce, as if he didn't want to let go. Even in his intensity, he was careful not to hurt me, and I reminded myself how different this behavior was from what I was accustomed to.

"I don't know what it means," I said, shaking my head in desperation. I pointed to my swollen, scarred cheek. "Look at me, Steven."

"I am," he said.

"This is not the same face you couldn't wait to kiss as we walked in the snow at Moscow University."

"Darya, can't you tell that I don't have eyes for anyone else?"

"You must be blind," I said.

"Just because you don't love yourself at this moment," he said, "doesn't mean other people can't love you."

456 Neville D. Frankel

He was still gazing at me, but the person he thought he was looking at wasn't there. I turned away from him, glared out over the patio at the couples seated around us. They seemed young and carefree, many holding hands. Their disjointed voices, interspersed with laughter, made me feel isolated and sad.

"I don't think I know you well enough to love you," I said. "And me—how can you love me? All the things that defined me—my marriage, my politics, my place in the world—are gone. I have to reinvent myself. You can't love someone who doesn't yet exist."

Steven took his hand from mine and sat up straight.

"We should eat," he said. "Our food's getting cold."

We ate without talking, the silence broken by restaurant noises—the conversation of other diners and the click and clatter of plates and utensils, and outside, tourists walking by, and the sound of street traffic.

"Last night," he said eventually, still looking down at his plate, "my father said we'd fallen in love inside a fantasy, that loving someone in the real world is very different. He said perhaps we need to give ourselves time to know each other. I didn't want to hear it." He paused and looked at me. "You and he must have been talking."

"I know you didn't want to hear it. I needed some help."

"Well, he didn't hesitate to step into the breach."

"What does that mean?"

"Never mind. It's just an expression."

"He's right, you know. The real world is all about jobs and sick children and hopping into bed at night exhausted. It's taking care of old people and doctors' appointments and going to the supermarket and the dry cleaners and making breakfast. We don't know how to do any of those things together."

"I've been living in my apartment while you've been in yours," he said. "We've been sleeping in separate beds. When you arrived I made no assumptions about how we would live. It was important that you feel free to do what you needed, and to act when you were ready. But we've been shopping and cooking and doing chores together, and planning and going to medical appointments. I thought that was taking care of each other, but I guess it doesn't count. Nor does my determination to take care of you. And," he said sadly, reaching across the table to stroke my cheek, "that I find you beautiful when you feel disfigured falls short of love, too."

"I appreciate it," I said. "All of it. Perhaps I just can't afford to believe anyone could love me when I have such trouble loving myself."

"Okay," he said abruptly. "Let's see what we can do to move this forward. What do you need from me?"

My first thought was that I wanted to be left alone, to find a lair and crawl into it like a wounded animal, and stay there, safe in the dark, until my hurts had mended. But that was only part of what I wanted, and anyway, it was not possible.

"I need time," I said. "Time to heal. And I need space, to find out who I am. I need to know that when you accept me into your life, it's because you can't live without my strength—not because you're afraid that I won't survive otherwise. I need some time to be strong again, without you. Then maybe we can learn to love each other in the real world. This time, slowly."

He nodded his head, taking in my words and trying to understand and accept how it had to be. Then he signed the check and rose, and as he stepped around the table to pull my chair out, there was the trace of a cheeky grin on his face. I loved it, and I was grateful for it.

"Why the big grin?" I asked.

"My father's right on all counts," he said, standing behind me. "I think you just want to be pursued and courted. That's exactly the kind of tail I like to pull. It's the only way to find out how big the tiger is."

I turned around and put my arms about his neck. "You're not pulling the tiger's tail," I whispered into his ear. "You're just flicking it."

I hoped that Steven would take my request for time and space to heart, without offense and without recrimination. He did, and I was surprised and relieved that he made no assumptions about our relationship.

He continued to live in his apartment, but he made himself available whenever we needed him. Sometimes I invited him for a family supper. He called and invited me to dinner, or to a Boston Pops concert outdoors, on the Esplanade. We took long walks along the Charles River, learned about each other slowly and naturally, as if we had just met. He kissed me gently when he walked me back to my door, and then he left. If I wanted more, I would have to ask for it. At moments, that gave me pause, and I wished he would be a little more aggressive. But when I found myself irritated by his willingness to subsume his own instincts to what he thought I wanted, I had to laugh at my own ambivalence. This was what I had asked for. He was simply granting my wish, even when I wasn't sure precisely what I wanted. I had no idea if he was correct in his assumption that I wanted to be courted, but if that was what we were doing, perhaps he was right.

The surgeon reset the ill-knit bones in my fingers. With physical therapy, I regained almost all my movement. I relearned to type on an American keyboard with the dexterity I once had on the Russian keyboard, and no longer felt that I had a deformed hand. The only deficiency was that no matter how hard I tried, I was unable to hold together the two broken fingers he had repaired. It was a minor problem, and I was the only one aware of it. I was happy to have a private wound, a touchstone, to remind myself that not everything in my life had always been so easy or so safe. It was only when I found myself saying those words in my head—that life had not always been so easy or so safe—that I realized how far I had come, and that healing was within my grasp.

The tumultuous affair we had fallen into in Moscow receded into the background. It had demanded such attention and so absorbed each of our energy and focus that at the time there seemed nothing more important. Now, the images of us together were like a faded curtain flapping slowly in a breeze, eclipsed by fresh air blowing through the open window, made transparent by the sunlight. When I remembered the passion of our coming together, I might have been watching a movie of two strangers, and for the life of me I couldn't recall the smell of his skin or the contours of his arms, or how his body looked unclothed. When I thought of him now, what came to mind was the touch of his hand. His deep, expressive laugh, and his teasing, boyish grin. The expression in his eyes when he looked at me. One Saturday morning in the fall as I was walking through Harvard Square with Larisa, I realized with a shock what it was about his expression that so moved me. When he looked at me, he actually saw who I was. I didn't remember ever having been seen before. Even with the movable lump in my cheek and the disfiguring scar, he saw me. And he recognized who I was.

The operations on my face were set for December, by which time we had been in Boston for six months. Steven had arranged his first painting trip since we arrived. He planned to spend most of the month in a remote cabin in the Canadian Rockies, doing a series of winter mountain studies. When I told him the dates of my surgeries, he was ready to cancel his trip.

"Absolutely not," I said.

"You're going to need help. I want to be here for you."

"If I need help, Lenny's here," I told him. "I want you far away as I go through this, and I don't want to see you until I'm fully healed."

"If that's what you want," he said, "I'll go along with it. But once I get back, I don't think I can abide by these rules anymore."

"What rules?"

"This courting business takes a lot of energy," he said. "I'm ready to move on to whatever comes once the courting is over."

"What's that?"

"I don't know," he said. "We'll just have to see."

❦

I sent him a card so that it would be waiting for him when he returned. It was an invitation to join me for dinner on his first Friday night back, at Café Budapest, an elegant Hungarian restaurant in the Back Bay. He called me.

"I thought you didn't like fancy restaurants," he said. "What's going on? Don't you want me to pick you up?"

"I want you to meet me there," I said, refusing to be drawn into conversation. "Don't be late."

I arrived at the restaurant before him, and made sure that the table I had requested was available. It was a corner table, and I sat down with my back against the far wall so that I could see him coming in, and he would have to walk the length of the restaurant to get to me. He had plenty of time to take me in, which is exactly what I wanted. I ordered a glass of Vouvray for myself, and a glass of Bordeaux for him, and I sat down to wait. I had found a dress very much like the one I wore on Steven's last night in Moscow, when I came to say good-bye at Juliana and Maxim's apartment. It was a little black dress, with bare shoulders. I was two years older, and what I had gone through had taken a toll. But my face had filled out, and the scar on my cheek was only a slight raised line. I could feel it with my fingertip, but it was virtually invisible to the eye. When I looked at myself in the ladies room, I felt as if I had been reborn, grateful to be pretty again. I allowed myself to feel desirable, and as Steven walked in and saw me, I also knew that I was desired. I stood up to kiss him, the perfume I was wearing the same one I wore that last night in Moscow. He breathed in deeply and as we separated, he looked at me and again, I felt known. It was a more sexual feeling than anything I had ever experienced in a bedroom.

"My God," he murmured.

"Hello, Stevie," I said. "Did you do good painting in Canada?"

He nodded, and sat down.

"So the butterfly has emerged alone from her chrysalis, unwatched and without assistance," he murmured.

"If that's how you see it." I smiled at him.

"That's how I see it," he said. "But be warned—now that the butterfly has emerged, she's fair game."

"What does that mean?" I asked.

"It means she's no longer earthbound. She can fly. She can't doubt her own perfection any longer."

"I'm good," I said, "but not perfect."

"Close enough," he answered.

"In that case," I said, "I'm ready to take the next step. It's a little step, but it's all I can give you right now."

I looked at his mouth. His lips were fine, and sweet.

"Do I get to find out what this step is?" he asked.

"I don't know if I will ever be ready to live with you." I said.

"That's not much of a next step," he said stiffly.

"Let me finish," I answered quietly. "I was going to say, I'm not ready to live with you, but if you invite me home with you tonight, I will probably accept."

He laughed. "You're a step ahead of me," he said. "But at least you're heading in the right direction." He stood up. "Anyway, I'll take what I can get." I watched him carefully fold his napkin and place it on the table. "I've got some delicious coffee at my place," he said. "Afterwards we can get to know each other again. Slowly. And we have all the time in the world."

We walked out of the restaurant side by side, his arm around my waist. He put his hand on my hip. I liked it. There was nothing tentative about his touch. Perhaps, I thought, I might even get used to it.

EPILOGUE

Lena

Boston, 1993

In America in summer I see old women walking about in plaid shorts. I shake my head when I see such ridiculousness. Each one looks like a dumpy little flamingo who flew through a washing line, and sailed out draped in someone's kitchen curtain. I've seen them on television playing golf—I could never imagine wasting my time on such a game. What kind of person would choose to spend a sunny afternoon swinging at a little ball using a long pole with a hammer at one end, and then chasing after it in a tiny cart? And that bag of long poles they carry around, each with a different-sized hammer at the end. They have serious talks about which pole to use, as if it makes a difference. You would think they would know, after hitting so many balls. I suppose this is a way they show how prosperous they are, but if I had such leisure I would spend it differently. Perhaps, they would say, I am limited by my own life. Work is all I know, all I want to do.

Anna and I have a wonderful time together. She pretends I am a nuisance, but sometimes, I let her take care of me. And I pretend to be the nuisance she teases, but I love her like another child. She has no one, but Steven makes sure she goes to school. She works now on her high school certificate, and as we cook together, she pretends to let me learn English with her. But this old tongue is not slippery enough to twist itself into a new language. And even if it were, the brain it is attached to has trouble enough remembering the present.

In the old Victorian house in Cambridge, I have my own bathroom. It seemed such a wonder, at first. But after a few weeks I realized, who needs such a thing? If I planned to spend half the day in there, perhaps. But no matter how much leisure I have, how much of it could I spend in the bathroom? I go in, do my business, and I leave. The excess is appalling. But I admit, once the children are off at school, and my Dasha goes off to work, I run myself a long, hot bath. Such a bathtub! I lie in it and drink my tea, and I think of all the years of standing in tepid water with a washcloth. But for me there is no local bathhouse in America, nowhere I can go to enjoy the steam, the ritual of bathing, the laughter and companionship of other women, as I have for most of my life. This I feel as a great loss, and I will miss it always. Especially in winter. I find now I am more and more affected by cold weather.

The kitchen is another luxury I will never get used to. Only the two of us most of the time, Anna and me, working in such a big space, with many gas plates on the stove, and a big oven; no shortage of space in the icebox, and a sink so big and with such quantities of hot water! And never, ever any shortage of food in the markets. I don't understand how a country so far behind the Soviet Union in so many ways, with such terrible social problems, can provide such quantities of electricity and hot water. The crime here, the violence, is terrible. Never in the Soviet Union did we see such crime reported in the news. At least in the Soviet Union we had standards of behavior, and children were disciplined.

The public transport here in Boston—the MBTA—is terrible. Dirty, old, slow, and unreliable. Such a wealthy country, and such shabby transport for its citizens. I take the MBTA to The Boston Museum of Fine Arts. They have some paintings by famous artists, but nothing to match what we had in Moscow. Nothing like Ivanov's masterpiece.

Steven bought me for my bedroom wall a reproduction of *The Appearance of Christ Before the People*. It is as wide as my open arms, a miniature—a mockery of the original. I took one look at it and told him to pack it up and put it in the basement until I could decide where to hang it. I think he was hurt. But I could not stand to see such a masterpiece, badly reproduced on cardboard, hanging in the bedroom of an old woman. I have spent my life laughing at religion, but this would feel to me like blasphemy.

It is strange to have such thoughts. I never had them when I was in

Moscow. I think all this freedom to say and do what you want without fear, it makes people sloppy and encourages wasteful ideas.

My thinking is filled with contradictions, I know. I find myself justifying events that happened in the past, even though they caused the ruination of many lives. And I am contemptuous of values and behaviors for which I have longed all my adult life. Past and present—Soviet Russia and this America where we now live—embrace such vast distances that they cannot be reconciled.   My great-grandchildren—and the children Dasha and Steven will have together, I am sure—will know me only as an ancient, shrunken old woman whose life they could never understand. Perhaps this is the fate of all of us fortunate enough to live long lives. As I say, we pay a price for everything.

I come now to the present, where I sit writing these words, and I read over what I have described. What hardship! I say to myself. How difficult my life seemed to me as a young woman. I ask, was it really so filled with terror and tragedy? And if it was, why am I surprised? Did I not know?

I would have no answer to the questions had I not undertaken this writing. We are each of us like a food prepared in life's kitchen, and I have had pleasure and grief in measures called for by my particular recipe. My long life has not been easy; I would have been a miserable soufflé. But I have thrived on being minced and mixed, mashed and pummeled and stretched, and as a pungent meat pie, a *pirozhok,* I have not turned out badly.

I seldom reflect on my mother, who died at our birth. Although I never knew her, I think she would be proud of the woman I became.

I remember as a young woman going ice skating on the Moscow River. I think I was on Vasily's arm, but perhaps I was skating with someone else. No matter. Of the men in my life, he remains at the center. I remember skating on the river, confident that the ice was thick enough to protect me from the frigid water rushing below. Like that young woman on the ice, today I skate comfortably on the surface of my memories, protected from the intensity of the past which remains deeply buried.

This act of remembering so long after the fact softens the frozen surface beneath me, and as it gives way I fall through the icy crust into my past. I relive the events of my life with emotions as powerful as they were when each one occurred. When I describe my love affair with Vasily, I feel the tender love of the young woman I once was flower within me. When I write of my daughter's birth, I fill with the emotions of that young mother, although it has been many years since I had such thoughts or feelings. I remember my helpless fury at those who betrayed Vasily, and the desperate sense of loss in which I felt myself drowning. And I feel them all as strongly now as I felt them then.

It is appropriate that this kind of story be told at the end of a life, when there is something to tell, when one imagines the teller being able to tell it dispassionately. But, at least for this old woman, it is impossible to maintain the boundaries between memory, and experience, and the passage of time. I have no dispassion—the act of retelling throws me back to the tumultuous, unprocessed memories of the moment. For an old woman the retelling is exhausting. Only the young have the energy to tell the story of their lives—but they have no past to share. Some would call it irony. Me? I trundle along in the middle of my ninth decade, and the older I get the more convinced I am that our world is a big mistake, walking around the universe wearing a sweater back to front, and boots on the wrong feet.

I have survived far more than the loss of my beloved Vasily. From the safety of America, my Dasha asks me to write down my story, so that the world will know the history of our family. Why, I ask her, do you think the world will be interested? We are one family among millions across the globe who have suffered under dictators and corrupt governments. What makes us special?

"We're not special," says my darling granddaughter. Yes, she is flawed, as we all are, but she has been, in so many ways, my life's salvation. "We're just lucky to be alive, and by telling our story, perhaps we honor all those who can't tell theirs."

So I ask the next question, the one that comes to mind whenever I think about my stepmother Esther, and all she suffered.

"How," I ask her, "do you think I was able to pick up and keep going, as one by one those I loved were taken from me?"

"I am here today because you refused to give up," says Dasha as she gently brushes my hair, white now, and thin, and as soft as her hair was as a baby. "Is it possible you kept going because you knew that without you I had no lifeline?"

"Maybe," I say. But I don't tell her that long before she came to me, my losses were already more than one small person should have had to bear.

"When I was a child, you told me giving up was not an option. You said keeping going was its own reward, maybe the only one. It was good advice. Perhaps you're just a survivor. Maybe it's as simple as that."

Before, there was never time to think about such things. But now I have time, and I realize what I have done, how I have survived. It is why I am always so tired, these days.

Today, I take a strange pleasure in vividly reliving my losses. It makes little sense, I know. Why, you ask, do I punish myself with unpleasant memories? The answer is that when these losses occurred, sadness filled every crevice of my being. There was no space for personal grief. Like many of those around me, I never mourned those I lost, never released a single one of them. Instead, I walled them off within me as they occurred, each one in its own separate tomb. Like a walking mausoleum, I carry my griefs with me wherever I go. And the weight of all the bricks I used to wall them off in my heart has taken a toll. This writing is my chance to break down the walls. As I release them, perhaps I can set myself free, too.

Last year the whole family gave me a birthday party. I think it was the first I ever had. Dasha says I'm eighty-five. She's probably right, but I'm not convinced. Who would believe I could reach such an age?

The children took me on the first vacation of my life—unless you count my trip to Lake Baikal during the Great Patriotic War with Klara. On that trip we were sent out of the city for a month with a trainload of women and children, in anticipation of the German invasion. This time we flew from where we live in Boston to meet artist friends of Steven's in Allentown, Pennsylvania.

They intended that I would stay at the motel, where I could waste the afternoon sleeping while they hiked and went fishing. I would have none of it. Soon I will have plenty of time for sleeping. How glad I am that I insisted on going with them! I remember the name of the place well—Beltzville State Park—because I fell in love with it.

"Steven," I told him on the second day, "we need a rowboat."

"Why, Babushka?" he asked with a smile. "You didn't catch enough fish from the shore yesterday?"

"Don't be grinning at me," I said. "You and Dasha and I have something we need to do out there."

So Steven hired a rowboat, and he rowed while Dasha and I sat beside each other. It was more a pond than a lake, but it was big enough. When we reached the middle, I told him to stop, and I opened my bag and withdrew the teapot, complete with its top, wrapped still in Esther's tattered shawl. When my nephew Lenny and I met, as we first arrived in Boston, we had together united the pieces, the teapot and the wine goblet. For the first time since my father separated it so long ago at the railway station and gave the goblet to his two sons, it was complete.

"My teapot has done its job," I said. "Time to let it rest." I handed it to them. "Go ahead," I said. "You have a new life, in a new country. You need to move forward. Let this be a new beginning for you."

Dasha's eyes opened wide. "You want us to throw it in the water?"

"Yes, Dashinka," I said softly. "And let it sink. Time for it to rest."

"It's not your teapot," she said, "and it's not right that you make this decision alone. When I was thirteen you told me it was mine. You said one day, when I had a house of my own, I would become its keeper. Now you want me to throw it away?"

I lowered the teapot to my knees, and I felt its cold metal hardness through my clothing. "It is a thing of the past," I said. "Sometimes we need to discard the past to move forward."

Steven reached toward me. I thought he was going to take the teapot from my lap and do as I asked, but instead he picked up Esther's shawl, and spread it out across his knees. It was threadbare, with holes in the warp and weft of the cloth, a little yellow and faded purple still visible in the ancient fabric.

"Esther's shawl must be very precious to you," he said in a soft voice, running his hands across it.

"Of course it is," I said. I saw that Dasha turned to him, puzzled.

"When you look at it," he continued, "it brings back all the rich memories of your childhood?"

I am no longer as patient as I once was, and I felt the beginning of irritation. "Why ask such questions when you know the answers?"

"This, too, is a thing of the past," he said. "All the time your teapot was hidden beneath the floorboards, this old shawl kept it safe. Don't they belong together?" He gently folded the shawl and handed it back to me. "Perhaps they should sink to the mud on the lake bottom together, wrapped around each other, as they were for so many years. Why don't you wrap them together the way you like them to be, and Dasha and I will put them over the side."

I felt rather than saw my hands trembling as I took the shawl from him. The thought of dropping Esther's shawl into the cold darkness beneath the water brought an unfamiliar wetness to my eyes, and I found myself dabbing at my cheeks with it. This was not at all what I'd planned. He was right, of course. There was nothing on earth that would make me drown the only thing I had left from Esther—and after what Steven had said, I couldn't very well keep the shawl and throw away the teapot. My natural response was to say something angry, but I had the sense to look at them both before I spoke.

Steven was looking at me, but my Dasha's head was turned towards him as if she were seeing him for the first time. Finally, I saw on her face some recognition of who this man was, and of how precious his qualities are. I had told her, over and over, to value his quiet gentleness, his caring, his humor, and I was fearful that I would die before she realized that the man she needed in her life was already there. All she needed to do was open her eyes, and take him in her arms. All he wanted—all any of us ever wants, really—is to be treasured. And if I didn't see the dawning of love in her eyes at that moment, I'll go out and buy myself a pair of plaid shorts and learn to play golf.

❦

When we got back to the shore, they helped me out of the boat and went off together for an afternoon hike. I watched them disappear down the path, hand in hand. They left me sitting alone in a folding chair beneath a huge pine tree, looking out at the water.

It was a hot, sun-filled afternoon, but it was September, a most beautiful month in the United States, and there was a cool wind that carried with it the smell of distant autumn. We seemed to be alone, and it was silent but for the cry of hawks circling above, and the sound of pigeons and mourning doves in the forest behind me. I looked out at the still water, reflecting the blue light of the sky and mirroring the fringe of white cloud on the other side of the lake, and I was suddenly aware of a long absent but very comforting presence. If I were a different person with a different history, perhaps I might have called it a celestial presence; nothing before or since has pushed me so close to recognizing the presence of an Almighty. But I think, finally, that I had come full circle, and I felt at peace with myself and with the world. This pine forest, with rustling branches and cooing doves and the whispered lapping of water, reminded me of the forest where Avrom was murdered.

I was still sitting on the folding chair watching the sun as it began to set, when Dasha and the others came to get me. It was late, and they were ready to go back to the motel for dinner. I refused to get up. She knows me better than anyone—once I make up my mind, there is no changing it.

"Babushka," she said quietly, waving the others off, "what do you need?" There was fear in her eyes, and I realized what she was thinking.

"Don't be ridiculous, child," I said. "Do you really think I'm the kind of woman to announce when she's ready to lie down and die?" I took her hand.

"I hope you'll be around a long time. I'm not ready to lose you yet."

"That's two of us, then. I'm not ready to lose myself either."

"So you'll come back to the motel with us for dinner?"

"You may think me crazy," I said, "but I want to stay here, on this shore, by the forest. For a few days, I want to sleep on the ground and collect wood and heat myself by the fire. If I must, I will eat squirrels and wild berries. But I'm not leaving yet. This is important," I said. "Please, do it for me."

"You know I would do anything for you," she said. "But can you tell me why you want this?"

"I don't know. Perhaps one day when I understand it myself, I'll write it down for you. But for now, this is what I need. I would organize it myself, but here, I don't understand the rules, or the money, and my English—"

"Shush, my Babushka," she said. "You don't need to explain. I'll stay here with you. Steven will go see what he can arrange."

When Steven returned, he had reserved a campsite just beyond the beach. He rented tents for us to sleep in, and sleeping bags. With Anna's help he packed up our things at the motel, bought food for us to cook, and then they all came back to the campsite with the children.

That night, and for some days after, I slept in the tent, cuddled in a sleeping bag as soft as the forests I began to recall from my childhood. I rose each morning with the sun, warmed myself at the fire, and spent my days wandering about the forest collecting wood. I listened to the silence, and experienced a feeling of safety unlike any I ever remember. Each afternoon I sat on a folding chair on the beach, reaching back into my mind for my lost childhood. With me were my brothers, Mischa and Yossel; and Esther, who became both mother and father to me; and Vasily, who loved me as I thought never to be loved; and Klara, whose loss even today I cannot fathom. With them around me, and with enough time on that perfect little beach, perhaps I would also find Avrom, my twin, and recall the experience of peering into his brown eyes, so similar to mine; the pleasure of feeling his hot, round cheeks between the palms of my hands.

I have time now, time to remember. There is nowhere else I need to be.

ACKNOWLEGEMENTS

To write a novel, all you need is the shadow of a story, something to write with, and something to write on. The rest is *sitzfleisch*. But it requires a village to make a novel as good as it can be. Here are some of the inhabitants of my village, to whom I am eternally grateful. Errors of judgment, content, history and context are all mine.

Rabbi Andrew Baker, for his particular view of the world. Professor Andrew Verner, for an education in Soviet history. Tibor and Helen Vais, whose personal experience illuminated the history. Victoria and Michael Turovsky, who provided early insight.

Sharon Nusbaum, for innocently sharing with me the idea of the teapot, which plays such an important role in the story.

To my early readers, whose feedback has been invaluable in rooting out errors and inconsistencies, and in deepening and intensifying the story. Book Group members Gail Close, Ellen Greenfeld, Kitty Howard, Carole Osterer Bellman, and Mary Close; Floyd Arntz, Maureen Costello, Leslie Elfant, Bonnie Foz, Jill Greenberg, Carol Remz, Larry Sagen, and David Sloan-Rossiter.

To my developmental editor, Alan Rinzler, whose wisdom and practical advice have been invaluable. Robyn Kasler and Linda Quigley, for detailed copyediting and finding mistakes missed by the previous dozens of readers. Louise Crawford and Marian Brown, for editorial and publication advice, and as publicists extraordinaire, whose warmth and enthusiasm have been an unexpected gift. Simone Kaplan, whose editorial insights were right on target. Carter Wentworth, whose artistry contributed to the design. Katherine DeHoyos, for an education in social media and for tireless support. Ed Velandria, whose website design and expertise have been a delight. Laura Grant-Hunter and Steve Andrada of Moltamedia, whose skills as filmmakers include making me sound wiser and more articulate than I could ever be in real life. In addition to technical skills, all the people mentioned above possess inexhaustible patience, for which I can only say a humble thank you.

This is, above all, a book about the strength of family bonds. To my family, for their constant love and encouragement. In particular, to my sister, Isabel and my parents Betty and Fred, for their close reading. To Danielle, for showing me how boundaries can always be stretched, for surprising insights and for never holding back; to Jessica, for editorial, copyediting, strategic and tactical marketing advice, as well as for unstinting availability. To both daughters, thanks for protecting me from myself as I dove into social media.

Lastly, and firstly, Marlene. Partner, muse, toughest critic. Pitcher, catcher, umpire, coach. I hit the jackpot.

About the Author

Neville Frankel is the author of two previous works of fiction, an apartheid-era novel, *Bloodlines*, and *The Third Power*, a well-reviewed political thriller about the transformation of Rhodesia to Zimbabwe. He is also the recipient of a 1984 Emmy for his work on a Frontline/BBC Documentary, *The Mind of A Murder: Part 1*, about the Hillside Strangler.

Born in Johannesburg, South Africa, he immigrated to Boston with his family at the age of 14. Frankel has three grown children, and he and his wife divide their time among Boston, Cape Cod, and Santa Barbara.

Visit him at nevillefrankel.com and on Facebook and Twitter.

CPSIA information can be obtained
at www.ICGtesting.com
Printed in the USA
LVOW11s2357140217
524305LV00002B/232/P

9 781944 884109